She unlocked the driv
locking the doors, he look

"Sure." She looked bemused. "Why shouldn't I be? I was locked safely inside a military-equipped Hummer. You?" Her silver-gray gaze narrowed and she scanned him—twice. Slowly. Every part of his body her eyes swept over burned with the heat of his unrequited lust. "I don't see any blood."

"Ve-very, um—" he coughed, swallowing past a constriction in his throat. God, just her eyes on him, her concerned attention, made him fumble like a damn school boy. The woman was dangerous to his control. "Unbloody confrontations. If those two assholes are the best Cruz has, his rep has been exaggerated." He turned away from her detailed scrutiny, shifted the running vehicle into first gear and pulled out of the parking spot.

"What did you do?" She touched his forearm, practically petting him.

His muscles flexed in response to her stroking fingers. His body yelled "more." It took every bit of self-control he possessed not to pull the vehicle over and order her to touch him all over, especially the part of him throbbing behind the placket of his suddenly too-tight jeans.

"I talked." He shot her a frowning glance then looked at his arm where she stroked him. She withdrew her hand. He breathed easier. "They listened."

"Uh huh, sure." She sniffed, a cute, very feminine sound which both amused and aroused him. *Shit, I'm in deep, deep trouble here.*

REVIEWS FOR *COLD DAY IN HELL*

THE ROMANCE REVIEWS TOP PICK.
"COLD DAY IN HELL is an intense suspense/ mystery romance story that is a must read. Believe me, you will not regret buying this book. I need to buy book one of this series and I will be on the look out for the next book."

—The Romance Reviews

"Non-stop action and wall-banging sex made it hard to put down."

—Chris for The Night Owl Reviews

"Readers will be swept away by the mad, bad hero Risto Smith ... the hot sex and fast paced action will make readers very glad they picked up this book."

—Dawn for RT BookReviews

COLD DAY IN HELL
A SECURITY SPECIALISTS INTERNATIONAL BOOK

MONETTE MICHAELS

ISBN-13: 978-1475274639
ISBN-10: 1475274637

E-Book, Published by Liquid Silver Books, imprint of Atlantic Bridge Publishing, 2012.

Copyright © 2012, Monette Michaels.

All rights reserved. No part of this publication may be reproduced, stored in a retrieval system, or transmitted in any form or by any means, electronic, mechanical, recording or otherwise, without the prior written permission of the author.

Editor: Sharis Mayer
Cover Artist: April Martinez

This is a work of fiction. The characters, incidents and dialogues in this book are of the author's imagination and are not to be construed as real. Any resemblance to actual events or persons, living or dead, is completely coincidental.

Dedication

To my husband, Tom.

Acknowledgements

Thanks to my beta-readers Holly, Ezra, and Sherry. Lots of hugs to Sharis for editing during a cross-country move. And as always, thanks to April for another luscious cover.

Chapter One

Rescue Day 1, the walled city of Cartagena de Indias, Colombia.

"Chin up, Calista!"

Mentally frowning, Callie followed Evan's instructions. Both of them had been dragooned into this one last modeling job before she hung up her Manolos forever. But unlike her, the photographer wasn't in the crosshairs of a paramilitary leader who wanted a new piece of arm candy. Evan was not Jaime Cruz's type.

Scared to death of the man stalking her and threatening to keep her in Colombia, she'd called in back-up who would assure she'd fly home to Chicago and not end up a prisoner on some jungle plantation. Once safely back home, she'd junk her top model image once and for all, become plain old Callie Meyers, and begin a real life.

For now, she was two days into a three-day shoot and she had a job to do—and the enemy to hold off until the cavalry arrived.

"Calista, love. Look at me, not the crowd."

Callie dragged her gaze away from the two thugs Cruz had assigned as her "guards." The huge men glared at anyone who got too close to the photo shoot.

"That's my girl. Now part your lips. Make love to me *and*

the camera, not the clouds, sweetie."

"Why, Evan, I didn't know you cared." She gave him the best sexy look she could muster under the circumstances. It must have been good enough because Evan nodded and hummed happily as he framed the shot. "Your Chad would bitch slap me into next month if I turned my wiles your way."

"Got that right." Evan chuckled. "My sweetie is one jealous hunk." He snapped six pictures in less time than she could think about it. "Although if I were going to play for the other team, you'd be the only woman I'd do. You are sex personified, dear one."

Yeah, right. What a joke. She might be a supermodel, but she hadn't had sex with a man in so long she forgot how. Raising younger twin brothers since the death of their widower father seven years ago had taken up the majority of her free time. Besides parenting the twins, she'd attended college part-time and worked as a waitress until she'd been "discovered" by Evan, a world-famous fashion photographer. That had been six years ago. He'd just been hired to photograph a new ad campaign for a major cosmetics line. Given *carte blanche* in choice of models, Evan had convinced the company to use her as their face. After that serendipitous meeting, there'd been little time for male-female relationships. It amazed her she didn't look as old and tired as she felt. If given the choice between sex and sleep, she'd choose sleep every damn time—and had.

"You." Evan turned and crooked a finger at the meek, put-upon Colombian fashion designer's assistant standing off to the side. "Fix the drape of the dress across Calista's hips."

The girl was in awe of her and Evan, but scared to death of the two goons in dark designer shades and jungle *haute*-design; their light-weight Italian wool sports coats were perfectly tailored to hide the guns holstered under them. Callie's guards glowered at the visibly trembling young girl as she approached Callie.

Thank God Cruz stayed away during the daytime shoots or

nothing would have gotten done. He was even scarier than his thugs since his harmless exterior hid the killer lying just under the surface. He was probably too busy raping and pillaging the countryside in pursuit of left-and right-wing terrorists while protecting his drug cartel bosses. Instead, Cruz chose to bother her during dinner. The last two nights he'd managed to corner her at the hotel restaurant for that evening's meal. She'd had indigestion her whole time in Colombia.

The designer's assistant smiled shyly as she smoothed the aqua-colored chiffon over Callie's hips with shaky fingers.

"It's okay, *pequeña.*" Callie hated the fear in the girl's doe brown eyes and suspected if anyone wanted to look closely enough, her own eyes displayed a similar emotion. They were both pawns in a male-dominated, failing nation. "They won't hurt you. They're here for me." The girl nodded as she backed away. Like any wary prey, she kept the goon squad in sight at all times.

Callie would've taken care of the smoothing of the dress herself and saved the poor girl the trouble of being the center of the bad guys' attention, but she was precariously balanced on her side on a crumbling wall of a UNESCO Heritage site, the ancient city of Cartagena de Indias. The drop from the fortification walls, which had prevented seventeenth century pirates from raiding the town, was over a hundred feet to a rocky, wave-beaten shore. Yet, as dangerous as her position was, the Caribbean Sea shined like a turquoise jewel in the background and the pictures would be fabulous.

Several more clicks and whirs and Evan put his camera down. He walked over to help her off the wall. "Sore, love?" He held on to her until she could step out of the five-inch-heeled, bejeweled sandals that probably cost more than most Colombians earned in a month. The little assistant snatched them up as if they were the crown jewels and placed Callie's own thrift-store flip-flop sandals on the ground.

Now barefoot, she wiggled her peach-colored toes on the

stones of the uneven walkway, polished to satiny smoothness by thousands of feet over hundreds of years, then slipped into her sandals. "As if you cared, sadist." Evan liked to make his models suffer for his art. She smiled. He winked, his lips twisted into his famous grin, but his eyes held concern and fear for their situation. "I'm fine except for those torture devices called shoes. They were killing me and I didn't even walk in them. We almost done for the day?"

They'd started six hours ago and she hadn't eaten. If it hadn't been for the vast quantities of fresh juice the assistant had provided, she would've fallen on her butt from low blood sugar and dehydration a long time ago. Then her guards would've probably shot everyone. Cruz wanted her in one functioning and decorative piece. His plans for her, ones he had shared in explicit detail the night she'd arrived, made her want to vomit.

"Almost, my precious one." Evan guided her behind the changing screen under the shade of a tent raised to protect her skin from the harsh equatorial sun and intermittent rain showers. While she changed out of the exorbitantly priced dress into her own chain store tank top and peasant skirt, Evan retreated to a perch on the wall next to the screen. "They're here again." His voice was whisper-low and tight with anxiety.

"Sort of hard to miss," she whispered back. "Think the Bears would want them for the offensive line?" She came around the corner of the screen and sat in the folding director's chair with her name screen-printed on it.

"Always the kidder, aren't you?" His lips thinned into a grim smile. His body blocked her from the gazes of the two tough-looking men who'd been her shadows since she'd arrived in Cartagena.

"Yeah, well, I grew up on marine bases all over the world and then raised two boys from pre-teen to college age. A sense of humor and a thick skin is a requirement." She sighed and swept trembling fingers through the mass of multi-hued blonde hair which had helped make her famous. She turned troubled eyes toward her friend. "Cruz won't let me go. It could get hairy."

"Jesus, Callie, I thought you were calling for help. Where is it? It's been almost two days!" He leaned even closer to her so as not to be overheard. He fussed nervously with the folds of her gauzy skirt, his hands trembling. "I read up on this Cruz person after you told me who he really was. He's bad news, my sweet."

"Yeah, I know." She stifled the beginnings of hysterical laughter. She tended to laugh at inappropriate times. Her childhood friends, the Walshes, used to tease her unmercifully. She'd spoiled many a war game of hide-and-seek/hostage rescue in the savannas and swamps contained within the borders and surrounding Camp Lejeune, North Carolina, by giving away her team's position. Because of that, she'd been made designated hostage. The irony when compared to her current predicament had her snorting delicately. "I called the US Embassy in Bogotá the night we arrived, the night Cruz threatened me, and told them the local para-leader was far too interested in me."

"And? What did our illustrious government representatives say?"

"To make sure I was never alone—and to get the hell out of the country as soon as I could. Big help, huh?" Callie swore under her breath. "We shouldn't have let Marv talk us into this job. I wonder what Cruz paid our slimy agent under the table to get me here?"

Evan fisted her skirt, realized what he'd done and then proceeded to smooth out the creases he'd made. "That greedy old bugger. Marv told me you wanted this job, that you wouldn't come without me, that you wanted to finish your career with the photographer who'd started it."

"He lied." *The asshole.*

He paused, his eyes narrowed. "Tell me the truth ... are

Chad and I in danger? From what I read on the Internet, kidnapping is a booming business for the paras."

"Cruz doesn't want you or any of the rest of the crew. He wants me." *Gracing his home. In his bed. Bearing his children. Yeah, like that will happen.* "Plus, he has other leverage to keep me here—my brothers. He won't use you." *Not if I can help it, anyway.*

She patted the hand mutilating her skirt once more. "He never mentioned you or Chad either time he cornered me." Not satisfied with threats, Cruz had also man-handled her as he outlined his agenda and what he expected of her. "At the end of the shoot, he expects me to go to his plantation and willingly…" *after he threatened to kill my brothers,* "…become his woman, as he put it."

"I said it before and I'll say it again … he can't stop you from leaving. You're a goddamned United States citizen."

"Which isn't worth crap in Colombia. Jaime Cruz is the law in this area. His paramilitary group, *Serpiente Negra*, is the only reason the FARC and ELN terrorist groups haven't overrun this part of the country." At the confusion on Evan's face she explained, "FARC is the main right-wing terrorist group in Colombia and the ELN, its communist counterpart. Both use threats, killings, kidnappings and other crimes to enforce their power, of which they have more than the sanctioned Colombian government. The only groups strong enough to keep them in line have been the paramilitary groups such as Cruz's. He keeps this area safe for the tourists. Wouldn't surprise me if he didn't take kickbacks from the hotels and resorts to do so. Hell, even the Colombian government probably appreciates his control of the region." Tourist dollars were almost as lucrative as drug money and a far better promo op.

Evan moved restlessly on the wall, his hands now fisted tightly on his thighs. "What are we going to do?"

She flashed him a brilliant smile. "I did it already. I told you I would get help and I did. After my first choice, the US Embassy, told me I was on my own, I called in private security last night while on my walk. He should be here today."

"He? One guy? Sweet Jesus, Calista! One guy can't fight off a paramilitary group. Even little old apolitical me knows that."

Callie had to chuckle. Evan was a political neophyte. If not for his lover Chad, Evan would've run into trouble years ago on his shoots all over the world. "I called my childhood friends, Keely Walsh-Maddox and her brother, Tweeter, who are principals in Security Specialists International. Their operatives are all ex-military Special Forces and trained for just these sorts of situations. One of their guys is equivalent to four marines." If she believed everything Keely had told her. She squeezed his cold hand. "I'll be fine—" *I hope,* "—and so will you, Chad and the others. Trust me?"

"You know I do." He shook his head, his eyes taking on a faraway look. "I remember that time in Kenya. Out of everyone on the team sent to protect us you were the only one whose brain seemed to work when the lions rushed us. But one guy? Come on, Calista."

"SSI could only get the one guy here today. But his back-up team should arrive at a safe house tomorrow on the last day of the photo shoot where we'll meet them to get me out of the country. I've been informed you'll be going out a different way. The operative will have the details for us when he arrives. The theory is Cruz will concentrate on me—not you and your people." She leaned closer to Evan. "Don't be surprised when a guy named Risto Smith arrives and claims to be my husband. Act as if you know him. Keely and I figured even Cruz might chill his jets a bit if he thinks I'm married. I guess this Risto is one mean-looking son of a bitch."

"Beauty and the Beast? I can see a photo spread for *Vogue*." He swept his hands in a broad arc. She could always count on Evan to find the humor in a situation. "By the way, how recent is the *marriage*?" He grinned at her raised eyebrow. "I'm a method actor, dear one. If you're recently married, I can be even more excited about seeing the new hubby. If it's a secret marriage of long-standing then I, as an old and dear friend, would greet Risto more casually."

"Recent … very recent. We eloped right before I left Chicago, okay? Is that enough inspiration?"

"Perfect … ah, and I think your hubby may have arrived." A commotion and angry male voices had Evan turning, which allowed her to see past him. "Oh my God, I hope that's him. He's…" Evan fluttered a hand over his heart, "stunning. All lines and angles. Rugged masculinity."

Holy crap! The picture Keely had sent to her cell phone had not done the guy justice. Her make-believe husband had just taken out the two, gorilla-sized thugs and wasn't even breathing heavily. He bent over and disarmed both men, throwing their weapons over the ancient wall into the sea. Her womb clenched and her lacy thong dampened at his show of strength.

Her pretend husband cast a narrowed glance over the area until he found her tent shelter. Man, he was impressive. She could practically feel his testosterone across the small plaza. Keely hadn't misrepresented Risto Smith at all—he was capable *and* dangerous. The tension she'd carried in her shoulders and neck since Cruz had threatened her and her brothers dissipated. She wasn't alone anymore.

"Sweet baby Jesus, he's huge." *And all mine.* Callie shook off the errant thought. The man didn't look like the type to belong to anyone but himself. She was just borrowing him for a short time. But damn, why didn't they grow men like him in Chicago? She reached for Evan who helped her stand. She dropped his hand then walked toward Risto Smith, taking her time to drink him in.

Keely had left some things out of her description. He was broad-shouldered, lean-hipped and far taller than her own five feet, nine inches. His face was all lines and angles with a sharp blade of a nose. Even though his name was Finnish-sounding, he looked to have some Native American blood. His collar-length hair was thick and dark as pitch, wildly layered about his head, giving him a medieval warrior look. His eyes were dark and glittering, focused only on her. She shivered and another small gush of moisture dampened her already soaked panties.

Shaking his head and muttering something she couldn't hear, he moved toward her in a ground-eating stride. Obviously, she wasn't moving fast enough to suit him. Her mouth dried as he stalked her. He moved like a jungle cat, aware of all potential danger surrounding him. His demeanor said it all: he'd handle whatever came his way and survive to tell about it. This was a man a woman could rely upon. He could be protective or destructive, depending on his mood.

Stopping a few feet from her, he sent her an imperious look, one dark masculine brow arched. It was a look she recognized, her father had often worn a similar look with her and her brothers; it said "what the fuck are you waiting on?"

Callie let out a sigh, forced her trembling lips into a wide smile and ran into his arms. "Risto! You made it!"

She buried her face against his throat, getting a whiff of citrus and clean male sweat. Her arms went around his neck in a vice-like grip; his went around her waist and back, taking her weight easily. He murmured something unintelligible against her hair. He lifted her until her feet dangled several inches off the ground, then swung her around, putting on a show for the crew, the lookee-loos, and Cruz's men who were slowly getting up. More likely, his act allowed him to continue to check for danger. Either way, the crowd seemed impressed. Callie knew she was.

Risto rubbed his beard-roughened jaw over her hair and spoke in a low tone, his breath wafting over her ear. "You okay, Ms. Meyers?" The rumble of his voice sent a frisson of sexual awareness down her spine, the sensations settling in long unused female parts. Her clit throbbed, matching the rapid beat of her heart. *God, what a time for my libido to wake up. Right kind of man. Wrong time and place.*

She angled her face then brushed her lips over his. Her tongue licked a small scar marring his upper lip. He started at the touch, exhaling roughly, his breath smelling of mint and coffee.

"Call me Callie." She whispered the words over his sculpted mouth, the tip of her tongue returning to trace the scar once more. His hands tightened on her body. "After all, we're supposed to be married. And, yes, I'm fine, scared, but fine. The bastard … well, let's say he has a sick way of courting me. His goons have kept their distance. But he…" A slight hitch in her voice, she stifled a sob threatening to erupt. She refused to let go of the control she'd kept on her emotions, the danger wasn't over yet.

He pulled her closer, so close her breasts brushed his chest. Her nipples pebbled from the casual touching. "Shh. It's okay. Keely and Tweeter fully prepped me." He nuzzled her ear. She shivered. "You did the right thing in calling them. Cruz would never have let you leave."

"I know … my brothers?" Her stomach clenched. She'd told Keely Cruz had threatened to kidnap her brothers if she didn't come to him voluntarily. Her friend had promised to get them to safety. "They're safe?" He nodded, his cheek brushing hers. She whimpered her relief, tears threatened to swamp her eyes.

Risto muttered a low, rumbling "fuck" and allowed her body to slide down his until her feet touched the ground. He kept a supporting arm around her until she got her balance. She hadn't realized how much the last two days of stress and worry had taken out of her.

He brushed his lips over her cheek, kissing away tears she hadn't even realized had fallen. He massaged her waist and back, soothing her. He played the role of a loving husband well. "Tweeter took them to Camp Lejeune. Colonel Walsh and his marines will protect them. Keely wanted to go with Tweeter, but Ren threatened to tie her butt to the bed if she dared to leave Sanctuary with the baby." Ren and Keely's son Riley was a little over three months old.

An inappropriate giggle erupted at the image Risto's words projected. "Sounds as if Keely has found herself a man who can handle her." She and Keely had been tomboys growing up. It would take quite a man to tame her friend. "Thank you, thank you, thank you." She punctuated her words with kisses to his chin, jaw and mouth. Suddenly, her knees gave way and she inhaled sharply as her vision dimmed.

Risto moved to catch her. "Stay with me, Callie." He swung her into his arms, cradling her against his chest.

Even securely held, the world spun for a few more seconds. She closed her eyes and took a few deep breaths, before opening them to his concerned gaze. "Sorry. I haven't slept much. Too much adrenaline. The heat. The humidity. No lunch."

He cursed, a litany of profanity the likes of which she hadn't heard since she'd stopped living on marine bases. She felt as if she'd come home.

Risto turned his back on the interested bystanders and began to walk. "Hell, woman, you can't do an op on an empty stomach."

"Cruz put me off my feed—and Evan has only one speed and that's fast forward."

"Fuck 'em both." His jaw clenched. "Excuse my language."

"No worries. I've heard and said worse." His snort of disbelief had her grinning. He'd learn soon enough. She might be a supermodel, but she swore like a marine and had often shocked the models and crews on photo shoots. Looking over Risto's shoulder, she found the astonished gazes of the photo crew and the hostile ones of Cruz's muscle. She returned her focus to Risto's sharply angled jaw line. "Where are we going? I don't think Evan was done for the day."

"You're done." He headed for the narrow path which led to the parking area. "We're going to your hotel."

The way he said "hotel" as if it were a nasty word had her narrowing her eyes. Something bothered him about the hotel. Had he tried to get into her room and they denied him? His next words negated that thought.

"I stopped by and put my gear in your *casita* and scouted around some."

Scouted around for what? She mentally shrugged. She'd find out once they got back to her, now their, suite of rooms.

"Okay. Can we get something to eat? I'm starving." He nodded. She wiggled. "Put me down. I can walk. I'm too heavy to carry."

"No." At her gasp and continued attempts to get down, he added, "Stop it! You fucking almost fainted. And you don't weigh all that much. You could add a few pounds." He hugged her more tightly against his body and continued to stride straight toward the *paseo* currently blocked by her erstwhile guards.

Risto swore foully, this time in idiomatic and very filthy Spanish. Loosely translated, he ordered the sons of bitches out of the way or he'd gut them and then drop them over the ancient wall to the rocky beach for the gulls to peck out their entrails. The thugs moved.

"Holy crap," she breathed against his neck, "effective threat."

He peered at her through thick lashes, his eyes glinted darkly. "You understood all that?"

"Yep."

"Shit." His mouth thinned and the muscles in his jaw tensed. "I apologize for…"

She placed her fingers over his lips. "Stop apologizing. I've wanted to let loose with some of the profanities my dad used. But since I couldn't follow up the words with the actions, I kept my mouth shut. It's been a real pain holding back."

"If you don't mind me asking, where would a lady such as you learn to swear in idiomatic Spanish?"

"Marine bases around the United States and the world." She smiled. "The best education a kid could get. I was a horrible tomboy … still am."

"You don't look like one."

"Appearances are often deceiving." She fluttered her lashes. Risto snorted and shook his head.

"Calista, dear." Evan's trilling tones came from behind them.

"Stop, please." Callie patted Risto's chest. He frowned, but nodded and turned to meet Evan. "Let me down." He refused even after she pinched his arm. Solid muscle that arm. "Yes, Evan? I thought we were done for the day. Risto and I haven't seen each other for four whole days."

Her pretend husband played his part by holding her against him with one arm, then turning her head for a searing hot, but far too short, kiss. She licked her lips, tasting him—mint and coffee and heat.

"Here's your tote bag, dear girl." Evan grinned and handed her the large, leather bag which held all her important papers—she hadn't trusted Cruz not to break into her rooms and steal her passport, traveler's checks and credit cards. "Ah, newly wedded bliss." Cruz's goons had followed and stood off to the side, interested observers. One had his cell phone out and was, she bet, making a report to his boss. "I guess this means you and Risto don't want to have dinner with me and Chad this evening?"

"Callie hasn't had lunch yet, Evan." Risto's voice held anger and a note of chastisement. "I'm taking her to get cleaned up and then I plan to feed her. Maybe we can meet later for drinks after she has a *nap*." The way Risto said "nap" was clearly meant to indicate to all who listened he intended to be in that bed with her and they wouldn't be sleeping.

Evan had the grace to blush. "Oh, yes, please take care

of our girl. And, definitely … a drink … later. Chad would love to see you again. He was so-o-o upset you two lovebirds eloped. He so wanted to plan a wedding for our Calista."

"I didn't want to wait for the hassle of a wedding." Callie stroked Risto's jaw. "I didn't want him to get away."

Risto coughed. "Callie tells me I have you and Chad to thank for keeping the Latin lovers away from her."

"No problem. Glad you're here though." Evan shot a nasty look at Cruz's men. "Some people can't take a hint that our lovely Calista is unavailable." He turned his back on their unwanted escorts. "Calista, dear one, we can probably wrap up the shoot tomorrow. We'll be doing some jungle shots—in the national park just outside of town."

"That's great," Callie said. "You'll have to tell us exactly where when we meet for drinks. Risto will drive me to the shoot."

"Sounds like a plan. See you two later." Evan saluted and walked back to the tent where the crew was packing things up.

"Señorita Meyers." One of the thugs must have grown an extra set of balls, because he approached them, fingering a large knife. "You will please stay. Señor Cruz is coming. He is not happy." The man glared. If looks could kill, Risto would've been dead on the ground, a bloody mess.

Before she could take the cretin to task, Risto jumped in. "I'm her husband, *pendejo*. Señor Cruz can fuck himself. Sorry, honey."

She kissed his chin. "No problem, tiger. I told you the man was persistent." Risto snarled, sounding very much like the predatory cat she'd just named him. He turned his back on Cruz's messenger boys and continued up the path toward the parking area. Either Risto was insane or had really big balls. She would never have turned her back on armed men. "Um, they're following us." She couldn't keep the shakiness out of her voice.

"Yeah, I know. Once I lock you in the Hummer, I'll take

care of them." His lips twisted into a nasty grin. Big *cojones* it was then. She was glad he was on her side. "Those two won't touch you."

"Well, I knew that—they wouldn't dare. Cruz wants me alive and unharmed." *Not quite true.* She had bruises on her ass and hips from where the bastard had pulled her to him when she'd tried to leave him in the hotel bar. "I'm more worried about you. I didn't think … Cruz will have you killed … he won't fight fair."

"Don't worry about me. Better men have tried. I fight to win." He stopped at a black Hummer with tinted windows and held her one-armed against his body as he punched in a key code. "Now, let's get you inside while I go take care of the trash."

Risto lifted her so she could scramble into the passenger seat. Waves of heat came off the dash and black leather upholstery. She flinched, the seat burning her skin through the thin fabric of her tank top and skirt. He frowned. "Fuck. You can't stay locked up inside a closed vehicle—it's over ninety degrees in there and like a damn sauna."

The man was a natural protector like her dad and Colonel Walsh. Damn, she loved marines. And even though he was an ex-marine, her dad had said "once a marine, always a marine, baby girl."

"Give me the keys." She wiggled her fingers. He handed them over. "I'll start the car and get it cooled off."

He swept a calloused finger over her heat-flushed cheek. "You need to eat and hydrate now. There are protein bars in the end pocket of my duffle in the back seat. Eat one to tide you over until I can get you a real meal." He pointed to the bottle of water in the cup holder. "Drink that. You need the water more than you need to worry about my germs. Got it?"

"Yeah, thanks, and I'm not worried about your germs."

"Get a bar now, Callie."

She scrunched her nose but decided it wasn't worth arguing

about his autocratic tone at this point—plus she was starving. She turned and pulled a peanut-butter-flavored bar out of his duffle, unwrapped it and took a bite.

He grunted. "Now, lock this door. Don't open it for anyone. If trouble comes, lean on the horn."

"What trouble?" She mumbled around a sticky bite of the chewy bar. She grabbed his water bottle and took a deep drink, helping the dry granola down her stress-constricted throat.

His lips quirked into a satisfied smile at her actions. "Remember? The badass said Cruz is on his way."

She swallowed another gulp of water then gasped. "Gee, you must think I'm stupid. This is…"

"*This* is outside your comfort zone. It is for most people." He leaned in and tapped the tip of her nose. "That's why you have me. If you do need to leave the vehicle, meet me at the cantina across the square. Sit in the back and try to blend in. I'll look there first before I start tearing the old city apart."

He turned to leave. She touched his arm. Flexing under her fingers, his skin was hot, hair-roughened, covering tight, steely muscles. "Be careful… Come back to me."

His lips twisted into a feral smile. "I'm planning on it." Risto shut the door and stood there until she locked it.

Callie watched him stalk toward the last sighting of his intended prey. He was all fluid muscle and lethal intent. She had no doubts the two men would regret pulling guard-the-supermodel duty today. Sinking low in the seat, she resumed eating and drinking and kept a wary eye out for Cruz.

Chapter Two

Risto wanted to take out Cruz's muscle: first, as a message to Cruz and, second, because they had frightened Callie. *Bastards.* He had to give her credit, she was holding it together better than most of the women he'd had to rescue from a hostage situation. Despite her current freedom of movement, this *was* a hostage rescue.

Cruz had the rep of taking what and whom he wanted and to hell with what anyone else said. The Colombian government was toothless and would do nothing to stop the para-leader from kidnapping a visitor to their country; they hadn't stopped the man in the past even when he'd kidnapped and held fellow Colombians. The government had good reasons for their lack of action: Cruz commanded a large number of well-trained and better-equipped men than the Colombian army.

SSI had gone up against Cruz's forces before. Although Risto had been in the country before as a marine on drug enforcement missions, he had only two previous visits to the region as a new member of the SSI team. From having studied all the case reports on previous SSI missions in the region,

Risto knew this wasn't Cruz's first go-round as a kidnapper of women for his sexual use. SSI and several other private security organizations had documented dozens of similar cases. Not all the women had been recovered. They were either dead or, as rumor told, sold into slavery in the Middle East. The ones rescued had shown signs of physical and psychological abuse and drug addiction. Cruz had extremely sadistic sexual appetites.

Risto fisted his hands. The bastard would never touch a hair on Callie's head and live. Taking a deep breath, he throttled back the rage threatening to consume him. He relaxed his hands and looked at them with a sense of disbelief.

God! He'd held and kissed Calista Meyers, world famous model. His buddies in his old Recon team would shit bricks if they learned of it. Was there a straight man on the planet that hadn't lusted after Calista? Probably not. He'd done so for over five years. He still had a copy of the first magazine on which she'd been the featured swimsuit model. She'd been in every annual swimsuit issue since and on the cover twice more. All his issues were well-thumbed, and Callie had played a role in many of his favorite fantasies. He'd never dreamed he'd meet her, let alone kiss her.

Callie was his idea of woman-personified. In flats, her head easily rested on his shoulder. She was all lean muscle covered by satiny soft, creamy skin with curves in all the right places. He could attest to the fact her breasts were full and firm; braless, they'd brushed his chest and arm several times. Her ass was two sweetly rounded and firm handfuls. Her eyes were the color of pale gray pearls rimmed in black. He could lose himself in the depths of those eyes.

And he damn well didn't ever want to see fear in them again, not like what he'd seen when she first ran into his arms.

But it was her hair which had fueled many of his sexual fantasies. Her famous hair was a hundred shades of blonde from light to dark and hung in loosely tousled waves halfway down her back. His fantasies had him fisting her hair as he took her from behind, his cock entering her pussy as he watched her mouth-watering ass meet his thrusts. He had images of her hair veiling his thighs as she sucked him off. Now that he knew how her hair felt—like the finest silk—and smelled—like flowers and female musk—he at least planned to indulge and touch it whenever possible.

She was a hundred times sexier in person—and so not for him. Not even for a one-night, get-it-out-of-his-system, living-all-his-fantasies bout of hard fucking. He couldn't make a move towards her, because she was, first of all, a client and, second, the Walsh kids' childhood friend. If Ren didn't kill him, Keely or Tweeter would. On top of those more than excellent reasons, her deceased dad had been a marine's marine, a hero killed in the field, decorated out the wazoo. *Semper fi.* She was practically family.

Of course, none of those reasons would stop him if she hinted she'd be open to twisting in the sheets with him. But that would never happen. Tomboy declaration aside, she was a lady from her sweet-smelling hair to her dainty polished toes.

Whereas he was a rough, scarred, mostly uncivilized former marine and a loner who'd spent most of his adult years in deep recon, living off the land with mostly himself for company. He was a stone-cold predator, albeit an authorized one.

When he managed to find the time to fit sex into his life, he did it with women who knew the score and could meet his needs in bed. Harder women who didn't mind that he liked to be in charge. He didn't have a romantic, gentle bone in his entire body. He'd scare the shit out of sweet Callie.

As he turned the corner of the *paseo*, Cruz's men were there. He expected from the look of worry on their stupid goon faces that Cruz had threatened them with emasculation if they lost Callie. Risto smiled evilly and motioned them forward. His body was loose and ready to fight. While he might not be a proper lover for Callie, he sure as hell was the best man to protect her. He'd begin with these two imbeciles.

He punched the first thug before the man could even let fly with the club he held. Cudgel-Boy fell to the ground and Risto finished him off with a vicious chop to the neck. Risto turned into the other man, kicking the knife from his hand. The goon looked at his empty hand then ran. Risto had to chase the fucker down. He finally cornered the pussy in a doorway of the ancient fortification.

After knocking Knife-Boy's head into the stone wall a couple of times, he held him up by his shirtfront. "Tell Cruz I don't like anyone threatening my woman." Risto shook the man a couple of times, causing his head to hit the wall again. "And I don't like strange men—that would be you and your sleeping *amigo*—following her."

Risto tossed the dazed thug to the ground with a grunt of disgust. "If I see you, hear you or even smell you near Callie, I won't be this nice next time." He leaned over and pressed the man's carotid artery just hard enough to put him to sleep. Then he moved away, stepping over the first man's body, and rushed back to the Hummer. As he approached, he swore. Callie was gone! Everything primal in him was ready to hunt, rend and kill.

"Callie!" His booming shout echoed off the buildings surrounding the small plaza and parking area. Several people looked at him askance and walked away quickly, the primitive part of their brains warning them a predator was about to attack.

He headed for the cantina. If Callie had run, he hoped she had remembered his instructions. Then her head popped up on the passenger side. Wide-eyed, she looked straight at him then smiled. *Sweet Jesus, she's beautiful and—safe.*

The adrenaline pumping through his system no longer required to fight switched over to the need to fuck. His cock hardened, threatening to burst through his jeans. Before this mission was complete, he was afraid his dick would petrify from over-exposure to Callie.

God, he was in so much fucking trouble. No woman had ever twisted his insides this way. He was always in control of his head, his emotions, his body, especially his cock.

She unlocked the driver's side door and he got in. After locking the doors, he looked her over. "You okay?"

"Sure." She looked bemused. "Why shouldn't I be? I was locked safely inside a military-equipped Hummer. You?" Her silver-gray gaze narrowed and she scanned him—twice. Slowly. Every part of his body her eyes swept over burned with the heat of his unrequited lust. "I don't see any blood."

"Ve-very, um—" he coughed, swallowing past a constriction in his throat. God, just her eyes on him, her concerned attention, made him fumble like a damn school boy. The woman was dangerous to his control. "Unbloody confrontations. If those two assholes are the best Cruz has, his rep has been exaggerated." He turned away from her detailed scrutiny, shifted the running vehicle into first gear and pulled out of the parking spot.

"What did you do?" She touched his forearm, practically petting him.

His muscles flexed in response to her stroking fingers. His body yelled "more." It took every bit of self-control he possessed not to pull the vehicle over and order her to touch him all over, especially the part of him throbbing behind the placket of his suddenly too-tight jeans.

"I talked." He shot her a frowning glance then looked at his arm where she stroked him. She withdrew her hand. He breathed easier. "They listened."

"Uh huh, sure." She sniffed, a cute, very feminine sound which both amused and aroused him. *Shit, I'm in deep, deep trouble here.*

The fingers which had stroked him now ruffled through her glorious hair, lifting it from her neck then allowing the silk strands to fall over her almost naked shoulders. One long curl lay over her breast. He fought the urge to move it.

"Are they dead?" She asked the question in the same tone someone might ask about the chances of rain.

While her voice might be calm and cool, her beautiful gray eyes still held all the stress and fear he'd observed earlier. She'd been living on adrenaline since she'd arrived two days ago. She'd crash soon, but he'd be there to care for her, protect her.

"They're breathing," he finally responded to her question. "It's hard to send a message with dead people."

"Very funny." She sighed, the sound so heart-wrenching he wanted to wrap his arms around her and promise nothing and no one would ever bother her again. She shuddered so hard he could almost hear it. "Cruz won't listen."

"How in the hell did you ever run across Cruz?" That issue had bothered him since Keely and Tweeter had briefed him on the case. They hadn't given him all the background, just the exigent circumstances. He doubted if they even knew it themselves. All the Walshes had cared about was their sister-by-choice was in severe danger.

"I didn't run across him. He found me ... in Chicago."

He stiffened. This was different than Cruz's normal modus operandi of kidnapping female tourists. He clenched the steering wheel. "How? I wouldn't think paramilitary leaders crossed bases with fashion models all that often."

"Yeah. Trust me, I didn't know who he was when I first met him. Just thought he was one of those guys who wouldn't take no for an answer. I didn't figure him or the situation out until after I arrived in Colombia. Dumb, huh?"

"No."

Her lips quivered into a small smile. "Thanks."

"What *have* you figured out?" He knew from the background Keely provided that Callie had undergraduate degrees in Accounting and Economics and had just finished work on her Master's in Political Science, all from the University of Chicago. So, Callie definitely was not dumb.

Keely also said Callie had a highly analytical mind—coming from Keely, a genius, that was lofty praise. Plus, Callie had real-world knowledge from having lived on marine bases. He'd bet his favorite fishing rod she'd examined and re-examined every single second of her interactions with Cruz *ad nauseam*.

"I've concluded this cluster fuck was a set up. Cruz had seen me somewhere. Who in the hell knows where or when." She twisted a curl around her finger, smoothing it out, and then did it again. Obviously, a habit she used to calm herself. "I began modeling six years ago. My picture has been plastered all over the damn world since then. Strange men approach me all the time." He shot her a glance. She wasn't bragging, just telling it straight. "Whenever it first happened, Cruz decided he wanted me—and set about getting me."

"Okay, I can see that. Lots of men probably fantasize about having you on their arm and in their beds." *And I'm right there with them.*

She shot him an annoyed look. "Yeah, trust me, it's not fun having men declare their undying love and following me home. It embarrassed my brothers when they were little and now that they're older, they think they have to protect me."

Good for her brothers. He'd like to meet some of those stalker asswipes and teach them a lesson. She'd been scared more than once, he could tell.

"Anyway, I met Cruz at a Colombian fashion designer's premier show and then later at the after-party held at the Colombian Embassy in Chicago. Not so coincidentally, the designer is the same one I'm doing this photo shoot for." She paused as if to let the significance set in. He grunted and she continued with a half-laugh. "At that time, I assumed Cruz was one of the Ambassador's staff or maybe associated with the designer's corporation."

"Do you get invited to a lot of foreign designer's shows and then go to parties at their diplomat's houses?" If he'd had the detailing of her security, those types of gigs would have been covered. Lots of nasty things could happen on embassy grounds since they were considered non-US land by treaty. Cruz would never have gotten near her on his watch.

"More than you'd think. However, if I'm not actually modeling, I don't usually attend, even when they are in Chicago. I have a life and responsibilities outside of the fashion world." She paused and shifted her curl torture to a new strand. "I didn't model in the Colombian show, just attended because my agent Marv twisted my arm. He said I had the chance to end my career on a high note with Evan taking fabulous pictures of me in the designer's beautiful clothes in," she let go of her hair to wave her arm around, "a magnificent World Heritage City." She let out another little snort and he couldn't keep the smile off his face. She sounded so indignant. "I never thought to look below the surface. I'm smarter than this, but I trusted Marv. So did Evan. Shit. Shit. Shit."

"So, you think this Marv set you up with Cruz?"

"Yeah."

"Don't beat yourself up." He glanced at his mirrors. They'd picked up a tail as soon as they'd left the parking lot. Cruz had sent in reinforcements to replace the downed men. "He was someone you'd trusted for years. You had the right to believe in him." He'd be looking up old Marv once he delivered Callie safely home. Just a little follow up, all a part of the SSI service, to inform the man not to fuck with her again.

She shot him a grateful smile. "Thanks for saying that. I still feel stupid, but I'll get over it." She sighed and angled her neck one way then the other. "As soon as I can get onto a secure computer so I can do some hacking, I plan to prove my former agent—I fired his ass yesterday over the phone—took money from Cruz to get me here."

"What makes you think he got paid?"

"Marv does not cross the street without getting paid. And because I accused him and he denied it. I can always tell when he's lying to me—and he was lying through his perfectly capped teeth. I'll find the money trail—and a side bennie of that is I'll have accessed one of Cruz's laundry accounts." She chuckled, a throaty sound which grabbed his testicles and gave them an arousing squeeze. "Once I find that first laundry account, I'll use my knowledge and skills and uncover some of Cruz's other accounts. I'll make that bastard sorry he bribed my chicken shit of an agent into betraying my trust. I'm also betting I'll find Cruz is a silent partner in the designer's company—another avenue to launder his ill-gotten gains."

He'd bet she was one hundred percent correct. Cruz had a lot of dirty money to clean. He shot Callie another glance to see how upset she was, but found her smiling and more relaxed than a few seconds ago. Talking seemed to calm her, so he'd keep her talking. Plus, the more he learned about her, the better he'd know her and how she'd react if they had to resort to any of his back-up plans to get out of the country.

"What happened in Chicago when you first met Cruz?" His gaze narrowed as another Range Rover joined the first one. Damn, he was a regular Pied Piper and the rats were joining in by the car loads.

"At the fashion show, he managed to sit next to me and then proceeded to tell me how much he'd admired me all these years." She stuck her finger in her mouth. "Ack!"

Risto couldn't help it—he laughed. "Bad, huh?"

She rolled her eyes. "He was so oily. He has movie-star looks and is a total narcissist. His conversation was all about *his* feelings and how I'd add so much to *his* experience in Chicago if I would show him around. As if I had that kind of time with two younger brothers to get ready to go to college and me finishing my Master's thesis. The jerkwad."

Risto just shook his head and smiled. He slid his left hand into the pocket on the driver's door and flipped off the safety on his Glock, just in case those following decided to go on the attack. He didn't think they'd endanger Callie, but he wasn't willing to be found unprepared. "Go on. After the show—at the embassy, what happened?"

"He put on the full-court press. He had the Ambassador praise him to the skies, probably a relative. Then the designer came up and fawned over the both of us."

"Why didn't you just walk away from the bastard?"

"He had his arm around my waist—" She startled when he growled. Shooting him a wary glance, she continued, "And, um, I didn't want to make a scene."

He swore in Russian. The bastard touched her, held her against her will. Her agent should be shot for putting her in such a situation.

"Um, I know filthy Russian swear words, too."

"All Russian swear words are filthy. Do you know Finnish?"

"No."

"Good. I'll do my worst swearing in that language then."

"I don't mind. You can swear in English. I told you—I swear." She batted her lashes. "Unlike Keely, I did not have a mom who made me pay up if I dropped f-bombs."

His lips quirked as he recalled Keely's amusing use of frick-fracking instead of fuck. He couldn't remember ever having this kind of conversation with any other woman to whom he was attracted. But then, this was an unusual situation. "So, tell me how you got away from the asswipe ... at the Embassy."

"The final straw was he asked me back to his hotel after the party—for drinks. As if I hadn't heard that line a hundred times before. Anyway, Marv, the fink, came over and did manage to extract me. He wanted me to sit down with the designer and talk about this photo shoot. Thank the Lord. Cruz was all smiles, kissed my hand. Blech."

"Kissed your hand how?" His words came out low and mean, he couldn't help it.

She shot him a "what the fuck" look, but answered anyway. "The palm."

He swore in Finnish. "I hope you disinfected it as soon as you could."

Her face turned solemn, but the corners of her eyes crinkled with impish laughter. "I had antiseptic wipes in my purse. I made sure he saw me use them."

"That's my girl. So, is that it? You got talked into doing this show and then you saw Cruz again here?" He'd bet his large Caymanian bank account, it wasn't.

"Are you kidding?" She leaned over and examined his face. "Yeah, you're kidding. He tried to see me several more times while he was in Chicago. In fact, he called the day after the show. I told him I did *not* date."

She flopped back against her seat and stared out the passenger-side window. "He didn't listen. He'd just happen to run into me several times when I was out eating with friends or shopping. The fourth or fifth time it occurred, he asked me out again." She laughed, and it didn't sound like a happy ha-ha. "As I mentioned before, men ask me out all the time. I don't think too much about it. I have a well-rehearsed and polite refusal. And it isn't a made-up excuse—I do have a busy life outside of modeling."

If I wanted you, I wouldn't let the story, true or not, stop me. I'd find a way to become part of that life.

"Obviously, Cruz didn't want to accept the story," he said, staring straight ahead.

The fact he shared a personality trait with Cruz didn't make him happy—and just went to prove neither of them deserved Callie.

He looked in the rearview mirror and noted his tails were maintaining at two to three car lengths. No shooting. Good. The Hummer was armored, but more and more of the terrorists of the world were arming themselves with armor-piercing bullets. They probably had instructions to do nothing unless he tried to take Callie out of the city.

"Yeah, he was persistent. Sent flowers. Sent gifts. Sent notes swearing his undying admiration and love. All of which I returned. Then nothing. I thought *good*, he's taken the hint

… finally." She shook her head. "I now realize his constant contact stopped when the final arrangements had been made for this trip. Dammit."

She hit the dashboard with her hand and shot him a glance filled with self-recrimination. "I bought into the trip. I mean, Evan and Chad would be here. They'd never willingly lead me or their crew into danger. They're my brothers' honorary uncles; we're family. The job looked normal. The crew was the usual one Evan used. *Elle* magazine signed on to publish the shoot. The designer bent over backwards to make modifications so the clothing would suit my looks and figure since I'm hippier and fuller breasted than most models."

Oh, baby, had he noticed. She was a straight male's walking wet dream.

"I couldn't imagine Marv setting me up." She began to play with her hair once more. *Shit, she's stressed again.* "He knew Cruz gave me the creeps. I told him so. But he did it anyway. Just wait until I get my hands on the dipwad, I'm making him pay."

Not if I get to him first.

"Yeah, sounds as if you were set up. When I get you home, you need to let this go, Callie. Let Keely and Tweeter follow the money trail. It's too dangerous for you to pursue the lead through your agent's under-the-table money. Cruz deals with some real badasses including one of the most ruthless drug lords in the Western Hemisphere. You don't want Paco's cartel after you. You could be…"

She cut him off by placing her hand on his thigh and squeezing. *Oh fuck me Jesus, save me.* Jerking off was now an absolute necessity if he were to keep his hands and randy cock off Callie—and as soon as possible.

"It's what I went to school to do—track terrorist and drug money," she said. "I'll be damn good at it. I plan on hunting down all Cruz's shell companies then tracking their bank accounts and getting them frozen until he has no access to the piles of money he's made from harming innocents. If that leads to his drug cartel bosses—and I sure hope it does—then fine. Cruz and all his associates are scum-sucking amoeba and I want them to pay for their crimes." She sniffed, not the cute little snort of disgust, but a sadder sound.

Risto looked at her. *Damn, she's crying.* He jerked as if someone had punched him in the gut. *Fuck. I'm an insensitive jerk.* He just recalled her father had been killed on a mission going after drug traffickers in South America.

"You sound like a taller Keely." His gently teasing comment had the effect he'd hoped for. She smiled and chuckled, a watery sound, but still better than crying in silence.

"Why thank you. I want to make a difference in the world."

"Tired of modeling, huh?"

He took a turn which would take them the long way back to the hotel—and his tails followed, closing in just in case he hopped onto Route 25. A third vehicle, a black town car with tinted windows, joined the parade. Cruz had arrived. If Risto had any doubts about the para-leader's seriousness in obtaining Callie before, he had none now.

He made a command decision. She wouldn't be at the photo shoot tomorrow. They needed to get out of Colombia as soon as possible. He'd advise his SSI back-up team of the change in plans once he got Callie safely back to the hotel so they could move the schedule forward. Cruz wouldn't make his move in broad daylight, he'd wait for darkness. By this evening, he and Callie would be safely tucked away at an SSI safe house in Cartagena where they'd get equipped and grab some sleep before setting out early in the morning to meet up with the SSI helicopter. Travelling the treacherous Colombian roads after darkness fell was not something he'd willingly put Callie through.

"Never wanted to model to begin with," she answered his question, "but the money was obscene. I had two younger brothers to house, clothe, feed, and put through college. Dad's marine survivor benefits and insurance didn't go far in Chicago which is where I was attending college on a full scholarship when he died." She absently stroked his thigh.

He clutched the steering wheel more tightly to resist the temptation to grab her hand and move it to the strained crotch of his jeans. Callie was very touchy-feely—a trait he highly approved of in women in general and her in particular. Her ease in touching him also led him to believe she might be open to return touching. He'd have to make it clear if she continued to pat him, she'd have to pay the consequences, pleasurable consequences for both of them.

"The boys agreed to move north so we could stay together as a family and I could continue my studies. Our Mom died after the twins were born. I was seven at the time so I was always more than a big sister."

He must've made a sound, because she reacted by petting his leg. His cock jerked and he mentally went through the procedures to field strip and clean his Barrett to keep from pulling over and taking her in the back seat of the Hummer. And the fact he even considered doing her in the vehicle with the enemy on their tail told him just how fractured his vaunted self-control was around this woman.

"Hey, don't feel sorry for me. Things weren't rough for long. Within a year of Dad's death, Evan discovered me at the place I waitressed. I was keeping things together, but I admit he really saved our lives. The modeling money kept us in our little bungalow and provided the boys with opportunities and a great private school education. I promised myself to model only until I didn't need the extra money any longer or I had finished my graduate education. Both those events happened earlier this year. I'd already given notice on all my cosmetics contracts and to Marv."

"When you find out how much he sold you out for, I'd be interested in knowing if it was more than thirty pieces of silver."

"I'll let you know. I expect it was far more than that." She moved her hand from his thigh to his arm. He let out a small sigh of relief and willed his cock to relax. "Um, we're being followed by two Ranger Rovers and a dark sedan of some kind. Is this why we're taking the scenic route back to the hotel?"

"Yeah. So, you noticed them, did ya?" She nodded, her face solemn. "They're making sure we don't hit Route 25 and make tracks to Bogotá and the US Embassy."

She raised a delicately arched brow. "We'd be safe there, yes?"

"If we could make it, there's a small squad of marines, plus some intelligence types on the embassy compound. We could hold off Cruz until the US Military came to chase them away."

"That's what I'd guessed, even though the Embassy told me they couldn't help me. Dad was stationed in Colombia before the twins were born. I was five and I remember living in a military-protected compound outside of Bogotá and Mom and Dad talking about the Embassy as the place to retreat to if we were attacked."

She paused and sighed. He glanced over to see her lay her head back against the headrest. Her eyes were closed, moisture coated her long lashes. Obviously, too many sad memories. He brushed a tear off her cheek with the back of a finger. She opened her eyes and stared at him.

"You wouldn't have made it, Callie."

"Yeah, that's what Cruz's terrible twosome told me when I went to the lobby to see about leasing a car. They said it wasn't safe for a beautiful señorita on the roads, especially at night."

Risto shuddered. The idea of Callie, alone, on a Colombian road, if you could call most of the tracks they had roads, exposed to any Tomas, Ricardo or Harry terrorist group scared him shitless. He didn't fear much in this world, but that scenario would rank right up there at the top of what did. "It's not. It's not safe for anyone on Colombian roads most days, but especially at night."

"I bet I'd be safe with you, right?"

"Yeah, you'll be safe with me. We'll be heading out early tomorrow morning to a small *finca* SSI uses as a safe house for operatives. We do a lot of work in South America. Our transportation out of Colombia will meet us there."

"What about the shoot and Evan and his crew?"

"No shoot. Cruz is moving faster now that another man is in the picture. Hence, the three vehicles following us. We'll be changing hotels tonight, also." For more reasons than the one he'd just told her about. "Once I have you safely tucked in with Conn Redmond at the SSI safe house, I'll inform Evan and Chad about their US military escort to the airport. Keely booked them a private charter flight out tomorrow night, but we'll need to bump that up to this evening. Once they get through Customs, they should be safe. If everything goes smoothly, Cruz won't even miss them until after their flight is in the air. He'll be too busy trying to find us."

"What about the charter departure area?" She scrunched her forehead and began twisting her hair again. "Won't there be some risk there?"

What a sweetheart. She was more concerned for her friends than herself. "We have some local contract operatives who'll stay with them until their plane takes off. They'll be fine."

"God, Evan and Chad will dine out on this story forever." She grinned briefly, then frowned, a puzzled look in her eyes. "Why can't we go with Evan and the rest if the US Military…" She shook her head and waved her hand in the air. "Enh, erase that. Stupid question. We need to be the diversion. Where I go, Cruz and his merry band of murderers will follow. Plus, Cruz is just stupid enough to attack a military escort. Casualties would then occur and the US would be drawn into an international incident. The US military might operate here, but we aren't supposed to be here."

"Basically. Most people know we have a large military and intelligence presence in Colombia, but we don't hit everyone over the head with it."

"Plus, we can't embarrass the Colombian government, shaky as it is." She swore under her breath. "I never expected that class on South American terrorism and real world politics would ever have applicability in my life. I just took it because Colombia has always been one terrorist group away from being a failed state and is a fertile ground for tracking drug and terrorist money trails."

"We'll get out of here." Risto patted her knee. "Trust me?"

"Yeah. And I think after I find all Cruz's laundries, Ren will have to offer me a job at SSI. Keely and I would be a super-analytical team and could prepare intel analysis for the NSA and other SSI clients."

Risto said nothing. Having Callie around 24/7, within arm's reach, at Sanctuary might be more than even his iron will could handle. Good thing Ren had okayed him heading up an SSI-East in Upper Peninsula Michigan.

Chapter Three

The Sofitel Santa Clara Hotel was situated in the core of the ancient city. Adapted from a seventeenth century monastery, it was the perfect blend of old and new, and if Callie had been here for any other reason, she would've enjoyed staying longer and exploring everything the ancient city had to offer.

She shot Risto a curious look when he pulled the Hummer into a temporary guest parking spot instead of driving up to the entrance and allowing the valet to park the vehicle. "Why are we stopping here?" She looked in the side mirror and saw the trail of vehicles following them had parked on the street illegally, hovering like predators to see what the prey would do next. "They're still there."

"We need to talk about some things while we have absolute privacy. Don't worry, I have my eye on them." He left the car running and turned toward her. "When we get to the valet, we need to put on a show for our friends back there. I suspect Cruz is in the town car."

She wrinkled her nose. "Exactly what kind of show?"

"I want you to kiss me as you'd kiss a new husband you hadn't seen in four days. You did okay back at the shoot location, but I'm pretty damn sure Cruz's men have given him a blow-by-blow, word-by-word description by now."

"And he might suspect the display was not lover-like enough. Gotcha. I can do that."

Boy howdy, could she. Her lips already tingled anticipating it. The last kiss hadn't been nearly long enough and she'd only gotten a hint of how he tasted. Hell, she was aroused just inhaling his scent in the short drive from the shoot location. A real kiss might push her over the edge into jumping his bones. It had been a long—a really long—sexual dry spell for a myriad of reasons. "Then what?" she asked.

"We'll go to the suite and get ready to go to a late lunch … out. Then we'll lose the tail and go to Conn's place." His formerly shuttered expression fell away. He hit the steering wheel with the palm of his hand, displaying the first real emotion she'd seen from him. "Callie, fuck it. I wasn't going to tell you something since I'd already given you a good reason for moving, but you have a right to … shit, there's no easy way—"

"What is it? You'll find it's easier to give it to me straight, Risto. I'm tougher than I look."

"The fucker has eyes and ears in your suite. Probably has had since you checked in."

"You mean," she massaged the too-tight muscles over her throat as she attempted to speak, "…h-he's … he's been watching me? V-videotaping m-me?" She thought of all the times she'd strolled around the *casita* naked. Hell, she'd used her vibrator the other night for a little stress relief, hoping it would help her sleep. And Cruz … his men … watched her!

"Not just taping, but real time, live eyes. When I scouted around earlier, I found their setup in the next *casita*." Risto's tone was coldly furious. Well, hell, he could join the friggin' club. She wasn't feeling exactly all happy-happy, joy-joy, either.

And now she knew why he'd sounded odd about stopping at the hotel before coming to get her at the shoot.

"Where did you make the call to SSI from, Callie?" He smoothed his hand over her arm, halting her fingers as she twisted her hair into corkscrews. His hand was warm and comforting.

"Not the suite. No clusterfuck in the making there." If she had, Cruz's guards would've known he was an SSI operative and shot him on sight. "I had a bad feeling after Cruz approached me two nights ago." *After he man-handled me and threatened my brothers.* "So, I made the call on the street as Evan, Chad and I walked off dinner and discussed the situation."

His lips twisted into a slight smile and the thunderclouds in his dark eyes lightened. He gave her hand a little squeeze. "Good girl."

She flushed with pleasure at winning his approval once again. She had a feeling it took a lot for a lay person to please him. "And you'll also be happy to know, Keely and I used a code we made up when we were kids," at his raised eyebrow, she added, "for when we played war games with her brothers and their friends." Her lips quirked. "Drove the boys nuts. As soon as I used the code words about big ears, we switched to Russian. We're both very fluent. I wasn't taking any chances one of the goon squad could overhear my side of the conversation."

She'd been intensely aware of the two men tailing her and her friends. That's also when she'd warned Evan and Chad about Cruz; they hadn't been present when the bastard had tried to intimidate her.

"That's good, excellent." He pulled her hand to his lips and kissed her fingertips, then released it. "We'll still have the advantage. They don't know who or what I am. They'll underestimate me ... hell, Cruz fucking underestimated you, sweetheart."

She blushed and wished she was his "sweetheart" for real

and not just for the job. "If Cruz thought you were muscle, he'd come in, guns a-blazing, and just snatch me. For now, we just get shadowed."

"Exactly, though his patience is waning."

She swallowed. "Um, where were the cameras?" Her face flushed rosy pink, a combination of fury and embarrassment.

"Everywhere. Full coverage." His voice was calm, but the look in his eyes verged on stormy again. It made her feel better to know he was furious on her behalf, that she wasn't alone in her anger.

"Shit. Fuck. Crap. I want ... want..." She hissed. "I'll kill the asswipe." A look of shock swept over Risto's face at her threat. She choked back laughter. He had totally the wrong idea about her. Better he learn who she really was sooner rather than later. She wasn't a prude or a pacifist. "Does it bother you that I want to kill him?"

"Not a problem, it's just you look so lady-like..."

"Get over that notion. While I may not look like soldier material, and it's been some time since I lived on a marine base, I can think and act like one when the occasion warrants." *And this occasion does.* She gave an abrupt laugh. "You need to know that Keely's brothers, their dad and mine trained me to defend myself. I excelled at the use of weapons. But while I'm coordinated enough and had the desire to learn martial arts, I just couldn't hit or kick people. Hell, I can't even punch a practice dummy. Wimpy, right?"

Risto's lips twisted into an amused grin. "No. Normal, I'd say." He looked in his side mirror. She did the same on her side and noted the Rovers and the town car hadn't moved. "Callie, Cruz will approach us while we're having lunch, you know that?"

"Yes. Why are we going out? Why not stick close to the hotel until it's time to move to the new place?"

"He could pay, or more likely coerce, someone to put something in our food."

"You really think he'd drug us?"

"Me, he'd poison. You, he'd drug. As you said, he wants you alive." As if he couldn't stop touching her, he lifted a hand and stroked a finger down her arm. She inhaled, goose flesh arising along his finger's path. She bit her lip to smother the gasp threatening to emerge.

"You're lucky he wants this photo shoot to come off for reasons of his own—or he would've taken you the first night." She shivered, not from his touch this time, but relief that she'd had the chance to call for help. "Hey, it's okay." His voice was just as gentle and soothing as his touch. "It didn't happen. Don't think about it. The fucker screwed up and now I'm here. He won't get you. I promise."

"I know. Keely and her husband trust you. I trust you." She worried her lower lip with her teeth. "Will you get rid of the eyes and ears … in the room? When we go to change? Please." She leaned into his hand as he moved to caress her neck. His words and touch warmed her, chasing away the throat-clenching fear she'd lived with over the past two days. On the surface, she'd called upon all her modeling skills and put on the performance of her life, but inside she'd been a quivering puddle of goo. Just having Risto here made her feel safe, feel as if she'd make it home and back to her life.

"Sorry, can't. It would tip him off…"

"…that you were more than just a husband." She nodded. "Sorry, I wasn't thinking. I've had some training about potential abduction. My dad saw to that. There was always the chance we military dependents might be kidnapped from the base housing in foreign countries. I have some survival skills, but nothing like what you're used to with Keely."

"Keely's unique. Don't compare yourself to her. From what she tells me, you're talented, just in a different way." He massaged the knots in her neck with a firm, but gentle motion. His touch, while it eased the tension in her neck, created new tension farther down her body. It was all she could do not to rub her thighs together to ease the aching in her sex. "As far as I can tell, you've done everything right to this point," he said. "You figured out you were in big trouble as soon as you saw Cruz and you called for your extraction and protection for your brothers. You held up."

"Thanks, I needed to hear that. I've been so afraid."

"Hey, fear keeps you sharp."

"Then I'm a Ginsu knife." She sliced the air as if she held a knife.

Risto grinned as he switched from massaging the back of her neck to feathering her hair through his fingers. It felt wonderful, and she wondered if he was acclimating her to his touch for the act they had to put on for Cruz or if he did it because he wanted to. "Callie, you said you had some training. What kind?"

"I told you about the failed attempts at teaching me how to take down an attacker. I couldn't even knee a guy in the balls." She frowned. "Although I think I have the proper motivation now. I'm pretty sure I could emasculate Cruz, the scum-sucking, Peeping Tom, lowlife fucktard."

Risto's lips broke into a full smile and he chuckled. Jesus, he was gorgeous when he smiled—not *GQ*, metrosexual attractiveness, but more *Field and Stream* masculine ruggedness. "Go on ... what else?"

"Um, I told you I excelled at shooting. Back at Lejeune, I was almost as good as Keely. I expect she's better now since she's attended Sniper School. My dad always said guns were the great equalizer for females in the military."

"What kind of weapons?"

"You name it, I've probably shot a version of it. Personal sidearm?" He nodded, his black-eyed gaze fixed on her face. No nerves or awareness on his face about the bad guys watching them, but she knew he was aware of where everyone was and would act instantaneously if needed. "I prefer a Glock or a Ruger. I own a ladies Ruger since it's lighter and fits my hand better. I like the Lapua or the Remington sniper rifles for long-range. And any of the submachine guns are just fine, though some of the Eastern European stuff is crap and gets clogged easy in wet and dirty environments." He raised an eyebrow. His eyes glinted with amusement. "We trained in the marshes and savannas surrounding Lejeune—very wet and very dirty places."

He nodded, chuckling. "Been there, done that. Jesus, you and Keely are unbelievable. Most women don't even want to touch guns, let alone crawl around in the muck and shoot them." His eyes filled with approval. "But have you shot anything in the last seven years?"

"Yep." His wider smile reappeared. God, she loved his approval. She could get addicted to it—she who hadn't felt the need to obtain a man's approval since her dad died. "I taught my brothers to shoot. We go to the range a couple of times a month." She shot him a broad grin. "I still rate expert—on paper targets." She frowned. She'd never shot at a live target. Could she? She pictured Cruz aiming a gun at her brothers—or Risto—and knew she could.

He pulled a submachine gun from under the driver's seat, keeping it below the level of the dash. "Can you shoot this?"

She studied it for a second then smiled. "An H&K MP5K. It has thirty-round mags. High velocity with stopping power. Bullet caliber is 9mm. And it weighs under six pounds." She nodded. "Yeah, I practice with the MP5A3 at the range—there's not much difference in how the two models handle. The MP5K is just shorter overall and has a slightly different grip."

"Very good. Put it in that huge tote bag you carry. It should fit easily. There are extra magazines and a box of ammo under your seat, get that out also. We'll be walking from now on. We'll pick up a new vehicle at Conn's. I figure Cruz will plant a bug on this one while it's in the hotel parking."

She took the gun, making sure to keep it out of the line of

sight of their watchers, and checked to make sure the safety was engaged. She popped out the magazine and checked to see it was full and loaded properly, then reinserted the mag. She put the gun in the tote sitting next to her legs then retrieved the extra mags and the extra ammunition from under her seat and added them to the bag.

Risto grunted his approval. "I'll have Conn locate you a light-weight handgun."

He stroked a surprisingly gentle finger along the pulse beating rapidly in her neck. Her stomach clenched and her pussy flooded. Who knew her neck was such an erogenous zone? She sure as heck never stroked her neck to get off, but if Risto kept at it long enough, she might come.

"Can you handle a knife?" he asked.

Before she could answer, he rubbed her earlobe between his thumb and a finger. She swallowed a moan at the pleasure sweeping over her upper body. Her nipples already tight from just being near him, puckered even more tightly. *Shit, this man is lethal.*

"Um, knife?" He nodded, no expression on his face and his thumb and finger still plying her earlobe. "No, not really. Only to cook. I chop a mean onion." She shoved his hand away from her ear.

He laughed and stroked his finger along her neck, then down along the clavicle. Pleasure shot down her spine and she had a hard time not wiggling in her seat.

"Funny girl. We'll keep the big knives away from you."

She grabbed the hand tantalizing her. "No, no! I want a knife. I need a knife. A big effing sharp knife."

He looked at her as if she'd gone crazy. "Callie, if you…"

She held up her free hand to halt his words. "I take it we may have to hit the jungle." He nodded and looked really unhappy about the prospect. "There are snakes and … stuff out there." She grimaced with distaste. "Dad and Colonel Walsh always had us kids carry knives when we played in the areas around the camp. Reptiles I can kill easily, in fact, I think it is my duty to do so—way too many reptiles in the world." Cruz being of the two-legged variety.

"Okay, one knife in a scabbard. You have any basic training in the wild?" He alternated idly stroking her neck and playing with her hair now. But she could tell he was still alert to the men watching them from the three vehicles. Glad he was, because all she was aware of was him.

"Yeah, Dad and the Colonel would take us kids on what they called wilderness vacations, but, in reality, they were toned-down versions of what the marine recruits went through." She smiled remembering how she and Keely would bitch and moan, but refused to let the boys do better than them. "I'm just okay in swamps, so that probably includes jungles. I need to warn you, I hate heat and especially heat with humidity. Something about my metabolism doesn't agree with it. So, jungles, deserts, I can make it, but I tire easily. My elements are the northern woods and mountains, and I just love snow. I should've been born a polar bear."

Risto smiled then sobered quickly. "Plan A avoids all roughing it and gets us out of Colombia the quickest. But if we have to go to Plans B or C, we might have several days in the rough as we head for the Panamanian border. We'll be properly supplied, though."

Picturing a map of Colombia in her head, she knew he meant to head for the port city of Turbo for sea travel or the Darien Gap for over ground. She shivered. No one travelled across the Darien area of Colombia and Panama if they could find another way. "I'll be fine. Just tell me what to do and when to do it—and I will. You're the boss."

"Yeah, I'm the boss." His words came out husky ... sexy. He glanced at his rearview mirror and stiffened. "Our friends are getting antsy. The passenger in the lead Rover is on his cell and gesticulating like crazy. Just remember, once we leave this vehicle, anything we say or do is probably being observed." He paused. "That means, I'll be touching and kissing you." He stroked the back of his hand over her breasts. She inhaled as sensation shot to her clit. "I'll be with you as you shower and dress. Keep your voice low and atonal. Whispers can be picked up by the mikes. I'll do my best to keep my body between you and the cameras."

God, he'd see her naked. More to the point, she'd see him naked. Her inner vixen said "yum." Her commonsense said "chill, it's his job to protect you, even from video cameras."

"Got it. Academy Award time. I'm not an actress, but I've played up to the camera often enough for fashion shoots. I think I can handle it. But can you?" She glanced at him as he turned away from her and put the car into gear. "You have a special lady? Will it be hard for you to make pretend love to me?"

Her damn mouth had a mind of its own. She really didn't need to know if he was seeing someone. She'd probably never see him again once they got back to the States—well, not unless she went to work for SSI, and then she'd come across him when he wasn't out on missions. "Forget I asked. It's none of my business. I apologize."

His gaze straight forward as he maneuvered the crowded valet lane, he replied in a gravelly tone. "No special lady. And no, it won't be a burden." He turned his head, his stare glinting and hot. "Just make believe I'm the guy in that perfume commercial you did. You burned up the fucking screen. Cruz sees that kind of emotion, he'll believe we're lovers."

Callie threw back her head and laughed. The first good laugh she'd had since she arrived in Colombia.

"What's so fucking funny?" He sounded aggrieved. "That commercial is hot enough to melt steel."

"The guy in the commercial?"

"Yeah, what about him?"

Was that a hint of anger she heard in his tone? Interesting.

"That's Evan's Chad—and he's gay. He hated every single

second of the commercial shoot. We had to break so many times because he kept muttering rude comments under his breath which had me laughing." She wiped tears of amusement from her face. "Man, I thought Evan was going to kill us. Chad told me later Evan made him pay big time for prolonging the shoot."

"Well, I thought it was sexy as hell."

"You and everyone else—except for the poor crew who had to stand around until we got it right." She rubbed his arm. A muscle in his jaw twitched and his hands clutched the wheel so tightly she could see white appear on his knuckles. She added, "I bet you can pretend better than Chad." *Geez, Callie, come on to the man, why don't you? He's here to do a job. You're the job.*

Risto pulled into the valet area, put the car into park and turned off the engine. He turned toward her. Framing her face with his hands, he pulled her to him then whispered against her lips. "I won't have to fucking pretend anything, Callie Meyers. You're a sexy woman. You'll have to set the limits here, honey, because once I start kissing you, touching you … I won't want to stop." He brushed a light kiss over her parted lips, once, twice.

The valet opened the driver's side door. "You staying in the hotel, *señor*?"

Risto didn't turn toward the interruption. Instead he took her lips in a rapacious kiss, thrusting his tongue inside her mouth as if he owned it. It was a kiss unlike any other she'd ever experienced, all dominant male laying claim to his female. She wasn't sure how long they kissed, time meant nothing as long as he kept stroking her tongue with his, as long as his fingers cradled her face, as long as his scent surrounded her. She was in big trouble, because a primal part of her didn't want him to stop ever. And he wanted her to set the frickin' limits?

"*Señor? Señora?* Do you wish me to park the car?" The valet sounded irritated and she wondered how long he'd been trying to get their attention.

Risto pulled his mouth from hers, placing a final, gentle kiss to the tip of her nose, his thumb massaging her kiss-swollen lips. "Stay put until I come around to help you out."

She nodded, touching his lips with a finger. He nipped the tip. Yeah, there'd be no pretending with him. He was all man—and his kiss told her she wasn't just a job, he wanted her. And she wasn't averse to letting him have her. Screw limits.

Kissing Callie had been a mistake. But he planned on doing it again—and soon. She tasted sweet and hot—and had definitely kissed him back. They had a highly charged sexual chemistry unlike any he'd experienced. His priority was to get Callie out of Colombia and back to Chicago—and he would. But until then, they were both adults, and if she was willing to walk on the wild side, he'd be happy to oblige.

"We won't need the car until tomorrow morning." He projected his voice so the men in the lead Rover, which was now two car lengths behind theirs in the valet lane, would think he and Callie would be spending the night at the hotel. He slipped the valet twenty dollars. The man smiled and nodded.

Risto opened the passenger door and lifted Callie out. He reached in and grabbed the tote and put it over her arm. His fingers trailed over her forearm. The valet watched Callie avidly, so he hadn't noticed when Risto added his Glock to her tote. Risto retrieved the duffle bag he'd left behind the seat, which contained his emergency evac kit.

He suspected the valet was in the pay of Cruz and would make a full report after he planted a tracking device on the Hummer. *Might as well play up to the audience.*

"God, I missed you, baby. No more trips without me." He angled his head to take Callie's mouth in another tongue-thrusting kiss. She opened to him immediately, her free arm going around his neck as she leaned into his body, rubbing her stomach against his hard-on. *Yeah, she tastes just as good as the first time. Sweet with just a hint of spice.*

Breaking away, he placed a kiss at the corner of her mouth, then spoke against the shell of her ear. "We need to take this inside."

Stroking his jaw with a shaky finger, she nodded and placed a nibbling kiss on his chin. His cock jerked and he swept a hand over his front under the cover of Callie's gargantuan tote and her body, nudging his unruly member into a more comfortable position. She snickered against his jaw line. *The little tease!* He placed her at his side, his arm around her waist, and her unencumbered arm went around his. They fit perfectly, just as he knew they would. They'd fit even better in bed. He maneuvered them out of the valet lane and toward the side of the building that led to her *casita*.

As they casually strolled the beautiful grounds, Callie slipped her fingers down the back of his waistband and underneath his shirt. Then she massaged his lower back and upper buttocks. "Watch it, Callie. I promised you'd be in control ... but if you keep tempting me, I'll take it as a green light." And to hell with the danger, her touch was incendiary.

Her eyes widened. "Sorry ... um..." She pulled her hand from the back of his waistband, but left her fingers lying lightly against his lower back. Her cheek bones were slightly flushed. "Define teasing." They continued to walk as if they hadn't a care in the world, their arms around one another.

Their unwanted shadows followed, always keeping them in sight.

"Touching me in more than a casual way." He angled his head to look at her. "Sticking your hand down my pants and massaging my ass is teasing."

"Um, I thought we were supposed to convince Cruz's men we're lovers."

"Was that what you were doing, Callie? Be honest." His voice was firm as he assessed her expression. He caught a look which he read as sexual hunger in her eyes. Good, he wasn't the only one attracted.

"Yes ... no. No. It just ... shit. It felt right ... okay?" She lowered her gaze to the hand clutching the tote bag. Her long hair hid her face from him, but her posture was rigid.

Dammit. He'd embarrassed her, put her on the defensive. She'd just started to relax, getting into the role she had to play, getting over her fear of Cruz now that he was here—now, she was stiff, upset. He could kick his own ass.

"Callie? Look at me." She shook her head, a single tear leaked from the corner of one eye. *Shit. Yeah, asshole, you embarrassed her. Now fix it.* "What you did ... it felt fucking fantastic. I want you to touch me however you want, whenever you want, but you need to understand I'll act on it. Right then."

A frown marred her smooth forehead. "I arouse you that much?" She angled her head. Her gaze seemed naively curious and ... she didn't believe him!

Shit, who were the assholes she'd dated? She could arouse a dead man.

He couldn't help it. He lowered his head and swept the single tear drop away with his tongue. She shivered and inhaled sharply. So responsive. He bet she'd make all sorts of sweet noises if he licked her from top to bottom.

"Yeah, you make me hot. Do you want me to act on this attraction between us, Callie?" He held his breath. Her response was more important to him than breathing.

"Yes."

He exhaled roughly. *If she knew all the ways I've fantasized about fucking her in my dreams, she'd run for the Ecuadoran border.* "You should have issues with me as a lover. I'm too rough. Too dominant. Plus, I'm not a permanent kind of guy."

She examined his face for what seemed like an eternity. She nodded, one short abrupt movement of her head. "Understood. I'll take what I can get, Risto Smith. Whenever

I can get it."

Sweet Callie had just given him *carte blanche*—and before he got her safely back to her door in Chicago, he'd take advantage of it—fully.

Chapter Four

After they reached the door of the *casita*, Callie waited as Risto retrieved his key card and opened the door. He ushered her inside, locking and bolting the door behind them. He moved about the room checking the locks on the French doors. "Take your shower and change, Callie. Wear something casual."

He moved to embrace her. She went into his arms and luxuriated in the solid strength of him. *Safe, I feel safe.*

"Pack only essentials into that huge bag of yours." He spoke in a low monotone against her ear.

She nodded and replied in the same tone. "Already done. I was ready to run if Cruz made his move. But I'll add some extra socks, underwear and some tank tops. Can you block my actions from the cameras in the bedroom?"

"Yeah." He walked her to the bedroom and stopped inside the doorway. He nuzzled her ear. "The cameras are aimed at the top of the bed, not the floors."

Her breath stuttered at the thought of what Cruz and his men must have seen.

Risto kissed her forehead and rubbed her back. "It's okay, I'm here now. Don't rehash the last two days. Forget the cameras. Let me worry about everything."

She kissed his jaw and stroked the back of his neck before she moved away. She dropped the tote on the floor next to the bed and casually added the items she thought she might need. She fastened the tote, then stood up with a change of clothes in her hand. When she turned around, Risto was there, his big body protecting her from the camera. His arms went around her waist and he rubbed his unshaven cheek against hers.

"I'm packed. You're going to get me a handgun more my size, yes? And a knife?"

"Yes, later." He kissed her ear. "Conn will get us anything we need. His voice increased in volume. "Let's get cleaned up, baby, so I can feed you. The cantina I told you about has these fish tacos I've been craving ever since you told me about the Cartagena shoot." He patted her bottom, his fingers lingering on her lower curves.

"Sounds yummy, tiger." Callie took Risto's cue and replied in the same carefree vein. She'd be damned if she allowed her rescue to fail because she hadn't held up her end of the acting. She angled her head and kissed him, tasting him as fully as he'd tasted her in the Hummer.

He muttered "tease" against her lips and took over the kiss. Her tongue dueled with his as he savaged her mouth. She loved his aggressiveness. His hungry kisses made her pussy ache and clit throb.

Reluctantly, she broke the kiss. His lips roved over her face, travelling to her neck as she arched to give him access. She moaned as he bit the juncture of her neck and shoulder then soothed it with his tongue. His hands shaped and caressed her breasts. Her nipples pebbled against the thin tank top.

"Shower. Feed me. Remember?" She gasped out the reminder while stroking the side of his jaw. She forced herself to move away from his talented hands. His heated gaze locked onto her breasts as if he were trying to decide whether or not he'd pull her back. She took the option off the table by stepping even farther away.

He scanned her body. "If you don't move that sweet ass, we'll be eating in."

She smiled, then turned to walk toward the bathroom. Casting a flirtatious look over her shoulder, she put a little extra motion into her steps. With her hips undulating from side to side, she recreated the scene from the commercial he so admired. Every few steps, she'd pause, cast him a sultry look, then strip off a piece of clothing until finally she wore only skin, bikini panties and her flip-flops. The flip-flops spoiled the effect; in the commercial she'd worn jeweled stilettos. Her entire body flushed from a combination of excitement and embarrassment.

His muttered "God save me" made her smile.

Reaching the bathroom double-doors, she stopped and angled her body so he'd get a nice look at her unfettered breasts. She skimmed his body from top to bottom through narrowed eyes. "Someone is way over-dressed." She paused, then added in her sexiest voice, "You are coming into the shower with me, aren't you?"

Risto's nostrils flared wildly as he growled something unintelligible. His eyes glittered like black opals as he zeroed in, first on her breasts, then on her bottom, exposed by the thong she wore. When he scanned her hips, anger replaced the lust in his eyes.

Shit, I forgot the bruises.

He reached her in several long steps and swept her into his arms, cradling her easily against his chest. She twined her arms around his neck. He adjusted her more comfortably within his hold, causing his jean-covered arousal to nudge her rear end.

Risto's tone filled with a combustible mixture of anger and lust, he muttered, "Did Cruz put those marks on your butt, Callie? What else did he do? Why didn't you tell me?" In a louder voice, he said, "I'll scrub your back, if you scrub mine." He nuzzled her ear, once more speaking so softly only she could hear. "I want answers."

She turned into his lips. "Cruz touched me…"

His narrowed eyes glittered fiercely through his dark lashes. "Mere touching doesn't cause bruises," he whispered against her mouth.

"Okay, so he grabbed me," she whispered harshly. "He didn't get the chance to do anything else."

"Fuck … just fuck." He placed a furious kiss on her lips. "You're mine to protect for the duration of this mission. I'll fucking kill any man who even tries to touch you."

His snarling tone of protective dominance aroused her even more, sending goose bumps over her flesh. Most men she came across in her world were metro-sexual or gay. God knew none of them had ever elicited this kind of primitive sexual response from her.

She petted his stubble-roughened jaw in an attempt to soothe his anger. "I didn't strip for Cruz." She tongued another of his scars, this one marring his jaw line. "I did it for you, Marine." He shuddered and closed his eyes. "Let's get cleaned up. I want out of this place."

"That's the plan, sweetheart." He nuzzled then licked the tendon on her neck. She arched her head back onto his shoulder to give him better access. He took the opportunity to lightly teeth the area. She gasped and moaned. Proving once again, her neck was a hot spot for her.

Risto carried her farther into the spa-like bathroom. Getting back into her role, she spoke in a normal tone of voice. "Put me down, you maniac. You promised to feed me. I'll start the shower while you get naked."

Her words may have sounded nonchalant, but her thoughts were anything but. All she could think about was Risto, soon-to-be-naked, his body close, surrounding her in the shower. The thought of going to bed with him had her practically panting. Her only fear? She wouldn't be woman enough for him.

Shoving her concern to the back of her mind, she turned on both showerheads and all the body jets. Efficient water heating had the glass walls of the huge bathing area steamy within less than a minute. Fuck the cameras, the watchers would only see silhouettes through the steam. She stripped off her thong and tossed it toward Risto, a very naked and aroused Risto. She almost swallowed her tongue. *God, he's built!*

He was all muscle, the kind nature built through hard work and not as a result of a gym and a personal trainer. A light smattering of dark hair in the middle of his chest extended from nipple to nipple then down to the bottom of his sternum. No manscaping. Callie's newly awakened inner vixen approved. Her appreciative gaze continued over his hairless, superbly-cut abs down to the strip of dark hair starting below his navel and leading to his… *Oh. My. God!* Risto had one of the largest cocks she'd ever seen—and as a model she'd seen a lot of men's sexual organs, clothed and unclothed, but none trumped Risto's for length and breadth. Her perusal continued downward over strong thighs and calves to … hell, he even had sexy legs and feet.

Risto bent over to pick up her discarded underwear. He eyed the minuscule ivory silk and lace thong appreciatively. Taking it to his nose, he inhaled. He closed his eyes and groaned. She was one hundred percent sure he wasn't acting for the camera's benefit.

"You smell so fucking good. You're ready for me, aren't you, baby?"

She said simply, "Yes," then turned to enter the shower. He was right behind her. His hands on her hips, he gently pulled her back against his torso. He caressed the bruises on the side of her hips and thighs with a light touch. Even with his rampant arousal nudging her bottom, he was taking care not to hurt her.

Risto kissed her shoulder and murmured, "I would kill Cruz for marking you alone."

She shivered and he pulled her even more closely against his body, warming her better than the hot water. He placed sucking kisses along her shoulder to her neck. Pushing her hair out of the way, he ran his tongue up the side of her throat, then gently traced the whorls of her ear. "Play or fuck? Your choice, Callie. How hungry are you—and for what? The assholes can't see you. My body is blocking the only camera in this room."

"Gawd, Risto. I want…" She gulped then hissed as he lightly bit her earlobe, then moaned as he soothed it with his lips. Yeah, she definitely had an erotic hard-wire from her neck and ears to her pussy. Her clit throbbed in synch as he tongued her ear. She leaned heavily against his strength as the world swirled and her knees gave way. He caught her before she fell to the tile floor, holding her up by the waist.

"Fuck me for being an ass. I keep forgetting you haven't eaten a real meal. Plus, you're probably dehydrated from being in the sun all day." He punctuated his words with biting kisses along her jaw. Cupping a breast as his other arm supported her, he cuddled it, his thumb brushing her puckered nipple.

She moaned. "Risto…"

"Sorry, I couldn't resist. I've wanted to do that since I first saw you." He moved the hand tormenting her breast down to her waist. "Let's get you clean, then I'll feed you. You'll need all the strength you can muster for later."

She noted he left open exactly what she'd need the energy for. Running? Or, sex?

"I'm fine. Just a wave of dizziness." She took several deep breaths. Her body was ready to combust from his touch. If she didn't move away, all his chivalrous self-restraint would go for naught, because she'd turn and attack him—then she'd never get her lunch.

She wriggled against his hold. He immediately released her. She twisted around to speak to him and all her good intentions went down the drain. His eyes blazed with lust—for her. God, she'd never been so aroused by a man in her life—not even for the guy who'd taken her virginity. She plastered her wet front against his, her breasts mashed against the hair on his chest. She rubbed, loving the feel of his chest hair against her peaked nipples. Throwing her arms around his neck, she fingered the wet hair curling at his nape. "I'm so glad you're here."

He opened his mouth to speak, to breathe ... who in the hell cared why he opened it? She seized the opportunity and kissed him, an all-out French kiss, deep and hot. He responded by pulling her into his erection, rotating his hips so his hard-on ground against her lower body. Her pussy clenched in response. Everything primal in her wanted completion. She curled one leg around his, then ran the arch of her foot up and down his hairy calf. The move opened her sex to him.

Risto took advantage immediately and snaked his hand between their bodies, nudging one finger into her wet slit, his thumb pressing the aching bundle of nerves at its top. She whimpered low in her throat, arched into his touch, then humped his hand as if she were an animal in heat. He added a second finger to the first. The pressure was a mixture of pain and pleasure and unlike anything she'd ever felt.

"Green light or red, Callie?" He began to pull his fingers out.

"No!" She moaned. *Why is he making me think?* She clenched his two fingers with her vaginal muscles and sobbed. "Please?" *Please take the decision out of my hands.*

"Fuck, baby, I'm a millisecond away from shoving you up against the tile wall and taking you hard and fast. Yes or no?"

Her heart pounded. Her breathing was rapid and choppy. She was so close to coming. But his question had her rational brain taking over, examining all the options. Did she want this? *Hell, yes.* But did she want her first time with Risto to be in a shower? With cameras taping every shadowy move, recording every moan, every cry? *Fuck, no.* But what if she never got the chance to have him? *God, no, I can't let that happen.* She might have gone around in circles forever, if her growling stomach and another wave of light-headedness hadn't made the decision for her.

"Red light. Sorry. Red. I'm so sor—" She allowed her leg to slip down his calf until it finally touched the shower's tile floor.

Risto's eyes glittered, the muscles in his jaw tightened. He removed his fingers from her pussy—slowly, their rough tips abrading every inflamed nerve over which they passed. She sagged as shallow spasms swept through her, a tantalizing taste of the climax she'd just missed.

Risto swore and grabbed her waist to hold her up. He held her body slightly away from his. She braced her forehead on his glistening pecs and glanced down and spied the purple head of his massive erection leaking precum. He had promised to allow her to make the choice—and abiding by his vow was costing him a lot of pain. His chivalry, his control of his desire made her want him all the more.

She looked up to apologize once more.

"Hush." Risto shook his head, his lips twisted into a smile full of self-recrimination. "I'm such a dog."

No! She shook her head and opened her mouth to deny that any of this was his fault, when he stopped her again. "Shh." He placed his fingers over her lips. "You're hungry. Stressed out. Tired."

He moved closer, hugging her to him until she was plastered against every throbbing inch of him. "Later." He rubbed his bristly cheek over her hair. "Conn's house will be safe. You'll be able to relax. You can make the decision without so much pressure."

He was protecting her yet again. She stroked his neck, soothing the tension she found there. He wanted her, but would deny himself. But it was unnecessary. "What if I give you the green light ... later?"

Risto inhaled sharply and his hands tightened briefly on

her waist. His mouth moved over her cheek to her ear. "I'll fuck you, Callie … I'm not like your other men. I'm not nice or sweet when I fuck a woman. I'll demand—and you'll give me everything."

"Good." She rubbed her cheek across his chest from one male nipple to the next. She turned her face slightly to place a butterfly-soft kiss on the bud lying under her lips. He groaned and she felt the rumbling in his chest. "I'm a woman, not a girl. And tonight, I want to be *your* woman," she angled her head and stared him in the eyes, "in every way possible. Yours."

"My woman." He nodded, his eyes filled with hints of dark fire. "All night. Mine."

Chapter Five

The *Jalapeño Rojo* was a little hole-in-the-wall dive bar near the edge of the old city. While on assignments for SSI, Risto had eaten there before. Trey Maddox, Ren's brother and co-owner of SSI, had introduced him to the place. It was clean, the food was excellent, and the owner, Tom Yates, was a former marine with dual US and Colombian citizenship who'd assisted SSI in the past. *Semper Fi. Semper Fraternis.*

The hostess, Tom's Colombian-born wife Rosa, recognized Risto from his previous visits and sat them at the gun-slinger's table, a booth surrounded on three sides by thick walls with the front facing the main door to the bar.

Risto guided Callie with a hand on the small of her back as they passed through the room to their table. No one stood out as a danger, though he nodded casually at another former marine who, he knew, was now a National Clandestine Service operative. You couldn't throw a knife anywhere in the major Colombian cities without hitting US military or intelligence operatives. The country was a hot spot ready to blow with just the right spark.

Risto smiled. "*Gracias*, Rosa."

"*De nada*, Risto." Rosa smiled. "We are always happy to see you."

He helped Callie slide into the booth, taking her tote bag from her and placing it under the table with his, then he slid in next to her. She was extremely pale under her light tan. Her gray eyes were clouded with fatigue and an over-abundance of stress. Despite that, she still looked as sexy as hell, wearing skin-tight, well-washed jeans and a navy blue, form-fitting tank top with no bra; a gauzy, pale blue, long-sleeved shirt was tied around her waist in case the rain brought cooler temps later. Without prompting, she'd left all her sandals back at the room and wore practical ankle boots just in case they had to trek into the jungle.

The longer he was around her, the more he admired her. Of course, his little brain just fucking wanted her. Something primitive in him needed to mark her so that any man seeing her would know she belonged to him. He shook his head ruefully. Thank God the Marines had trained him to use his larger brain at all times and that organ counseled patience and restraint. But it was damn difficult. Something about Callie touched him in ways he wasn't familiar with.

"What do you want to drink, sweetheart?" He picked up her left hand. It trembled slightly. Hunger? Fatigue? Fear? Or, most likely all of the above. He closed his hand around hers and brought it to his lips, kissing the ring she'd dug out of her purse and put on her finger before leaving their suite of rooms. It had been her mother's wedding band, she told him, and she never traveled without it.

He leaned over and brushed a kiss over her ear. "Guy across the way—end of the bar?" She casually glanced in the direction he indicated and nodded. "He's a good guy, former marine, as is the bar owner. If Cruz follows us here and shit happens, run to them. Tell them who you are and ask for protection. Got it?" Her eyes narrowed. Anger colored her cheeks as she shook her head rapidly. He touched his forehead to hers. "Got it?"

She stared at him for several seconds then nodded, her expression still rebellious.

"Good." He kissed the tip of her nose then looked up at the patiently waiting Rosa. "Sorry for the wait, Rosa." He looked at Callie. "What do you want to drink, sweetheart?"

"Um, the house Sangria. Lots of fruit and ice. I'm not much of a drinker." She shot the hostess a radiant smile, but her trembling body told him she was still upset by his instructions. Bless her, she still managed to put on a show.

He placed an arm around Callie's shoulders and idly stroked the exposed skin. She was soft and smelled so sweet and feminine. It was hard to imagine her trekking the wilds of Colombia. He would do all he could to avoid that happenstance.

"I'll take an *Iguana Roja, por favor,* Rosa." It was the local microbrew on tap. He'd had it before and it was good, refreshing. The day had turned even more humid, more miserable. It would rain before nightfall. September was still the rainy season. The forecast predicted an all-day rain for tomorrow. The good news was the rain would make it harder for Cruz to track them. The bad news was the roads would be treacherous, making their travel more complicated than the norm—and the norm in Colombia was pretty darn fucked up to begin with.

Rosa placed menus in front of them. "I'll get your drinks. The special is fish tacos with fried plantains, rice and beans. I'll be your waitress this evening, also." She winked. She knew what he did for a living; she'd made the assumption he was on the job.

"That sounds good to me," Callie said as she snuggled into his side.

Callie's hand brushed over his T-shirt clad chest, just missing one of the nipples she'd teased earlier. The contrary fucker puckered to alert and demanded more. He inhaled, then exhaled sharply, moving her hand away from his sensitive nubs and farther down onto his ribs.

"Two of the specials, Rosa."

"*Sí*, Risto." The woman smiled and walked away from their table.

Suddenly, Callie stiffened. Her hand on his rib cage flexed, her fingernails digging into his muscles. He followed her anxious gaze to the entryway, the view previously had been blocked by Rosa. Cruz and two of his men stood in the opening, scanning the room.

"Rosa," he called out in a voice that carried to every nook and cranny in the restaurant, "could you add an appetizer? Some chips and some of Tom's famous queso? And let him know I'm here. I want him to meet my wife."

Rosa's eyes widened at his last words, but didn't show her shock in any other way. "*Sí*, Risto. I'll let Tomas know you are here." She hurried off.

Callie nuzzled his neck. "Cruz wants you dead. Look at him. Jesus, I'm so sorry to pull—"

"Fuck it, Callie, just hush. Don't worry about me. This is my job. Do you doubt my ability to take care of a two-bit terrorist?" He brushed his lips over the top of her head. His narrowed glare never left the enemy entering the room. He felt her shake her head. He squeezed her shoulder. "That's my girl. Just keep up the act. If all goes as planned, you'll be home by this time tomorrow. Safe and sound."

Cruz and his bodyguards were seated by Rosa at a table straight across the room from theirs, just inside the door. He bet there were at least another two of the para-leader's soldiers outside, one on the front and one on the back. If it hadn't been for Callie's presence, Risto would've looked forward to taking them out. It took more than a few terrorists to take down an SSI operative.

Rosa placed their drinks and the chips and queso on the table. Her troubled gaze flickered over Callie whose face was burrowed into his shoulder, her hair covering her expression from any interested eyes. Risto mouthed, "She's fine." Rosa nodded and left.

"It's okay." He rubbed her arm, trying to impart his warmth to her too-cool skin. "No reason to be afraid. Cruz won't do anything in the bar."

She turned her face up, a look of heated indignation and not fear in her eyes. "I'm not scared. I said I trust you and I do. I'm just so cold all of a sudden. I hope I'm not catching a virus." He suspected her chills were a result of an adrenaline crash.

"Kiss me," she ordered, then delicately licked his lower lip. Her hand massaged his stomach above his waist and his dick strained to escape his jeans, a heat-seeking missile searching for her hot little fingers. "Warm me up, Risto. Make me think only about later ... about us."

Fuck. The images her words created had him momentarily forgetting where they were as he debated whether Tom would let him use the bar office. *Shit.* He needed to get his brains out of his pants and act like the highly trained marine he was.

"Callie, I need to keep my head in the game and not in bed with you." He picked up a chip and scooped some queso onto it. "Here, eat something. You need fuel. I can't have you fainting on me if we need to run for any reason."

"Okay, but I'm damn well giving the green light later at this Conn's, and if I have to attack you, you will fuck me." She was damn cute when she was pissed. She bit into the chip he offered, chewing, then licking her lips. "So good." Under her breath, she muttered, "But I bet your cock tastes better." He groaned. She smiled sweetly then sucked his fingers clean of every trace of salt and cheese. "Yummy."

In that instant, he had clear, 3-D, Technicolor images of her using that tongue on his horny cock. *Fuck. Just fuck.* The little tease. His dick was ready to shoot.

Callie turned her head away, a calm, almost beatific look

on her face. She moved the hand from his abs to pick up her glass of wine, then took a sip. The sexy hum she made in the back of her throat had him groaning and adjusting to a more comfortable sitting position. If he got any more aroused, he'd have permanent zipper marks on his dick.

He leaned into her, forcing her back against the upholstered banquette, then took her lips in little biting kisses. She tasted like wine, queso, and Callie. "God, I want you, minx." He took her hand and placed it on his cock. "This is what you do to me." Her opalescent eyes filled with heat and need.

He folded her hand back around the stem of her glass. "But that's for later. So, behave. No more teasing little strokes, no more husky little hums and definitely no more kissing while the enemy is present. We stay alert, eat, and play the game. Maybe—" he doubted it, "—Cruz'll go away and we can leave Colombia without a fight." *Not gonna happen.*

She kissed his chin. "I understand and I'll try to behave." She settled back onto the seat, her side glued against his as if she were afraid he'd disappear.

Cruz had stared daggers at them during their little byplay.

"He wants to hurt me now."

Yeah, Callie was damn observant and had read the enemy's emotions well.

"I can see it in his eyes," she said. "He, uh ... threatened me, told me what he'd do to me if I ran, what he'd do to my brothers. Then he bruised me on purpose, a taste of what could happen, he said. He scared me, but he also made me mad—so I called Keely."

Risto fought the need to go across the room and kill the fucking bastard. Instead, he carefully smoothed away some hair which blocked his view of Callie's beautiful face. "You're standing up well. You don't look frightened."

"I put on faces for the camera for a living. I was scared to the bone until you arrived. But I'm not scared now. I'm royally pissed. So, fuck him."

She was lying through her teeth. He sensed the fine tremors travelling through her body, but she maintained a calm face for their audience. She had courage. He was fairly sure she would hold her own if the need arose. Retreat was not in her vocabulary—just like a marine.

Then Callie shocked the shit out of him. She lifted her head and coolly, regally, acknowledged Cruz with a short nod. Observing her face, you'd think she was greeting a casual acquaintance and not a raping, murdering paramilitary leader and wanted terrorist who'd terrified the hell out of her.

"God, you are so sexy."

She glanced at him, confusion in her expressive eyes. "What?"

He leaned into her and whispered against her lips. "Sexy, because you're facing a monster, your nemesis, with that royal-princess-to-peon attitude. Your courage is a turn-on."

"I think I just pissed him off even more." She snuggled into his side, one hand gripping his thigh, the other hand on his neck twisting the hair at his nape, both actions telling him how stressed she really was.

"I think you sucking my fingers did that, baby." He tucked her even closer to his side. He stroked a finger over the top of her shoulder. "He's underestimated you from the beginning. Because you're a woman," *My woman. For now,* "and he's a chauvinist, he didn't foresee you fighting back."

"Yeah. Well, get me a sniper rifle and some high ground and I'll show him his equal." She aimed a frosty glare at the topic of conversation. "Right between his vile, slitty snake eyes."

Risto chuckled and squeezed her. "Blood-thirsty wench."

"You have no idea." She rubbed her cheek against his shoulder and sighed. "If I could've gotten my hands on a weapon sooner, I would've shot the bastard and run for Ecuador."

Risto was glad that hadn't happened. While there might

have been enemies of Cruz between here and Ecuador who might have aided her in getting out of the country, she would've never made it out of Cruz's territory to get to them. The para-leader controlled the area from Barranquilla to Cartagena along Route 25 to outside of Medellín. A huge chunk of Colombian real estate.

"*We'll* make it out of Colombia, but not to Ecuador." He tucked an errant lock of hair behind her ear so he could see her face. "Just follow my lead and you'll be fine."

She angled her head, her gaze fierce. "You can't guarantee we'll make it out of the country. I'm not stupid. All sorts of things could go wrong. We need to work together. Let me at least pull my weight. Share the driving. I'm good with a GPS and maps."

"You're running on nerves and adrenaline. You'll nap and I'll drive." She opened her mouth and he put his finger over it. "Hush. I want you rested. You promised to follow my orders. We'll do this my way."

Her eyes glittered with some strong emotion. "Then we won't have sex. You need to…"

He glared her into silence. Everything primitive in him screamed at the thought of not taking her, marking her. "Tonight, you're getting thoroughly fucked—and tomorrow, I'll be driving and you napping. Understood?"

She nodded, lowering her lashes, a slight flush on her cheeks. Her breaths were shallow, but rapid, and he could see the pulse beating in her neck. His authoritarian tone had either excited her or pissed her off. He could live with either emotion just as long as she wasn't scared.

Risto's lips quirked with a satisfied smile. Callie, while brave, game, and possessed of a strong feminine temper, had been raised to respond to strong authority figures. The years she worked in the fashion world to support her brothers were years of survival, of always being the strong one for her younger and needier brothers—years of sublimating her desire for a strong man to love and care for her. She was a strong woman who needed a strong man, a good man—one who knew about building a home and protecting a family.

Risto would like to be that man, but knew himself well enough to know he wasn't a forever kind of man. But he'd do for now.

Rosa interrupted them. "Tomas says to tell you he'll be out to sit with you after you have eaten." She placed their meals in front of them. She leaned over and adjusted the place settings. "Tomas will take you on a *very special* tour of the kitchens later." She winked and straightened. "Enjoy your food."

Risto nodded. He'd always suspected Tom had a hidden way out of the bar. "Thanks, Rosa. We'll look forward to speaking with Tom. Won't we, honey?"

"Yes." Callie took a bite of the rice and beans. She licked her lips and moaned. The sound was so sensual, his cock jerked within the confines of his jeans. "This is so good. My compliments to Tom."

"*Gracias.*" Rosa left to greet a new customer.

Ignoring Cruz and his thugs, they sat silently, companionably, and dug into the food. He cleaned his plate then noted Callie had stopped with more than half her food left.

"Eat it all, baby, or I'll feed you. You need the fuel."

She smiled and it was as if the sun had broken through the clouds. "I think I'd like you feeding me, but we might get finished faster if I feed myself. Maybe another time?" She arched a brow, sending him a look full of mischief and promise. "I'm just pacing myself, okay?"

"Damn, and I was looking forward to feeding you now." He wiggled his brows, causing her to giggle. The fact he'd made her laugh sent a warm feeling to the pit of his stomach. God, it would kill him to let her go after this assignment was over. But he would. She deserved someone with a safer livelihood and more civilized.

Callie picked up her second fish taco and took it to her mouth. He kept a peripheral eye on the enemy as he watched her enjoy the food. An indulgent smile crossed his lips as he took a drink of his beer. She made better progress now that he'd lightened the atmosphere.

He hadn't ever thought watching a woman eat would be a sexual experience, but it was proving to be with Callie. Her little sounds of enjoyment. The licking of her lips. Sucking food off her fingers. All were rife with sexual connotations. He shifted in his seat. *Keep your fucking head in the game.*

Callie's little snort told him she knew exactly why he fidgeted. He'd make her pay for her amusement later. He smiled evilly at the thought of arousing her and all the ways it could be accomplished.

Movement from across the room had Callie stiffening. She laid down her fork, the hand closest to him went to his thigh again, her nails digging into the denim. She swallowed hard. "I can't eat any more. He's coming over."

Risto's warm breath feathered across her cheek. His hand covered hers as she clenched his thigh. "Let me handle him." He patted her hand and then moved his left arm around her shoulders and idly played with the curls lying there.

She brushed her cheek against his upper arm. "I'm sorry. I can help—"

"No. I'll handle it. You sit there and sip your wine." He turned to face the approaching enemy. He had his Glock in his right hand, under the table, pointed at Cruz's gut. If FUBAR happened, he'd shove Callie under the table and take out at least Cruz and one of the others. His peripheral vision told him Tom stood behind the bar. The former marine nodded; he had their backs.

"Calista." Cruz loomed over her side of the booth. His two men stood behind him, their hands hovering over their sports coats where their weapons were concealed. "Who is this man?" The Colombian's possessive rage came through clearly in his harsh raspy tone and the icy glare of his eyes.

Callie buried her face against Risto. He hugged her closer and placed a kiss on her forehead. "Her husband. Who the fuck are you?"

Cruz hissed an ugly profanity.

"Sweetheart, is this the *pendejo* you were telling me about?"

"Yes," she mumbled into his neck. She turned her face to the side so her next words carried clearly into the restaurant. "He's the one who's been stalking me."

Cruz's furious gaze swept over Callie; his lips thinned in anger. Then he redirected his ire at Risto, which was exactly where Risto wanted it. He didn't want the bastard to look at Callie, let alone breathe the same air.

"You are *not* her husband. She has no husband. This I checked."

Yeah, you bastard. You checked and saw she had no family but for two teenage brothers. No one who could make you pay if she went missing. Well, buddy, you fucked up. She has me.

Risto stroked Callie's tense shoulder with a gentle finger, while inside his rage roiled and rumbled, threatening to explode into overt violence against Cruz and his men. Only the danger of Callie getting hurt stopped him. The object of his concern placed a kiss at the base of his throat, the small gesture calming him. "The marriage certificate says I am." His tone was even but scalpel-sharp.

"I do not believe this. You are hired muscle, yes? You have the look of a soldier." Cruz leaned over the table, invading Callie's personal space. "Look at me, Calista."

The dumb fuck reached to grip her face. Risto growled.

Cruz withdrew his hand and eyed him cautiously, then turned to glower at Callie. "You hired this man? After I warned you what would happen?"

Callie dismissed him with her I'm-a-queen-and-you're-nothing look. Then she turned her face back into Risto's neck. Under the cover of the table, her hand gripped his thigh until he could feel the prick of her nails through the denim. She trembled, but he got the impression it wasn't fear this time, but rage which shook her. Good, he'd rather her be mad. The bastard still needed killing for causing her one single second of fear.

A predatory smile twisted his lips at the thought of hunting down Cruz and taking him out permanently. Not that he would do so while Callie was near. His smiled turned to one of satisfaction when Cruz backed away as he recognized the hint of predator in Risto's face.

"Like I said, I'm her husband. And not that it's any of your business, but I am a former marine. An angry marine who can take care of his own. Callie is mine." Risto stroked her hair, running his fingers through the tangled curls. "You want to see the marriage certificate, *chingado*? Look it up online. Cook County, Illinois, Recorder's Office."

He loved the look of shock on Cruz's face. Good thing Tweeter and Keely temporarily added a marriage certificate and its concomitant license to the records in Cook County for this op. Callie let out a small sigh and relaxed into his chest, hiding her face from Cruz. Risto smoothed a hand over her hair.

"Stay away from my woman. Stay away from her family." Risto snarled the words. "The twins are in a safe place. You try for them, you're dead. You touch Callie, you're dead."

"Who are you really?" Cruz took another step back at Risto's outright threat. His thugs moved in to surround their boss, the jackets now open, revealing their weapons.

Inhaling sharply, Callie lifted her head and glared at Cruz. "He just told you. He's my husband, you moron. Now, get the hell away from us. I never want to see you again."

"Naughty little hell cat, I told you I'd handle this." Risto lifted her face and kissed the tip of her nose.

She leaned into his touch, her arms twining about his neck. The little minx was purposely placing her body between his and the weapons. His finger tightened on the Glock he held under the table. He kept Cruz and his thugs in sight as he attempted to nudge her out of the line of fire. He'd told her he'd handle this—and now she'd placed herself in danger of getting shot. They'd be discussing her disregard of his orders later. He turned to address Cruz who'd signaled his men to stand down when Callie's body got in the way. The jackets were now closed over their weapons. "Leave. Next time I see you anywhere near my wife, I won't be giving any warnings—I'll act."

Cruz's face darkened as Risto kissed Callie's cheek then nuzzled her neck. The Colombian's hands fisted but he backed down. The man realized he would not come out looking good in this confrontation. No, the sneaking coward would attack at night. Too bad for Cruz they wouldn't be found easily later that night.

Risto smiled and kissed Callie's cheek again. *Yeah, fucker, we'll be burning up the sheets tonight while you chase your fucking tail trying to find us.*

Casting one last smoldering glare at Callie, Cruz swore, turned, then walked out of the restaurant. His men backed out, their hands ready to go for their weapons as they covered their boss's ass.

Callie turned and brushed a kiss against his jaw. "I'm sorry. I couldn't stand it. He didn't believe you." Her breath stuttered and tears streaked down her cheeks. "He was going to order them to shoot you!"

Her tears wiped away what was left of his iron control. "I fucking didn't care if he fucking believed me or not." Risto squeezed her until she squeaked. "Don't you ever fucking put yourself between me and a fucking bullet again. You will follow my orders to the fucking letter." It would take a long time and a lot of thrusting into her sweet pussy before the icy fear in his gut melted away. She could have been shot protecting him. Unacceptable.

Sniffing loudly, she shoved away from him. "Very impressive use of the f-word. And being a typical fucking, macho-ass marine, you missed the fucking point." She glared defiantly. "If Cruz's men had fucking shot you, you'd be fucking dead and I'd be at Cruz's fucking mercy." She jabbed her finger into his chest. "So, I'll do what I think is necessary to protect your tight fucking ass."

With the knowledge that Tom hovered in the background, covering their asses, Risto did what he'd wanted to do ever since the last kiss during their joint shower. He covered her mouth with his. Anger, lust and fear driving him, he mounted an all-out assault. The little cat refused him entrance. He snorted then bit her lower lip. When she gasped, his tongue thrust inside and claimed what was his. He poured every strong emotion he'd held back during the confrontation with Cruz into the kiss, making sure she knew she was his and that he was the alpha in this partnership.

When she whimpered, he released her mouth. She gasped for breath; her eyes glazed. His labored breathing rasped over her swollen lips. "Promise me you'll never scare the shit out of me that way again."

Blinking, her gray eyes glittered, losing the dazed expression of a second ago. Her kiss-swollen lips tightened into a thin, mutinous line. She shook her head. "No."

He swore under his breath every foul word he knew in three languages. All through his litany of curses, Callie petted him, massaging his neck in a soothing manner. The obstinate look on her face remained. When he growled "stubborn brat" and swore some more, she had the audacity to snicker.

He stopped cursing and shot her an angry glare. "What's so damn amusing?"

"Um, some of your swearing struck me funny." She wrinkled her nose. "Hey, I can't help it. I appreciate creative swearing. Marines seem to corner that market of all of the Armed Forces."

He shook his head, his anger disappearing as swiftly as it had arisen. He tugged one of her curls then rested his hand on her shoulder as he settled her back against the booth and as close to his side as he could without her being on his lap. He cast her a sideways glance. "Just a heads up, I plan on being in bed with you all night, Callie. Maybe I can fuck that sassiness out of you. You might want to finish your meal so you'll have the energy for the evening's activities."

Before she could come back at him—and he found he was anticipating what she would say or do to put him in his place next—they were interrupted. "Making new enemies, Risto? Trey and Ren know about this? Cruz is one vicious bastard."

"Tom." Risto turned to greet the man. "Ren sent me to rescue Callie from the A-hole, so they knew I'd have a hard time avoiding his treacherous ass."

Tom slipped into the booth next to Risto. He reached around Risto's body and offered his hand to Callie. "The world-famous Calista in my little dive bar. I'll need to get a picture for my bar wall." He waved a hand to a row of pictures of local celebrities and a few international ones.

"Callie is a special friend of the Walshes." Risto told the bar owner. "Her dad was Lieutenant Commander Meyers."

"I knew your dad." Tom took Callie's hand, pulled it across Risto's body, and brought it to his lips. He pressed a lingering kiss to the back until Risto growled and took Callie's hand into his own. Tom laughed then his face turned solemn. "Your dad saved my ass once, Callie. Anything I can do to help, I will." He turned to Risto. "Word is on the street that Cruz has himself a new woman. Your little Callie?"

"Shit. He made it public?" The para-leader would lose all face if Callie didn't end up on his plantation as his woman. Cruz would pour everything he had against them in order to take her. Colombian terrorists were all about the *machismo*. Good thing Risto had planned to move up Callie's extraction by twenty-four hours.

"Yes." Tom's mouth twisted as if he tasted something foul. "Cruz leaves me alone since Paco, his cartel boss, is related to my Rosa and likes my fish tacos. Cruz has a bad rep with women, goes through them like water and they don't wear his attentions well. Good thing you're here to make sure he doesn't slurp this little lady up."

"Yeah, good thing." Risto massaged Callie's hand with his thumb. "My intel says he's a city boy. Cruz tends to stay away from the jungle and swamps. True?"

"True. FARC and ELN own the jungles, but Cruz has some jungle boys. So, if you're heading southwest for a Darien coastal extraction, watch your ass. There are all kinds of predators between here and there."

"I know." Risto smiled grimly. "But even predators are prey sometimes."

Tom snorted. "Yeah, Trey told me he was impressed with how you handled yourself on SSI's last little mission in the Darien. Said you must have leopard blood running in your veins." He turned to Callie. "Just listen to what this man says, Callie. He'll get you home safely. I'd trust him with Rosa out there—and that's saying a lot." He began to slide out of the booth. "Whenever you're ready to leave, let my wife know. I'll give you the special tour and take you out my escape tunnel."

"Escape tunnel?" Callie asked in a low, non-carrying tone.

Tom grinned. "Yeah, ya never know when Paco might decide he doesn't like my cooking. It probably would never happen since Rosa's one of his favorite cousins and Paco loves to protect women. Plus, I also stay out of *active* covert ops. But my trainers always told me 'shit happens,' so I cover my ass." He turned to Risto. "My little tunnel will take you to a vacant building I own three doors down. Cruz's men won't see you leave. I suggest you two don't go back to your hotel."

"We aren't. Now that Cruz has seen me, he'll make his move to grab Callie as soon as he can. But we won't be there." He stroked the back of Callie's head, loving the feel of her silky hair against his calloused and scarred palm. "Call Evan now, Callie. Tell him I'll meet him and Chad at the cantina across from the hotel in two hours. I'll give them their departure instructions then. Anything you might have forgotten from the suite, let me know. I'll be paying it a final visit to tweak Cruz's nose by unhooking those cameras and microphones."

"No!" She gasped then grabbed her throat as if she were choking.

"Callie? What's wrong?" Risto rubbed the back of her neck.

"Y-you're … uh, not … going … back … th-there." She coughed and gasped for a breath.

A panic attack. Shit. She was stressing out, worrying about him. He didn't know if he was pissed because she thought so little of his ability to slip in and out of the room without Cruz's men knowing or if he was happy about her caring so much. The same kind of caring that had had her putting her body between him and danger.

Probably a little bit of both.

"Sip some Sangria, baby. The alcohol will help relax your muscles." He held the glass to her lips. "Slowly." She took a sip, then another. "That's a girl." He helped her swallow past the constriction in her throat by gently massaging it with the back of his finger. "Good girl. Now, take slow, deep breaths."

She nodded and did as he'd asked.

Tom hovered in front of the table, blocking them from curious eyes.

Tears filled her beautiful gray eyes. Damn, he hated to see her tears. Holding a hand to her throat, she took over the massage, then finally managed to whisper, "There's nothing there I…" She grabbed the glass and sipped some more of the wine.

"Shh, I understand. I was going back anyway. By shutting off the cameras, it'll drive him fucking crazy. He'll double his efforts to find us, keeping his attention off the others."

She frowned, but he knew her natural instincts to protect

Evan and Chad were roused. He saw it in her eyes.

"Plus ... the bastard has videos of you."

Tom snarled an ugly phrase aimed at Cruz.

Risto concurred with the sentiment one hundred percent. "I'm shutting the cameras off. Then I'll retrieve any back-ups."

He wouldn't mention to Callie that anyone unlucky enough to be on porn duty tonight would die. That additional message would promise death to anyone spreading ugly rumors or any other surviving video about Callie. If something happened to Risto, SSI would back that promise up for Keely's sake alone.

Callie gasped. Her face went ashen, her eyes, distressed. She turned her hand under his and gripped it tightly. "It isn't worth risking your life. I don't mind about the videos."

"I do." Risto squeezed her cold hand.

"Don't risk yourself ... whatever the bastard has recorded can't hurt me. I'm not going to be in the public eye any longer. I'll either be employed in the basement at NSA or possibly at Sanctuary with SSI. It's hard to embarrass a person who doesn't care what the public thinks about her any longer."

He cared. He cared a hell of a lot more than he should.

"You've already been hurt. I saw the expression on your face when I told you about the cameras. I wanted to kill Cruz right then and there."

What was on those tapes? Had Callie been attacked by Cruz in her room and not in public as she had told him? Had she had some other man in her room since her arrival? He had to know. Bottom line, he didn't want any risqué tapes of Callie out there.

"Risto?" Callie stared at him, her eyes pleading. "Please tell me you aren't going."

"I'm going." Callie stiffened and opened her mouth, probably to argue even further. He wasn't having it. He pulled her into his arms and nudged her head to his chest. "Shh. I'll be fine. You'll be fine." He stroked her hair and looked up at Tom, who nodded. At least a fellow marine agreed with him.

"Callie can count on me and, I suspect, Conn?" Tom asked. Risto nodded. "We'll make sure she gets to safety if something happens to you."

Callie sniffed then glared at Tom. "I need *him*. Alive. Period."

"Understood, darlin'," Tom said. "But once a marine sets his mind on something, he doesn't back down."

"Hell, Callie, Cruz will never know I'm there." He stroked her cheek with his thumb. "Just fucking trust me. Now, call Evan, baby. Set up the meet."

"God, I hate this." She rubbed her forehead on his chest. He soothed the back of her neck. "If I'd checked Cruz out when he first bothered me in Chicago, I'd never have taken the job here—and none of this would be happening."

"No. You can't think that way." Risto practically growled the words. "Cruz would've found another way. A way which could have put you in a worse position. By luring you here and revealing himself, he played his hand too soon—and allowed you to get help. A dumb-ass move on his part. We're smart—you and me." He tipped up her chin and looked her firmly in the eye. "We'll beat him and on his own turf. Just think how humiliating it will be. He'll lose even more face. Who knows? Maybe one of his rivals will use our distraction to wrest power from him?"

That was a very great possibility and one he, Trey, Ren and Keely had kicked around when planning the mission.

"Fine. Go to the hotel. Send the bastard a message. I hope he chokes on it." She glared, silver sparks glistening in her eyes. "And, dammit, come back to me or I'll get really pissed."

Risto threw back his head and laughed, hugging her to him. "Count on it. Hoo-rah."

"Hoo-rah." Callie and Tom echoed simultaneously.

Chapter Six

Callie paced the small, but luxurious, suite she and Risto had been shown to several hours earlier. The rooms were located in a private residence which was a quasi-bed-and-breakfast operated by SSI for private covert operatives. The mansion was situated in a quiet neighborhood adjacent to the old city. The place was definitely not open to the public. The grounds had safety and security measures to rival some embassies she'd visited. From the outside it looked like every other palatial residence on the quiet, tree-lined boulevard. The manager for SSI and an operative himself was Conn Redmond.

She and Risto were currently the only guests. Their host had supplied them with gear for a potential trip into the rain forest, found her a ladies model Ruger, and was securing a new all-terrain vehicle for their trip, just in case shit happened and they needed to go off-road. He'd also provided a secure computer connection with video-conferencing capability and she'd spoken with her brothers and Colonel Walsh. Risto had held her as she cried tears of relief to see her brothers safe in the Colonel's care.

After ordering her to stay put, Risto had taken off on foot for his meeting with Evan and Chad and then his mission at her former hotel. That had been almost three hours ago. Her gut told her something was wrong.

A knock on the door startled her. Had Risto forgotten his key? That didn't make sense, he could've gotten another one from Conn or one of the guards on duty. She walked over and peered through the peep hole. It was their host. She opened the door. "What's wrong?"

Conn's facial expression was blank as he took her hand and pulled her to the small sitting area in front of the fire he'd built for her earlier. Releasing her hand, he sat and patted the cushions next to him. "Sit, Callie."

Dread settled over her like a lead blanket. She sank onto the sofa. "Tell me. Is it Risto?"

He shook his head. "I haven't heard anything from him yet."

She frowned. If not Risto then… "Is it Evan and the others?" Sickness pooled in her stomach. She looked at her watch—it was ten o'clock. The escort should've already picked them up for the ride to the Barranquilla airport.

Again he shook his head. "I got confirmation that your friends are on their way. So far, no one has attempted to stop them."

"Then what's wrong?"

Conn, a tough-looking blond, leaned forward, bracing his elbows on his knees. "Cruz has his men tearing the city apart to find you. This makes your situation even more dangerous since there are people in this town who'd sell out their mothers to get on Cruz's good side."

"But we expected that … it makes a good diversion for Evan, Chad and the others."

He let out a rough breath and rubbed a hand over his face. "It's worse than we expected. Cruz has offered a large reward for Risto's dead body and your live one. This means every free-lance mercenary in town will be on the hunt. The fact he's willing to bring in outsiders indicates this is more than business as usual. Hate to say it, sweet cheeks, but Cruz is a tad bit psychotic about possessing you. And when crazy people do crazy things, innocents get hurt."

Her breath hitched but she managed to stifle the moan threatening to erupt from her throat. "He's hurting people to find me?" She gasped. "Tom and Rosa?"

"They're fine. They've gone to visit Rosa's cousins in the cartel. Paco is the head of Rosa's family and understands loyalty to family and leaving innocents out of business whenever possible. Cruz wanting you is not business as far as Paco is concerned—and I got that straight from Tom who got it straight from Paco."

She let out the breath she'd been holding. "This makes it more dangerous for Risto? With more people hunting for him?" He nodded, his mouth a thin grim line. "We have to go get him."

"Not *we*, me and one of my men. I just wanted to let you know I'd be out of the house for a while."

"But…"

Conn shook his head and chuckled. "Risto told me to tie you to the bed and not let you come after him if he was late—or if something happened. My job, and my only job, was to make sure you kept your sweet ass here."

"But he didn't need to go back to the hotel … the meeting with Evan and Chad was necessary, but the rest … he did for me. And I asked, begged him not to go." She began to cry. "He's out there risking his life for nothing."

Conn stared. "What in the fuck did he go back to the Sofitel for if it wasn't necessary? Did you leave something important in the room? Your passport? Money? Jewelry?"

The man must think she was some sort of high-maintenance bitch. "God no, nothing like that. I made sure I had everything I needed when we left to eat at Tom's place. Why didn't he tell you?" she asked the question more of herself than him. Then she knew, Risto had been protecting her again—from humiliation. He didn't want his friend and associate to know about the videotaping. Damn him, her feelings weren't more important than his life.

Conn snorted. "I asked. The asshole told me it was none of my business."

But it was his business. Conn risked exposure of this operation if Cruz expanded his hunt to this area of town. Someone could've seen them arrive and sold them out just as Conn suggested.

"Cruz was videotaping me. He had the whole room wired."

"Well, fuck the perverted son of a bitch."

She swallowed past the lump in her throat and willed herself not to blush at Conn's intense scrutiny. No time to get embarrassed. Risto could be in danger—they all could. "Risto wanted to disconnect the cameras to keep Cruz focused on us so the others could get away."

"That wasn't the real reason. Cruz was always going to be focused on finding you. The damn chivalrous idiot wanted to destroy any copies of the videos, didn't he?" She nodded. Conn rubbed a hand over his face and swore some more. "Well, hell, I can understand his motivation, but the shithead could've told me—that's more than a one-man job."

She nodded. "I didn't care about the video or who saw it. But he said he wanted to send a message about what would happen if any copies of the videos were released."

"Sounds like him. Always the lone wolf, our Risto. Fucking Force Recon marines, think they're bullet proof." Conn stood. "I'll take my second in command, Berto, and go after him, cover his ass."

"I'm coming along." She stood. "Just let me put on something dark so I blend in with the night better." She had on a white T-shirt of Risto's and a pair of his plaid boxers. She had few clothes and had used Conn's laundry to wash her jeans. They were still in the dryer.

"I believe we've covered this ground already." He towered over her in an attempt to intimidate, but she'd been raised around larger men than Conn and didn't intimidate easily. And she'd hurt Conn if he tried to restrain her in any way. No man touched her that way, well, maybe Risto if he wanted to play, but not this man, not for real.

"I can help. I can shoot. I was taught to slink around in the shadows by the same men who trained Force Recon operatives. I'm pretty sure I can keep up with you and help keep watch outside the *casita*."

"Babycakes, I don't care if you're the second coming of Rambo." He tapped the tip of her nose with a finger. "You aren't coming. Risto told you to stay put and he meant it. Both our asses would be chewed to hell and back if we disobey that particular order."

"But…"

"No buts." Conn placed his hands on her shoulders and rubbed. "Risto is fine. He's been in far worse situations than this and lived to tell about it. He's probably holed up evaluating his options. He'll have more options with me and Berto to help. You'd be a distraction, divide his concentration. You don't want to endanger him or us, right?"

Damn the man knew just where to dig in the knife. Conn and Risto had done SSI missions here in Colombia together—they knew how each other thought and reacted. She'd be an unknown in the field and they'd feel the need to protect her. Her shoulders sagged and Conn gave them a gentle squeeze as if he'd followed her every thought. "No, never, it's just … he's risking himself for me—for nothing."

"Hell, I know that. And I plan to ream him a new asshole over that little thing. He damn well should've asked for backup. Another reason you can't go is we can't take the chance someone might recognize you and let Cruz know. Risto wanted you safe—and safe you'll stay."

Shit, he was right, and she hated it. She hadn't thought, just reacted. She needed to get her head in the game or they wouldn't make it out of Colombia. She took a breath and nodded. "Fine, but call me when you're clear. I'll go nuts waiting."

"As soon as we're away from the hotel with Risto in tow, I'll call the phone in this room."

She hugged him. "Be safe." *Bring Risto back to me.*

After Conn left, she sat on the couch, her shaking knees no longer able to hold her. Then she prayed as she'd never prayed in her life.

Risto held perfectly still and listened to the two men in the other room. He'd dismantled the cameras in Callie's former suite of rooms easily. The *casita* next door had been empty when he entered, but just as he started to dismantle the computer to remove the hard drives, he heard the thudding sound of feet and men's laughing voices coming toward the room. He quickly put the computer back to the way he'd found it, including the USB back-up drive, and fled to one of the bedrooms off the main salon.

Cruz's surveillance team was not only derelict in their duty, but also sloppy. They immediately sat down without clearing the rooms and shot the shit in crude Spanish about two women they'd just met in the bar. Their monitors remained dark. Risto could see the red flashing lights telling them their feed was dead or interrupted, but the bozos hadn't seen the warning lights yet or just didn't care. From what he could surmise, they'd taken a drink-and-tittie break together against orders.

Such disregard for duty told him they weren't "real" soldiers but merely hired help, doing work for which Cruz's battle-tough soldiers had no aptitude. They'd be easy to take out—

and take them out he would, brutally. He didn't care that they were geeks; he didn't appreciate the way they spoke of Callie. The talkative twosome also commented on the fact Cruz was out for Risto's blood and had instituted a city-wide manhunt for him and Callie. He'd expected as much and was glad Callie was safe at Conn's.

Patience being a virtue and having saved his ass many a time, he waited to make his move on the men until after he was certain no one was coming to relieve them any time soon. He'd hate to get interrupted while taking their asses down.

And once again, patience proved to be a good move. The door to the suite opened and two men joined the others. The new guys were loaded for bear; these two were soldiers.

One of the soldiers, the leader from his bearing and the way the other men reacted to him, said, "We've just come from Señorita Calista's room. The cameras have been destroyed." One of the surveillance team woke up his computer and turned pale when the screen showed no feed. "Where were you two when this happened?"

"We were here," one of the computer geeks said, his face as white as the stuccoed walls.

Wrong answer, bozo.

"Liar. If you'd been here, you would have seen someone entering the room." The lead soldier struck both men, knocking them to the floor. *Fuck, this could get ugly really fast.* "You were both seen in the hotel bar, flirting with the waitresses, stuffing your faces and drinking tequila." The leader kicked the downed men in their ribs, repeatedly. Their groans and pleas for mercy didn't faze the soldier at all. "Because of your incompetence, we have missed the chance to capture this person and make him tell us where Cruz's woman is."

Not Cruz's woman. My woman.

"No … no … please don't…"

Two shots rang out. The surveillance team was dead. Risto wasn't sorry. They would've bragged about seeing Callie naked, and he would've had to kill them himself. Cruz's man had just saved him the hassle.

"Pack up this equipment," the leader ordered the other soldier who'd stood guard as his superior had taken out the two men. "I'll take the jump drive with the film images. Señor Cruz wants it in a safe place."

"*Sí*, patron. The DVD? Do you wish this also, or shall I leave it in the computer?"

"I'll take it. Señor Cruz will not want it lost." The leader removed the USB jump drive from the connection on the back of the computer and popped out a DVD Risto would never have thought to take. He had to get those from the man before he left the hotel grounds. Risto would return to get the hard drives. The guy packing up the equipment would have to make more than one trip.

Decision made, Risto moved as silently as a hunting cat. Exiting by the French doors to a small patio, he slipped through the privacy landscaping and slid around the corner of the *casita* just as his target left.

Blending into the shadows, he paralleled the man's movements. When his prey took a path which led toward the main part of the hotel, Risto made his move. He grabbed him, one hand over his mouth and the other grabbing his jaw. With a quick snap, he broke the man's neck. He dragged the body to the bushes and searched him to find the storage media. Finding them easily, he also confiscated a nice double-edged knife and a semi-automatic pistol and extra clips. Never knew when he and Callie might need the extra weaponry. Scanning his surroundings and finding no one, he slipped into the shadows and headed back to get the hard drives.

Re-entering the *casita* through the patio doors he'd left open, he halted just inside. He raised his gun. Two large forms were in the room; their weapons were trained on him. An amused chuckle reached him. He knew that laugh.

He inhaled, then exhaled, and lowered his weapon. He

moved closer to the two. He could see them clearly now with the light coming in from the other room. "Fuck it, Conn. I could've shot you and Berto. What the fuck you doing here?" He had a horrifying thought. "Is Callie okay?"

"Callie's fine. You were late, old buddy. Plus, you should've told me what you were hunting for. This was a two-man job at the very least. And you know it." Conn scowled at him.

"I don't need a fucking babysitter." The other man raised an eyebrow, his lips twisting into a sardonic smile at Risto's sarcasm. "I was just being cautious."

"Which is what I told your woman. And since I agree you needed to get the nasty videos of Callie, I won't be reaming you a new asshole." Conn looked over his shoulder toward the main room. "The two dead guys? Your work?"

"Nope. But I did just break the neck of the guy who did them and retrieved the back-up drives I came for. You take care of the guy hauling out the equipment?"

"Yep. Me and Berto took the opportunity to dismantle the computer and retrieve the hard drives. We were just coming out this way to hunt for you."

Berto grinned and held up three hard drives. He wondered what else might be on the drives. "We took them all. We figured there might be other information on them SSI might find useful." Great minds think alike.

"Good thinking." Risto fingered the single USB drive and the DVD in his pocket and wondered if there were any other portable back-up media out there, but decided to deal with the fallout from those, if any, when it occurred. He'd accomplished what he'd come for. "Then we're good to go." He smiled grimly. "And I think all the corpses will send Cruz a serious message."

Conn smiled. "I just love it when a plan comes together. We have a car parked on a side street. We need to get out of here before Cruz decides to backtrack and re-cover old territory. He set the jackals on you and they weren't told to bring you back alive."

So Cruz had taken the game to the next level. Damn, every mercenary or mercenary wannabe in Colombia would be trying to get a piece of him. He'd be a moving target.

Maybe he should leave Callie with Conn and set off on his own, act as a decoy, and let the extraction team come into Cartagena and slip her out after he drew the hounds away.

Something twisted in his gut at the thought. No, he'd stick with the plans he and Ren had worked out. Since he'd already moved Plan A up by twenty-four hours, they had the tactical advantage. Cruz would expect him to take a woman like Callie to a city with an airport and hire a private charter. Instead, they'd be going to a working cattle ranch south of the city and flying to Panama City and safety. Plans B and C were moves he'd rather not make, but neither were they ones Cruz could anticipate a beautiful woman such as Callie attempting. They were riskier since she'd have to do some trekking. But Keely and Tweeter, and Callie herself, had assured him she was up to the job.

"Risto?" Conn tugged on his sleeve. "You planning on spending the night? As much as I'd like to take out some more of Cruz's assholes, I think we need to go. Your woman is waiting."

"Sorry, just thinking about the next moves." Conn was correct—the *casita* could soon be crawling with Cruz's men. When hunting quarry, a good hunter never forgot that prey tended to return to the place where they were first flushed out. It was a territorial thing—prey had their comfort zone. Smart prey, those who deviated from this zone, proved Darwin's Theory about adaptation. Only the strongest survived.

"Well, think about them later in the safety of my house." Conn led the way to the patio doors. They exited and worked their way through the landscaping, staying away from the landscape lighting but using the ambient light to show them the way.

Berto took point as Conn dropped back. "I had to talk Callie into staying put. She wanted to come."

Risto grinned. "Told you."

"Yeah, you got that woman figured out all right." Conn shot him a sideways glance. "You keeping her?"

"No." Risto thought he heard Conn mutter "stupid son of a bitch." Well, he didn't disagree, but it would be better for Callie to find a normal guy, one who didn't break necks as easily as twisting off a bottle cap. One who didn't carry a lot of emotional baggage from a shitty childhood with a dictatorial, stern paternal grandfather and an adulthood of fighting and killing in wars no one understood.

The three stopped at the corner of the hotel property and a small side street. Lots of people out and about. No way to tell who was just out for a fun evening of bar hopping and who was hunting. Berto signaled he'd go ahead and bring back the car.

Risto turned to Conn who was on his secure sat phone. "Who you calling?"

Conn grinned. "Callie. The sweet darling made me promise to call when I had your ass out of there. It was part of the deal in keeping her million-dollar butt at my place." He held up a finger. "Callie. We're clear. He's fine. Not a scratch. We'll be there in about thirty minutes. Yeah, a light meal sounds good. My kitchen is your kitchen. Bye."

"Thanks for making her stay put." His gut clenched thinking about what could've happened if they'd run across some of Cruz's men on their way to cover his ass.

"Not a problem." Conn's smile dimmed and his expression became more serious. "You do know she's halfway to being in love with you, don't you?"

"No, she isn't." At Conn's snort, Risto added, "Hell, you've done hostage rescue and personal security. The women victims usually get a hard case of hero worship. Once they get back to civilization and their lives, they go back to their usual type of men. Callie's a lady. I'm not a gentleman. 'Nuff said."

Conn grunted. "You keep on lying to yourself. Callie wants you. She was ready to strap on a gun and come with us to pull your ass out of whatever trouble it had gotten into. The fact she stayed put was because she didn't want to divide your concentration and get you killed." He slapped Risto on the back as Berto angled the car next to their hiding place. "Face it, buddy, she wants you. You just have to get over whatever in the fuck bug you've lodged in that tight ass of yours and decide whether you want her."

Risto glared. "Of course, I want her. What man wouldn't want Callie in his bed, in his life? But I'm not the man she needs."

"You're too hard on yourself. You're an honorable man doing dirty jobs which need doing. Callie isn't stupid or naive. She grew up on marine bases. Her dad was one of us. I'm betting the little lady knows exactly what she wants in a man—and I'm looking at him." Conn climbed into the passenger seat. After Risto got in the back, his friend turned and looked over the seat. "I want an invite to the wedding."

Risto snarled and said nothing. There'd be no wedding. He'd take Callie home and never look back. It was best for both of them.

He'd take any sex she offered him tonight; it might be his only chance to have her, to live some of his fantasies. Tomorrow night, she could be home in her own bed. After that, he'd leave and stay out of her life. Even if she went to work for Ren, Risto would be spending most of his time in Michigan. He'd very rarely run across her at Sanctuary, only when he attended meetings and trainings.

He laid his head against the head support. God, he hoped she hadn't changed her mind about the sex. The adrenaline running through his body made him horny as hell—and only Callie could help. Then he glanced at his hands and swore silently. Shit, he shouldn't touch her, shouldn't be anywhere near her. He'd broken a man's neck, would've taken out the other men if someone else hadn't done so.

Wearily, he closed his eyes. Fuck! He'd man up, bunk in another room, and take a cold shower. He'd use his murdering hands to pleasure himself. The way he felt right now, he'd be too rough on Callie, rougher than his usual. He'd scare her, possibly hurt her—and he'd break his own fucking neck before he did either of those things.

Chapter Seven

After the all-clear call from Conn, Callie felt as if a load had been lifted. She grinned and did a happy dance around their suite of rooms. The offer to make a meal for the returning men had been a spur of the moment decision. She wanted to feed them, these men who placed their lives on the line to save her future embarrassment. Plus, she'd recalled something her dad once told her about post-adrenaline crash—"Baby girl, men after a mission want three things: food and maybe some alcohol, getting their rocks off, and sleep, in that order." Her dad had never shied away from telling her like it was, even when it came to sexual things. He wanted her to know what to watch out for, especially since she lived on a base with so many macho and horny marines. He also made sure his men knew that "no meant no" when it came to women—and that Callie was hands off, which is why she hadn't had sex until Tweeter Walsh asked her.

Turning back to the here and now, she could easily handle the food and drink for all three men—and later she'd take care of the sex then sleep for Risto. Conn and Berto were on their own for the latter two needs.

Slipping out of the room, she raced down the back stairs to the kitchen. She poked around and began assembling a small make-your-own-taco mini-buffet with rice and beans on the side. She fried the corn tortillas on the state-of-the-art restaurant-grade stove and put them in a warmer drawer until the men got home. The shredded pork she'd found in the fridge was simmering in a pot. Someone had already chopped the toppings, which led her to believe Conn and his men often ate tacos as a quick, easy meal. She grinned. Made it easier for her. The beans needed to cook longer, but the rice was done and she placed it in the warming drawer.

A slight noise from the great room reminded her that Conn had left two men to guard her and the house. Javier and, um, Ricky. She'd just check to see if they wanted to eat also. She'd need to fry up some more tortillas, if so.

She took a minute or so to make sure the beans were simmering and not ready to boil over, then left the kitchen by the door leading to a hallway running the depth of the house. The great room was off this hallway toward the front of the mansion. When she reached the room, she heard no sound. The room was dark, only the flickering light of a muted television and the security monitors lit the room. One of the men, she couldn't tell which, was sitting on the couch; it looked as if he was resting. She didn't see the other guy, probably outside doing a perimeter check. Conn told her they did so every hour unless something showed on the monitors.

Walking quietly, so as not to disturb the man's short nap, she moved until she was next to the couch. Her stomach heaved. Swallowing hard, she took a step back. Javier wasn't resting. Necks weren't meant to bend that way. God, was the killer still in the house? She looked around. Saw nothing. Heard nothing. Who'd killed him? The sound she'd heard must have been the killer leaving the room, but where was he now?

A thump upstairs answered the question of where. He'd

gone up the main stairs as she'd approached from the back of the house. Why hadn't the killer looked in the kitchen? She wasn't going to seek him out to ask him, she was just glad he hadn't.

Several more thumps from above. Some louder, some softer. Shit, there had to be more than one of them. Were there others outside? Where was Ricky? Had they killed him, also?

She needed to hide. The men were on their way home. She couldn't chance going outside and running into more bad guys, so she'd have to hide and make her stand here. Hold out until Risto and the others got back.

She needed a gun. The Ruger Conn obtained for her was upstairs, dammit. She glanced at poor Javier. He had a gun. It was in his shoulder holster. Clenching her teeth against the whimper threatening to erupt, she gingerly removed the gun from the dead man. A Glock. She checked the clip, 9x19 parabellum cartridges, seventeen-round magazine. It was full. She left the safety on for now and went back to remove the extra mags Javier had on his belt. She had three full mags including the one in the gun; that was fifty-one rounds. She could shoot a lot of bad guys.

An abnormal calm settled over her. She could do this. She'd pretend the bad guys were the targets she annihilated at the range—or treat this as a live single-shooter video game such as the ones she played with her brothers. She beat their scores every damn time. She could do this—but prayed she didn't have to.

Thuds and angry shouts from upstairs told her whoever was up there was tearing the place apart. They were looking for her. She searched for a hiding place and decided upon a very dark corner behind a huge, leather wing-backed chair. She'd have the wall to her back, the chair with its stuffing to slow down bullets to her front and the French doors to her one side as a possible escape.

She ran on tip-toes to the corner and set her gun and clips

down behind the chair, then unlocked the French doors and opened them slightly. No alarm went off, which told her the intruders had either disarmed it—and she doubted it, Conn had a good system—or, they'd forced Conn's men to disarm it—again she doubted it, Javier and Ricky were hardened soldiers. Or, and the most likely occurrence, Ricky had sold out, which meant he'd killed Javier and was one of the men upstairs looking for her.

Callie's gut told her it was Ricky. As for whom he'd sold out to was anybody's guess. She vibrated with anger. Javier had never had a chance. He'd trusted his buddy.

Thudding feet came down the front stairs. She scurried to her hidey-hole, picked up the gun and flicked off the safety. Kneeling, she used a two-handed grip and braced a shoulder against the wall so she could aim around the side of the chair. She could hear her dad's voice as clear as the day he'd instructed them on how to wait out an enemy when you were out-numbered and trapped: *Single shots, Callie. Breathe calmly. Assess the situation. Pick your targets. Get them in your head. Once you shoot, baby girl, they'll zero in on your position. Make every shot a kill shot—or you're dead.*

She whispered as the steps came closer. "Thanks, daddy." She swore she felt him sweep a hand over her hair. Shaking the feeling off, she took a deep cleansing breath and watched the entry to the great room. The hallway light would backlight her enemy, making them easy to take out. Her ears took in every creak, crack and thud now. She could even hear the drapes as they rustled in the humid breeze coming through the opening in the French doors.

Two, no, three men, approached. As soon as she thought it, the first one came into the room, low, his gun hand sweeping. The second came in high. The third, the murderous traitor Ricky, hovered in the double-width doorway. *Move into the room, asshole.* She wanted to move her shots from the lead man through the second to Ricky before they separated too much.

Didn't look as if Ricky would cooperate.

Good news for her was Cruz wouldn't pay for her dead body, so Ricky would be the most likely to hesitate to kill her—and that would be his mistake. She could easily save him for last, even if she had to chase him down. However, the other two looked like hired guns, the kind of battle-hardened mercs she'd seen during her travels in third-world countries for her charitable work. She knew their type. If she shot and didn't kill them, Cruz wanting her alive wouldn't matter. They'd shoot to kill whoever shot at them.

"*Chica*? Señorita Calista?" Ricky called her from the doorway where he partially sheltered himself. The scumbag. She remained silent.

The lead merc straightened and spoke to the others in bad Spanish, "she isn't here." Not one of Cruz's men; Cruz only hired Hispanics according to her research. He sounded Eastern European and looked like a Serbian or a Croat. He'd be the worst one, experienced from a long and bloody civil war. He'd die first.

"She is here," Ricky insisted. "*Chica*, we won't hurt you. Come out now. The bad men who killed Javier are dead."

As if she'd trust the murdering coward. She remained still. The second merc pointed to the open door. "She left that way." His English was highly accented, definitely not a Spanish speaker, maybe South African.

Both the mercs believed she'd left. Ricky moved into the room. *Gotcha now!* She inhaled, let it out slowly and took the first two shots. The lead merc and his buddy were down. She'd aimed for their heads and was pretty sure she'd hit them dead on. If they weren't dead, they should be incapacitated with the 9 mm jacketed hollow points loaded in the Glock.

Ricky had dived for the floor as soon as he'd seen his companions go down. She peered around the edge of the chair and spotted his legs extending past the sofa. Sighting down on the Glock, she shot him in a kneecap before he could figure out what happened and return fire. His scream of pain echoed loudly in the room.

Callie moved away from her initial firing position to the other side of the chair. Ricky shot wildly. One bullet hit the wall, just missing her shoulder. Plaster splinters struck her cheek. Another shot struck the French doors, shattering the glass. She peered around the chair and saw a part of his body as he moved behind the sofa. The man really wasn't very good at this. She shot and missed. *Damn! Maybe I'm not either.*

His curses filled the air. From the sound of his voice, he was on the floor just beyond the sofa, at the opposite end from Javier's body. Good, she'd hate to desecrate the poor man's remains.

She lay on her stomach and emptied the rest of the seventeen-round magazine through the space under the sofa. Even if half the bullets embedded in the sofa, the other half might make it through the narrow space and hit Ricky lying on the floor, doing enough damage to keep him from getting up and shooting her.

Smoothly, she ejected the mag and shoved in a new one, then began to belly crawl toward the French doors, giving herself a bail out position if Ricky were still mobile. No shots. No movement from the other side of the sofa. She stopped and listened. Multiple bursts of weapon fire outside. Risto and the others must've returned and found the rear guard. But she couldn't let her guard down. As far as she knew, Ricky was still mobile and playing possum.

Baby girl, slow that breathin' down. You don't want to hear your heart thuddin' in your ears when you need to be listenin' for anything out of the ordinary.

Blocking out the sounds of the small war zone in the background, Callie slowed her breathing. Her heart rate soon followed until she could once again hear the drapes rustling in the breeze. Then a swoosh sound. She frowned. What was that? Another swoosh-swoosh. Fabric moving over fabric.

Somehow Ricky was on the move, crawling just as she was. Which end of the couch would he come around? Poor Javier's end or the other? She stilled her breathing even more, forcing all other noises out of her mind, praying no one would come in from the veranda and shoot her ass.

Swoosh-swoosh-swoosh, then a groan. He'd turned and headed for Javier's end, the end of the sofa farthest from her current position. She checked the other two who'd fallen as they'd headed for the French doors. They were dead; her head shots had hit true, so no trouble from that quarter.

She got up slowly, cautiously, ready to dive for the floor at the slightest noise from Ricky's position. She heard nothing, no sound, no movement, but she knew he was on the floor in front of the sofa, near Javier's feet. Blessing her long legs, ballet lessons, and her track and field experiences in high school, she took a running leap and hurdled over the sofa, away from Ricky's location. As she cleared the couch, she twisted in the air as if taking a high jump and then, using the only part of martial arts training she was good at, fell to the carpeted floor and rolled. Coming up onto her knees, she let off two quick shots, one hitting his gun arm as he lifted his weapon.

Quiet settled over the house.

Her breaths now came fast and furious. *Aftermath, baby girl, don't let it beat you. Use the rest of that adrenaline. Check and make sure the bad ass ain't gonna shoot at you anymore.*

She moved slowly, gun aimed at Ricky's head. His arm was flung out, his hand gun lying in his lax fingers. He still breathed, painful-sounding gasps. She'd grazed him in the upper fleshy part of his dominant arm with one of the last two shots. His eyes were slitted, hatred burning in their dark brown depths.

She didn't need to recall her daddy's words about wounded animals. She approached cautiously and watched for any tells. Ricky inhaled sharply, his nostrils flared. Before he could raise the gun, she let off two more shots, one decimated his hand

and the other sent the gun skittering just out of his reach.

His eyes flew open and his gaze was filled with shock, pain, hatred—and resignation. "Kill me, *puta*." He gasped the words, blood trickling from the corner of his mouth.

"Would've earlier. Not my call now. Conn will want to talk to you." She kneeled down and shoved his gun even farther away from his bloody hand. Her breaths were ragged and she used every bit of strength she had not to succumb to the blackness eager to take her over. She'd survived, her daddy would have been proud, but she was sick to her stomach and just wanted to forget the whole night ever happened.

A noise behind her, from the front hall, had another rush of adrenaline sweeping through her system, momentarily clearing her head, settling her stomach. She dove to the side of the entrance to the great room, then rolled behind a chair near the fireplace and took aim at the door. Anyone entering the room wouldn't see her.

Risto came into the room, his body crouched low, his gun sweeping the room. His fierce glance took in the scene in a single swift glance. "Callie!"

She opened her mouth to tell him she was fine when a noise at the French doors had her turning her head. An unknown man, gun in hand, stood just outside, out of Risto's line of sight.

As she took the shot, she yelled to Risto, "French doors!"

CONN'S ESTATE ENTRANCE, MINUTES EARLIER.

Berto drove to the gate leading to Conn's. The gate was open. The security panel was disarmed.

"Shit," Conn swore. "There's been a breach."

Leaving the car outside the gate, the three bailed out and checked the small guardhouse. The guard was dead, one bullet to his forehead.

Using the many trees on the estate grounds as cover, Risto made his way toward the house with Conn and Berto running to keep up. As they got closer, he spotted men on the perimeter, watching, waiting, which meant the enemy was in the house already.

He turned and motioned the other two back. Once they were out of hearing range of the enemy guards, he turned to Conn. "How did they get into the fucking house? Your security system is almost as good as the White House's."

Conn thought for only a second. "Traitor on the inside. Ricky, most likely. Javier is Berto's cousin and has reasons to hate Cruz and everything he stands for." The expression on Conn's face was ugly. Berto looked even meaner. "Shit. Callie's a sitting duck. How do you want to play this, Risto?"

I promised she'd be safe at Conn's and now this. He'd failed her.

He ruthlessly shoved down the urge to rush the house. "We need to take out the perimeter guards, then go in and find Callie. They won't hurt her. She's worth money alive." The other two nodded. "Berto, you go round back. Try the silent approach first. If they spot you, all bets are off. *Comprende*?"

Berto's answer was a wide evil grin as he slithered into the bushes and began his way toward the back of the house.

Risto turned to Conn. "We'll eliminate the forces at the front of the house."

Conn drew his knife. "She's fine, Risto. You said it yourself, Cruz wants her alive. Do your job and she'll be even better."

Risto nodded. He refused to think about what the kidnappers could do to her before they decided to deliver her. "Not one of these asswipes leaves alive."

"Hoo-rah," whispered Conn as they began to make their way to take out the intruders.

It only took him and Conn less than five minutes to kill two men apiece, slitting their throats. As they approached the last four of the enemy, two in a vehicle and two others leaning against another vehicle, smoking cigarettes, shots sounded from the back of the house. Berto must've been spotted. Their four targets began shooting at air. *Fucking idiots.*

He shot a disgusted glance at Conn who shrugged and mouthed "dumb asses."

Picking their shots, they easily took out the two men outside the vehicles and disabled the vehicles. Then Risto heard shots which sounded as if they came from inside the house. Not semi-automatic fire, but single, well-placed shots as if someone were executing targets. Then came a flurry of shots. His blood chilled at the implications. "Fuck, Conn. Someone's shooting inside the house."

Conn looked murderous and nodded. "Yeah. Let's finish clearing the path. We need to get in there."

Conn taking the lead, Risto followed. They stayed in the shadows and approached the vehicle in which the two men had hunkered down with a perfect angle to shoot anyone attempting to enter the house. With their vehicle disabled, the men were stuck, probably counting on the armor-plating to protect them, hoping they'd get lucky and take out him and Conn first, or got help from their buddies inside the house.

His friend signaled he'd go to the driver's side. Risto nodded. As Conn moved from bush to bush along the drive, using the enemies' other vehicle to cover his movements, the passenger side door opened and a man dove out, firing blindly.

Risto yelled, "my side," and took the man out.

"Fire in the hole!" He warned Conn to stay down and stay put, then peppered the passenger-side opening with semi-automatic fire.

"Guy's toast," Conn called out. "I'm on cleanup. Get your ass to Callie."

Risto took off, running toward the open front door. He heard several more shots from inside and then nothing. His heart in his throat, he cleared the entryway and the den, then approached the great room. Through the doorway he spied a scene from Hell. Javier dead on the couch, broken neck. Two unknown men lying on the floor near the French doors. Their heads had taken large caliber rounds and they lay in a pool of blood and brain matter. And Ricky, with several wounds, lay on the ground near the sofa. He was alive, in visible pain, glaring at something or someone Risto couldn't see. *Callie?*

He surged into the room, going low, sweeping his weapon from side to side. "Callie!"

Before he could even begin his search for her in the bloody wreckage, a movement at the French doors captured his eye. Simultaneously, Callie's voice cried out, "French doors!" He dove, shooting at the black silhouette, as shots rang out.

From his position face down on the floor, he felt bullets whizz over him and thud into the wall next to the opening to the hall, then nothing. Staying on his stomach, he crawled to the side of the room from where Callie's shots had arisen. She was on her belly by a chair, in shooter's position, a Glock held steadily in a two-handed grip, with her gaze fixed on the doors to the patio. She muttered under her breath, "Possum or not? Possum or not?" She shook her head and sighed in despair. She ignored his presence, possibly didn't even register he was there, and began to belly crawl toward the patio doors.

"Callie. Sweetheart?" He kept his voice low and calm so as not to startle her. She stopped crawling. She breathed heavily, but seemed to be holding it together. She was in the zone. He recognized it because he'd been there many times. Not knowing when to stand down. Wondering if the enemy was defeated or not. Knowing he needed to make sure and put another shot in each and every enemy's head.

"Baby? I can check the enemy. Callie, love, you've done enough." He touched her arm.

She gasped and blinked then looked at him. At first it was a blank, icy stare, then her gray eyes warmed to their normal color. "Risto?" Her voice was soft, breathless, broken. It was as if she'd forgotten how to breathe and talk at the same time.

"Give me the gun, honey." He held out his hand.

She shook her head. "Could be more. Can't stand down yet. Need to check…"

"I'll check, Callie." Conn stood in the doorway to the great room, his gun at the ready. "You let Risto check you over, sweet cheeks. You've got blood on your arms and face."

She frowned, confusion in her gaze. "I do? I wasn't hit. Ricochets, maybe? I was behind cover the whole time." She swiped a finger over the blood on her forearms and scowled. "Maybe glass from the patio doors—I had to stay low so Ricky couldn't get a bead on me."

Risto let out a sigh of relief. She was back and thinking. Not that she wouldn't collapse sooner or later, the adrenaline crash and the fact she'd killed tonight would hit her. But he'd be there to help her through it. The fact she'd survived, and survived well, again confirmed Keely and Tweeter's assessment of her ability and her innate courage.

He crawled closer and took the gun from her hand and set the safety, tucking it in his waistband at his back. He swept a shaky hand over her face. No holes, just scratches from flying bits and pieces of the room.

She smiled and leaned into his touch, then frowned as if she just recalled something. "You okay?" She touched his face. "I heard shooting outside right before I shot the first two guys. It took me longer to get Ricky, since the coward hung back. But the other two were more dangerous. Had to shoot them first. Daddy always told us not to shoot until we knew which were the most dangerous targets and then to take them down fast and hard. No mercy. Dead man can't come back to kill … kill…" Her face went white, her eyes glazed over, and she began to cry. "Ohmygod, ohmygod…"

Shoving his gun in his shoulder holster, Risto pulled her into his arms, then stood. He headed for the hall. As he carried her away from the carnage, he peppered kisses over her hair, her face, anywhere he could reach. Rocking her in his arms, between kisses, he muttered nonsense words, words of praise. As he walked, he thanked God for keeping her alive. He also added a few silent words of appreciation to her dad for teaching her how to defend herself.

Her loud, heart-wrenching sobs hurt him to his very soul. He walked into the kitchen where Berto stood, pulling a steaming pan off the stove. Obviously, Callie had been cooking when the bad shit went down.

Berto caught his eye. "The little one did good. She survived. Upstairs is a mess. She must have been down here when it went down. This is good, yes?"

"Yes. She took out three mercs. Ricky is seriously wounded. I'd say the little one did very well."

"Berto," Callie lifted her head from his chest. She sniffed, wiping her eyes. "Ricky … he … killed Javier."

Shock then anger colored Berto's face. "Did you shoot Ricky, Callie?"

"Yes. But I didn't kill him… I wanted to … but knew Conn would need to … uh, question him about who he sold out to." She buried her face in Risto's chest and shuddered.

"She may not have killed him, but she did a number on him. Blew out his knee. His gun arm and hand are a mess." Risto stroked her hair, smoothing out the tangles and picking out pieces of plaster. "He probably wishes he were dead." And if he didn't now, he would after Berto and Conn got done with him. Callie's instincts had been good; they needed to know how far the damage from Ricky turning traitor went. If Ricky had exposed Conn's operation, then they wouldn't be safe here and would have to move out tonight. More than just Javier's death or Callie's thwarted kidnapping was involved.

Berto's expression was deadly as he left the kitchen to check for himself.

Risto settled into a large club chair in the hearth room just off the open concept kitchen. As he cuddled her on his lap, he stroked her hair and let her compose herself. She'd had a hell of a time over the last two days and probably needed a good cry just for the emotional release. Hell, there'd been times after a bloody battle he wished he could cry. Instead, he got drunk and had sex. He couldn't visualize Callie casually indulging in booze and sex to excess.

Conn entered the hearth room and covered Callie with a throw from the great room sofa. His friend swept a shaky hand over Callie's hair before Risto shoved it away. "She took the two mercs out with single head shots," Conn said.

The first two shots I heard.

"Ricky, the fucking traitor, is a mess."

Probably the exchange of shots that followed the first two.

"She did a good job on him. He's belly-aching. Said 'who'd have thought a *chica* could shoot like a black ops soldier.' Said he thought she would kill him, instead she shot his hand and then moved his gun out of reach with another shot."

The last two shots I heard, which drove me insane with the need to find her.

Conn snorted back a laugh. "I heard she saved your ass, too, taking the guy out at the French doors?"

Risto shrugged, stroking Callie's back. "I took a shot."

"Well, buddy, you weren't shooting a Glock with 9 mm jacketed hollow points, she was. She took the fucker out with another perfect head shot. Damn fine shooting. Don't know too many soldiers aside from special forces who could've done as well."

Risto shook his head and smiled. "Well, she was trained by the best."

Callie sniffed and turned her face to lie on his chest. "I … I heard Daddy's voice in my head. Remembered what he taught us. I … I … had to take them out." She looked up at Conn then him, her fingers digging into his shirt. "You were coming back. I didn't know how many were outside … couldn't worry about them at that point. But inside…"

She inhaled and blew out a breath, then took another

full breath before continuing. "I found poor Javier ... heard intruders upstairs searching. Alarm was off. All wrong ... knew someone ... not someone ... Ricky ... just knew..." She shrugged.

Risto stroked his hand down her side. "You put it all together. Smart girl. Then what, Callie? Get the rest out, sweetheart."

She sucked in a breath and exhaled noisily, noticeably calmer than even seconds before, but the horrific knowledge she'd taken lives was in her eyes. "I couldn't run. They probably planned for that."

She looked at Conn who'd knelt by the chair. A grim-looking Berto had come back into the room and leaned against the wall. Both men nodded, acknowledging her thinking. She'd done well. If she'd run, she would've been caught instantly.

Her lips twisted into a slight smile at the two men's agreement. "So, I took ... took Javier's gun and hid behind the chair ... then waited ... waited to take my shots ... make them count. Dead man can't shoot you." She shuddered and rubbed her cheek against his shirt. "Could I have done it any differently?" She looked at him, then the other two, tears welling in her eyes. "I was ready to kill Ricky. I looked right at him, waited to see whether he'd go for the gun..."

Callie started, gasping for breath. Risto growled, angry he hadn't been there to take the burdens off her slender shoulders, angry that she had to kill to stay safe. "Shh, baby." She was in danger of hyperventilating. "Slow breaths."

"I c-can't..." She shook her head, a wild look in her eyes.

He took her mouth in a kiss and breathed for her. When her breathing changed and she began to respond to the kiss, he pulled away. He smiled at her dilated eyes and pink cheeks.

"You did the right thing," he said. "Ricky would've gone for the gun, and if you'd hesitated..."

Licking her lips, she stroked his jaw. "I didn't hesitate. It all happened so fast and I just acted. It was as if it wasn't me doing the shooting but some alternate Callie." She shrugged, her lips turned down into a grimace. "When Ricky's nostrils flared and his fingers twitched, I knew he'd kill me. He was livid and in pain and wanted me dead. So, I shot his hand, then the gun. I thought about a head shot ... maybe for a split second, then thought no, he wouldn't get off so easily." She looked at Conn and then Berto. "He killed Javier in cold blood, killed him for money. He sold you all out so I left him alive for you."

"And Berto and I thank you. We will take justice for Javier." Conn leaned over and kissed her forehead. Risto hissed and Conn grinned. "And we'll find out what else he might have told the enemy."

"I already did. The coward told me all." Berto's lips twisted into an evil smile. "The *pendejo* didn't sell us out to Cruz. He hooked up with a bunch of mercenaries who were out for the reward Cruz was offering. He swears they were the only ones he told of this place. I believe him. He was greedy and didn't want anyone taking away his prize." Berto spat on the floor. "He will never sell anyone out again. My *familia* will take care of the *espuma*.

Berto came off his position near the wall and knelt in front of the chair. Shooting Risto a "fuck-you" grin, he gently picked up one of her hands and raised it to his lips. "Javier was my cousin." Callie gasped. Risto kissed the top of her head, offering what comfort he could. "On behalf of my *familia*, I thank you for honoring his death by taking down his killer. You are now family. If you need help, me, my brothers, and all my cousins will come and fight for you." He placed her hand back on Risto's chest, got up, bowed and left.

"He meant that," said Conn. "And I'll be there right alongside them if you need me."

Callie shook her head, the saddest sigh escaping her lips. "If only I'd checked earlier, I might've stopped Javier from being killed."

"Don't think that way. It'll only make you crazy." Risto

brushed a kiss over the side of her face, swearing silently at the bloody scratches on her smooth skin. Wanting to divert her attention from self-recrimination and the battle she'd just survived, he sniffed the air. "I smell something good. Think you could eat?" He didn't figure the traumatic side effects from the evening's events were over yet or had even all appeared, but he knew from experience, the sooner a soldier could get back to normalcy, the better. "You want me to fix you something? How about a glass of wine or maybe something stronger?"

Callie laughed, so hard he sent a questioning glance toward Conn who shook his head and looked concerned. "Callie, baby, you okay?"

She waved a hand in the air then raised one finger. "Give me a ... um, a minute." She chuckled for a few seconds longer then wiped the heels of her hands over her face, rubbing away the newest tears from her laughing jag. "Um, you offered to feed me."

Risto frowned. "That set you off?"

She nodded and choked back another laugh. "Um, after a big battle or a tense situation, my dad said soldiers want three things: food or alcohol, sex and sleep. You just offered me food and wine."

"Well, I can offer a bed and some…" Conn looked at Risto and laughed.

Risto shot him an ugly look. "Well she sure isn't getting the sex from you, old buddy, so shut the fuck up—and she's sleeping with me."

"Never doubted it, old buddy." Conn leaned over and looked Callie in the eyes. "Callie, if this dumbass decides to let you get away, call me."

"Over your dead body, asshole." Risto glared as he shoved Conn on his ass. The loon laughed until he choked.

Chancing a glance at Callie, he found a slight smile on her face. "Callie?"

"I only want you, Marine." She kissed his chin and then

licked the small scar on his lip.

He grunted. "Good, that's good. Now, let's see about feeding you. We have a long day tomorrow. We need to get to bed soon."

"Yes, Risto." She snuggled into his chest, let out a yawn, and fell instantly asleep.

Conn smiled fondly at Callie. "Put her to bed and crawl in with her, Risto. She'll need you when she wakes up." All soldiers understood nightmares, especially after first kills. "The food will still be here later. Berto and I will do cleanup and then eat. We'll store the leftovers in the refrigerator. I've called in extra guards. No one will get to Callie again."

"Thanks." He stood up and carried his exhausted little soldier to their room.

At the doorway, he stopped. The room had been ransacked by Ricky and the mercs. Well, at least the bed was still standing and mostly made. He carried Callie to it, laid her down, efficiently stripped her, then retrieved a damp cloth and wiped off all the blood on her skin, checking to make sure she didn't need stitches. After cleaning her up the best he could, he stripped and climbed in next to her. Pulling her butt against his thighs, he dragged the comforter over them and fell asleep, his nose against her neck, his arm anchoring her waist.

Chapter Eight

Blood and bodies littered the floor. She moved from the corner where she'd shot the men who'd come to hurt her, to take her away. The house was deathly quiet. She was safe—for now.

She lowered the gun to her side and walked to stand over the dead mercenaries. Her aim had been true—single shots to each of their foreheads. She kicked their guns away, just in case they came back to life.

Mixed emotions swept through her—satisfaction at surviving, regret at having to kill, and grief for the loss of life. A half-laugh, half-sob came from her throat. She'd killed. She took several deep breaths and the sickness threatening to overtake her subsided. Backing away, she kept the men in sight. Would the images of them falling to the ground and their empty unseeing eyes haunt her forever?

As she retreated, a hand grasped her ankle. How could she have forgotten? There'd been a third man, Ricky, the traitor. She lost her balance and screamed as she fell to the ground. Hitting the floor, she lost control of her gun. Ricky dragged her across the surprisingly rough silk rug. He was strong and held her ankle in *an unbreakable grip. She clawed at the floor to slow his progress, but the rug came with her as he pulled her ever closer.*

She yelled obscenities, kicking out with her free leg as she attempted to grab her gun, just out of finger reach. An unearthly growl came from her attacker. With almost super-human strength, he pulled her the last few inches. He held her tightly against his naked torso, his cock erect and nudging the crease between her buttocks. He'd rape her! Hurt her!

She found a well of strength and turned to fight her captor—it wasn't Ricky. It was Cruz. His fingers bit into her waist, jerking her closer. His dark, cruel eyes gleamed with lust as he shoved his cock...

Callie woke, her cry of fear echoing off the high, beamed ceilings of her room at Conn's house. A naked male lay against her back, surrounding her, trapping her. A fully erect cock rubbed along her ass. *Cruz!* She whimpered and began to struggle. It was her nightmare come to life. Had he killed Risto and the others? Had she killed for nothing?

"Ssh, Callie. Wake up. I've got you, sweetheart." A familiar voice whispered over her cheek, the tones soothing and calm. Strong but gentle hands held her as she fought her way out of the nightmare to waking lucidity. "You're safe. It's just a dream. Just a dream." Firm male lips pressed warm kisses along her tense, cold neck.

She inhaled, scented the clean male musk unique to one man. She exhaled shakily. "Risto?"

An amused chuckle vibrated against her throat followed by a small nip on the pulse point. "Who else would be naked and holding you in his arms?"

"No one." She let out a noisy breath then stiffened as she remembered. Tears formed in her eyes. Not everything in her nightmare had been imaginary. "I killed those men. I would've killed Ricky..."

Risto's arms tightened, surrounding her with his strength, with safety. He took a gentle nip of her shoulder. "Don't second-guess yourself. You did nothing wrong. They would've hurt you. Delivered you to Cruz." He nuzzled a path to her ear. He licked, then took the lobe between his lips, sucking it. The sensations shot straight to her clit, and her pussy grew wet.

His mouth caused intense feelings, ones she couldn't keep up with in her current frame of mind. He fondled one of her breasts, first cupping its fullness as if testing for ripeness then teasing the nipple with his finger and thumb.

"What are you doing?" Her voice sounded weak and so unlike herself. A low simmering ache roiled within her body, beginning with the ear he gently tortured, then to her breasts, and finally spreading to her sex where it grew into full-blown arousal unlike any she'd ever felt.

Risto released her earlobe and smothered an amused chuckle against her shoulder. "I'm distracting you with sex. Is it working?" She nodded. He pinched her nipple. "Talk to me, Callie. Do you want this?"

He moved his hand from her breast to her mound. Dipping a finger into her opening, he spread her moisture over her labia and clit. "Oh, yeah, you're wet." Her arousal gently simmered as he lightly and rhythmically traced her labia. When he thrust a finger into her, then ground the heel of his hand over her clit, she yipped and arched against him. He sucked on her earlobe. "Callie, do you like what I'm doing to you?"

"Yes-s-s. Can't you tell?" She arched her head back onto his shoulder so she could kiss his jaw. She couldn't hold back the gasp of pain as his finger went even farther into her with her movement. God, it had been so long ... she hadn't realized it would be so uncomfortable ... that it would hurt.

"Callie? Did I hurt you?" He began to withdraw his finger.

"Um ... don't stop." She covered the hand on her sex. "Please? I want you ... want this."

Risto brushed a kiss over the side of Callie's sweat-sheened face. She was in pain, but refused to admit it. So, he'd go slowly if it killed him. He wanted her as hot and ready as he was.

"Hush, sweetheart, I won't stop, but you need to tell me what feels good, what hurts. Tell me if I'm going too fast." He tried to add another finger and managed it only after spreading even more of her juices around and several seconds of delicate stretching with the finger already inside her.

"God, you're so tight, baby." Kissing along her jaw, he observed her as he thrust his fingers in and out in a slow, gentle motion. Her discomfort was evident in her winces and the teething of her lower lip as she attempted to stifle her gasps.

He frowned. Jesus, had she ever even had sex before? He'd assumed ... shit. He pulled his fingers from her, turned her upper body toward him and cradled her head on his arm so he could see her face. His cock throbbing against her ass protested the halt in action.

"Callie, look at me. Please tell me you've had sex before." She opened her eyes, her lashes glistened with unshed tears. He found a mixture of lust and distress in her all-too-innocent gaze. She was either a virgin or really inexperienced. *Fuck, just fuck.*

If she were a virgin, he'd fucking kill himself before taking her. Ren, Keely and Tweeter and every other Walsh male would resurrect his carcass and kill him again for even thinking about taking her innocence. He was not the man to introduce a complete novice to sex play.

"I'm not a virgin..." She hesitated.

Thank you, Lord. Then he scowled. "Honey ... it sounds as if there's a *but* in there somewhere."

"My first and last experiences were when I turned eighteen." She spoke softly, her eyes closed against him. "My dad died the next week—and I sort of had to become a mother, the breadwinner—and, you know, had to deal with everything. Then Evan discovered me and I started modeling and really didn't have a lot of time … and the men I attracted…"

"The men what?" he snarled.

Her eyes flashed open, their silver gray darkened with the storminess of her feelings. "The men wanted my sexy, sophisticated image—and I'm not Calista. I'm plain old tomboy, marine brat Callie Meyers who's only had sex twice in her whole life with one guy who…" She sniffed as tears slid onto her cheeks.

Damn. She was fucking crying again. He wanted to kill someone—preferably the incompetent jerk who'd taken her virginity. God, she hadn't had sex in over seven years? What did the fucker do to her? "Did he hurt you?"

She shook her head, her hair slid over his supporting arm like a silken shower. "No. No. It wasn't like that. He was sweet … nice. We were both inexperienced and wanted to know what it was like." She blinked and another tear trailed down her cheek. He caught it with his lips. "I'm afraid I won't be up to your speed—and I want to be."

Risto cursed silently in three languages. Jesus H. Christ, she was more worried about disappointing him than him hurting her. How to explain to her that there was no way in hell she'd ever let him down. God knew, she deserved a gentler reintroduction to sex, but damned if he'd allow another man to have her. He was here and to hell with good intentions, he wanted her, she wanted him.

"I don't want to hurt you. Try to relax for me. I need to stretch you out a bit."

He reinserted his fingers into her slippery channel, this time with more ease than before. He gradually increased the depth and vigor of his thrusts, watching and listening for her body's cues.

When she whimpered at one particularly deep thrust, he withdrew his fingers slightly and rotated the heel of his hand lightly over her clit. "Sorry, baby. I need to stretch you so you can take me. I am quite a bit larger than my fingers." She nodded and rubbed her cheek affectionately against the arm under her head.

He reintroduced his fingers as he licked and nibbled her neck just below her ear. When she let out a sigh and relaxed into him, he bit the spot where her neck and shoulder met. She arched into him. He noted the sensitivity of her neck and shoulders.

"You just got wetter. You like me sucking on your neck." He licked the spot he'd bitten, causing her to shiver.

"Yes … it makes my clit ache."

He massaged the nub and chuckled as she yipped and thrust her pelvis against the heel of his hand. "Let's add some more sensations to those. Hold your breast to my lips."

"What?"

His stern order seemed to rouse her from the haze of sensations he was giving her. Good, she'd need to be floating in pleasure when he took her with his cock. She was too fucking tight and he'd come as soon as he was in her.

"You heard me." He licked her jaw. He curled the two fingers in her pussy and stroked. She sucked in a sharp breath and let it out on a whimper of need. He'd hit a sensitive spot. "Do it."

With a shaky hand, she offered him the breast he'd fondled earlier. He continued to fondle her sex as he leaned over her and licked his way around the nipple in slow, concentric circles, never touching the tip. Her inner muscles clenched his fingers tightly and he wished they were his cock. She'd feel so good.

"Risto? Please?"

He stopped his teasing of her breast and rubbed his cheek over its upper curve. "Please, what?"

"Suck my nipple."

"My pleasure." He captured the tip with his lips and suckled it with a strong pulling pressure. She made increasingly urgent noises in the back of her throat. Her body moved, always seeking his touch as he teased her sex with his fingers and her mons against the heel of his hand. When he lightly teethed the tender nub, she let out a tiny shriek. He felt her clit throb against his hand.

He allowed the puckered tip to slip from his mouth and then brushed a light kiss over the peaked bud. She shuddered and moaned. "Oh yeah, you liked that. My hand is soaked with your juices." As he continued to nuzzle and lightly kiss her breast, he added a third finger to the two in her vagina. She took the extra digit easily. Soon, she would take his cock, but first—

"You have a choice, sweetheart. I can bring you to orgasm just like this, with me dividing my mouth between your neck, your breast, and my fingers playing with your clit and your pussy—" She whimpered as he demonstrated for several seconds. "Or, I can take you from behind with my cock. The second choice involves me letting you go long enough to snag a condom from my pants."

Callie released the breast she supported and covered his hand on her mons. She was afraid getting a condom was just an excuse to leave her. Afraid that he'd stop completely, that she was too much work. He could easily find a dozen women in the bars of Cartagena to have sex with him with half the effort. "Don't go. Don't leave me ... I'm sorry I'm not like your other women…"

"Hush, just hush. I'm not fucking going anywhere. There's nowhere else I want to be." He rubbed his chin over her shoulder, his beard stubble scratching her over-sensitized skin and adding to her arousal. "No one else I want. I want you to be safe. And I refuse to hurt you."

She looked at him. His sharp cheek bones were flushed from his arousal. She blinked. He wanted her. She saw his desire etched in his gaze, felt it in his touch. He was all masculine heat and tightly leashed desire mixed with possessiveness. She'd seen Colonel Walsh look the exact same way with his wife when they hadn't known she and Keely were spying on them. Both girls' sex education had gotten a leg up that lazy, hot afternoon at Lejeune.

If Risto took her now, it would be a primal mating, a claiming—even if he didn't know it. He might tell her he wasn't a permanent kind of guy, but in that instant she knew she'd do her best to change his mind. For the first time, she'd found a man worth fighting for, a man who saw "her," not the marketed surface. He was her mate.

"Callie?" His voice and eyes held concern. He moved the hand now smelling of her from her mound to cup her chin. She whimpered at the loss of fullness. She reached for his hand to put it back when he angled her face closer to his. She saw remorse in his dark eyes. "Fuck, I'm pushing you, aren't I? You could've died tonight… I'm hurting you … shit, it's too soon." He kissed the tip of her nose. His body trembled against hers as he began to pull away. "We'll save the sex for when you're more up to it."

"No!" If he didn't take her now, her gut told her there'd be no sex later. He'd find a way to put distance between them, treating her as just another job. She needed him to mate so he'd remember later when he tried to leave her.

Firmly, decisively, she captured the hand cupping her chin and held it tightly within hers. Her gaze never leaving his face, she trailed his fingers down her body, tracing a path over her breasts then down her torso to her mons. He didn't fight her, just stared so intently she swore she felt him probe her mind.

She flattened his hand over her needy sex. "I'm on birth control and am clean—and I trust you're clean. I want you in me. I want to feel your seed flooding me." She pressed his hand harder against her clit and rubbed her ass over his steel-hard penis. "Fuck me, Risto. I want to lose myself in you."

He stared into her eyes for what seemed like forever. Finally, the cool examination left his eyes and they glowed with an internal flame. A low growl rumbled through his body and vibrated along her back. "God, I could've lost you tonight. I need to lose myself in you, too, baby." He took her lips in a deep thrusting kiss, eating at her mouth as if he were starved.

Her lips curled with satisfaction he as plundered her mouth. No more gentle and soothing kisses, his control was gone and she loved it. He broke off the kiss. He shifted the arm under her down her body, allowing her head to sink back to the pillow, then pulled her bottom back to cradle his hard-on. His other hand stroked her from breast to hip in long, firm strokes as he licked and nibbled pathways between her neck and shoulder.

"Risto! I want you in me … now!"

Risto paused, his breath rasping over her shoulder. "You'll take what I give you … all that I give you … when I choose." He nudged his hips forward, his cock shoving in between the juncture of her thighs, sliding easily through the vaginal fluids wetting her mound.

Callie arched from the sensation of his cock rubbing against her naked labia and teasing her clit. The simple *frottage* had her whimpering and gasping. Her labia and clit were sensitive to the lightest touch. Risto took her mouth, thrusting his tongue inside, drinking the noises she made as he rubbed his penis over her pussy. He left her mouth from time to time to place sucking, biting kisses along her exposed neck.

"What … oh shit, Risto!" She moaned through an explosion of pleasure, not quite an orgasm, but a tantalizing hint of what would come. She needed more. She clenched her vaginal muscles, needing something solid to assuage the empty achiness. She wanted his cock, his fingers, his anything, filling her, heightening the pleasure. When the contractions died away, she still throbbed, her nerve endings simmering, waiting for more heat to take her to a roiling boil.

"We can do better than that." He petted and stroked her

body, his hand smoothing over all her erogenous zones, first lightly, then with more and more pressure. Already, she sensed the need to come, the urge building with each sweep of his hand and nudge of his cock against her sex. "Let's see if we can make your next climax a screaming one."

She moaned at his words and arched into him, demanding more. She wasn't even sure she could vocalize what she required from him at this point. She just needed.

"I know, baby. I know." He moved the arm under her body so his hand covered her sex. Pressure at that opening had her looking down to watch as he inserted two, then three fingers inside her with his thumb angled to cover her clit. "Good, you're taking me more easily now." His other hand played with her breasts, cuddling and shaping with an occasional tantalizing sweep over her turgid nipples.

"Risto!" The combined sensations and the addition of his lips, tongue and teeth paying homage to her ear had her rapidly climbing the steep peak once more. Her vagina clenched his fingers as he gently thrust them in her tightness with short, rapid jabs.

"Just go with it." He pinched her clit. "Come now."

"But … but…" Her words were lost when a wave of pleasure crashed through her senses. The vibrations built upon one another, rolling through her again and again until like a tsunami the pleasure swept away everything. All thoughts, all sense of time were consumed as she floated on the waves of sensation. Through it all, Risto held her securely, her anchor to Earth. He played with her body, drawing out the pleasure until she collapsed bonelessly against him.

He kissed her cheek. "Eyes on me, baby. I want to see the look I put on your beautiful face." With some effort, she managed to open her eyes and angle her face toward him. "Ahh, now that's the look of a pleasured woman. Now, while I take you up once more, tell me what the 'but' was for."

She shook her head. "I don't remember." She stroked the

hand at her breast with a wobbly finger. "Risto, I'm not sure … I think I'm climaxed out. Come in me, take your pleasure."

"Not how it's gonna work." He touched his forehead to hers. "You will come again and this time I'll be in you." He pinched the nipple he held and then soothed it with his lips. The fingers of his other hand had never left her pussy and once again began small, rhythmic thrusts, stimulating already over stimulated nerve endings. He stroked all around her oversensitive clit, but never quite hit it.

Amazingly, despite the lassitude the previous two orgasms had engendered, a throbbing neediness built within her once again. Her body was as limp as overcooked pasta. Lying quietly, she floated on the feelings his lips and hands had created. His hard, hot cock pulsed against her ass.

She frowned, her mind as limp as her satiated body. There was something she should be doing, wasn't there? Sorting through the pleasure-swamped fog in her brain, she finally realized what the "but" had been all about.

She stayed the hand playing with her sex. "Shouldn't I be kissing your penis? Touching you?" She scowled when he chuckled and nipped her ear. "What's funny?"

"Callie, I've had a hard-on ever since you leapt into my arms this afternoon. If you put that sweet mouth or hands on me, I'd explode. I want to be inside you when that happens."

His words made her smile and confirmed her gut. The part of him that was dominant, alpha-male, wanted to mark her with his seed. "The next time we make love, I want to take your cock in my mouth."

He laughed, a low, sexy sound which sent a frisson of pleasure over her body. "Oh, fuck yeah. I'll insist on it." He sucked on her neck then bit down. She'd have a mark later. "I'll have you on your knees with your lips around my dick. My hands holding your head as I fuck your mouth."

She moaned at the images his words created. She licked her lips as if she could taste him now. Her pussy squeezed the fingers inside her and coated them with even more moisture.

He scraped his teeth along her jaw line. "Oh, yeah, we'll definitely put that mouth to use later. But right now—" He added a fourth finger to her pussy and stroked the spongy part of her vaginal wall. She made a guttural sound and moved into his touch. "I want you to come on my cock."

He pulled his fingers from her pussy, flipped her onto her back and entered her with one powerful thrust of his hips.

Callie's eyes widened as the pressure deep inside her exploded. The feel of Risto's thick cock plundering her sex was pain and pleasure. Far sooner than she thought possible she soared toward another orgasm. Then she was flying, the only thing keeping her anchored to the earth was Risto's large body over her, pressing her into the bed with each thrust of his hips. The animalistic sounds she heard were coming from her. She was so overcome with sensation, all she could do was ride the strong waves of pleasure and hope her lover would catch her if she fell.

Risto alternately kissed and muttered "fuck yeah" against her breasts, her throat, her hair. "More, I need more."

He pushed away from her body until they barely touched, his cock in her sex. He lifted first one of her legs then the next and braced them on his shoulders. Now, his entry was even deeper. He played with her clit as his hips moved faster and faster and so deeply he hit her cervix. Breathing and intelligible sounds had long since abandoned her and she could only catch shallow gasps of air between making grunting sounds. Amazingly enough, she came again—her inner walls rippled incessantly around his cock as he threw back his head, a rictus of pleasure sweeping over his face. His hips thrust harder and animal-like growls came from the back of his throat as he filled her with his seed. Pressing forward until her knees were almost alongside her head, he kissed her, muttering earthy compliments and praise against her lips as he rode out his orgasm until his hips slowed to lazy undulations. His pubic bone rubbed over her swollen clit with each inward move and had the effect of drawing out and prolonging her pleasure.

After her orgasm fully subsided, she could finally breathe. She took in several breaths and waited for Risto to pull out and move away. But he continued a slow, rhythmic, almost dreamy thrusting. He was also still hard.

"Risto?" She reached one limp hand toward his face and petted his cheek. He turned his head and kissed her palm.

"Yeah?" He smiled and leaned into her mouth and licked along her open lower lip.

She shook her head. This couldn't be normal. He'd come and he'd come hard. She could feel his semen added to her own fluids leaking down her leg and onto the bed. Her only experiences had indicated that men came quickly and needed recovery time. Very young men could get hard again fairly quickly, but Risto was over thirty years old. "Um, you're still hard."

He nuzzled her hair, his breath hot against her throat and ear. He licked and sucked on the tender skin under her ear. "Yeah." He chuckled. "You inspire me. One more time, baby?"

She moaned. "God, you beast, I don't think I can. I'm so tired." She attempted to move her legs from their position over his broad shoulders. The pressure on her diaphragm wasn't allowing her to take full breaths—plus he was heavy. Shit, he wasn't budging. She wasn't going anywhere unless he allowed it. She whimpered in the back of her throat.

"Shh, baby. You can do it. You're so fucking beautiful when you come." He nuzzled her damp cheek. "I'll do all the work. Just lie in my arms and enjoy."

Callie laughed, a hysterical note tingeing the sound. "Easy for you to say. Coming is hard work. Plus, I can't breathe. You weigh a freaking ton."

He laughed and kissed the corner of her mouth and then trailed kisses over her face, back to the sensitive area on her neck. "I can fix that."

He moved her legs off his shoulders until they lay on either side of his body then rolled them over, his cock still lodged inside her. As she settled on top of him she swore she had a mini-climax as his penis hit a new spot inside her tender passage.

"How's this?" He stroked her back and sides with strong, soothing strokes. "Just use me as a bed like those magic fingers types in cheap motels. Just lie there and I'll do all the work."

"How?" She braced herself on his chest with her forearms and looked into his slumberous, sexy eyes.

"Like this." He grasped each side of her hips and moved them to meet his in-and-out hip movements.

"Oh ... yeah that should work." She collapsed onto his chest, then nestled her head on his shoulder and closed her eyes. She idly stroked a hand over his shoulder and up his neck, taking small nibbling kisses. She was happy to let him do all the work. His cock was huge and throbbing within her and it felt good, as if it belonged there.

Callie floated along on a gentle sea of pleasurable sensations. But all too soon the sensations became sharper, shooting up and down her body. God, she was going to come again. She panted into his neck where it joined his shoulder. "Ohmygod." She bit then sucked on the skin under her mouth. Risto's hands massaged her ass as he moved her up and down, rotating her to hit pleasure spots she never knew she had. When one hand drifted to the seam of her ass and he swept a finger over her anus, she let out a mewling sound as she tightened her inner muscles around his cock.

"That's the way. God, you're so fucking tight. So warm and wet ... just for me." He inserted the tip of a finger into her anal opening.

She cried out, a breathless sound of pain and pleasure. She tossed her head side-to-side as he teased the tender rosette, pushing her toward a pinnacle she wasn't sure she'd survive. Trying to catch a full breath, she failed abysmally. "I don't ...

think…"

He kissed her forehead gently, almost sweetly, as he drove her body to where he wanted her to go. "Don't think. Just feel."

He withdrew partially then thrust. The only thing keeping her from being tossed off his body was his hands on her ass and her fingers grasping the balls of his shoulders. It was like riding a bucking bronc lying down. Each upward move of his lower body rubbed nerve endings, sending shards of pleasure throughout her entire body. With her voice strangled by the intensity of sensation, she could only gasp for breath and moan.

Then Risto stopped moving, his cock buried in her sex. His chest heaved as his breaths sawed in and out of his mouth. Under her ear she could hear his heart pounding, feel the pulse against her vaginal walls from his throbbing penis. *God, I'm so close to coming again. What's he waiting for? Armageddon?*

His cock twitched within her and her body pulsed around him. They breathed in unison, her heart matching his speed and rhythm. It was as if they were one living organism.

"Look at me, Callie."

She lifted her face away from his neck and gasped at the heat and possession she saw in his dark eyes. He took her mouth with a hard thrust of his tongue. After several sweeps of her mouth, he broke off the kiss and licked a trail along her jaw until he reached her ear. Sucking in the tender lobe, he began to move his hips in a circular motion, thrusting his already buried cock even farther within her.

The combination had her screaming soundlessly as a massive tsunami of pleasure took her over. He held her to him, one arm across her hips and one hand on her head. She had no choice but to ride until he was through with her. God, she never wanted him to be through with her. He'd ruined her for every other man. No one could be as in tune with her body as this man.

Risto cursed and snarled unintelligible words against her shoulder, her jaw, the corner of her mouth. Then finally he shouted "Callie!" His roar of completion sounded against her ear. His upward thrusts were rapid and deep, violent, jerky. Warm moisture flooded her, his cum filling her, marking her with his scent. "Mine!"

Callie angled her head to tell him of her joy at his possession. Before she could utter a word, Risto thrust his tongue inside her mouth, matching the rhythm of his hips as he rode out his climax. He groaned into her mouth as his big body shuddered and shook under her. Her vaginal muscles spasmed in response to his post-orgasmic shudders, each organ milking all the pleasure it could from the other. She moaned into his mouth, returning his breath.

Finally, he stilled his thrusting motion, his chest heaving under her as if he had run a race. He held her to him and gently rolled them over on their sides, his semi-erect cock still lodged within her. She moved to pull away from his arms, dislodging his cock.

"Stay here, baby." He tucked her along his side, one arm under her head and one over her waist. He gently shoved her head onto his chest and rested his cheek on the top. She sighed happily and snuggled against him, placing little kisses over his sweaty pecs and playing with his silky dark chest hair.

"You okay? Did I hurt you? Scare you?" He rubbed her back.

"Mmm, that feels good. I'm fine." She yawned and patted his chest, daring to smooth one finger over a hard male nipple. Her move elicited a rumbling sound similar to a rough purr. Not sure what the proper post-sex protocol was, she pushed against his chest. She was sticky and wanted to clean up before going to sleep.

"You need to use the facilities?"

Well, yeah, but she wasn't going to tell him that. Hell, she was blushing just thinking about it. "Well, uh, no … maybe a little…"

"You're thinking too much." He pulled her to him for a deep kiss and then whispered against her lips. "Now, let's get you cleaned up." He got up and then lifted her into his arms and carried her into the bathroom where he gave her just enough privacy to go to the toilet before he gave her a sponge bath.

"I can do it." She tried to grab the wash cloth from him.

"Nope, I got you sticky," he winked at her as he smoothed the cloth over her breasts and down her stomach toward her mons, "I get to clean you up. Lover's privilege."

He gently and thoroughly wiped between her legs and down her thighs and then around to her bottom. She had a full body flush by the time he was done. He quickly swiped the cloth over his torso and then his cock and balls. "There, that should hold us until a shower later this morning. Right now you need sleep." He pulled her back up into his arms and carried her into the bedroom. "You're sleeping with me just in case you hadn't realized it." He laid her down and then climbed into bed with her, pulling her into his side. "Rest against me."

"Okay." She settled her head back onto his chest. She rubbed her cheek over his tanned skin and inhaled. He smelled … right. She was happy, replete—and proud. She'd satisfied this man with her body despite her relative inexperience. And, wow, had he satisfied her. Multiple orgasms and so much pleasure she was surprised she hadn't spontaneously combusted. She closed her eyes and snuggled into Risto's furnace-like warmth as he pulled the covers over them. His hand immediately returned to hold her tightly against him.

As she drifted on a warm dark cloud of lingering pleasure into sleep, lips brushed her ear with one last order, "Sleep, sweetheart."

Risto cuddled Callie. Her shallow breaths whispered across his chest as she practically lay on top of him. He moaned low in his throat at the memory of her lying atop him as he lodged himself so far into her body they had become like one entity.

Boneless in sleep, Callie's long legs tangled with his; her bent knee rested against satisfied cock, soft for the first time since he met Callie. He ruffled his fingers through her tangled curls, then smoothed the hair over her naked back. She sniffed, then murmured something against his skin. His cock jerked at the movement of her lips right above his nipple. While his body gave an indication it would be up for another round of sex, Callie was exhausted and needed her sleep. Today would be just as rough as yesterday.

God, the way she made him feel was unlike any other woman he'd ever been with. He'd never come so hard and so quickly by just entering a woman's pussy. He'd never recovered that quickly. He was always in control, but this time, his own games had sabotaged him. No, he needed to be honest, it was all her. She responded beautifully as if she were made for him. Just the thought of another man tasting her, taking her, sharing her orgasms, made him crazy. She filled a hole in him he hadn't even realized existed.

Mine. Fuck, no, he couldn't think that way. She wasn't his. This was only temporary.

Yours, a voice inside his head insisted.

Shutting out the taunting voice, he turned toward Callie and found a position which would allow him to continue to hold her and catch some much needed sleep. As he settled into the mattress, Callie's body adjusted so she touched him all along his torso. She sighed and her lips brushed his skin as she snuggled her nose into his clavicle, the top of her head just under his chin. He refused to think about how well she fit within his arms or he'd want to take her again. Dawn was a couple of hours away, and they needed to get some rest so they could handle whatever the day might bring.

With her light, feminine scent surrounding him, he closed his eyes. He rubbed soothing circles on her back as he drifted to sleep. He didn't know if he was calming her or himself. All he knew was he needed this closeness, something he'd never shared with any other woman in his life. *Mine—for now.*

CHAPTER NINE

*Rescue Day 2,
Cartagena then to somewhere outside of Montería.*

Callie entered the kitchen. Risto, Conn and Berto stood up. All of them stared at her, concern the predominant emotion on the men's faces. Risto's gaze also held lingering heat. She blushed. She couldn't help it. The memories of their lovemaking last night and then again when he'd joined her in the shower this morning were all she could see when she looked at him. She stopped and self-consciously rubbed her damp palms on her jean-covered thighs. "Hi."

Risto came to her, placing his arm around her waist, then lifted her to a stool at the kitchen island. He tucked some errant hair behind her ears, his fingers lingering to caress her face. "How are you feeling?"

Stiff. Sore in places she hadn't been sore in ... well, ever. Her cheeks heated up even more. His eyes crinkled with silent laughter. "I'm fine."

He brushed a kiss over her lips. "You're more than fine." He stepped away and sat on the stool next to hers. "Berto is cooking. What do you want for breakfast?"

She wrinkled her nose. She was starving. Sex burned a lot of calories, well, at least, the way Risto performed sex it did.

"Depends. When will we get a chance to eat again?"

"Around noon. We're only travelling a little southwest of Cartagena to a *finca* outside of Montería. The roads are mostly good since we'll be taking the main highway."

"We're going to a ranch?" She'd thought they'd head to the Andean foothills and some place in the middle of nowhere.

"Yeah. It's a working cattle ranch. Great cover for men coming and going." Risto bumped her shoulder with his. "Now, tell Chef Berto what you want to eat."

Berto smiled and winked. She smiled back. "Whatcha got?"

"Traditional American or local?" He flipped the spatula he held. "Risto is getting my *huevos pericos*." At her raised brow, he added, "Eggs scrambled with onions and tomatoes."

"That sounds good. Could you add cheese?"

Berto nodded. "For you, *bonita*, anything. Cheddar okay?"

"Sounds great." She picked up a warm corn tortilla from a towel-covered basket, folded it in half and took a bite. "Oh, yum. These are good. Did you make them, Berto?"

The Colombian looked over his shoulder and nodded. "Yes, my mother taught all her sons to cook."

Conn sat on the other side of the island. He looked her over, his gaze touching her bare arms then her head. "You have a cover up? Something for your head? The sun will be brutal today, even through the tinted windows of the Land Rover."

"I've got one of Risto's button-down shirts to go over this tank and a hat." She took another bite of the tortilla. "I need to either put my hair up or braid it. It will be too hot and heavy in this weather to hang on my neck." She pulled up a length of hair that covered her breasts and flipped it back over her shoulder. "Now that I'm not required to keep it a certain length for my cosmetic and shampoo ads, I may just cut it all off."

Three loud "no's" rang throughout the spacious kitchen/hearth room. Risto turned toward her and glared. "That would be drastic, considering you don't live in a tropical climate year-round. We'll find something to put it up with." He stroked a hand over her hair. She shivered at his possessive touch, at the lustful way he eyed her hair. Something told her she'd have a battle on her hands if she attempted to cut her hair right this minute. But, hell, he didn't have to wash and dry and deal with the damn stuff.

"I agree with Risto," Conn said. "It takes forever to get that kind of length. One of my sisters cut hers and regretted it the minute after she did it." He came around the island. "If it's okay with Risto, I can French braid it for you. I used to do my sisters' hair all the time."

"Why does he have any—"

Risto cut her off, a finger on her lips. He skewered his friend with a narrowed gaze. "Braid it. But, Conn, if you touch anything other than her hair, you'll lose some fingers."

Callie pushed Risto's fingers away. "You have no say in this matter." She looked at Conn. "Thank you. I've never gotten the hang of French-braiding so please do. It will be cooler and out of the way."

Conn chuckled. "If you think he has no say, sweet cheeks, then you don't know the man very well." He pulled a stool behind hers and began to divide her hair into the sections needed to do the braid. "Do you want me to braid it in more of an up-do or just a tail? And do you have anything to tie it off with?"

She twisted to look at Conn. "You can do an up-do?" Her awe at his expertise had to show on her face because he chuckled and nodded. "Heck, we'd need some pins for that," she frowned, "that's too much trouble. Just a braid. We can use any piece of cloth or string."

Conn nodded. She turned back to find Berto had placed her meal and a glass of juice in front of her. She was intensely aware that Risto's gaze strayed to Conn's surprisingly agile fingers every few seconds. When one of Conn's fingers stroked the nape of her neck, Risto muttered, "fucking asshole."

Conn's snort of amusement rustled over her hair.

"Risto, behave." She concentrated on eating and keeping her eyes forward. Nothing was worse than a crooked French braid because the recipient hadn't sat still. Berto caught her gaze and winked. "The food is delicious, Berto. My compliments to you—and your mother for teaching you. Did you use any special herbs in the tomatoes or onions? There's something extra here."

Before Berto could answer, Conn spoke, "Berto, find me a string or something to tie this off with."

A hair tie flew past her head. At her questioning glance, Berto smiled. "I use them on my hair. It is a clean one," he assured her.

"I'm not worried." She smiled. "Thanks."

"*De nada, chica.*" Berto indicated her clean plate. "You wish more?"

"No. I'm fine. I expect my marine wants to hit the road." She turned toward Risto. He wore a ferocious frown on his face as he stared at the man still dealing with her hair. "Risto? Are we ready to go?"

He glared some more at Conn then looked her way. "Yeah, let's get out of here." He slid a finger over her cheek and then under one eye. "You're too pale and have dark circles. Hold up a hand."

She blinked at the scowl on his face and the self-recrimination underlying his words. When she held her hand up for his perusal, she was shocked to see the fine tremors. Risto enclosed her cold hands between his and chafed them.

"Just as I thought, you're still recovering from the adrenaline overload and crash." And in a low tone, but loud enough that Conn could definitely hear. "We should've waited to have sex. You needed more rest. I'm sorry, baby."

God, could he embarrass her any more? He had to beat his chest in front of the other men. But she refused to let him regret what for her had been lovemaking. "I'm fine. You didn't do anything I didn't want you to do." She blushed as she felt Conn's piercing examination of her face and body. Berto stood across the counter from them, an expression of interest on his face. "You said I could take a nap in the car?" Risto nodded. "Then I will. You can wake me if you need me to drive."

"Won't happen. Like I said, we aren't going all that far. Montería is around 146 miles down Route 25. The *finca* we're travelling to is about another thirty-five miles outside of the city, but those roads are rougher. Total travel time will be around four hours, depending on weather and traffic."

Callie looked outside and observed that a steady rain fell. "Isn't that area of Colombia fairly low?"

"Yeah." Conn came into her line of sight. "It's savanna with some tropical scrub. The ranchers cleared the area for their cattle and the crops to feed them. It is hot, humid and will flood this time of the year."

"So, there's a chance of water rushing across the road like a gully-washer?" she asked the men.

"Let me worry about it." Letting go of the hands he still held, Risto smoothed a palm up-and-down her arm. "I'd never do anything to endanger you."

"I know," she said. Risto pulled her off the stool and into his body, his arms anchoring her in front of him. She snuggled against his warmth, her hands braced on his chest. "Just wondering, that's all. I was on a photo shoot once in the Hill Country of Texas and saw a huge truck swept off the road by what was only about a foot or so of water. It was amazing—and terrifying. The only good thing is the high water usually subsides quickly once the rain stops."

"It is the same here," Berto said. "The water, it drains quickly. You can easily wait it out if such a thing should occur."

"We'll be fine." Risto placed her next to him, his arm around her waist. "Let's go. Conn and I loaded the car. With any luck, Cruz and his lackeys are chasing their tails to the north and the Santa Marta area."

"Why Santa Marta?" She knew the city was a port city with a regional-sized airport, up the coast toward Venezuela. "Why would they think we'd head that way? We wouldn't be able to cross into Venezuela. US citizens aren't welcome there."

Risto grinned. "A little bird told Cruz."

"What little bird?"

"Tom had one of Rosa's cousins pass the word. Seems Paco doesn't like Cruz's womanizing ways, feels it hurts their drug business for Cruz to bring so much attention to himself."

A drug lord was helping them out because he believed in family values? She began to laugh. Risto and the others joined in. "That's priceless. And I don't suppose we can tell anybody. One, they wouldn't believe us, and two, once I get back to the States, I'll be tracking Cruz's money and some of it will lead back to Paco." She turned a sober face to the others. "I can't take it easy on him just because he helped us."

"I don't expect you to. Even though he has chosen to ignore us for the moment, he is still a murdering drug trafficker." Risto leaned over and kissed her lips. "Plus, I think we have a head start for you on finding the money trails." He handed her a DVD he pulled from his pocket. "Found this last night when I retrieved the videos of you. Conn looked it over and found what looks to be Cruz's back-up files for corporate shells and financial records."

Shocked, she looked at Conn. "With bank account numbers and everything?"

"No, he was dumb but not that dumb," Conn said. "But there do seem to be account ledgers. Some entries are from companies I recognized as fronts for Paco's cartel."

She took the DVD and then kissed Conn on the cheek. "This, added to what I'll get from Marv's financials and the designer's dealings with Cruz, gives me a great place to start."

Muttering threats at his friend as Berto chuckled, Risto pulled her into his arms. "Behave, Marine." She patted Risto on the chest. She scrunched her nose and looked at Risto.

"Does Paco know we have this?"

"No, and that's why we need to get you and it out of the country. If Cruz tells Paco the DVD is missing, we'll have both of their troops after us."

"Well, hell, we'd better get going then." She walked out of the kitchen, the three men behind her. As she passed by the room where she'd shot the intruders, she stumbled. Images of the previous evening played across her vision. Blood. Bodies. She shook her head, her hand reaching for something. For someone.

Risto caught hold of her hand and turned her to face him. "Callie?" She couldn't answer, could only see the room, now mercifully free of bodies and blood. Berto and Conn must have deep-cleaned all night. She swayed.

"Fuck, Callie. You're white as a ghost." He swept her into his arms and continued walking down the hallway into the foyer and then outside into the gray, rainy morning.

Vaguely, she was aware of Conn running ahead and opening the passenger side door. Risto placed her on the seat then carefully swung her legs inside and buckled her seat belt for her. She hated being such a wuss, but lack of sleep and the emotional stress had ganged up on her. She just needed some rest, then she'd be back to her normal strong, can-deal-with-anything self.

Risto's hand caressed the side of her chilled face. "Just lay back, rest." He reclined the seat.

She attempted a smile and raised a limp hand, wanting to touch him, reassure him she'd be okay. He captured her hand before she had it halfway to his face, placing a kiss on the palm before laying it on her lap. "Rest, little soldier, that's an order." He shut the door.

Closing her eyes, she rested her head against the seat. She was barely aware of Risto entering the car and the men's voices. Her mind had decided to shut down. No matter how much she wanted to thank Conn and Berto for their assistance, she couldn't. Her body had run on fumes for days and, now, had finally given up the ghost. She exhaled softly and drifted into sleep.

Risto checked Callie's condition once more, as he had many times since they'd left Conn's. She was breathing easily and looked to be in a deep sleep. Her satiny skin was pale, cool and dry, not clammy as it had been earlier. There were no signs of shock or nightmares, but he would stay alert to the slightest change in her condition. His little soldier was damn resilient, but even the hardiest soldier succumbed to the horrors of battle now and again. And what she'd survived the previous evening had been a battle. The sexual release he'd given her had allowed her—and him—to rest for what had been left of the night. Although he could kick himself for waking her so early for the morning shower sex; she'd needed the rest more. The only thing he didn't regret was the gorgeous smile she'd given him afterwards.

He shot her another glance. He couldn't help himself. She looked so beautiful and at peace. So far, she'd had no more nightmares, made no noises, but for an occasional cute little snore. He grinned and smoothed a hand over her thigh. Once Callie went to sleep, she did it big time. She hadn't even roused when he'd pulled over several times due to heavy downpours and once because of foot-deep water crossing Route 25.

His eyes turned back to the road ahead. The highway might be the main road between Cartagena and Medellín, but it wasn't engineered to drain well, unlike the Federal interstate system in the US. At one point, he and the other vehicles on the road were detoured off then back on. That had been a tense moment. Often terrorists would use such a tactic to rob and cherry pick kidnapping victims. In this case, the Colombian army had enforced the detour and been present along the detour route.

He checked the portable GPS plugged into a cradle on the dash and realized they were maybe twenty-five miles away from the *finca*. He was hungry and bet Callie would be also once she awakened. He'd let her rest until they reached the ranch; they'd eat there.

His sat phone rang. The noise caused Callie to move and murmur something unintelligible, but she remained asleep. He pulled over to the side of the road and answered the call.

"Smith."

"Risto? It's Trey. We've got a problem, buddy."

He stiffened. "What?"

"The ranch was attacked by FARC guerillas. It isn't safe to take Callie there." Trey spoke to someone in the background. "We got the call and then diverted to Turbo and traded out the plane for an assault helicopter so we could provide air support to our guys and the Colombian army on the ground. The area won't be safe for a while." It was business as usual in Colombia.

"Fuck." He leaned back in his seat and shot a glance at Callie. Her gray eyes were on him. Worry creased her brow. He traced a finger over the line in her forehead, smoothing it away. "Can we count on Plan B? Or, should we go straight to Plan C?"

Plan B was a boat out of Turbo to a safe house in Puerto Obaldo on the coast of Panama where Tweeter Walsh was with the SSI jet. Plan C was a twisted and far more dangerous route. It involved following the Río Atrato through the Darien region of Colombia and ending at the Atrato river delta on the rugged Colombian coast near the border with Panama. Once there, Tweeter would pick them up by helicopter. The latter route would mean travelling by dugouts and possibly by foot through some of the most uninhabitable territory in the world. The benefit of Plan C was Cruz would never anticipate him taking Callie out that way. He hadn't been sold on the idea, but Keely and Tweeter had insisted the girl they grew up alongside of could do it. So far, she hadn't proven them wrong.

"Trey? What Plan am I using, man?"

"Go to B for now. You might have a narrow window. Conn just called and told us Paco is now after you. Guess Cruz fessed up about the DVD you appropriated."

Risto had brought the back-up team up to speed last evening after Callie had fallen asleep and before he'd made love to her. He yawned, tired all of a sudden. God, he should've left her alone this morning in the shower and caught the extra sleep. But if he had it all to do over again, he'd do it the same way. He might never get a chance to make love to her again—and he'd wanted to absorb as many memories as possible for later, after he left her in Chicago.

"Plan B it is. Tell Tweeter I'll let him know what's going on when we get to Turbo and assess the situation."

"Got it. Luck to you, buddy. Use Corona's on the Turbo waterfront. The owner has been informed you need his safe room until dark when your boat will be available."

"Corona's, got it. Out."

"Out."

Risto punched off the phone and set it back in its charger.

"What's wrong?" Callie touched his thigh, massaging it. And his damn cock got hard. Well, he should be used to his reaction to her by now.

"Some FARC terrorists attacked the ranch. Our ride is providing them air support so the situation is fluid and dangerous right now."

"So, what's Plan B again?"

He looked at her face. She had some color in her cheeks. Her eyes were alert, calm, and he could almost see the wheels in her head processing and reassessing the situation. Damn, she was wonderful. "To Turbo then out by boat under the cover of darkness, then up the coast to Puerto Obaldo where Tweeter is waiting with the SSI jet."

"Sounds good." She looked in the back seat. "We have any food?"

"No, I'd planned to eat at the ranch. I passed a small town about fifteen minutes ago. It had a place to eat. Since we need to backtrack to catch the road to Turbo, we'll grab something there."

"Okay. How long to Turbo?"

"Depends on the rain. While you slept I had to pull over a couple of times and take one detour around the water. The elevation isn't much higher going to Turbo." He looked at his GPS and plotted the trip. "Maybe ninety miles and potentially two to three hours."

"Okay. What do we do when we get there? Play tourist?"

"No. Paco is on our tails now." She grimaced but remained silent. "We'll go to ground at a place called Corona's until it gets dark, then we can meet our boat. Trey has already given the bar owner and our ride a head's up."

She wrinkled her nose. He couldn't help it. He swept a finger down the length to the tip then traced a path over her lips. She kissed the tip of his finger and he swore he felt the sensation on the tip of his cock. "Won't that be dangerous?" she asked.

"How so?"

"Either of these men could decide to sell us out."

"SSI has used them in the past or they wouldn't be using them now. Plus, if they attempt to screw us over, I'll handle it." It wouldn't be the first time he had to get himself and those under his protection out of a goat roping.

"That's good to know." Her gaze travelled over his face. "You look beat. Want me to drive? I can drive a stick and follow the route you've plotted." She tapped the GPS on the dash.

"Let's talk about it once we've eaten." He cupped her face and his thumb smoothed over her chin. "You look more rested but still too pale."

She covered his hand with hers. "I'm fine. I just had a four-hour nap which puts me ahead of you in the sleep column. But we can always talk."

He read between the lines and heard "but I will be driving to Turbo." He shook his head. She hadn't figured him out yet. She'd learn. He had to be in control.

Chapter Ten

Rescue Day Two, on the road between Montería and Turbo.

Callie chanced a glance at Risto. He slept like the dead in the passenger seat. They'd eaten in a tiny village boasting a decrepit, one-pump gas station, a bus stop consisting of a covered bench, and a tiny café. The local eatery had a basic Colombian menu, and the special of the day had been a cornmeal pasty of spiced beef, cattle being the main product of the area, with a local cheese and some grilled vegetables washed down with a local wine. She'd had two of the filling pasties and Risto, four. The meal was delicious and provided the boost of energy she needed.

As they'd dined, she'd demonstrated her ability to use the GPS and read the maps. She also argued he needed the sleep in order to be on top of his game in case of trouble in Turbo, a rough coastal town and one of the main ports of Colombia at the base of the Gulf of Urabá. Finally, he agreed to let her drive as long as she promised to wake him at the first sign of trouble or when they reached the outskirts of Turbo, whichever occurred first.

So far, the drive had been boring. She was used to the cutthroat and high-speed driving in and around Chicago. The Colombian highway had very little traffic and what there was,

was mostly the busses that traveled the major roads connecting the larger cities. The sun remained behind the clouds, and a light but constant rain fell, adding to the already over-inundated drainage ditches along the road bed. She'd had to go off-road twice to avoid deeper water where the road dipped and once to avoid cattle taking a siesta in the middle of the road. Risto had slept through it all.

What in the world was that? Was that a roadblock ahead? She blinked dry eyes and squinted against the glare filtering through the clouds.

It was a road block; that couldn't be good at all.

"Shit, shit, shit." She checked behind her and saw no one coming. She braked to a stop, made a U-turn and headed back the way they'd just come. "Risto. Wake up. Trouble."

His eyes opened instantly and he glanced around, then at her. "What's wrong?"

She noticed his Glock was in his hand as if he expected to shoot someone. He might just get his wish. "Roadblock on the road, just outside of Turbo. I made a command decision and turned around."

Risto twisted in his seat and looked behind them. "Did they see us?"

"Don't think so. And there wasn't anyone behind us to tell whoever they are about the U-turn." She tapped the GPS. "You want to get out the maps Conn gave us and check them against the GPS? I saw a couple of small local roads back this way. Maybe we can go cross-country and come into Turbo by a back road."

"Maybe." He stroked her arm. "Quick thinking."

"Thanks." She shot him a worried glance. "I hope I didn't overreact. They could've been police or Colombian army looking for drugs or terrorists, but my gut said no. I think they were looking for us. But how could they have known we'd be coming from Montería?"

Risto had his nose in the map. "They couldn't. This is

the main road to Medellín and Cali, both of which have major airports. A branch of the highway also goes to Bogotá. Cruz, and Paco, too, would guess we're heading for a major transportation hub. Trey and I figured we had a narrow window to avoid just such a situation. Guess it was narrower than we thought."

"Okay, but won't they cover the major ports, also?" Turbo was as major as you could get in Colombia.

He looked up, his face grim. "Yeah. We're ditching Plan B and going to C." He didn't sound thrilled. "I've found a road which will take us close to Puerto Cava, the small village on the Atrato River where we'll pick up a *piragua* from one of our local contacts for the next leg of our trip." He keyed something into the GPS and hit the plotter button.

"A *piragua*? That's like a dugout canoe." They'd be on a river. Mosquitoes. Alligators. Piranha. No wonder he was worried. He probably thought she'd freak. Well, she'd prove him wrong.

"Yes." He massaged the back of her neck where she hadn't realized every muscle had tensed. "Callie, it'll be dangerous. Hell, taking this back road will detour us completely south and west around Turbo and then due west to the base of the Gulf of Urabá—smack dab in the middle of FARC and ELN disputed territory. Then we'll be travelling north by river through the Darien, an area which always lands in the top ten most dangerous areas in the world."

She nodded. "I know. But you've been through here before or we wouldn't be going this way. I trust you—and I'll do what I can to hold my end up."

"God, sweetheart, this won't be anything similar to a field trip at Camp Lejeune. People go into the Darien and some never come out." When she just shrugged, he heaved a disgusted breath and rubbed a hand over his face. "With luck, we won't have to get off the river and we'll take it all the way to its delta at the north end of the Gulf. At that point, we'll be close to the Panamanian border. Once we get to the coast,

Tweeter will fly a helicopter out of a stronghold we have near Puerto Obaldo, Panama, and pick us up."

"Sounds straightforward. I can paddle."

"If it were just paddling a small boat, I wouldn't be so concerned." He ran a hand through his thick, dark hair. Hair she now knew felt like raw silk against her skin. "The Río Atrato runs through dense rain forests and ends in a swampy river delta. Worse than the hostile environment, the route takes us through the middle of drug-smuggling central in Colombia, not to mention all the local guerillas fighting one another and the Colombian army. We'll have to travel fast and be ready to take cover and avoid hostiles. This could add days to the trip and mean we'll be camping in less than agreeable conditions."

She'd been correct: he worried about how she'd handle it. Truth be told, she wasn't thrilled, but she'd deal. Now to put things in perspective for him, she asked, "What are the other choices?"

He opened his mouth. She held up a hand and cut him off. "The way I see it, there aren't any. Cruz, and now Paco, will have the main roads covered to the larger Colombian cities. Any secondary road into a bigger city puts us in danger of meeting up with any of a number of armed locals who would kidnap us and sell us to Cruz for shits and giggles. The sooner we get out of what stands for civilization in Colombia, the better." He winced at her words but nodded his agreement.

She continued, "You didn't take us toward Venezuela, the closest border with Colombia, because Chavez is hostile to the US. Brazil is out because it's too far away and the terrain between here and there involves the Andes, deserts and rain forest with hostile, dart-shooting natives. Running to Ecuador is also too far and wrought with danger of being trapped by Cruz or any number of other paramilitary groups. So, there were no alternatives but escaping into Panama after Plan A tanked—and the safest route by boat is now out, correct?"

"Yes." The worry in his eyes, while not gone, was now

overshadowed by respect.

"The route you've plotted will get us to the closest friendly border," she said. "I understand the journey will be extremely hostile, but Cruz and his ilk will also have to deal with the same dangers. We have the advantage of knowing where we're going and he doesn't. That about it?"

"Yeah, pretty much. I can see why Keely said you were a natural analyst." He closed his eyes and let out a rough breath. "I've used this egress twice since starting to work for SSI. It took four to five days including time out to remain below the radar in order to avoid active guerilla patrols. There's a possibility about midway, at Ungaía, to pick up an outboard motor for the dugout to speed up the trip. That stop would depend on how quiet the local guerillas are. Bottom line, the whole area is just plain dangerous."

Callie took his last statement as meaning "dangerous for her." If alone or partnered with another SSI operative, he wouldn't think twice about taking the route. She promised herself not to make him regret having to use this alternative. She shot him a grim smile. "It's a good plan, stronger for the fact that Cruz and Paco are chauvinists and it would never cross their minds you'd take me this way."

He emitted a choked laugh. "Yeah, that was the other reason we included Plan C. Keely said men think with their little brains all the time and don't give women credit for being adaptable."

She laughed. "Sounds like Keely." She pulled to the side of the road. "The road you marked is just ahead. Unlike Keely who thinks she is an Amazonian super-woman, I know when I can't do something. I think you should take over the driving." She arched her neck and winced as she wiggled her fingers to get feeling back into them. "I had three short detours off-road and the rough conditions took all my upper body strength." She shifted the car into neutral and set the handbrake.

"Why didn't you wake me?" He grabbed her hands.

Turning them over, he stared at the livid red creases in the palms from where she'd held on to the steering wheel with a death-like grip. He muttered several pithy curses as he brushed kisses over the angry-looking welts. "Fuck, baby, you're already bruising."

"I'm fine. You needed your rest, and I handled it. Problem with that?" She arched a brow, daring him to belittle her efforts to carry her weight on the mission.

Risto shook his head, a bemused look on his face. Drawing her to him, his hand firmly on the nape of her neck, he kissed her. Moaning, she leaned over the center console into the kiss, her arms twining around his neck. She groaned deep in her throat as the kiss turned from sweet to heated and hungry.

After what seemed like minutes, he pulled away. "In case I forget to tell you later, you're a wonderful partner. Any other woman would've complained about … well, everything."

"I'm not a complainer." Whining had never gotten a job done and was a waste of time. She leaned her forehead against his. "I won't say I'm not scared, because I am."

"Callie…"

She brushed her mouth over his to halt his words. "Shh, let me finish. I'm far less scared than if I'd had to do this on my own. What helps keep the fear manageable is doing the things I can to carry my weight. Just driving kept me from thinking too much."

"I understand. I'll try to keep you involved. But if you don't tell me when something is hurting, I'll paddle that sweet butt." He nipped her lower lip. "Understood?" She nodded. Risto smiled and rubbed his nose over hers. "Once we get under way, your next duty will be to call Tweeter and let him know we are now on Plan C."

"Is the safe house another *finca*?"

"No, the coastline of Panama in that area is very rugged. It's a small, rehabilitated Spanish fortress overlooking the Caribbean which we share with the US Military and several private security organizations. There's just enough flat space to land a small jet. We use it as a base for fighting drugs and hostage rescue in the region."

"I've never heard of anything like that before." She unlocked the car in preparation to changing places with Risto.

"And you'll forget about it once we leave it. This is black ops stuff, baby. The fortress is vital to stopping drugs from moving north through Panama and is operated with the full knowledge and cooperation of the Panamanian government. They realized a long time ago they couldn't police the area for drug smuggling so they allowed the US and chosen private companies, SSI being one of them, to do the job."

She nodded. She'd known SSI worked for foreign governments from time-to-time. She exited the car. The light rain had turned to a heavy mist. The air was saturated, all thick and steamy. She felt as if she'd stepped into a steam bath. Risto waited by the passenger door and lifted her into the vehicle. He grabbed another quick kiss, then buckled her in and closed her door.

When he got into the driver's seat, she asked, "Do we have enough gas to get where we're going?"

"Yeah. That fill-up when we ate lunch helped and I have four gallons of gas in the back of the Rover. As long as we don't have to take too many detours off the plotted route, we'll have fuel to spare."

She breathed a sigh of relief. "That's good to know." She pulled the satellite phone from the charger in the console between them. "I'll call Tweeter now. Anything I should tell him other than go to Plan C?"

"No and no chitty-chatting. While I'm pretty sure the sat phone is as secure as it can get, you never know who at NSA might be listening and to whom they might be selling info."

She frowned. "What do you mean? Why would we be concerned about NSA listening in on our transmissions?"

Risto took the car off-road and was silent for several

minutes as he negotiated a couple of deeply rutted, washed-out areas just off the main highway. "There's a traitor high up in the DOD selling out US military and private security operatives doing work for NCS. Keely discovered him while she was working on a project for NSA. She had to go to South America to warn Tweeter and that's how she met Ren."

"Keely told me about it right after she got married. But I thought the traitor had gone under. You mean he's still causing trouble?"

"Yeah."

"You think this traitor has someone listening to all SSI transmissions over the NSA satellites. Why would a traitor to the US care about a private hostage rescue mission?"

Risto shot her a glance. "Money. I'm sure Cruz has made it clear to all and sundry by now he'll pay for information about you—and if not you, for the DVD I stole. We know the traitor has serious connections to the South American drug trade and the terrorist activity in Colombia. He sells intel to all sides. He also likes to cause SSI problems. This fucker doesn't like us at all. We've curtailed or sabotaged his lines of communication—and put a serious damper on his commerce stream."

"Scum-sucking bastard." She viciously punched buttons on the phone. "One more asshole I can help Keely and Tweeter put away, well, that is, if Ren agrees to take me on at SSI. There'll be money trails—there are always money trails." She spoke into the phone. "Go to Plan C." She listened to Tweeter's response and looked at Risto. She covered the mouthpiece. "He wants to know the time table."

Risto grimaced. "Right now it's fluid. Tell him we'll contact him when we know better."

She nodded and uncovered the speaker. "We'll get back to you on that." She punched the off-button and put the phone back in its charger. "Extra batteries?"

"In my backpack." He patted her knee. "We're well supplied. Conn and I planned on the potentiality of Plan C.

We won't use the phone unless we need to. Its feed is off NSA satellites through Keely's contract work so we should have access throughout the Darien."

Callie wrinkled her nose as she thought things through. "We need to let Keely know that it's possible her traitor sold info to Cruz. She can back trace the transmissions made about this mission. If there is chatter lying outside of normal channels, she can set up a trap so we can obtain the IP address of the NSA computer used. If we can pinpoint the leak in the NSA we could follow it back to the DOD traitor."

"They tried that route already." He rubbed her leg. "The leak is as shifty as the traitor. They found the monitoring of SSI was done on several different computers, all of which were used by multiple NSA analysts."

"Okay. Then who in the DOD has the authority to command NSA monitoring of SSI transmissions and to send Ren and the guys to that fake meeting in Argentina? Not many people in the DOD have that kind of authority to influence the NCS hiring of private security organizations and sending them on covert ops. I mean, NCS is part of the CIA and not even under direct DOD authority."

"It has to be someone high up in the US intelligence community. Keely and Ren think they have it narrowed down to four or five people. But since the bastard has laid low since Ren and Keely's baby was born, they haven't gotten any other data to help pin him down. Keely has her trapping program running 24/7."

"Well, he's active now. Keely needs to know what we suspect."

"It can wait, Callie. The data will still be there, right?"

"Yeah." She yawned and jiggled her hands, massaging them to get the stiffness and soreness out. Risto's rumbling snarl had her looking at him sideways. His gaze fixed on her hands and not the treacherous road. "Just stretching them out, Marine. Eyes on the road."

"Little liar." He shifted his narrow-eyed scrutiny back on the sorry excuse for a local connector road. "Check the first aid kit out for some pain relievers."

"I have some in my tote." She retrieved her bag from the floor of the back seat, found the ibuprofen and swallowed a couple dry. After putting the bottle away, she pulled out a small bottle of lotion and poured some on her sore palms and massaged the cream in, then stored that bottle also. She tucked the tote next to her legs. The ladies Ruger was in the side, zippered pocket; she wanted it within reach in case they ran into trouble. She looked out the window at the thick greenery as it passed and yawned several times in a row. "Not sure why I'm so sleepy."

"Stress and not enough rest." He rubbed her shoulder. "Take another nap. Things will get rough later once we abandon the Rover and have to hoof it to the riverside village to pick up our next ride. Plus, we'll be camping out tonight—and will need to take watches. Get as much sleep as you can now."

"What about you?" His look of shock at her concern hit her hard. Tears formed in her eyes and she quickly turned away so he wouldn't notice them. Hadn't anyone ever taken care of him before? Ever worried about him?

"I'll be fine. You don't need to take care of me, Callie."

Like hell I don't. Even if she weren't so attracted to him, she'd still take care of him. He was risking his life to get her away from Cruz. The least she could do was assure he got rest and carry her own weight on the trail. Maybe she wasn't an ex-special ops marine, but she knew how to nurture males. She turned back and considered Risto as he concentrated on the track masquerading as a road. He was strong, courageous and so alone. She'd never seen a man in more need of nurturing than Risto. She fell asleep with her gaze fixed on his strong profile.

Rescue Day Two, on the Atrato River.

RISTO PROPELLED THE *PIRAGUA* FORWARD and away from some vegetative detritus clogging up the river. The long pole used to steer the flat-bottomed boat had proven to be too unwieldy for Callie who was used to canoe paddles. She sat in the back of the boat with a shorter pole which she used to shove the boat away from the shore when the river narrowed.

Aware she was sensitive about carrying her weight, he hadn't voiced his relief that she couldn't handle the long dugout pole. He admired that she knew her strengths and weaknesses: she'd admitted within the first half mile on the river she didn't have the strength or the knack. It took a lot of man-handling to keep the boat in the middle of the river. The current moved steadily and, at times, swiftly, to the sea, but with eddies and submerged debris, the passage was fraught with danger. At this point of the Atrato, and because they were in the rainy season, the river was extremely navigable with the shores almost twenty feet from the middle. Later, they might have to get out of the boat in order to ford areas of the river's tributaries where silt and plants grew thickly.

Callie had proven she was strong enough to handle the weight of the dugout by helping him launch it at the small village where they'd picked up the boat. Fording, if required, would be easy.

"Do you think Cruz realizes we've headed into the Darien yet?"

Risto checked her face for any signs of additional stress and was relieved to see only mild interest. In her waterproof poncho and floppy hat, she looked like a jungle queen set off against a backdrop of the thickly treed shoreline. Her gaze met his and she smiled. She was enjoying the journey. He hoped to hell she'd still enjoy it once they stopped for the night. He hadn't decided whether to anchor in the middle of the river or attempt to find a secure shelter on the thickly vegetated shore. There were many abandoned river houses on stilts, left vacant when the local farmers fled the guerillas and drug dealers who'd taken over this area of northwestern Columbia. Even if he could find such a shelter, he wasn't sure it would be any safer than taking turns sleeping and keeping watch in the boat. Plus, the middle of the river in a boat kept them away from the insects which swarmed the shores.

"Risto? Something wrong?" Callie leaned forward as if she wanted to touch him.

"No. I was thinking about tonight and where we should stop." He looked up at the overcast sky and the clouds which had chosen not to drop their moisture for the time being. "We have about two more hours of light with the cloud cover being as thick as it is. And, as for your question about Cruz, no, I don't think he knows yet. But someone in the village where we bought the boat will talk, however innocently, to the wrong person and he'll know soon. We're still in his paramilitary area."

She nodded and grimaced. "Yeah, not too many tall, blonde *norteamericana* females running around the Atrato River. You, they wouldn't even remark on—your tanned skin, hair and eyes are dark enough to pass as a native."

"Don't worry about it. As you said before, we know where we're going, he doesn't." He steered the boat. The rhythmic movements were soothing, as was the constant hum of the marshy jungles surrounding them. "Our biggest danger could be Ungaía since it's a fairly large town and has some of the mod cons such as a residence hotel and some small restaurants."

"Then we should give that place a pass." Her words were spoken in a firm and calm tone.

"We'll stop if it looks quiet. SSI's local contacts will let us know if Cruz or Paco have had anyone asking questions. If we can get a motor for this boat, we could be at the coast three times faster. Plus, after spending the night in the rainforest, you'll want a shower and some real food." He'd picked up enough local fruit that, along with the MREs Conn had procured for them and any game or fish he could catch, they wouldn't starve, no matter where they stopped.

"Risto, look at me." He looked up. She had a fierce look in her eye. "I'm not a hothouse flower. I may not have done this kind of camping in a while, but I did accompany my brothers on extended camping trips to Montana and the North Woods in Minnesota. I can handle this. So, if you don't feel Ungaía is safe, we don't stop there. We stay on the river and it takes what it takes to reach the coast. I'm far more concerned about Cruz catching up with us than roughing it with heat, bugs, and wild animals."

"Good."

"So? What *are* the choices for camp tonight? Do we need to stop to build a shelter? There's definitely enough wood and palm leaves to build a snug one." She gestured to the thickly treed shores. "Although we might have to build tree houses, the land looks saturated on both sides."

"We have two choices: middle of the river or taking over an abandoned river house."

She scrunched her nose. "Well, the problems camping on the shore are the flooding, bugs and wild animals. On the river, there's the danger of the anchor not holding and getting swept away if the current increases because of the weather behind us."

"And the river anchorage also has the problem of a guerilla or drug smuggler coming along and seeing us."

"Yeah, they'd have outboard motors and lights." She stayed silent for a second or two. He wondered what brainstorm she'd come up with. "We should've gotten torches from the natives. Don't they use them for night fishing?"

Risto laughed. "I thought of that but ruled it out. Too many dangers on the river at night. I can always rig up something if we need to move fast to stay ahead of hostiles, but I wasn't taking any chances."

"If the river is dangerous at night, won't it be just as dangerous if we're stuck in the middle of it?"

"Yeah, but we'd also be in the boat and all packed and ready to go." Risto poled away from a log lying ahead. "Staying on shore takes making-and-breaking camp time."

"Time we could use to be down river and closer to the coast. Let's just take it as it comes." She arched her back and moaned. "I hate just sitting. I'm really ticked off that I can't handle that damn pole thing."

His lips twitched. She looked like a grumpy kitten. "You're doing an important job. I have to pay attention and make sure we don't get caught on debris. While I'm doing that, I can't watch the shores for trouble."

Callie's face broke into a wide smile, the smile which had sold millions of dollars of cosmetics and designer clothes. He eyed the Ruger which was now holstered under her left armpit. Somehow, Conn, or maybe Berto, had found her a shoulder harness which could be adapted to fit her. He shook his head and silently snorted back a laugh. If her fans could see her now, dressed in jungle chic with a gun snuggled against her perfect breast and a wicked knife sheathed along her thigh. She was a cross between Lara Croft and Sheena of the Jungle.

"What were you thinking?"

"What?"

"That look on your face," she prompted, "what thoughts made you look that way?"

"How did I look?"

She bit her lower lip and he almost groaned. He wanted to bite that lip and other various places on her body, then soothe them with his tongue.

"Happy. Peaceful. Like a man who had found his place in the world and knew it." She waved an arm around. "You like the jungle?"

What should he say? He hated jungles. He did fine in them, but as she did, he preferred cold northern woods like the ones surrounding his home in the U.P. He couldn't admit he was thinking about her and that she was every man's, most especially his, idea of a perfect woman. And the fact that she was also a great companion for an adventure was icing on an already delicious cake.

"Risto?"

"I was thinking about you." He went with honest. Something deep inside him wanted her to know how he felt.

"Oh?" She studied his face then said, "Thanks. I like being with you, too. Even though it is in a hot, humid jungle." She sighed. "Want some water? You're doing all the work and must be sweating off all your body fluids." She dug in the packs at her feet and brought out one of the canteens. She moved one seat toward him, carefully balancing her weight and barely rocking the boat. She had a great sense of balance, probably from learning to walk on those high-heels models always wore. "Here take this. And here are some electrolyte tabs. I don't want you getting sick on me."

He took the canteen one-handed as he maintained the boat's trajectory with the pole and set it by his feet. He held out his palm and accepted the tablets she gave him. He swallowed them dry, then chased them with a drink from the canteen. He closed the canteen and handed it back to her. "Where did you get the salt tablets? From Conn?"

She moved back to her seat in the bow. "No. I had them in my tote. I told you I didn't deal well with tropical weather. I always carry them on shoots where it's hot."

He chuckled. "When we camp for the night, I have to see what else is in that tote."

She grinned. "Maybe. If you ask me nicely, I might just let you."

"Oh, I'll do more than ask nicely, sweetheart." He'd kiss her until she'd let him do whatever he wanted, and what he wanted, but couldn't act on while they were surrounded by danger, included more than looking inside the tote bag.

Chapter Eleven

Callie helped Risto tie the dugout to the stilt legs of an abandoned riverside house they'd found on a small, side tributary. By staying away from the main channel, the hut on stilts was a safer bet than one on the main river shore. The ground surrounding the hut was saturated to the point there was a foot or so of water covering what in dry season would be a rocky clearing. With the boat hidden in the thick shore foliage and positioned next to the crude ladder leading to the hut's entrance, it couldn't be seen from the main tributary. To enter the single-room dwelling, all they had to do was climb from the boat right onto the ladder. No need to get their feet wet.

Risto climbed onto the ladder. "You can hand the packs to me and I'll carry them up. You'll need both hands to climb. The ladder has some loose rungs."

She snorted and Risto laughed.

"What?" she asked.

"I love the little noise of disgust you make." He winked. "It's all cute and huffy. Now, why the attitude, sweetheart?"

"Stop thinking of me as a super-model and start thinking of me as an over-grown tomboy. Since I can climb trees, I can make it up a rickety ladder with a pack on my back."

"I'm sure you can, but with me here, you don't have to." He stepped off the ladder back into the boat and made his way to her. Tipping her chin up with a calloused finger, he looked into her eyes, then nipped her bottom lip. "I've wanted to do that all day. Every time you thought better about sassing me, you teethed your lip."

He licked the seam of her mouth until she let him in. His kiss went from zero to a hundred miles an hour in a split-second. She whimpered as her nipples budded and the crotch of her pants got wet. Her arms twined about his neck like kudzu on a tree trunk. She wanted to stay in his arms forever, but ... the boat rocked dangerously under her.

"Hey, hold my place." He set her gently away from him, holding her until she found her balance and the boat stabilized. "We need to get situated before I can give you the kind of kiss I want."

"Holding your place, gotcha." Following his instructions like a good soldier, she handed him a pack after he climbed back onto the ladder. He ascended one-handed then tossed the bag into the little hut and reached for another pack.

Something had been eating at her since the early morning shower sex. "Will you want to collect on that blow job I owe you?" *God, nothing like blurting out every prurient thought in your head, Calista Jean.* She looked anywhere but at him, not wanting to see his amusement at her embarrassment over talking so bluntly about sex.

"Oh hell, yeah ... but not tonight. I'll collect once we're safe and have someone to cover our asses. We need to stay alert. I'd hate to get us killed just so I could get my rocks off."

Callie felt all hot and achy at just the thought of taking him into her mouth and making him go crazy, of taunting the dominant male in him to claim her. Since he was concerned about potential danger and staying alert, she bet all she'd get later were some tame kisses—dammit. In only one day of knowing him, the man had seriously addicted her to his kisses and love-making—and upset her usual commonsense.

Risto stared down at her, a frown on his face. "Callie, you with me? Hand me the last pack."

"Oh, sorry." She leaned over and attempted to lift the last bag, a big black duffle. "Um, what's in this? Lead weights?" She used her strong leg muscles and lifted the bag to her waist, then juggled it until she got both arms under it. The boat rocked violently until she redistributed her weight properly. "Oof!" She lifted and offered the handle to Risto with trembling arms.

"Shit, I forgot how heavy it was. You okay?" She nodded. "No lead weights—just a sniper rifle, ammo for same, and another submachine gun and ammo for it—and some extra perimeter alarms." He took the bag, one-handed, and easily lifted it into the doorway above him.

"Show off," she muttered. She shook her arms out and then arched her back, both hands massaging her lumbar region. *Note to self—do more weight-lifting once you're home. Pilates and yoga ain't hacking it.*

Risto leapt the few feet from the ladder into the shallow water on the other side of the boat. "Here, let me make it better." He waded to a point parallel to her position in the *piragua* and pulled her against his upper body as she remained in the boat. Her head on his shoulder, he rubbed her back and shoulders. She inhaled his musky scent of clean male sweat and the citrus-based soap they had used at Conn's. She sighed, her aches and pains gone at his scent and his touch. Yeah, she was addicted to him all right. He was better than muscle relaxants and anti-inflammatories.

He kissed the top of her head then held her away from him. "Go on up. I made sure there were no nasty critters inside. I want you to pull out the sniper rifle and check it over, make sure it's one you know how to use. It has two scopes, one for night-vision and another for thermal imaging. Set it up for night-vision, we'll be using it for guard duty."

"Okay. What are you gonna do?" She picked up her tote and slung it over her shoulders in preparation to climb the ladder.

"I'll scout around the area and make sure we don't have any two-legged neighbors." He patted his backpack. "I'll also be setting up perimeter alarms and some traps. And, if we're lucky, I'll find some fruit to supplement our supply and maybe snag a fish or two. We can chance a small fire before it gets too dark since we're not on the main channel of the river. I make a mean fish wrapped in plantain leaves cooked over an open fire."

"Sounds yummy." Risto lifted her from the boat then swung her over the marshy shore toward the ladder. He held her until she placed her feet on the rungs. She began climbing then stopped and turned her head. He was watching her just as she knew he would. "Give me a time frame."

His eyes narrowed. "You don't need a time frame. You sit and wait for me."

"Unh-unh. Not gonna happen. Tell me when I need to start worrying." She glared at him, anger boiling up so quickly she wanted to explode. "If you don't come back within a reasonable time, I'll start hunting—so give me parameters. What did you think I'd do if you never came back, sit here forever?"

Risto tossed his pack into the boat and waded toward her, fury in his eyes. He pulled her from the ladder. Her feet brushed over the water's surface as he gathered her against his torso. A show of his manly strength and dominance. She snorted, and he scowled.

"I'll be back. You'll stay put." He shook her gently. "And if … and I mean if … something should happen and I don't return by dark, you'll use the damn sat phone and give Tweeter your status and GPS location. He'll alert Conn who'll come to get you. Got that?" He shook her again then returned her to the ladder, holding her until she grabbed the sides and had her feet set in place.

His controlled vehemence ratcheted her annoyance even higher. "Oh, I heard you." She stared at him. Hooking an arm around the side of the ladder, she poked him in the chest, punctuating her words. "But it doesn't make sense. You could be down with a frickin' twisted ankle and I could do something about it. So ... to keep me from going bonkers and coming to look for your macho-stubborn ass, you'll promise to check back before full-dark. You can pick fruit while you're scouting. I'll fish." She pointed to the trees near the hut. "Those are plantains. I can wade just as well as you can. I can pick leaves. I can cook. Got that?"

The last finger to his chest was grabbed. He engulfed her hand and pressed it over his heart. All his iciness gone, his eyes crinkled at the corners with suppressed laughter and something else. It looked a lot like lust. She glanced down and spied his monster erection outlined by his jeans. *Yep, definitely lust.*

"Got it." He leaned over and whispered a kiss over her ear. "By the way, sassy little spitfires get their asses spanked. Think about that while I'm gone." He backed off. "Now get your adorable butt up the ladder. You can fish off the side of the hut just as the natives do. It's safer. The alligators will be hunting for food this time of the day. I'm the only living thing who gets to take a bite out of you."

She swallowed, hard. She had images of him feasting on her breasts and pussy, leaving little love bite marks on her skin. Every sexual organ in her body jumped up and shouted "hurrah" at the thought. "Got it." She scurried up the ladder and crawled into the hut on her hands and knees. She turned to see him watching her, a superior male smirk on his lips.

"I'm in, okay?" She waved her hands in a shooing motion. "Go. Hunt. Do manly things. I'll be here when you get back.

The little woman, taking care of the home fires."

He shook his head. "Unh-unh, baby. I'll take care of the fire and getting the plantain leaves for cooking the fish when I check back. If you haven't caught anything, I'll catch the fish also."

The man thought she was a helpless idiot. She'd bow-hunted and skinned rabbits in North Carolina and deer in Minnesota. A little fishing then cleaning and cooking would be a piece of cake. She looked at the sky. "Aargh, men!"

Risto's shout of laughter echoed around the small clearing. She snorted. She should cut him some slack. After all, he didn't know she could survive in the wild. She'd told him, but he needed to see it to believe it. She'd just have to prove she could carry her weight making camp. She might not be able to lift and carry seventy-five pound duffle bags or set perimeter alarms, but she could do this much and lighten his burden.

A quick glance around the hut showed her what she needed to know about the cooking possibilities. "There's a small cooking area in here." As if he didn't already know, after all she'd sat safely in the dugout as he'd checked out the hut. "And decently dry fuel. I can start a small fire so the ashes are hot enough to cook anything *I catch*. Get me some plantain leaves now…" she stared down at him, "…so I don't have to disobey your orders and get my dainty little feet wet."

Risto's lips twitched. "Yep, bossy, sarcastic spitfires get their asses spanked, too." He splashed over to a plantain plant and picked some leaves, then brought them to her. When she went to take the leaves from him, he held on to them until she looked him in the eye. "Any other orders before I leave, baby?"

"No."

"Good. Now be an obedient little soldier and stay put."

She saluted with the leaves still in her hand. "Sir, yes, sir!"

Risto chuckled and lowered himself down the ladder using just his upper body strength. *Show-off.* "Callie." His voice was sober, all laughter gone from his expression. "Don't let anything happen to you. If you need me, one single shot from the Ruger will bring me on the run."

"Got it. Be safe. If you need me, a single shot will lead me to you, too. Don't be a macho idiot. I can help."

He shook his head as if he couldn't believe she just called him an idiot. "I'll be back, Callie. Trust me." It wasn't a question but an order.

Dammit, had he heard the fear she thought she'd hidden under all her brave talk? Not the fear of being left alone as he probably thought, but her real fear, that something would happen to him and she wouldn't be there to help.

"Marine, I've trusted you since the first second I met you. But shit happens—and you need to learn I can be counted on in a crisis even if I'm scared. Even if I'm thrown into a situation I've never experienced before." There she'd said it. Trust was a two-way street.

"You've already proven yourself. But, for my peace of mind, I need to know where you are. I need to know you're as safe as I can make you. And, I need to be in control of what is controllable. Unfortunately for you, you're the only one I have power over in this jungle." He saluted and melted into the jungle so quickly she lost him immediately in the layers of dark green shadows and the misting rain.

She shivered. It was as if the jungle was alive and had swallowed him whole. She thought she'd known what to expect on this excursion. Some of the swamps and marshes around Camp Lejeune and other areas her dad had taken them to camp and practice survival skills were pretty dense and rough. But the rainforests of this area of Colombia had them all beat. And, she couldn't imagine the terrain getting worse, but as they travelled down the river, Risto had told her stories of him and Trey Maddox hunting in the Darien Gap toward the mountainous Panamanian border. Their quarry had been a small squad of leftist guerillas, a splinter group who'd broken away from a larger group and were only in it for money and the joy of killing and terrorizing. SSI's clients had been a small group of foreign businessmen who'd invested in banana plantations in the region. Their farms had been harried by the group. Some of their workers were killed and some of the workers' wives, taken.

SSI's job had been two-fold: to get the women back and eliminate the small band of terrorists. They had, but the look of hell in Risto's eyes had told her the real story—it had been grim, deadly and dangerous work. In the Darien, nature was more dangerous than even the human element and the human element here was often the dregs of society. His eyes had also promised nothing bad would happen to her if he could prevent it. The man had a surfeit of responsibility. Control or no control, he needed to learn to share burdens.

Callie set about making the small hut a little bit more comfortable. She laid out the sleeping mats, placing them next to each other, and then hung the netting she'd found in one of the packs over them from a hook in the ceiling she imagined was there for just that purpose. Finding fishing line in one of the survival packs and a hook, she used a small piece of fruit for bait and hung the line out the window on the tributary side.

She started a small fire using the bits of stacked dried wood, some pieces of what looked like dried peat, a piece of paper from a notebook in her tote, and the matches she always carried in foreign countries. She tended the blaze until she had it burning to produce the most heat and the least amount of smoke.

Sitting by the window, she kept an eye on the fire and another on her line.

The rain had started up again with a vengeance and was now a downpour. Her outer clothing was getting wet from the spray as drops hit the window frame.

Callie stripped down to her tank top and boy short panties. She hung the button-down shirt on a hook away from the hut's openings, but close enough to the fire to dry out, then draped her jeans over the black duffle bag after removing the sniper rifle, the night-vision scope and a couple of magazines for the rifle.

Before she could check over the rifle, something tugged her line. "Duh, Callie. It's raining. Fish come to the surface during rainy periods." She went to the window and pulled the line in carefully. "Yes!" She landed the wiggling fish on the hut floor. Looked like a catfish similar to the ones found in the US. Probably in the same family, but much larger. She silently crowed at her success.

Unhooking the fish, she rewound the line, removed the hook and put them on the pack for repacking later. She pulled her knife from its sheath and took the fish to the doorway and cleaned it, then scraped the garbage out onto the bank-side of the hut. As the parts they wouldn't eat hit the shallow water covering the bank, some scavenger fish or other animal came to the surface and gobbled them down. Nature hated waste.

She took the fish and filleted it, then found some spice packets in the kit. After flavoring the fish, she wrapped it in the plantains then wrapped it again in foil from the very well-equipped survival kit. She buried the package in the hot ashes and glowing wood embers.

That done, she sat and tended the fire to keep it burning hot, turned the fish, and checked over the rifle. It was almost dark now. Risto had been gone for over an hour. No one had passed by the hut on the small offshoot of the river. And no one had approached from the jungle side. She felt a momentary sense of panic. It was as if she were the only person in the green, wet world of the Darien Gap. "Stop it, Callie. Risto will be back any minute."

"Talking to yourself, baby?" Risto smiled at her from the ladder.

Callie shrieked, her hand going to her chest where her heart pounded rapidly. "God, you scared me. Make some noise the next time." She frowned. "I was worried … it's almost dark."

"Sorry. It took longer than I thought. I snagged us some bananas. Had to climb to get them." He shoved a small bunch of semi-ripe bananas into the room and then followed them in. "Damn, it's wet out there." He took off his button-down shirt and hung it on a hook next to hers. He pulled his T-shirt over his head and hung it on another hook. His gaze swept the room, lingering over her naked shoulders and legs. He nodded with approval when he saw she'd kept her socks and shoes on. "Comfortable?"

"Yeah. I wanted my stuff to dry before tomorrow." She nudged the foil packet with her knife. "Supper should be done. We're having what looks like catfish. You hungry?"

"Yeah." The tone of his voice and his glittering stare said it was for more than food, but his body language showed he was in full control.

Her pussy clenched and her nipples stood at his thorough examination. Damn, the man should come with a warning label.

He walked over and gracefully sat Indian-style next to her. His jean-covered thigh brushed her naked one. He leaned over and kissed her shoulder. "Anything happen I need to know about?"

She swallowed past the lump in her throat. How could a kiss on the shoulder have her ready to explode into orgasm? She shivered and wiggled her bottom to assuage the ache in her cleft. "No. No one passed by on the water. The whole Colombian army could've been in the jungle and I wouldn't have known it." He grinned. "The rain forest is really dense. How could you stand it?"

"It's not bad once you get away from the clearing where the sun can promote the lower vegetation to grow. The upper canopy blocks out the sun so much that the forest floor is mostly vines, air ferns, and detritus from the bigger trees."

She nodded. "Okay, that's what the swamps are like around

Camp Lejeune. They do controlled burns to clear out the forest floor so any forest fires won't spread as easily."

"Doesn't burn much here because of the moisture. Farmers sometimes clear-cut and burn, but it's frowned upon. Whoever cleared around this hut will be back after the rainy season is over, but we'll be long gone."

What he didn't say had her guessing whoever had built this place was cultivating coca crops nearby for the local drug cartel.

He took her knife and rolled the foil packet from the fire. "Let's eat, Callie. Then we'll take shifts sleeping and watching." Without warning, he leaned over and kissed her. She moaned and leaned into his lips. He broke off after thoroughly tasting her and just before the slow burn in her womb flared into a blazing bonfire. "Good, you kept my place." He opened the fish and unrolled the plantain leaves. He inhaled. "Damn that smells good." He picked a piece of the fish off. "Shit, that's hot." He blew on it, then touched it to his lips to test it for temperature. Satisfied the fish wouldn't burn her lips, he fed it to her.

"It's good." She licked his fingers clean and then her lips. When she reached for a piece, he pulled her hand to his lips and kissed her fingertips. "Ah, ah, ah. I feed you. You cooked." He fed her another piece. "Damn good fire. Your dad taught you well."

If she'd had buttons on, they would've burst. His praise made her feel ... well, special. Appreciated. His kisses and hand-feeding made her feel adored, cared for ... desired.

All of those feelings were new to her. Oh, her brothers cared for and appreciated her, but they were blood. Risto was ... was ... her lover, her protector, and someone she was coming to care about—and need—more and more with each second they spent together. He might plan to leave her once they got back to the States, but she'd make sure he didn't forget her. Once home, she'd place herself in front of him every chance she got. She'd enlist Keely's help. This man was hers and she wouldn't let him get away.

"Callie, open your mouth." He nudged a succulent morsel over her lips.

She took the offering from his fingers, managing to lick the tip of one of them before he pulled his hand away. His eyes burned at her touch, promising with just a look she'd pay for teasing him. She licked her lips. His low "save me Jesus" was music to her ears. He desired her as much as she did him—and maybe, just maybe, he was starting to need her, too.

The fish was soon gone. Risto alternately fed her a bite then took one for himself. It was one of the most romantic and sexy meals she'd ever eaten. That bit of news would shock all the men who'd taken her to five-star gourmet restaurants, hoping to get her into their beds. She choked back a laugh.

"What's funny?" She told him and his lips quirked with amusement. "So? Now that I've wined," he held up his canteen and she took a drink from it, "and dined you. It's time to bed you down, baby. Strip, I want to see all of you before I douse the fire."

"I thought you wanted to stay alert." Her words were cautious, but he was happy to see she quickly followed his orders and pulled her tank over her head. She wasn't afraid of his sexuality at all. Her breasts looked beautiful in the firelight. Her dusky peach nipples were puckered and ready for his lips.

"Just looking. I meant put out the real fire, not sexual fires." Risto groaned and reined in the need to take her to the mat, strip off the sexy underpants and fuck her sweet pussy until she came screaming around his cock. He'd had a hard-on since entering the hut and seeing her near nakedness. Finger-feeding her had made it even worse, especially when she'd teased his fingers with her nips and licks.

"Risto?" Her hand on his arm called him back to the here and now. Shit. He needed to stay alert. Making love to her, whether it was with his mouth or his fingers or his cock, was not conducive to hearing the enemy approach.

He took the hand she touched him with and raised it to his mouth. He nibbled on the knuckles before brushing his lips over them. "I want you ... more than any woman I've ever met. And I'll have you—and you me—before I take you home. I shouldn't have asked you to strip ... I just ... wanted."

She leaned over and kissed his chin. "Hey, I understand. When you make love to me, I lose all sense of who and where I am. Time has no meaning. It's not safe here. I can wait. All I need is…" She slipped her tank top back on.

He breathed a sigh of relief even as he groaned at the loss of the view. Her breasts were far too tempting. God, she was wonderful. Unspoiled with a feminine strength and a brand of courage unlike any woman he'd ever met. "What do you need, sweetheart? I'll do my damnedest to give it to you."

"I want one goodnight kiss and—"

"And what?" He caressed her neck.

"And I want you to hold me until I go to sleep—and promise me you'll wake me for my watch." She turned a stern gaze to his. "No molly-coddling. You're doing all the hard work with the boat. The least I can do is take a shift so you can sleep."

"Sounds like a deal." He pulled her into his body.

Unlike their other kisses, this one was meant to reassure and calm, not incite. He nibbled her lips until she opened for him, then sealed their lips together, sipping at her mouth, giving her his breath and taking hers in return. Her eyes were closed, her naturally dark lashes fluttering on her pale ivory skin. He held her face, his thumbs gently massaging her sun-tinged cheeks. Her hands came to his wrists and held on to him as if she were afraid he'd pull away too soon. Her tongue traced his lower lip then tangled with his. He groaned at the back of his throat and broke off the kiss, his lips a whisper away from hers.

"Careful." He kissed the tip of her nose. "Your hot little tongue makes me want to fuck you until you can't walk."

"Sorry." She licked her lips.

He snorted out a laugh. "Minx. Don't tease me when I can't do anything about it." He released her face and slid a finger down her nose, then moved to trace her lips. "Be aware. I'm keeping a tally of every teasing look, every tongue appearance, and each teething of those lips. I'll get you back for every infraction. Count on it."

She smiled. "I look forward to it." She yawned, and instead of looking like a sultry sex goddess, she looked like a kitten needing a nap.

He chuckled and pulled her into his arms, holding her against him, her face buried against his naked chest. He breathed in her scent, memorized the feel of her supple, toned body against his for when he no longer had her near. "Time for bed. How do you want me to hold you?"

She sat back on her heels and looked him over. "You're right-handed. So we need to keep your gun hand free." She scooted over on the mat and sat next to his left side. "Arm around my back so I can lean my head on your shoulder. Then after I fall asleep, you can shift me to the mat. Okay?"

"Your wish is my command." He raised his left arm and gathered her into his body. She snuggled and sighed, closing her eyes. He liked her in his arms. She fit him perfectly. And she must have felt safe, because her breathing slowed almost immediately. She fell asleep as fast as a Special Forces operative.

Callie's only problem was she slept so deeply. That could be a life-threatening issue if they were on the river too long. She needed to be battle-ready at a moment's notice. He stiffened with his concern. She woke with a start, her left hand going to her side and to the gun he hadn't notice her placing there.

"What's wrong?" She looked around.

He smiled. "I could barely wake you up at Conn's and here you fall asleep instantly and awaken just as quickly, what gives?"

She blinked and yawned. She reached over and pulled her Ruger closer to her side. Her non-dominant side. "Um, I was safe at Conn's. You said so. I sort've learned to program my brain to be aware when it needs to be. Mothering two pre-teen and then teenage boys, I had to be alert twenty-four seven. They often pushed my limits, the rules, and their curfews." She wrinkled her nose. "Everything okay?"

"Yeah." He kissed the top of her head and pulled her back into his body. "Go back to sleep, little soldier. I'll wake you in about four hours and you can take the shift to just before dawn." She nodded, snuggled into him and fell asleep on another cute little yawn. He noted her left hand lay lightly on her gun.

God, it will kill me to leave her in Chicago. No matter how adaptable she proved to be on this escape through Hell on Earth, it didn't change the fact he wasn't the right man for her. Being with him would constantly bring her into the danger zone. His life was rough and not one in which a woman and the inevitable family belonged. And, she was definitely a woman meant to have children. Just hearing the affection she had for the brothers she raised proved that. He wasn't father material. He knew nothing about families. He'd been raised by an irascible, unyielding paternal grandfather who'd kept him away from his more loving maternal grandparents who'd desperately wanted to raise him. Living in isolation on his grandfather's island, he was often left to his own devices, with only a few year-round residents' kids for friends. The Marines had parented him more and provided the socialization he needed to exist in society.

Callie deserved a man who could provide a safe and loving environment in which to raise a family. He wasn't that man, wouldn't know how to begin to be that man.

He brushed another kiss over her hair and smiled at her grumpy little murmur. He laid his head against the wall, pulled on the night vision goggles and examined the darkness outside their shelter. Nothing and no one would take him by surprise, not while he had Callie in his keeping.

Chapter Twelve

Rescue Day Three, somewhere along the Atrato River.

It would be another hot, rainy day. The only reason Callie knew it was near dawn was a slight lightening of the sky to the east and her watch. She let out another yawn and stretched her neck. She hadn't realized how boring and tiring sitting watch was. She glanced at Risto who'd stretched out next to her and fallen instantly asleep several hours earlier. His dark eyes were open and his stare fixed on her, the only part of him completely alert. The rest of his body was relaxed. The man had less than four hours of sleep and he'd awakened himself by the internal clock Callie knew all special forces operatives were trained to use.

"Hey, you're awake."

"Yeah." He sat up, a smooth movement, all controlled muscle, and stretched like a large cat. "Anything happening out there?"

"You'd have awakened if there had been."

He nodded. "But I still would like to know why you think nothing has happened. Consider it a test of sorts."

"Okay." She glanced through the netting which surrounded both of them; coated in an insect repellant, it had kept them from being eaten alive by mosquitoes. "It's still raining. Some periods were fairly heavy. It would be difficult in the dark, even with night vision goggles, to maneuver in the weather."

"That's the brain talking. Now, tell me what your senses tell you."

"The birds are making their usual greeting-the-day noises. I heard several night predators hunting. Three jaguars came from the forest to the water to drink. I heard the grunts of tapirs as they rooted nearby. And the howler monkeys just started to call to one another at the sun rising. If there were any humans out there, the animals would be silent and hiding." She turned to look at him. "That do it?"

He pulled her to him. "Yes, you get an A."

"What if I want something other than a letter grade?" She arched a brow and tentatively touched his bearded jaw with one finger, liking the scratchy roughness against her skin.

Risto smiled, a slow upward curve of his lips. He angled his head and took her mouth. He skipped any gentle exploration and demanded immediate entrance. She let him in and lost all sense of control from that second forward. His tongue swept through her mouth, touching every square millimeter, imprinting his taste, his claim upon her. She wanted to hold on to him, touch him, claim him back, but still held the sniper rifle, cradled in her arms between their bodies. All she could do was allow Risto to take what he wanted, give him the submission his will seemed to demand.

Breaking away, he held her upper arms, not allowing her to advance or retreat. His lips now touched hers gently, reverently. "That do it?" She nodded and licked her lips, tasting him. He groaned then sucked her lower lip between his. "I'm keeping count, baby. For every lip sucking and teething, I'll make you beg for release. We'll be in bed for quite a while at the rate your teasing infractions are mounting up."

"Doesn't seem fair. It's a habit and I can't control it." She rubbed her cheek against his beard-roughened one. "Plus, you tempt me—and I react. Do I get to make you beg also?"

Risto nipped her chin with his teeth. "Only if I let you—and I think I'd like how you'd make me beg."

She smiled. "Oh, I can guarantee it." She rested the rifle on her lap and freed one hand to massage his morning hard-on through his jeans. "I bet you taste good there, too."

He groaned and removed the rifle, placing it on the sleep mat on the other side of her, then pulled her fully against his body until her breasts rubbed his chest. "Please tell me you want me as much as I want you."

"I want you. And when we're safe, you can have me for as long as you want me." Forever would be nice, but she'd take what he offered and use the opportunity to convince him this attraction between them was more than a result of propinquity and danger.

Risto nodded and allowed her to move away. Retrieving a bottle from his pack, he handed it to her. "Coat your skin with this insecticide before we get out from under the netting. We'll eat some trail bars and some of the fruit, pack, then take a relief break and head out after I retrieve the perimeter alarms."

Callie poured the DEET-infused lotion into her hands and coated her arms, legs and neck. She hated the stuff, knew it was dangerous if over-used, but it was about the only thing effective against the man-hungry, malaria-carrying mosquitoes. She'd worn the stuff even in Cartagena since the mosquitoes in the urban areas in Colombia often carried dengue fever. So far, she'd been lucky, only a few bites and no fever.

"All done." She handed the bottle to Risto who shook his head.

"Let me get the backs of your arms and under your hair. You missed them." It was scary how closely he observed her. He turned her away from him and massaged the repellant into her skin. "You can do my back."

"Okay." She retrieved a trail bar from her tote and another for him. She ate hers while he coated the exposed areas of his body. When he was done hitting the areas he could reach, she handed him a bar. "Here, eat."

He took the food and turned away, presenting his broad back for the lotion. She loved smoothing the lotion over his muscled shoulders and back, taking special care to knead out any knots she found in his muscles. Even though the Atrato River was the swiftest moving river in the world, he'd still used the pole to keep them from being drawn into tributaries and to move them around obstacles. He had to be sore.

"God, that feels good. How about adding a massage to the blow job you promised me?"

She rubbed her cheek against his back. "Deal."

"Drink." He handed her the canteen and took the repellant from her and put it away. "You got any more of those salt tablets?"

"Yes, you want some?"

"Please. Once we use up all of yours, there are some in the med kit in my pack." He swallowed the tablets she gave him. "And, Callie, at the first sign of chills, body aches or even a slightly elevated temperature, let me know. I have Levaquin and you'll need to take it. I don't want to take any chances with you. Even the best repellants in the world still allow some mosquitoes to get through. We'll reapply the lotion frequently just to be safe."

"You let me know also. We can share the Levaquin." His lips turned downward. He was pissed. "I mean it. If you get sick, I'd have to take care of you. So, no macho-bullshit, Marine. Okay?"

"You this bossy with those brothers of yours?"

"Yeah, and they turned out just fine—so I can't hurt you any."

Risto stared for several seconds. All sorts of expressions swept over his face. She couldn't begin to imagine what he was thinking. Finally, he said, "I bet they're fine young men. They have a wonderful sister." He punctuated his statement with a light brushing of his lips over her forehead. "Now, put on your shirt and pants—and your hat."

She changed her socks before donning her clothes. She was happy to note that while not absolutely dry, the pants and shirt weren't all that damp either.

Risto grunted, drawing her attention. "Glad to see you had the forethought to pack extra socks. I know all the clothing is hot, but between the sun and the insects, you need to stay covered."

Callie watched avidly as he got dressed. His movements were swift and economical. Within a minute he'd changed his socks and put his boots back on, then pulled on a T-shirt and his long-sleeved tropical-weave cotton shirt. As he packed away his dirty clothing, he looked at her and smiled. "Ready to leave our abode?"

"Yes. Can we make the coast, today?"

"With the speed of the current and some luck at avoiding drug smugglers and guerilla patrols, it's doable, but I wouldn't count on it."

"Gotcha, potentially another night camping out." She buttoned her shirt all the way to the top button. "Um, about this potty break." She couldn't help it, she blushed. Risto had the decency not to laugh. He just shot her an inquiring, almost indulgent, look. "Where will we, um, do it ... and how do we avoid the insects? My dad had some horrible stories." She wrinkled her nose in disgust. "We kids thought he made them up until Keely read some books on surviving in jungles and they were confirmed."

Risto's humoring look turned serious. "Sweetheart, do you think I'd let your adorable bottom come anywhere near anything harmful?"

"I don't ... um, no."

"Good answer."

"But how can we avoid them? I read these fleas burrow into the skin while a person is um, well, you know."

"They're called tungas. Usually the fleas hang around a

pre-dug latrine. If we were staying here for a while, we'd just spray the latrine area regularly and that would take care of it. Just using a spot once won't be a problem. And we'll both use different areas just in case, okay?"

She nodded but she must not have convinced him, because he added, "I have never had an issue with a tunga infestation, and I've had bodily functions in jungles all over South America. You're in far more danger of having a mosquito bite that lovely butt than a jungle flea. Just make it quick and you'll be fine." He stood and picked up the heavy duffle and his pack. "We'll move farther from shore to higher ground where there are some drier areas. That's where I placed the alarms. You can help me pick them up once you've taken a bathroom break."

"Okay." Callie packed her stuff into her tote then helped Risto fold the netting and the mats and pack them away. "What about water?" She jiggled the canteen she carried in her tote. "I'm getting low and I suspect you are also." She wouldn't let him know how thirsty she'd been even with drinking regularly. She'd forced herself to sip all night, but the treated water was hard to get down and didn't seem to help with her thirst. She hoped they could stop in the town he'd mentioned last night—Ungaía—and get something good to drink.

"There's an underground stream flowing from a slight escarpment about two hundred yards into the forest. We'll fill our canteens there. With the addition of the iodine tablets, we'll have fresh water until we reach Ungaía where I think we should try to take a short break if the coast is clear."

Callie said a silent "yippee."

"If we had to, the Atrato is not a dirty river," Risto said. "It has a lot of volume and runs too swiftly. So, if needed, we could fill our canteens in the middle of the channel."

"I know that makes sense intellectually, but," she made a moue, "it makes me feel all squicky, thinking about drinking river water."

"I know, but trust me, we'll be fine. The iodine tablets take care of any bad stuff and these canteens also have filters in them. Conn got us the state of the art purification system."

"I'll have to thank him once I get back to the States." She turned to pick up her holster to put it on. She'd already strapped her knife sheath to her thigh.

Risto gripped her arm and turned her to face him. "The son of a bitch actually gave you his number?"

Other than when Cruz's goons had threatened her and the attack at Conn's, she'd never really seen Risto anything other than calm. He was definitely furious now. "Yes." He swore an ugly oath under his breath. She flinched and hurried to explain. "Um, he told me I could call him any time I needed help, that he and Berto would come. He said they owed me for taking care of the men who killed Berto's cousin."

"Callie, if you ever need help, you call me first … not them. Understand?"

His hands on her arms, he shook her lightly. The look on his face was a mixture of anger and pure male possession. His inner animal had claimed her. He didn't want any other man to take care of her. *Good.* She hid her satisfaction. She wanted him present, every day and every night, for the rest of her life, taking care of all her needs. Mr. Risto Smith might not want to acknowledge it, but he was all but hers. He just hadn't realized it yet.

"Callie? Do you understand? Call me … not Conn or Berto." He shook her again.

"Call you. Got it." She looked at his hands still clenching her arms then up at his flushed face. "But what if I can't find you? What if you aren't there?"

"Ren will know where I am."

"And if he doesn't?"

"Then you can call Conn—but only as a last resort. Ask Ren or Tweeter for help first if I'm unavailable. Understand?"

"Yes, I understand." *More than you want me to.* His demands went against his "not a permanent kind of guy" statement and his insistence that he'd leave her once he got her back to the States.

"Good. Now let's get this show on the road. Hand the packs down to me so I can put them in the dugout. Once the boat is loaded, we'll go ashore and take care of business before we shove off."

Risto shook his head. He'd all but beat his chest and marked Callie as his woman. She seemed to accept his pronouncements, but who knew what she really thought. She was a modern, independent, intelligent woman who was used to taking care of herself and those around her. She didn't need him, and she sure as hell didn't need the baggage which came with being with him. But something inside him had urged him to force her to acknowledge his right to care for her needs.

With their bodily needs taken care of without a single hitch, he left Callie packing up perimeter alarms while he obtained water. The area was heavily treed and he didn't want her getting hit by an errant branch or anything the monkeys in the trees decided to toss at intruders. Shoving aside a large fern, he located the small waterfall created by an underground stream. The water was as clear as any he'd ever seen in the mountains of North America, but he'd throw in the iodine tablets to be safe. Neither of them needed dysentery.

After filling the canteens, he set out, back to where Callie waited on him. Without any warning, something dropped onto his shoulders and immediately twined about his chest, crushing him in an unbreakable hold. *Fuck!* An anaconda. An adult by the size of it. He must've threatened it in some way— or it was hungry.

One arm was secured to his side by the rapidly coiling body. His other arm had instinctively moved to hold off the snake's head and the unhinging jaws which had opened to take a bite to hold him to be swallowed. He couldn't let go of the head to get to his knife and his other arm was useless.

"Callie! I need you." And didn't that go against every male instinct he possessed. He didn't want Callie anywhere near this monster reptile.

Callie's approach was swift. "Risto! What's wrong?" Her voice was tight with fear and he could hear her gasping for breath as she crashed through the low-growing foliage and volunteer saplings.

"Slow down, sweetheart. I don't want you falling." God knows what was lurking on the ground. The snake might have a mate or friends nearby. He spied her clothing in the dim green-gray light of the jungle. "To your left a bit. Get your knife out and approach slowly." He also didn't want the snake startled into deciding he wanted a smaller, easier prey. Anacondas moved fast.

"Oh … my … God." Callie stopped about four feet from him, a look of pure horror on her face. She stood for what must have been only seconds but seemed like an eternity. Her gray eyes darkened with too many emotions to categorize, but underlying them all was something almost feral.

"I need to cut the head off." She looked to him for affirmation.

"Yes." He gasped out the answer. His diaphragm was being constricted with each breath he took.

"Don't talk. Breathe shallowly." She shook her head. "God, I never thought all those pop quizzes Dad and Colonel Walsh gave us kids from the Marine Survival Manual would ever have a use."

Knife in hand, she approached him slowly and at an oblique angle. To the snake, she would seem non-threatening—he hoped. "Careful."

"Shut up. Every time you talk, the snake tightens. God, your poor ribs." She looked down, and he could tell, forced herself not to jump back and away from him. "Fuck that is one long-ass snake." She shuddered and turned pale green. Swallowing loudly, she took a deep breath and visibly shook off whatever she was feeling.

God, I love her courage. I fucking love her.

A determined look entered her eyes and she muttered under her breath, her undivided attention on the snake and not him. *Good girl.*

"Just like cutting through a piece of meat, Callie," she muttered as she inched closer. He didn't know how all that courage could be packed into one slender female, but he thanked God it was. "Just think of the stories you can tell your friends." She raised her hands and covered Risto's hand, holding the anaconda's head with one of hers, adding her strength to pull the head away from his face and steadying it for the cut. Her calm, determined gaze switched to Risto. "I'm going to cut through the body just below the snake's skull—away from your and my wrists. So hold tight, I will slice on three."

He nodded and mouthed the word "careful." The move she intended to make placed her upper body in danger of being cut. One slip … if she cut herself … no, he wouldn't think about it or he wouldn't be able to move when needed.

She took a deep breath. "One." She tightened her hand over his wrist and slipped the knife between his wrist and the snake's body. "Two." She placed the knife a mere inch away from the snake and stiffened the arm holding on to him. "Three." She struck swiftly and strongly, with so much control she managed to cut through the snake and avoided cutting herself.

As Risto tossed away the head of the anaconda and pulled off the snake's coils, the reptile's nervous system still synapsing, he kept his eyes on Callie. She had turned whiter than freshly bleached white bed linens. She held the knife, dripping with snake blood and tissue, away from her. Blood spatter covered her shirt and face. Small whimpers came from Callie's throat and her body began to shake. Violently. She dropped the knife and turned to the side to vomit.

Swearing a blue streak, he shoved away from the snake's body as quickly as he could then closed the few steps separating him from Callie. He surrounded her with his body, one arm supporting her and the other hand holding her hair away from her face as she lost what little was in her stomach. The sound of her dry heaves hit him in the gut and he swore even more.

"Shh, baby. My brave woman. You saved me. So brave. So brave." He held her with one arm and stroked her hair, her back. She cried now, great heaving sobs. "Hush, love, you're killing me."

She shoved at his arm and moved away from him. He released her reluctantly. Turning, she shuddered, once, twice then stiffened her spine. She touched his ribs then seemed to notice the blood on her arm. "God, get it off me." Pleading eyes turned to his. "Please, please, get it off me." She stroked a trembling finger over his torso. "Off you."

Shoving his way through the heavy foliage, he led her to the small waterfall. He pulled off his shirt and hers, hanging them in the flow of the small waterfall on a jagged piece of rock. Then he placed her hands under the water to clean them and used his to wipe her face clean of the blood. "Lean your head over, baby. I want to get the blood out of your hair." She let him move her where he wanted, and he rinsed her hair until no blood and snake flesh was visible. He stood her back up and carefully wrung the excess water out of the long strands. He clumsily wove a braid which he tied with a piece of vine he cut from a tree.

Watching him with dazed slate gray eyes, she stood completely still but for the constant tremors sweeping over every muscle in her body. "You, too." Her voice was a mere wisp, strained as if she were holding back screams. "I can't stand seeing the blood on you. Knowing the snake could've killed," she managed to choke back a sob threatening to escape her throat, "could've eaten you." She touched his arm with shaky, ice-cold fingers. "I wouldn't have survived if that had happened. I'd have died right here with you."

"No, you wouldn't." He sluiced off the snake remains, all the while talking to her in a calm tone in an attempt to keep her from freaking out. "You'd have called for help just as I ordered. You are not to die … ever."

"Everyone dies." Her eyes turned silver with a flash of heat. Good, he'd rather her be mad than scared shitless or in shock.

"Not you. Not now. Especially not here." Risto pulled her into his arms and brushed frenzied kisses over her face, her hair. "You were so brave, braver than any woman I've ever known."

She rubbed her cold nose against his wet throat. "I detest snakes."

He chuckled. "I know, baby, so do I. You sure taught him a lesson." She sniffed and held on to his waist as if she never wanted to let go. He massaged her back from her neck to her bottom, long soothing strokes. Her body trembled constantly, a combination of shock and the icy water used to clean her off. He needed to get her dry and off her feet before she crashed.

"Damn right." She nuzzled his throat, licked and teethed his pulse point. "Kiss me. Make me feel something other than bone-chilling fear. I could have lost you." The last words came out as a wail.

He took her lips in a searing kiss, warming them. Her fingers digging into his waist, Callie clung and sobbed into his mouth, meeting his tongue with hers. With every touch and kiss, with every act of courage and intelligence, this woman burrowed ever deeper into his body, his heart, his soul. *How will I find the strength to leave her?* It was a question for another time, another place. Right now, he had to calm his little soldier's fears and get her out of this fucking Hell on Earth and to a place of safety.

Slowing the kiss from the speed of light to lazy, soothing kisses and nibbles, he finally eased Callie away from him. "We need to get going. We'll be safer on the river."

She nodded, her forehead brushing his chest. "I know. I'm fine." Another full body shudder shook her.

"Like hell you're fine." He swept her into his arms and began the walk to the boat. He'd get her situated and come back for their gear.

"Risto? I can walk."

"No." He rubbed his cheek over hers. "Let me take care of you. Christ, Callie, I watched, couldn't do a damn thing as you conquered your horror to save my ass. This is twice you've saved me. I came to Colombia to save you and have only brought you more hell."

"No!" She jerked her head up, cupped his face with a fierce grip. "You saved me." She gasped, her breathing fast and erratic, as fear once again appeared in her beautiful eyes. "Cruz would've hurt me, beaten me down." His angry snarl had her caressing his face, soothing the beast in him who'd kill anyone daring to hurt her. "So, I have to face some fears, so what? Cruz drove both of us into Hell. You aren't the bad guy." She turned her face into his neck and her hand clutched his shoulder as if he were a lifeline to sanity.

In silence, he carried her back to the boat. He gently placed her in the middle, using the duffle and a pack to support her in a reclining position. He pulled out another one of his long-sleeved shirts and helped her into it. He placed her hat on her head. Through it all, she hadn't said a word, uttered a sound.

He tipped up her chin so he could see her eyes. Her pupils were so dilated, only a thin silver-gray rim was left. Despite the sauna-like heat, her skin was cool to the touch and clammy. She shivered with each rasping breath. He swore and pulled out a thin solar blanket, blessing Conn for being an efficient son of a bitch, and wrapped it around her. She hummed her pleasure at the added warmth as she snuggled into the nest he'd made her. Since it was a fucking ninety degrees even under the cloud cover, she had to be cold from the inside out to tolerate the extra layers.

"Sweetheart? Look at me." She lifted her head, her eyes finding his. At least she was responsive. "Once we get started, if you need to stop. If you need anything, you let me know. I don't want you ... suffering alone. These arms are always here to hold you."

Her lips twisted into a slight smile. He breathed a sigh of relief. If she could attempt to smile, she'd be fine. She just needed time—and TLC, which he'd provide if he had to take on every fucking guerilla in the Darien. They'd definitely be stopping at Ungaía so he could see she got proper food and could clean up properly. A chance at some small amount of normalcy after all the abnormal curveballs thrown at her.

"Don't worry so. I'll be fine. No s-s-s-stupid snake is going to get me down." She clenched her jaw against the chattering of her teeth and patted his face. "Now, go get our stuff." She reached for his Glock, her Ruger still back at the waterfall, and took it from his holster with a steady hand. He wondered what that must have cost her in control. "I'll guard the boat."

"You are fucking amazing." He kissed the top of her head and left the boat to get the rest of their gear. When he looked back, Callie held his gun on her lap, her gaze quartering her surroundings. He shook his head and muttered, "fucking amazing."

Chapter Thirteen

Rescue Day Three—Ungaía, Columbia.

Callie sat in the dugout while Risto and a helpful young man pulled the boat onto the ground. With all the rain, the shore was a quagmire. She wasn't sure if she was to get out or just wait in the boat. "Risto?" She struggled out of the nest Risto had made her.

"Stay put, sweetheart. I'll carry you." He turned to the young man, a dark-skinned native whose skin tones had to do more with the African slaves the Spanish brought to this area of the New World many centuries ago than the native Indian tribes here when Bolivar and his ilk mapped South America. The Ungaía citizen smiled and took the money Risto slipped him. "Teo will watch our boat and things until we get back. He says the guerillas have been quiet lately. It's also market day so you will see Ungaía at its best." He lifted her from the boat, tote bag and all, and carried her to an area where the rain had not managed to wash away the rocky pathway.

"What about the duffle?" She looked toward the boat and saw that Teo had already found a comfortable spot to stand guard. A machete was in his hand and his gaze examined everyone walking by as if they were thieves and thugs.

"I know Teo, Callie." Risto placed a hand under her elbow

and supported her up the incline, then guided her toward the central part of the small town. "SSI uses him each time we come to the Darien. He is on a retainer of sorts. Our stuff will be safe with him."

Callie concentrated on placing one foot in front of the other. The footing was tricky and she was a bit dizzy from hunger, thirst and heat. She was glad to have Risto's support. Once they reached a more level surface, she felt steady enough to take an interest in her surroundings. Most of the buildings were one- and two-level wooden structures. As they walked away from the river landing, she spied a church tower then the church itself on the far side of a small tree-shaded plaza. The church was a typical Spanish missionary-style with two bells in the stuccoed, arched bell tower. The plaza was a pleasant surprise. Besides trees, someone had taken the time and effort to plant flowering bushes. The reds and fuchsias of the blooms made the plaza appear very festive.

"Pretty plaza. But why did we stop? I could've made it to the coast." *What a fib, Calista Jean.*

He massaged the small of her back. "I could see you fighting shudders ever since we set out this morning. I wanted to give you some semblance of normalcy before the last mad dash to the sea—and before another night in the rough."

"Mad dash?" She chanced a glance and saw Risto wasn't making a joke. "What's the problem with the last part of the trip you haven't told me about?"

"Nothing you didn't already know." He angled her to a small seating area for a walk-up restaurant. "Between here and the sea is the most-travelled part of the river. That means drug smugglers, Colombian military, guerillas and all sorts of other bad asses. Teo is getting us a motor for the *piragua*. A motor will give us a fighting chance if we encounter trouble."

Callie sat in the seat he held for her. She looked around at the people crowding the plaza. It looked like every other small farming town she'd ever visited in her travels around the world. Some had been more primitive than others, but all in all the feel and the sounds were similar: people laughing, talking, bartering and just living. The scene of common people doing everyday things eased the tension in her shoulders. Risto, the man who thought he was too rough for her, had sensed what she needed and produced it. For that alone, she loved him.

Risto leaned over and kissed her lightly on the lips. "What do you want to eat? The food is good. The owners are relatives of Teo so I can vouch for the cleanliness of the food and drink."

She was parched and her sickness earlier in the day had added to her dehydration. Her body needed more fluids than she'd been giving it. The iodine-laced water had left a bad taste in her mouth. Her stomach gurgled, telling her the trail bar she'd eaten after the anaconda incident had long since been burned up. "Fruit juice of some sort. Bottled water if they have it. Any sort of empanada or tamale is fine."

"They have ice, so I can guarantee you'll love the *champús*."

"*Champús*?" She scrunched her nose. "Never had that, what is it?"

"It has a corn syrup base with lemon and other fruits. Very sweet but refreshing, sort of like lemonade with a twist."

She smiled. "Sounds good." She stretched and looked around. "Think I can take my hat off? I'm so hot." She couldn't remove her shirt since she had her gun holstered under it. The knife sheath on her leg wasn't as much of a problem since it seemed as if everyone sported some sort of knife.

"Leave it on." Risto scanned the plaza then angled his head toward a brightly colored, two-story building caddy-cornered from the church. "On the roof of the hotel."

Moving slowly, she idly perused Ungaía's central plaza. She spotted two armed men on the roof of the hotel and then three others strolling the area with their guns cradled in their arms. All of the men were scrutinizing the crowds.

"Who are they? Do we need to get the food to go?" Fear tightened her throat so much she had to force the words out.

"They aren't looking for us." Risto hunkered down next to her seat and put a comforting arm around her waist. "Teo said the FARC unit in the area is looking for Colombian military operatives chasing *narcotraficantes*. Just business as usual in Ungaía. We'll be fine for the short period we're here, but if anyone does start shooting just get under cover and let me handle it."

"Okay." She stroked his beard-rough cheek. "Go. I'll be fine. The sooner we eat, the sooner we leave." He looked into her eyes and must have seen what he needed to see because he nodded and stood. She watched him stride to the counter and sighed. The man looked good coming and going. Obviously she'd recovered from her battle with the anaconda, because her pussy dampened at the memory of the power of those lean hips.

A feminine voice speaking in Spanish commented on Risto's manly attributes. Callie turned and caught the woman eyeing Risto's tight buns also. Callie smiled. "*Sí, mi marido es todo hombre.*" She kept the fiction going that Risto was her husband, her *marido*, so the locals wouldn't think of them as a single woman and single man travelling together, just in case someone asked questions later.

The woman, who could've been anywhere from thirty to fifty years of age, it was hard to tell since her skin was wrinkled from too much exposure to the sun, smiled and nodded. "*Todo hombre.*"

Risto strolled up to their table and smiled at the other woman as he handed Callie her drink. "What's up?" He whispered the words next to her ear under the pretense of kissing her neck.

"She likes your ass." Callie patted the body part and smoothed her hand over it. "So do I."

"What did I warn you about teasing me?" She inhaled sharply and swiped her lips with her tongue. Risto's eyes heated. He nipped her earlobe. "You're playing with fire, sweetheart. I know the owner of the hotel and he rents rooms by the hour."

"Sounds good to me." She smiled at the flare in his nostrils. His cheek bones flushed red over his tan. She fluttered her eyelashes and trailed a single finger down his arm. "What are we eating?"

It took Risto a second or two to answer. He seemed to be distracted by her lips. She laughed silently.

"Um, some meat pies with a mix of beef, corn, peppers and potatoes in them. I've had them before and they're more than a meal. Then Teo's aunt makes delicious fruit pasties. Today's are banana and papaya. Sound good?"

"My mouth is watering. You marines sure know how to treat a girl right."

"Oh, baby, you are tempting me again."

She grinned and took a sip of the cold lemony drink then sighed. "That is just to die for. I wonder if I could make this at home."

"I'll get the recipe from the owner. She'll be flattered." He leaned over and kissed her. "Don't look, but the guerillas on the hotel roof are watching us. If anyone asks, we're married and eco-tourists. They're used to that here."

She kissed him back. "I already confirmed to the lady next to us that you're my manly husband."

He barked out a laugh and buried his nose against her neck. The whisper of his breath across the sensitive area had her nipples perking and her vaginal muscles clenching. She wondered if he'd been serious about renting them a room at the hourly rate. The more involved they became sexually, the harder it would be for Risto to walk away.

The woman working the counter called out their order and Risto rose to get it. Callie noted the soldiers watching him, then they shrugged and began to scan the midday crowds once more. She let out a sigh of relief.

Risto scanned the crowds as he and Callie ate their food. The guerilla soldiers were only mildly interested in the two of them. So far, his idea to stop and give Callie some rest from the debilitating tension and fear of the last couple of days was a good one. She looked more relaxed already. Her skin was still too pale under her tan and she hadn't been drinking enough. They'd stay here long enough so she could replenish the majority of her body fluids. With the potential of another night camping in the rainforest, she'd need to be as equilibrated as possible.

Teo's assurances that no one had been asking after a tall, blonde *norteamericana* woman had taken a lot of the pressure off. Cruz was most likely looking in all the wrong places. He smiled as he imagined the man and his minions scurrying to chase them down in the main cities and toward the Ecuadoran border, the safest crossing out of the country other than by plane. By the time Cruz figured out he'd taken Callie out by the more dangerous route, she'd be in Chicago and he'd be on his next assignment for SSI.

Risto laughed silently. Cruz would be beside himself losing Callie—the embarrassment alone should turn his attention to easier female prey.

"I'm done." Callie pulled a wet wipe from her seemingly bottomless tote. "You said I could get a shower some place?"

"Yeah, the hotel has public showers. Just like the rooms, they rent by the hour." He stood up and collected their trash.

"That sounds wonderful. I still feel that snake all over me." Callie followed him to the trash receptacles.

Risto noted that while she stayed close enough to touch him, she stayed away from his gun arm and was highly alert. He smiled. She was sharp and had good instincts. Like Ren's wife Keely, Callie could more than handle herself when needed. So what if she couldn't street fight as Keely did, she hadn't hesitated to shoot to kill the mercs at Conn's house, and her response to the anaconda despite her intense aversion was more than many soldiers could've done. He'd seen hardened warriors turn pale and puke at the thought of touching a snake that large.

"Let's go, sweetheart." He took hold of her arm and kept her close. He led her through the crowds in a slow, but steady pace so as not to call any more attention to them than was necessary. He nodded to a local man he knew from a previous trip, a farmer he'd helped escape from a drug smuggler who wanted to use the man's small holding for drug storage. The man nodded in return.

He guided her through the dark, open doorway of the hotel. The place was clean, but basic. He wouldn't trust the cleanliness of the beds for Callie and had been teasing about renting one for an hour. He'd seen the flash of arousal in Callie's eyes and his cock had hardened at the idea of some afternoon delight. If they were in one of the larger cities with a more modern hotel, he'd be tempted to stay the night to give them both a break and Callie more rest. But they weren't, so Callie would just have to settle for a nice shower. The shower facilities, he knew, were cleaned regularly and worth the few pesos to give her some privacy and the chance to get the rest of the snake blood off her and change into some cleaner clothing. He knew it bothered her that she hadn't been able to clean her body as well as she would've liked. Hell, it bothered him.

"*Hola!*" The clerk smiled at them. "Welcome back! Do you need a room this trip, Señor Smith?"

"No, we just need to use the *baños*." He handed over the correct amount of money plus some extra.

The clerk handed over two keys and gestured toward the doors. "Please. They are unoccupied. If you require anything, please ask."

Callie touched his arm. "What does he mean by that?"

"They have some shampoo and the like. You need anything like that?" It was then he noted the intense interest of the majority of the men in the adjacent bar area. They weren't looking at him. He stiffened. Callie might not be safe with just a cheap lock on the door. "I've decided I'll share your shower, baby." He leaned in and whispered against her ear. "I don't like the way some of the men in the bar are looking at you."

Callie inhaled sharply and nodded. "I have my own bottle of shampoo and shower gel. I'll share."

Risto handed the clerk one of the keys. "We've decided to share. Keep the extra money."

The clerk smiled, his avid gaze travelling Callie's long legs and picking out the blonde hair escaping her hat. "Is probably a good idea, Señor Smith. Your woman is a temptation, *sí?*"

Risto nodded then turned to guide Callie to the shower room for which they had the key. He glowered at the men whose stares followed them.

"You're growling." She laughed, the first time he'd heard her laugh since the anaconda incident. It made him happy—and even hornier. "Men are the same everywhere. They're just looking." She kissed him on the jaw.

"Well, they can just stop. Colombia is playing Brazil in soccer on the television. They can watch that, not you."

She laughed and patted him on the butt. "Maybe they play for the other team?"

Risto snorted. "In the wilds of Colombia? Odds of that happening are slim to none. They are definitely hetero and they definitely are looking at your butt." He placed a hand on her bottom as he unlocked the door. "And this butt is mine."

She turned to eye him as she entered the room. She licked her lips then sucked provocatively on the lower one. "Definitely yours."

Risto urged her inside then shut and locked the door. Before she could say a word, he picked her up. She dropped her tote and grabbed onto his shoulders for balance.

"Put your legs around my waist." She must not have moved

fast enough for him because he pulled one leg up then the other. "Keep them there." He moved so her back was supported by the rough wood door. She swore she could feel each seam of the poorly constructed door along her spine.

"Risto?" She stroked the back of his neck, finding the muscles tense. "What's wrong?"

"That was one lip licking and teething too many, Callie. I need you ... now." He took her mouth with a deep thrust of his tongue before she could answer. His hips shoved against her in the same rhythm. His hard-on rubbed the juncture of her thighs in almost the right spot.

She groaned, excited by his need for her. She twined one of her arms around his neck, holding him close. Her other hand snaked between their bodies and fumbled with the opening to his jeans. Unable to open them one-handed, she rubbed her hand up and down his length from the outside. Risto broke off the kiss and groaned. "Callie, no. Honey, you've been sick ... we can't ... just needed to kiss you."

Her answer was to nip his chin. "Put me down."

"God, baby, I'm so sorry." He gently set her down.

"Don't be. I'm not." She dropped to her knees, her back sliding down the rough wood door with its peeling paint. Thank God she had on Risto's shirt. She undid the snap to his jeans and had him unzipped and her hand and mouth on his erect cock before he could stop her. She hummed in the back of her throat as she fisted him with one hand and licked his length. She licked him like an all-day sucker, relishing the feel of him against her tongue. Her other hand fondled his balls, getting the feel for their size and weight.

His hand gripping her hair, he attempted to pull her away from her prize. "Callie..."

She glared at him. "Mine. You promised." She took his cock into her mouth and licked and sucked, using her hand to hold him steady.

"Fuck, just fuck." A low guttural sound rumbled from his

chest. His hands tugged her from his cock. "I need to be in you."

Before she could protest, he pulled her up and unfastened her jeans then pulled them off. His fingers found her wet. "Thank you, Jesus, you're ready for me." He licked the moisture from his fingers then lifted her once again as if she weighed nothing. One arm around her back and another under her hips, he ordered, "Put your legs around my waist."

As soon as she did, he walked forward until she was braced once more against the door. "Put me in, Callie."

She circled his cock with one hand as she held on to him with the other. As soon as she had the purpled wet head at her slit, he shoved into her with one hard lunge of his hips.

Callie let out a soundless scream, her head thumping against the door as she received each movement of his hips. "God, that feels so good."

"Can't go slow ... sorry."

"Not asking you to, Marine ... fuck me ... take me." She moved her hands to hold on to his steely biceps.

At her words, Risto began to thrust hard and fast. All she felt was the drag and pull of his cock inside her aching channel. Her back shoved solidly against the rough door, she could not move away from his hips, even if she wanted to. All she could do was hold on, breathe and feel.

It didn't take long for the simmering arousal she'd felt ever since the last time he'd made love to her to explode. She screamed "Risto" and then came and came and came.

Her orgasm seemed to be the signal giving him permission to come, because as she rode his hips, he threw back his head and grunted, his hands gripping her hips even more tightly, holding her to receive his seed. Even after his cum had flooded her and his hips slowed, he held her to him, riding her through the small after-spasms of her climax.

When the last of her tremors subsided, she sighed and rested her forehead on his shoulder and her arms shifted to twine around his neck.

"Let go, sweetheart." He nuzzled the top of her sweaty hair. "We both really need that shower now."

"I can't."

"Did I hurt you?" He unwound her arms and helped her to stand, his arms going around her waist to hold her against him. "God, please tell me I didn't hurt you."

"No." She looked up, tears in her eyes. "I loved it." She peeked up at him from under her lashes. "I was loud." She blushed.

He chuckled. "Yeah, so was I. Don't worry about it." He nuzzled the top of her head. "My *machismo* quotient probably just increased by a thousand percent with the locals."

"I'm so glad I could help." She winced as she looked up. Damn door bruised her back and shoulders. Bet she had splinters, too. Of course, she hadn't felt a thing while he'd given her the best orgasm yet in their short relationship. She'd never known she would like it rough and ready.

He frowned. "Are you sure I didn't hurt you?" He kissed away an escaping tear.

"Just a little stiff. You get the door next time."

"Fuck." He started to pull her shirt off when she stopped him with a hand to his forearm.

"I'm okay. Let's take that shower before I fall asleep standing up." She yawned. "I'm tired all of a sudden. I get weepy when I'm tired." She braced her forehead against his chest. "I'm still thirsty. Can we get something else to drink?"

He stroked her hair. "After our shower. Come on, let's get you the rest of the way naked and clean."

He unbuttoned her shirt. This time she didn't attempt to stop him. She wasn't sure she had the dexterity right that moment to deal with the buttons. Plus, she sensed he needed to care for her.

"You can nap in the boat, baby."

"Okay." She kissed his chin then stepped away to shrug off

the shirt. She pulled her tank top over her head.

His worried gaze never left her as he undressed. "You got any clean clothes in that tote bag?" Risto asked as he hung his clothing on a hook by the door.

"A tank and some socks." She looked her jeans over before she passed them to him so he could hang them with his. "I can live with these. This shirt is clean enough. Mostly I want to wash off all the sweat and then get the snake blood out of my hair." She pulled some bottles out of her bag and a large-toothed comb.

Risto started the shower then held out his hand. "Come here, let me bathe you."

"Yes, please." She took his hand and stepped into the cracked but clean-looking tub/shower combination.

RISTO EXITED THE SHOWER ROOM, leaving Callie to get her hair de-tangled. He took the key with him since she could unlock the door from the inside. He left the key with the desk clerk and headed for the bar. He took a seat at the end of the bar, farthest from the front entrance and with a good view of the door where Callie was. He spied several of the men in the bar watching the door and swore under his breath. There was far too much interest in Callie. Her unusual height and blonde hair would've attracted even a dead man's attention in this backwater town.

He turned to Dario, the bartender and Teo's older brother and also owner of the hotel and in a loud, carrying tone, he ordered. "A beer—and a Pepsi-Cola for my wife, *por favor, Dario.*"

A small smile twisted his lips when the men watching for Callie's reappearance noted his height, his muscle, and the bulge under his arm. Their attention shifted back to the soccer match, although he knew they listened for Callie. These were farmers for the most part; they wouldn't challenge him over his wife. The guerillas he didn't trust farther than he could throw them.

Dario placed the drinks on the bar and took the money Risto had placed there. "Your woman is beautiful. You should not have brought her here, Señor Smith."

"Yeah, Dario, I agree. But it couldn't be helped." The man nodded and headed for the other end of the bar to take care of another order.

The minute Callie walked out, the tension in the place upped three levels. Every man in the place watched her long-legged, graceful walk across the width of the room. She'd left her shirt open over the tank top which hugged her full, firm braless breasts and nipples like a second skin. Her eyes were only on him, but the heightened color on her cheek bones told him she was aware of the ogling men. He snorted and shook his head. Shit, she was used to men staring, but he didn't have to like it.

He stood and reached for her. She walked into his arms, swayed slightly until he steadied her against him, then allowed him to button her shirt, covering some of the tempting sight. The men's moans of disappointment could be heard over the annoying announcer of the television soccer match. She leaned into him and let him lift her by the waist and place her on the stool next to his. Nuzzling her neck, he whispered, "You're more of a draw than the soccer match. We should charge."

"They know what we did in there and I'm not talking about the shower. We were loud." She laughed, her pale eyes twinkling like silver stars. "I think they're trying to picture the act." She was probably correct. He swept the bar with an ugly glare.

Callie snickered. "They're only looking, Marine. Leave them alone. What did you order me to drink?" She reached for the glass in front of her, her hand trembling slightly, and took a sip. "Yum, my favorite. Can we get one to-go?" She drained the glass and carefully, almost too carefully, placed it on the counter.

He narrowed his eyes and examined her face. Under the color the orgasm had put in her cheeks, he spotted fatigue. He could kick himself for taxing her strength, but when she'd dropped to her knees and taken his cock in her mouth … no, he wouldn't think about it. He mentally ordered his cock to stand down. She didn't have enough reserves to go round with him again. He was a sick randy asshole.

Never looking away from her face, he called out as he took his seat. "Dario, another Pepsi and one to go for my woman."

"Sí, señor."

Callie, a hand on his thigh, sighed. "Thanks for this stop—and the um, penalty for all my teasing. I needed it. I'm sorry you had to stop whe—"

"No apologies." He removed her all-too-distracting hand from his leg and kissed the tips of her fingers before placing it on her own lap. His little brain was disappointed, but it would survive. "You've done a damn good job. If your dad was still around, I'd tell him what a brave daughter he raised."

"Really?" She eyed him. After several seconds, she let out a breath. "Well, damn, you mean it. Wait until I tell my brothers, they won't believe it."

"Send them to me. I'll make sure they do." He tossed back the beer and set the bottle on the bar. "Now, finish the second Pepsi and we'll go."

She nodded and drank the second soft drink almost as quickly as she had the first. While not the best hydration, it was better than nothing and had the side benefits of sugar, caffeine and sodium. She then reached for the to-go cup Dario had slid onto the counter. "I'm ready to leave." She slipped off the stool.

Risto held her when she wobbled slightly. He pulled her in between his legs and rubbed a hand over her ass in soothing motions, a territorial claiming to the men still watching Callie. Her eyes drifted shut on a sigh. "Christ, baby, you're ready to fall asleep standing up. Let's get back to the boat so you can take a little nap."

"'Kay." She leaned her head on his shoulder. "Sorry, not sure why I'm tired all of a sudden."

"Want me to carry you?"

"No. I can make it. I feel the caffeine and sugar flooding my system already." Callie made a move to step away.

Risto placed his hand on her waist and halted her. He glared at one man whose eyes were on Callie's firm and nicely rounded ass. *Bastard. She's mine!* The man turned his eyes to his beer. The tension in Risto's shoulders dissipated somewhat, but he needed to get Callie out of here before one of these men grew some steel balls. Plus, she was ready to drop no matter what she said. But they couldn't rest here any longer, his spider senses were freaking out. They'd be safer on the river.

"Risto, what's wrong?" She kissed the chin he'd shaved for her.

"Nothing." He placed his arm farther around her waist, to claim and to provide support. He guided her to the door leading to the plaza. "Cross your fingers, baby, for our continued good luck."

"I haven't uncrossed them since we left Conn's."

Risto laughed and led Callie out of the bar into the sunlight and Hell.

Chapter Fourteen

Callie blinked against the brightness of the sun after the dark interior of the hotel lobby. As she gingerly stepped onto the uneven packed stone and dirt of the square, the sound of automatic gunfire sounded from above. She momentarily froze and watched as dirt and branches went flying as the crowded plaza was inundated with bullets and panic. People shouted and screamed and dove for cover. Some men began shooting back at the men on the hotel roof, the men who had started the carnage.

Risto yelled and grabbed at her arm. Callie's focus tunneled and all her senses fixed on the woman who'd smiled and exchanged conversation with her earlier. The older woman was on the ground, her body in a fetal position, surrounded by an ever increasing puddle of blood.

"No!" Tossing her to-go soda to the ground, she broke away from Risto's grasping hands with a strength she hadn't known she had. Then she stumbled the eight or nine feet separating her from the injured woman. She fell to her knees and touched the woman's back. "*Señora?* You need to get up."

The only response to her urgent words was a pained moan.

Bullets hit near them, rock and dirt spraying them both. "Shit, shit, shit." Her fight or flight response finally kicked in with a vengeance, fueled by adrenaline, sugar and caffeine.

Slinging her tote over her shoulder, she got to her feet and found the strength to drag the woman toward the relative safety of the hotel. Something sharp and hot hit her high on the back near her shoulder, close to where her tote's handles lay. She ignored the stinging pain. Her arm still worked so she continued to tug the woman inch by inch as chaos surrounded them.

It seemed as if she'd been in the battle zone forever, but it could only have been mere seconds when she heard Risto yell, "Goddammit, Callie. Fucking get your ass in the hotel." He tore her away from the woman and flung her toward the hotel. As she half-ran, half-tripped into the hotel, she sensed him on her heels, carrying the woman and shouting words which she couldn't process above the sounds of gunfire and the frantic pounding of her heart.

"Come, come." Dario met them at the door and pushed her ahead of him, toward the back of the bar area into the kitchen. She prayed the kitchen with its metal equipment would give them some safety from flying bullets. "Put the injured woman on the prep table," Dario instructed Risto. "Teo called. The ELN guerillas landed. The FARC guerillas are shooting at them. My brother has moved your boat to our mother's house. You know this house, yes?"

"Yeah." Risto placed the seriously injured woman where Dario indicated then turned to locate Callie. "You okay?"

She nodded, breathing heavily. "I think so." She glanced at the counter. "The woman needs a doctor."

"The desk clerk is EMT-trained," Dario told them. "He'll see to her." The bar owner walked to the rear of the hotel kitchen and looked outside. "It is still clear back here. You need to go. This isn't your fight. You would be a prize for either side to ransom or…"

"Over my dead body." Risto's furious gaze pinned her down. "Fuck, Callie, what did you think you were doing?"

She waved a hand toward the woman. A short, sharp pain bit her shoulder where her tote bag straps rubbed; she probably got hit by shrapnel from all the flying bullets. She'd have Risto look at it later when he had calmed down some. "I was being human and helping another. I know it was crazy, but…" she eyed the moaning woman as the hotel desk clerk competently took over from Risto, "…she was nice to me and she didn't deserve to lie there and bleed to death. Plus, I knew you'd have my back."

"Next time let me save the innocents, okay?" Risto grabbed her by the arms and shook her. "You could've been killed." She winced and let out a groan. "Callie?" His slitted gaze swept over her front, then he turned her and swore as only a marine could. "You're fucking shot!"

Risto tore off the long-sleeved shirt, forcing her to drop her tote. The straps abraded the wound as the bag fell. *Holy shit that hurt. Do not faint, Calista Jean. It's just a scratch.*

She angled her head to look over her shoulder and saw a bloody gouge across the upper part of her shoulder. "I'm fine." She bent over to reach for her bag, but Risto's iron grip on her arms held her still. "Risto," she smoothed a hand over his tense jaw, "my injury can wait until we get to the boat." She broke away from his hands, picked up her bag, and started toward Dario. The wound hurt like a throbbing sore tooth, but it was bearable—just. She dug deep into reserves she never knew she had and headed for the back way out of the bar.

Risto pulled her back to him, this time avoiding her wound. "Don't ever fucking pull away from me, woman. Now, drop the fucking bag, hold the fuck still and let me look at it. You're bleeding like a stuck pig."

He was exaggerating since she knew the wound only bled sluggishly. But with all the f-bombs flying, she decided she'd better do as he said. The usually calm and controlled soldier was well on his way to freaking out. Pissing off an irate marine never produced good results. She wouldn't be surprised to see steam pouring off his body.

Risto held her uninjured arm and angled her so he could see the back of her shoulder. Despite his anger, he was exceedingly gentle as he pulled away the fabric of her tank top and probed what she knew was only a deep graze. If a bullet or shrapnel were in her, she'd have more pain and wouldn't have been able to drag the woman as she had.

As Risto swore and fussed, Callie checked the injured woman's status and found pain-filled golden-brown eyes fixed on her. The woman's lips formed the word "*gracias.*" She nodded and whispered, "*de nada.*"

Risto's sigh of relief was hot on her bared shoulder. "Only a graze. It needs to be cleaned and treated because even scratches can fester in the tropics, but otherwise it looks minor. It will scar, though." His thumb massaged the arm he held.

She threw him an incredulous look over her shoulder. The room swirled around her but instantly settled. She mentally swore not to move so quickly again. "You think I care about that? A life is far more important than a scar. I'd do it again. I was closer. She could've died before you got me to safety and then went back for her."

Risto's gaze still held fire, but the kiss he placed on her good shoulder was gentle and even if he wouldn't admit it, loving. "I know. But you gave me quite a scare." He shook her. "Don't fucking do it again." He released her. He cleaned the wound with something the hotel clerk handed him. She bit her lip so she wouldn't cry out at the sting of the antiseptic. Risto applied some pressure and taped something over the wound. "This gauze pad will help control the bleeding until we can get to Teo's mother's house. My first aid kit is in the duffle in the dugout."

Dario waved at them. "Come. It is as safe as it will get. You must leave now. Some local men are here to help you get to your boat safely."

"But why? Shouldn't they be taking cover?" asked Callie.

"The woman you saved is the Mayor's wife. The people of Ungaía are in your debt. They will protect you as much as they are able. Go now. Quickly. And safe journey to you both."

Callie allowed Risto to lead her from the hotel kitchen. The sound of gunfire, which had been muted by the thick adobe walls and the metal kitchen equipment, was now louder. It sounded as if World War III had begun in this small backwater of South America. Twenty locals formed a perimeter around them as soon as they exited the building. All of them armed to the teeth with older model submachine guns and hunting rifles and lots and lots of knives and machetes. Risto sheltered her with his body as he hustled her along the rutted ground.

"My tote!" It had all her identification and supplies they might need, including the submachine gun Risto had given her in Cartagena and her Ruger and holster.

"Fuck the tote." He kept her moving along.

"But my passport, the guns…"

"Here is your bag." A young man had caught up to them. He handed it to her and smiled shyly. "You saved my mother. Thank you, Risto's woman."

Callie smiled as she accepted the bag which Risto immediately took from her with a muttered oath about clueless women. "I hope your mother will be okay."

"With God's grace." The young man stayed by her side, his hand on his weapon, his too-old eyes scanning for guerillas.

She chanced a glance at Risto who also scanned for imminent danger, his Glock in his free hand. He must've sensed her gaze, because he looked down, a look of concern in his dark eyes. "You hurtin', sweetheart? Want me to carry you?"

"No, I'm fine." Of course, at the moment of her denial she stumbled on the uneven ground and jarred her injury. She gasped as blinding pain shot through her. The wound hurt worse now than it had when it occurred. Risto and the teenage boy both reached for her before she fell to her knees.

"Fuck!" Risto swung her up into his arms and began to run. He yelled at their escort. "Cover us."

For several minutes, all she could do was hold on with her good arm and bite her lip against the moans and whimpers threatening to erupt from her throat. Damn, she'd managed the incessant pain just fine until he'd picked her up and began his marathon run. Instead of an occasional throb, now the pain came in unceasing waves. "I … was…" she gasped, "… doing fine."

"Like hell." His words came out on a snarl. "You're in pain and I won't have it."

She decided nothing she could say would convince him otherwise, so she just laid her head on his shoulder and held on the best she could, hoping they'd stop soon before she threw up.

Finally, she spied a woman waving at them in a hurry-up motion in front of a small, pink shack built out over the river. Their boat, now equipped with what looked like a new and powerful motor, was tied to the dock attached to the small river house.

Risto carried her into the small house and laid her on her good side on an over-stuffed sofa covered in a brightly colored, flower-print fabric. He ripped her tank top off and tossed it to the floor.

Callie squeaked. "No, I'll get the couch all bloody." She sat up, covering her naked breasts with her crossed arms, and refused to lie on what had to be the woman's pride and joy of the scantily furnished house.

"Is okay." Teo's mother smiled and placed a thin olive-drab blanket behind Callie. "Please. Lie down. We clean wound, yes?" The woman looked first to her then to Risto.

"Yes. Get my black duffle," Risto instructed a worried-looking Teo who stood just beyond the sofa. The teen got an eyeful of her breasts.

Callie buried her face in the blanket. "Naked here." Well, not exactly, she still wore her jeans, but still.

Risto swore. "Forget you saw those breasts, Teo, or I'll … never mind." He took the duffle the boy had retrieved and swung it, one-handed, over the top of the couch and Callie's body. Knowing how heavy it was, she was impressed. "Thanks, Teo," Risto said. "Keep watch, would you?"

"*Sí,* Risto. I hope your woman is okay. She is a heroine in our village. We will all pray for her." The youth left the room.

She could still hear gunfire, but it sounded as if it was getting farther away. She must have spoken her thoughts out loud because Risto answered. "The FARC guerillas realized they'd ticked off the villagers when they accidentally started a war in the middle of the fucking plaza on market day, so they took their fight outside of town into the hills and the forest. The ELN could care less, but the FARC rely on this town for shelter."

Teo's mother gently cleaned Callie's wound with something cool and herbal smelling. She nodded her head and added, "The Mayor … he is related to the local FARC leader. There will have to be … what is the word…" she spoke rapidly in Spanish.

"Reparation," Callie supplied a second before Risto did. She looked over her wounded shoulder and smiled. He closely observed what the Colombian woman was doing to her, ready to take over. "I guess we're both pretty good with Spanish."

Risto's face lightened somewhat from the grim, angry— and worried—man. "Yeah. How's the pain, sweetheart?"

"Bearable now that I'm not being jostled." She laid her head down on the couch, leaving her shoulder tilted so the Señora and Risto could finish tending to it. "It's just a dull thud now. Whatever the Señora used is numbing it somewhat. I feel sort of woozy." She'd bet there was some narcotic in it which her open wound allowed to get in her bloodstream. At the moment, she could care less. All she wanted to do was sleep.

"It is a local remedy." The Señora probed the wound gently. "Looks clean. What do you think, Señor Risto?"

Risto's much hotter fingers poked and prodded. "Looks good. I'll put an antibiotic cream on it and we'll tape it up so nothing gets into it. I'll check it again when we stop for the night. In this environment, I don't want to take a chance. Insects will be attracted to the smell of blood."

After about a minute, Risto came around to the front of the couch. He helped her lie against the cushioned sofa back. Then he pulled the blanket under her around to cover her breasts once again. She clutched at the covering and wished he would hold her; she wanted his heat and touch. She was so very cold all of a sudden and to prove the point she shivered.

Risto sat on a low table in front of the couch and handed her a couple of tablets. "Take these."

"What are they?" She took them and examined them for any markings.

"One is a pain killer and the other is a Levaquin. I'm not taking any chances. We'll treat for infection ahead of time."

She nodded and absently wondered how the painkiller would mix with the stuff the Señora had used on her wound. She tossed the meds back, took the plastic cup the Señora offered, and drank whatever was in it to help swallow the tabs. It was an icy cold Pepsi. Callie raised her eyebrows. "Where did this come from? I dropped mine to help the Mayor's wife."

Risto cracked a smile for the first time since their interlude in the hotel restroom. "The Mayor's son ran back and got you a fresh one." He sat next to her and pulled her uninjured side against him, then brushed some stray hairs from her cheek. He kissed her hot forehead, his lips felt cool and refreshing. "You have a devoted admirer—and that was before Dario told him you were the world-famous Calista."

"Well, there goes anonymity." She felt the pain killer take effect and kind of liked the floating feeling the drug cocktail in her body provided. She yawned, then took a sip of the Pepsi, careful to use both hands so she didn't drop the cup.

"It would've been gone anyway," she arched a questioning brow and Risto laughed, "all the soccer fans at the bar recognized you. Those swimsuit issues find their way all over the world." He rearranged the blanket so none of her upper torso showed at all. She wrinkled her nose at his possessiveness. "Baby, do you have any other clothes in that bottomless tote bag of yours?"

"Not clean and I don't think…" her words trailed off and she frowned. She couldn't think. Damn, the drugs had knocked her on her butt.

"No, we don't want anything which could possibly infect the wound. We're fighting time and nature in this climate as it is." He yelled over his shoulder. "Teo, bring me my backpack, *por favor.*" He turned to her and swept a finger down her nose and tapped the end. "You can wear one of my T-shirts and cover it with another of my long-sleeved shirts. I always pack extras for just these sort of situations—except I'm the one usually getting shot. We also need to reapply the insect repellant."

She licked her lips. Why was she so dehydrated? She could barely swallow. And what had she wanted to tell him? Oh, yeah… "Um, I'll swim in your T-shirt." She took another sip of her drink and sighed at the cool liquid as it slid down her too-dry and suddenly too-tight throat.

"Tough." He looked out the doorway. "Plus it's started to rain again. We need to keep you—and especially the wound—as dry as possible."

She yawned. A gray fog had sneaked into the edges of her visual field. She tried to reassure Risto that she hardly ever got sick, but words took too much energy. She closed her eyes and let her head fall onto his shoulder.

"Callie, honey, you okay?"

Risto's voice came from far away. She could feel his arms holding her, feel his blessed heat and smell his unique male scent. She was safe. He would take care of her. He started to swear again—and the fear in his voice made her want to reassure him, but the grayness in which she floated turned to black.

Risto kept checking Callie's pulse and respirations as he waited for Tweeter to call him back and let him know where between Ungaía and the coast he planned to infringe Colombian airspace in order to pick them up. When Callie had slipped into unconsciousness and began to struggle for breath he lost it for a few seconds before realizing she was having an allergic reaction to something in the concoction the Señora had used and that her airway was constricted. Since he had epinephrine, he used one of the portable pens and gave her a dose. It helped almost immediately.

He swept a finger over her hot, sweaty forehead, attempting to figure out if she was cooler than the last time he checked. He alternately swore and prayed under his breath. Why the fuck hadn't Tweeter called him back? He told the man it was a medical emergency. He checked his watch and realized it had only been five minutes since he placed the call, but it seemed like an eternity.

As it was, unless someone in SSI could get permission for Tweeter to invade Colombian airspace, SSI would be violating international law to come in and retrieve them. They really had no choice. Callie needed a hospital. She was out like a light and wouldn't wake up. She had a fever of 102. He'd started an IV to administer medications, including more epinephrine, if needed, and to keep her hydrated. Once they got her to Puerto

Obaldo, they'd fly her by jet directly to Panama City and to the US Military hospital there. Colonel Walsh was paving the way for her admission.

All Risto needed now was to know when and where Tweeter would meet them. Ungaía was out since the FARC and ELN were still fighting and would happily shoot down any helicopter, uncaring whose it was.

His sat phone rang. "Give me good news."

"Take the Río Atrato fork to Tigre. You'll see the helo on the southern banks before you get to the village."

"ETA?" Risto stroked Callie's sweat-soaked hair away from her face. She moaned.

Thank God, she hadn't made a sound since she lost consciousness over fifteen minutes ago. He could kick himself for not asking what the Señora had used on Callie *before* she used it. He obtained a sample of the herbal mixture so the doctors at the military hospital could test it in case her reaction was not merely allergic. The fever—well, that could be caused by anything. The Levaquin had been the maximum loading dose so he didn't dare give her anything else other than acetaminophen for the fever and electrolytes until the docs had a chance to see what was going on.

"I'll get to the rendezvous before you will," Tweeter told him. "Colonel Walsh pulled some strings and our people called their people. Bottom line, we have permission to land anywhere along the Atrato as long as we stay out of the current fight in Ungaía. Colombian military does not want the international incident potential."

He breathed a sigh of relief—at least the Colombian Air Force wouldn't try to shoot them down and they could take the faster more direct route back to Panama rather than flying evasively. "Got it. We're heading out now."

"See you soon. Take care of our Callie."

"Count on it." Risto shut off the sat phone and looked at Teo. "You sure you want to pilot the boat while I hold Callie?"

"*Sí.*" A solemn Teo watched as Risto picked up Callie.

"Our stuff all loaded?" Teo nodded. "Callie's bag also?"

"*Sí, sí.* All of your items are on the boat. We go now. She is too pale. Maybe it is the heat?"

"That's part of it." He brushed a kiss over her clammy forehead as he followed Teo out the door. Teo's mother stood guard over the loaded boat. "Thank you for all your help, Señora."

"*De nada.*" She stroked Callie's head. "Bring your woman to see us when things are better. We will throw her a party on the plaza."

"I'll let her know." But she'd never return if he had anything to say about it—the Darien wasn't a healthy place to make social calls.

Teo and the Mayor's son, who would also be accompanying them to ride guard, steadied the dugout so he could step into it without relinquishing his hold on Callie. He sat down carefully and shifted her so she'd sit between his legs, her back supported by his chest. Teo hung the IV bag from a makeshift pole over Risto's shoulder, then arranged a rainproof poncho around the two of them. It was like a fucking sauna, but he'd deal—Callie was shivering like an aspen in the wind and she did not need to get chilled from the rain.

Callie moaned and tried to shove the poncho off. "Hot ... dizzy."

"Shh, baby." He captured her flailing arm and re-tucked the poncho around her injured shoulder. He whispered against the damp curls near her ear as she shuddered incessantly within his arms. "Tweeter is coming to get us. We'll get you to a hospital as soon as we can."

Her face twisted into a rictus of pain. "Hurt. So tired. Sorry."

"There's nothing to be sorry for." He nuzzled her forehead. "I should've taken better care of you. Forgive me?"

"Nothing to ... forgive. Sleep ... now." She went boneless

against him.

"Callie?"

Scared shitless at how quickly she'd fallen unconscious again, he checked her pulse. Slow, but strong. Took her temp. Lower now, 101 degrees instead of the 102 he'd taken ten minutes ago. He let out a sigh of relief.

Lifting his face into the rain-laden breeze created by the boat moving swiftly down the river, he thought about the immediate future. He'd get her to safety then fade out of her life. Let her get on with hers. While she might not blame him for what happened, he blamed himself. He'd failed to protect her. His life was filled with the potential of violence every time he went on a mission and he didn't want it to touch Callie, even indirectly. She deserved a man who could guarantee she'd always be safe—and he couldn't. Leaving her with Tweeter in Panama City would be the best for both of them.

He ignored the pain in his heart, the wrenching in his soul. He knew from the beginning of the op that this interlude would end, but hadn't realized how much it would hurt. He'd survive. He always survived, but this time it would be harder than ever.

Chapter Fifteen

Two months later, Chicago, Illinois.

Stunned, Callie walked out of the doctor's office in a fog. Sinking into a chair in the lobby, she stared into space. She was pregnant, two months along. Even on birth control she'd gotten pregnant, probably in Ungaía. The doctor said, "It happens, Callie. The patch has a higher rate of failure as compared to the other birth control methods, especially if you miss changing it by a day or two." And that had happened in Colombia.

Tears streaked down her cheeks. She'd been crying at the drop of a hat since Risto abandoned her in Panama City. *Damn hormones.* She hadn't heard from him since, not a card, not a call or even a frigging e-mail. And how that hurt—she'd been miserable.

Tweeter had been the one to bring her home after they'd detoured to Camp Lejeune and picked up her twin brothers. Once home, Ren offered her a job at SSI as an analyst specializing in forensic accounting and economics. She took the job and had been working from her home office with an occasional trip to Idaho. She'd been extremely successful in tracking drug and terrorist money for SSI's NSA contract projects. Her success rate drew even more government contracts to SSI. Ren had already given her a raise plus a percentage of the reward SSI got for finding the dirty-money accounts. It was a lucrative and satisfying use of her education.

With Keely's help, and on her own time, she'd pointed the US government to four off-shore accounts directly connected to Cruz. The US had them frozen, depriving the para-leader of over forty million USD. That had to hurt the bastard. From those leads, she'd also helped the Colombian government seize some of Paco's drug cartel monies.

But even with all Callie's contact with SSI, Keely never said anything to her about Risto other than that he was on jobs for other SSI clients. Pride had kept her from contacting him or asking Keely too many questions. Now, she was pregnant with his child and didn't know if he'd even care. She sniffed and swiped at the tears trailing down her face. God, she'd become a regular watering pot.

As she fumbled for a tissue, her cell rang. "Callie speaking."

"Calista, dear. It's Mrs. Morgan." Her brothers' landlady. With Thanksgiving Break coming up, the twins had cut out early for a week-long ski trip to the Rockies. So this call couldn't be about complaints over loud parties and beer cans on the lawn.

"Hi, Mrs. Morgan." She sniffed back some more tears and cleared her clogged throat. "Is there some sort of problem? Did the boys forget to pay the rent or something?"

"No, dear. Their apartment was broken into. I called the police, but we couldn't tell if anything was taken." The older woman paused then added, "But the crime scene watchamacallits did find something had been left behind. Now, what did the nice detective call it? Um, something-ware. Eyewear? No, that's not it. Uh, spyware."

"Spyware? You mean they found cameras and recorders?" A niggling of fear swept over her, chilling her to the bone.

"Yes, both. The detective removed them. He wants to speak with your brothers. I gave him their contact number in

Colorado. I hope that was the right thing to do."

"That's fine. I'll also call them." Nausea hit her and it had nothing to do with the early pregnancy queasiness she'd been experiencing for over a month. The people living in the building could be at risk. "Mrs. Morgan, how is your security?"

"Oh, I'm covered. My son saw to it months ago. But thank you for the concern." The older woman paused. "As I told the officer, I've noticed some strange men watching the place lately. I reported them and the area patrols have been driving by more frequently. One of the other tenants also noticed the men and took down the license plates and gave descriptions to the robbery detective when he was here this morning."

"What did the men look like, Mrs. Morgan?" *Please be local thugs.*

"They were Hispanic, Calista. Your brothers told me all about your bad experiences in South America. I just wanted to let you know about the break in, but also to warn you."

Fear stole her breath for an instant. Her free hand covered her stomach. "Thank you, Mrs. Morgan. I'll take precautions."

"If I were you, dear, I'd leave town. After what happened the last time, can you afford to stay in Chicago?" Her brothers must have dropped the whole story on their landlady. She wouldn't be surprised if Mrs. Morgan had also told the police every detail. But the woman had a valid point, Chicago wasn't safe now—especially since she had another precious life to consider.

"That's exactly what I plan on doing." She forced herself to take one complete breath when she realized she had been panting and in danger of hyperventilating. "Don't count on seeing my brothers until this situation is taken care of. We'll, of course, continue to pay the rent. And would you please call in a security company to put in a complete system in my brothers' apartment? I'll pay for it."

"No need to do that. I've asked my son, who owns a home security company, to upgrade all the apartments. One can never be too secure these days. I've been meaning to do it ever since I did my own—this occurrence just makes it more urgent."

"Thank you, Mrs. Morgan. I'll be in touch when the boys are coming back."

"Take care, dear. And tell the boys to take care also."

"I will. Goodbye." Callie disconnected. Her mind was in a whirl. She didn't know what to do first. *Breathe, Calista Jean. You and the baby need oxygen. Calm down and use that analytical brain.*

First, she needed to call her brothers. Then call … who? Risto is who she wanted to call, but he hadn't shown any interest in her wellbeing since Panama. *He did tell you to call if you needed him.* That had been one of his male-chest-beating moments, a reaction to Conn's offer of help and flirtation. *Call Risto, Callie. If he blows you off, call Keely.* No, she'd call Keely first, feel her out as to whether Risto was even in the country. Yes, that would work. If he wasn't, then she could proceed in another direction.

She called her brothers and made them promise not to come back to Chicago. She also asked them to cut their Colorado trip short and head to Idaho and Sanctuary until Ren and Keely gave them the all-clear to come home. They could ski there just as easily. If for some reason Cruz found out where the boys were, Ren and his men would protect them. They weren't happy, but they agreed. They wanted her to come to them, but she refused. Cruz or his agents would follow her. She wasn't leading the man to her brothers. She promised to call and let them know where she ended up.

Now to let Keely know. She placed the call. "Keely? It's Callie."

"What's wrong?" Keely's alarm came over the phone clearly.

"I sound that bad?" Callie idly watched people move in and out of the massive office building lobby. No one paid any particular attention to her, but she needed to stay alert.

"Yes, you sound as if you've been crying. Tell me what's going on."

"My brothers' apartment was broken into and spyware, planted. The landlady said Hispanic males were seen watching the building."

"Shit." Keely called to Ren, then came back on. "You think Cruz is coming for you again?"

"That's my take. He couldn't know I was the one who got his assets frozen, could he?" She heard Ren's baritone and the baby sounds of their son Riley in the background as Keely brought him up to speed.

A beep on the line, then Ren said, "We're on speaker phone now. I wouldn't count on Cruz not being fully informed. The DOD traitor is pretty highly placed and has access to NSA and other intelligence community sources. He could've sold the intel to Cruz." Ren sounded calm. Good, she needed calm because if Cruz knew that particular piece of information, he'd be coming to hurt her, not fuck her. "Where are you, Callie?" Ren asked.

"I'm in the lobby of a building on Michigan Avenue. I had an appointment." They didn't need to know she was pregnant. They'd add two and two and come up with Risto as father. She wanted to tell him herself, face-to-face.

"Don't go back to your apartment," he said.

"I hadn't planned on it." Her gaze swept the building lobby and the noon-time crowds coming and going to lunch. One man, not Hispanic, but tall and Teutonic-looking, watched her closely. He smiled when her gaze paused on him for a second. Probably just someone who recognized her, but she didn't want to take the chance he wasn't a merc hired by Cruz. She stood, making sure her tote was securely on her arm, then walked away from him. She exited onto Michigan Avenue and headed for the Water Tower mall. "I'm walking and talking now. I want to see if anyone follows me."

"Good, that's good." Ren mumbled something to Keely she

couldn't quite make out. The baby cooed in the background. Callie's womb contracted at the sound. Nothing could happen to her baby. Risto's baby.

Finally, Ren spoke to her. "We can't send anyone to you right now. All our regular operatives are on cases and we haven't fully vetted the probationary operatives yet." Which meant Risto was on assignment—and Ren didn't trust his new recruits. And after a couple of close calls in the last year, she didn't blame him. So, she was on her own for now.

"I'd come myself—and Keely argued that point adamantly—but with the new baby, I'm uncomfortable leaving her alone." With the "unknown new recruits" implied.

"No, Ren, you need to stay and take care of your family. Plus, I *need* you there. I'm sending my brothers to Sanctuary until it is safe for them to go home. They're coming from a ski trip in Colorado and could be there this evening."

"We'll be happy to have them," Ren said. "Keely's parents told me they loved having them in September, said they are marvelous kids. Keely and I will keep them safe."

"I know you will." Callie wiped away more tears threatening to fall. The moisture would freeze from the cold wind off Lake Michigan. At least she was dressed for the inclement weather. It was supposed to snow later in the day.

"Callie," Ren said. "I'll get someone from the Chicago FBI office to check your house. They'll secure it and remove any video or audio devices and see if they can trace the feed. They can also touch base with the Chicago PD about the break in at your brothers' place and let the locals know this is connected to a federal crime. Cruz is now wanted by the US government for your attempted kidnapping, drug trafficking, money laundering, and terrorist activities. If they could catch him on US soil, that would be a coup."

She let out a breath. "That's good. And if Cruz isn't here, whoever is doing his dirty work could be picked up and turned on him." She entered the Water Tower mall, stopped in the lower lobby, and looked back the way she'd come. She didn't see the man who'd smiled at her. Nor did she see anyone who singled her out. She took the escalator up and headed for the top floor and a lunch place. She was light-headed from hunger after what had become her morning ritual of vomiting. "Once I find a place to go, I'll let you know where I am."

"Come to us," Keely said, her voice insistent. "We can protect you here."

"Idaho's so far away." Her stomach revolted at the thought of a plane ride. She wasn't a good flier to begin with and the thought of holiday-crowded planes and airport layovers exhausted her just to think about them. She hesitated, how could she explain it and not reveal her pregnancy?

She fell back on the Thanksgiving travel excuse. "I doubt I could get any tickets west which wouldn't involve a ton of layovers. Flights have to be sold out, and quite frankly, I have some sort of a tummy bug," *well, it isn't a complete lie*, "and can't face the crowds and the inevitable getting bumped because of over-sold planes. Plus, I'm afraid Cruz would have people covering airline and train reservations. And, at this time of year, a car trip would be dicey, weather-wise."

Not to mention she'd have to do it in stages. She was tired all the time. The doctor had told her that her symptoms seemed to be exaggerated—and then had delicately asked about stress, worry—and the father of the child. Callie had declined to share.

"So, what are you going to do?" Ren asked.

"Greyhound bus, I think. It would be unexpected. Cruz has a vision of me as a sophisticated model—not a Joe-bag-of-doughnuts person who takes a bus."

Plus, with the open-ended ticketing option, she could pick a long-distance destination and get off anywhere along the way and stay in a small, no-name town. The bad guys would have no way of knowing where she got off—if they even discovered she'd taken the bus.

Entering one of her favorite cafes in Chicago, she sat at a table so that her back was against a wall and her view of the entrance unimpeded. "I'll withdraw lots of cash for food and motels on the road and use my credit cards one last time in Chicago to shop for some extra clothes and toiletries. Then I'll find some remote place, take the bus, and disappear until you give me the all-clear to come home to Chicago."

"What if we don't catch him, Callie?" Ren's worry was clear in his voice.

"Then I'll wait for an SSI escort and plan on an extended stay in Idaho."

"Sounds like a good plan for now," Ren said. "How will we contact you? He might have someone monitoring your phone accounts."

"I'll buy a throw-away or use a landline. I have my laptop. I can use the secure satellite connection you set me up with for work to retrieve e-mail." She patted her tote bag and reassured herself that her small computer was still inside. Sometimes she forgot. It was there, thank God, or she'd have had to buy a netbook or a tablet.

"It'll take some time, but eventually we can set it up to bounce your cell phone signal, Callie. Tweeter will take care of it as soon as he gets back from Boise today," Ren said. "We'll send you an e-mail letting you know when you can use your cell again. Keely says she'll use the code you girls used as kids in any e-mails so you'll know it's from her. We still have the trapping program on all our incoming and outgoing messages over the NSA satellite."

"Great. I'll send an e-mail with my itinerary in code once I'm on the bus." If the bus was one of the new ones with WiFi that is; it all would depend on the destination. Maybe she should get a network card for her laptop. She could then sign on to the secured SSI server through it.

"Callie, I want you to check in with us every eight hours," Ren said. She knew he and Keely would try to free up one of the regular operatives to come get her as soon as possible.

"Gotcha, every eight hours, beginning now." She checked her watch. "It's eleven central standard time. So, I'll check in at seven central time this evening."

"Got it, and good luck, Callie," Ren said.

Keely chimed in, "Take care of yourself, Calista Jean. Sorry, we couldn't be of more immediate help."

"You've helped. My brothers will be safe. I have a plan—and you'll come through if I do get in actual danger. Nothing has happened yet. This could all be a lot of hassle for nothing." And, God willing, it would all be a false alarm, but she didn't really think so. "Bye. Talk to you this evening." She ended the call.

"What would you like to eat?" Her favorite waitress, Sissy, smiled at her. "We have potato soup today. Sandwich special is a tuna melt."

"I'll take a Pepsi." To hell with what the doctor said about caffeine, she needed the boost. "A cup of the soup and a grilled cheese sandwich, whole grain bread, please." All of a sudden she was ravenous. Her stomach grumbled loudly. The baby was hungry. She smoothed a hand over the place where her child lay.

"Want chips, fruit or coleslaw with the grilled cheese?"

"Fruit, please. Thanks, Sissy."

"Got it. Be right back with your soda."

Callie stared at her phone. She didn't think Cruz would suspect she would know to run so she should be safe making one more call. So, who to call?

Her gut told her she should leave Risto a voice mail message, letting him know she was on the run. He'd want to know. Her earlier maudlin doubts about him not caring enough to call she chalked up to hormones and shock at being pregnant. Dammit, the man wanted her. She wasn't sure what bug he'd gotten up his butt that caused him to dump her in the hospital in Panama City, but she suspected it was some dumb macho-idiot thing.

Tweeter had also told her when he'd dropped her and the twins off in Chicago that he thought Risto wanted her. Her childhood friend and brother-by-choice advised her to give the man time to miss her. Men like Risto, Tweeter had said, didn't like being chased. They liked to do the chasing. That would be the last time she took romantic advice from an alpha-geek who had no steady woman of his own. She'd wasted two months, waiting on Risto to decide to chase her.

She refused to wait any longer. She'd pursue him—but indirectly.

Her lips twisted into a slightly evil smile. She wouldn't leave Risto a voice mail message. Instead, she'd call Conn for help and let him call Risto. She snorted back a laugh. If that didn't light a fire under Risto's stubborn tight ass, then he really didn't want her and she'd know once and for all. At the thought he might not care, she started to cry. Pregnancy had turned her into a Grade-A wuss.

"Here's your Pepsi, Callie. You okay?" Sissy patted her on the back.

"Just a little blue today. Thanks for asking." She attempted a smile. It must've been a pathetic one because Sissy looked even more concerned and patted her back once again before leaving to wait on another table.

Callie took a sip of her Pepsi. Aah, the elixir of life—pregnancy be-damned, the baby would just have to acclimate his diet to caffeine and sugar. Taking a slow calming breath, she punched the speed dial number for Conn. She smiled, recalling how jealous Risto had been when he discovered she had Conn's private line. Yeah, the marine cared all right.

"Conn?" she asked when the call was connected and she heard only silence.

"Callie? What a pleasant surprise? How are you, sweet cheeks."

She smiled at the endearment and got all teary again. It was so Conn. "Not good. I'm in trouble. I need help."

"Talk to me." His voice had gone from happy to concerned and all business in a nanosecond.

She sighed and knew this call had been the right move. "Cruz is after me again." She heard Conn's snarling "fuck", then him yelling for Berto to get his ass in there.

"Where are you?" His voice echoed and she realized he had put her on speaker phone.

"In the Water Tower mall in Chicago ... eating."

"What the fuck are you doing in a fucking mall? It's like a fucking shooting gallery in those fucking places." He sounded like an angry marine; his f-bombs were an indication of his concern and frustration at being too far away to help.

"I'm fine." She laughed nervously. Yeah, hysteria was imminent. "No one followed me here."

"Then how in the fuck do you know Cruz is after you?" She could almost see him ruffle his fingers through his hair. The snarl in his voice was so familiar, so alpha, so like Risto. It centered her.

She quickly filled him in on the break-in at her brothers' apartment and her call to SSI. "I'm afraid Cruz wants to use my brothers to get to me—just as he threatened before."

"Maybe, or maybe he just wants to fuck with your head before he comes after you directly." He sounded calm, but his intense anger still thrummed over the connection.

"The security of my apartment is better than my brothers'. Plus, if they'd been casing my place, I would've sensed it." She paused. "Ren's notifying the Chicago FBI to check my place out just in case they do try to break in and wire it."

"Go to Idaho, Callie. Sanctuary is a fortress." His words sounded like an unconditional order.

"I can't." She swallowed, taking the biggest chance in her life. He'd seen her with Risto—he might guess her condition. "I'm sick."

"Sick? What kind of sick? Did you pick up a bug in the

Darien? Risto told me you'd been wounded, had heat stroke and some dehydration…"

The news that Risto had talked about her to Conn made her happy. "Yeah, something like that. Just the thought of the plane ride, well, I can't. I'm dizzy, weak, sick to my stomach … I'd be afraid to chance it. I'm not all that good on planes to begin with." *What a liar you are, Calista Jean.* "Plus, the weather here is getting bad—so no car trip. And Amtrak wouldn't get me close enough to Sanctuary to be worth it. I was thinking about a Greyhound bus and getting off at one of the stops and hiding in some rural motel until Ren can get someone to me."

"Callie, you aren't telling me everything." She remained silent. *Damn,* he was putting it together just as she feared—and hoped. "Why didn't you call Risto? You're all he talks about. He bragged the other day about how you're nailing Cruz's secret accounts right and left. And let me tell you, Paco ain't too happy about his drug profits being taken by the Colombian government. Only good thing is Paco's blaming Cruz, not you. Tom and Rosa made sure of that."

"Risto is unavailable, according to Ren." The tears in her voice were real and not forced at all. "I haven't seen or heard from Risto since Panama City. He doesn't want me, Conn." Her sob was loud. Sissy looked over, a frown on her face. Callie waved the girl off when she started to walk toward the table.

"Bullshit. The man would give both his nuts for you. As much as I like the guy, I'll admit he's a stubborn shithead." Conn exhaled loudly. "Okay, this is what is gonna happen. Berto will set up your Greyhound itinerary and pay for it out of one of my accounts so Cruz's minions and the fucking DOD traitor can't track it to you so easily. Hold the line, Berto just came in. I want to bring him up to speed and get him on that detail." Mumbled masculine tones and the slight hum of the connection were all she heard for a few seconds. "Okay, he's working on it."

"Where am I going?" She nodded at Sissy who set her lunch order down.

"For starters, Watersmeet, Michigan in the U.P., um, the Upper Peninsula. I expect Risto's sorry butt will pick you up at one of the stops before you even get to Watersmeet. He owns an island in the Cisco Chain of Lakes on Thousand Islands Lake."

And wasn't that a shocker? She knew a lot about Risto—his courage, his protectiveness, his possessiveness, his intelligence and that he made love as if she were the only woman in the world—but she didn't know much about his private life. A whole island? Amazing.

"What if he doesn't meet me, Conn?" Her breath hitched. "What will I do?"

"Callie, are you pregnant?" She didn't answer, but continued to sniff back the tears threatening to explode, Conn sighed. "I'll take the lack of response as a *yes*. How long have you known?"

"Since a little over an hour ago. I'm so scared. If Cruz got me, my baby…"

"Nothing's going to happen to you or the baby. Do you want me to tell Risto about the baby, Callie?"

"No! He'd be so upset. I need to see him, Conn. I miss him like crazy. I want to tell him face-to-face to see if…"

"Callie, the man loves you. Period. I had a bet with Berto that Risto would look you up by Thanksgiving. So, don't think he doesn't want you. He does. Count on that."

"When did you see him last? Maybe he changed his mind." She sniffed, wiping her face with her napkin.

"Four days ago and he hasn't changed his mind. Trust me on that one, sweet cheeks. I would've won that bet."

"So is he still in Colombia?"

"He should be in the States by now. He would've flown into Marquette out of New York."

The knowledge Risto was on his way home and she could

possibly see him in the next day or so unwound the knot in her gut and eased her renewed nausea. But something nagged at her. "What if SSI sent him somewhere else? Ren was crystal clear that all his operatives were busy."

"Risto got done early. Wanted some down time. So, Ren doesn't know." Conn chuckled. "And I'm damn sure the down time included a side trip to Chicago and you. He loves you, Callie. He's just not sure you should want him back."

"I love him, Conn."

"Well, hell, Callie, I knew that. It's Risto you have to convince. He doesn't think he's good enough for you."

"Why in the hell not?" She had all but crawled all over Risto the entire time in Colombia. Did he think she just had sex with any man?—especially after she'd been celibate for seven years before him.

"He's a loner, always has been. You sort of set him back on his heels. You fit him—and he never expected to find a woman, especially one who looks like you and is as smart as you, who could deal with his lifestyle. He's pretty much a throwback, Callie. One of those rugged males who explored and settled the Wild West. He won't change. He'll have to wear the pants in any relationship."

"I don't want him to change. I liked his bossiness. I thoroughly enjoyed my time in the Darien—well, except for the anaconda, the heat stroke, and getting shot—but at heart, I'm tired of travelling the world and having adventures. I want to stay home, do my analyst work and make a nest for Risto and the children we'll have."

"Well, sure looks like you'll be nesting. Risto won't allow you to be exposed to danger—he was kicking his own ass because you were hurt on his watch. The man would kill the tree that gave you a splinter. Hold a sec, Berto has something."

As two low male voices mumbled in her ear, she took a bite of half of her sandwich and then gobbled the rest up in four bites by the time Conn got back on the line.

"Berto has us on a plane to the US. We'll be in Watersmeet by tomorrow, shortly after the bus arrives there. We'll let Risto know when we talk to him. If he can't get to you before Watersmeet, we'll be there to get you and take you to his island."

"You're flying here? I didn't ... you don't have to..."

"We're coming, Callie. If Risto doesn't go straight home, you still need back-up. Plus, even if Risto picks you up first, we need to deal with Cruz once and for all. Risto will need us covering his ass."

"Thank you." She sniffed. "Sorry, I've been crying at the littlest thing—happy, sad, depressed, mad, makes no difference, I cry."

Conn laughed. "I've heard tell pregnant women are very emotional."

"Yeah, damn hormones." She snorted. "When does my bus leave Chicago?" She needed to get cash and some clothing and personal items, plus get the vitamins the doctor recommended.

Berto's voice chimed in. "Hey, little *mamacita*. Your bus leaves Chicago at 4:54 p.m. (CST) today and will get to Watersmeet, Michigan, weather permitting, tomorrow morning at 6:16 a.m. (CST). I made the reservations in your name. It's all paid for, *chica*. You just pick up the ticket at the will-call window."

"Thanks, Berto." She sighed. She'd have time to do all she needed. The bus station was downtown so she didn't need to worry about rush hour traffic to get there.

"See you soon. Don't worry. We'll protect you, *bonita*."

Conn came back on. "I'd count on being dragged off the bus, scolded, soundly kissed, and then scolded again by your man long before Watersmeet. That marine loves you. It'll drive him bat shit crazy when he hears you're sick, in danger, and on the run. He'll move mountains to get to you ASAP."

That was what her evil inner Callie had hoped for. But to hear Conn confirm her gut feelings about Risto made her happier than she'd been since Colombia when she was last in his arms. "Thanks. I really appreciate…"

"Not a problem. You're family now, just think of Berto and me as honorary uncles for the baby, okay?"

"Absolutely. See you soon."

"Watch your six, Callie. Call me if something unusual comes up."

"I will. Bye." She shut off the phone and powered it down. Then she finished her meal with an appetite she hadn't had in weeks. She needed to fuel up and get her errands accomplished before she picked up her ticket at the bus station and started her trip.

Tuesday, 11:54 p.m. (EST), Marquette, Michigan.

RISTO DROVE HIS JEEP OUT of the long-term parking lot at the Marquette airport and headed toward home. In about four hours or so he'd be back on his island where he could sit and ponder what to do about Callie. Conn and Berto had double-teamed him the whole time he'd been on assignment in Colombia. Teo and the citizens of Ungaía had asked about her when he'd stopped by and took them some much needed medications and money, his and SSI's way of thanking them for their kindness to him and Callie.

He'd made the decision to take some time off and visit Chicago, take Callie out on a real date, and court her. Then if he thought she'd have him, he'd ask her to marry him and put him out of his fucking misery. He'd missed her every damn day since he'd left her in Panama City. There wasn't a single hour he didn't wonder if she was happy, healthy, safe.

Blunt as always, Keely had called him a "frick-fracking asswipe" for not calling Callie during the last two months. Because of employee privacy and client confidentiality—and the need-to-know philosophy SSI worked under—he knew Ren had instructed Keely not to tell Callie anything about him or his missions. But that hadn't kept Keely from informing him about everything Callie had been doing to shut Cruz down.

Damn, he was proud of his woman. She single-handedly had put Cruz on the defensive, weakened him in the eyes of his own men and of Paco and his cartel. But a humiliated Cruz was a dangerous Cruz—and if the para-leader ever figured out Callie was the instrument which had destroyed his nice little world, he'd kill her, after he tortured her first. Risto wouldn't allow that to happen. He'd marry her and hide her away on his island or at Sanctuary.

Pulling into a McDonald's, he ordered a burger and some coffee for the road. He wanted to sleep in his own bed tonight before heading to Chi-town tomorrow. The weather was okay now, but would worsen to blizzard conditions later tonight and on into tomorrow morning. The sooner he got home, the sooner he got off the snowy roads. And getting to his island in this weather would be cold, wet and bone-rattling rough.

As he picked up the order, his phone rang. He hit the send button on the steering wheel for his blue-tooth connection. "Smith, here." He pulled onto the access road and ate his burger one-handed.

"Risto, where the fuck are you?"

"Conn?"

"Yeah. Berto and I are about to board a plane for New York. We'll be in Marquette tomorrow and then Watersmeet as soon as we can fly a charter there."

"What the fuck you coming here for? It's snowing—blizzard warnings for tomorrow."

"Callie called."

Icy fear swept down Risto's spine and he gripped the steering wheel so tightly his knuckles turned white. "What happened? Is she okay?"

"Someone broke into her brothers' place and planted surveillance equipment. Hispanic someones."

"Fuck. Did they try to grab her? Are her brothers okay?" He pulled over to the side of the road so he wouldn't crash. He tossed the burger into the bag, no longer hungry. "Where is she?"

"She's on a Greyhound bus to Watersmeet. What time is it, there?"

"About midnight."

"Eastern or central time?"

"Eastern. My house and Watersmeet are in the Central time zone."

"She'll be hitting Escanaba, Michigan at 3:57 a.m. eastern time, and changing busses for Watersmeet, departing at 4:40 a.m. Can you intercept her? She's sick, scared, but maintaining. Your woman is courageous, but neither Berto nor I were really happy about her travelling alone."

Out of all the words coming out of Conn's mouth, he zeroed in on one. "Sick! What's wrong with her? And why in the fuck did you send her north in this weather when you didn't even know I'd be here?"

"Because we would've picked her up in Watersmeet and taken her to your island. She didn't think she could drive to Idaho and had already ruled out flying because of her illness."

"Tell me—what's wrong with her." His insides turned to ice. She'd fucking needed him and he hadn't been there for her. Never again—that would never happen again.

"Not sure. I took her word for what she could and couldn't do and helped her figure out how to get the fuck out of Chicago without leaving bread crumbs for Cruz to follow."

"Did she tell you why she didn't call me?" He distinctly remembered ordering her to call him first if she needed him.

"You haven't contacted her, you dumb fuck. No communication at all, she told me. You hurt her. She thinks you don't want her."

God, his gut hurt. He'd just wanted to give her some space, not make her doubt how he felt. He *was* a dumb fuck. He'd make it up to her—once he got to her, she would never doubt he loved her.

Conn added, "By the way, she did call Ren and Keely, before she called me. You might want to check in and get a sit rep concerning Cruz and his whereabouts. They were scrambling to find someone to cover Callie's ass. I called them after I spoke to Callie and told them she was covered, but they're sending us the Walsh twins for extra back-up. They resigned their commissions and are in Chicago right now."

"Damn right, she's covered. Nothing and no one will touch Callie. I appreciate the help, Conn, and thank Berto for me, also. Call when you get to Watersmeet. I'll come get you in the SSI helicopter housed on my island."

"Good, that'll save us trying to find a way from Watersmeet in the middle of a fucking blizzard." Conn paused. "What are we going to do about Cruz and his band of hired guns?"

"You sent her north, because my island is an easily defended fortress."

"That, and she needs and wants you—and you, you thick-headed fuck, need and want her."

"I love her."

"Well, hell, Risto, I knew that, wasn't sure you did."

Risto sighed. "To answer your question—we'll set a trap for Cruz and his men." One the fucker wouldn't escape alive. "I want this asshat out of her life."

"Good, we're all on the same page, old buddy. Now, go get your woman off the damn bus, take her home, and tuck her in bed, you with her. We'll call when we need to be picked up."

"Thanks, Conn. Safe journey."

Risto ended the call, then made a U-turn and headed back

east to pick up the road to Escanaba. With any luck, he'd be there, waiting, when Callie's bus pulled into the station.

Chapter Sixteen

Early Wednesday morning, Greyhound Bus Station, Escanaba, Michigan.

Callie stood up and swayed slightly. She arched her back and moaned, then bent to pick up her tote bag sitting on the floor of the bus. Behind her she heard, "Here, let me get those bags for you." The owner of the voice reached over her and retrieved the shopping bags containing the items of clothing and toiletries she'd purchased for the trip.

She groaned and muttered, "persistent bastard."

The voice belonged to the man who'd attempted to sit next to her when she changed busses in Milwaukee. She'd declined his company, and since there were lots of empty seats, he had to accept her refusal or look like the jerk he was. At each stop from Milwaukee to Escanaba, he'd hung over her seat and talked at her. Since she was battling nausea, it wasn't hard to keep her replies to monosyllables. Rude? Yes, but she'd told him several times she was tired, sick and taken. He had yet to take the hint.

"Here." He offered her the shopping bags and smiled. "You meeting your party in Escanaba?"

"Thank you." She took the bags and couldn't avoid his hand stroking over hers. She purposely ignored his nosy question and followed the other passengers disembarking in Escanaba. They were early and the bus to Watersmeet wouldn't leave for another hour. The good news was the bus station was a full-service one and had a place to eat and real restrooms. She wanted to wash her face and brush her teeth. Then she planned on eating something light; she prayed the diner attached to the station had something like chicken noodle soup and lots of saltines. A kind woman on the bus had offered her a couple of small packages of her now favorite cracker. Those, along with a bottle of water, were all she'd had to eat since Chicago. She'd been too sick in Milwaukee to eat anything and had spent most of the three-hour layover there spewing her guts out in the restroom and trying to keep clear fluids down.

As she entered the bus station, she sensed the pushy man from the bus on her heels. She headed straight into the women's restroom and hoped he'd take the hint and leave her alone. She also prayed he wasn't travelling on to Watersmeet. Having this creep breathe down her neck for most of the journey made her miss Risto all the more. Her marine would've scared the persistent bonehead off with just a glare.

Taking her wool hat off, she stuffed it into her tote and pulled out the items she needed to cleanse her face and teeth. She looked pale, but that could be the crappy fluorescent lighting. And if it wasn't, she had a right to look pale—she was tired and in the early stages of pregnancy. She washed her face with the pre-moistened towelettes she pulled from her tote and then moisturized. After a quick brushing of her teeth, she felt almost human and actually hungry. She put the toiletries she used away and then unbraided her hair and brushed it out. God, that felt good. She'd leave her hair down for now, it might help ease her throbbing head. If that didn't solve the problem, she'd try some acetaminophen. It wasn't a coincidence that the throbbing in her head had arisen when the man had begun to bother her after Milwaukee.

Under her breath, she lectured herself, "Okay, Callie, no

eye contact. Find a place he can't sit near you. Ignore him." She left the restroom and spotted him right away as he'd taken an unavoidable position at the end of the hallway leading to the small diner. "Geez Louise, why me?" she muttered. She took a deep breath and walked purposefully toward the food service area, fully intending to pass by him without a glance.

Of course that would've been too easy. He stepped to her side and grabbed her arm, pulling her in the direction he wanted to go—away from where the other passengers were.

She dug in her heels and shot him an angry glare. "No. Stop." He paused but didn't let go of her arm. "Listen, I've tried to be polite, but you aren't taking the hint. I *do not* want to socialize with you. I want to sit by myself, eat some soup and work on my computer without you hanging all over me. Leave me alone or I will report you to whoever runs this station. Understand?"

"I like women who play hard to get. No man wants his woman to be an easy mark." He smiled, an expression two levels above slimy and heading into freaking creepy. *God, the man is certifiable. His woman? In what universe?* He pulled her against his side, his exceptionally strong arm anchored around her waist. "Come on, Calista. I'm a nice guy. Really. Get to know me." His hand slid down to grab her ass and squeeze.

"That does it!" She jabbed his gut with her elbow with as much force as she could muster and attempted to twist from his grasp. But he was too strong. Her heart pounding, she wriggled against his hold as he dragged her toward a side door away from the main area of the station. "Let go!" she shouted.

Why wasn't anyone helping her? Couldn't they see him dragging her away? Obviously, shouting wasn't enough. She opened her mouth to scream, but he pulled her back against him and covered her mouth with his other hand.

"No, you beautiful bitch. I tried to play this nicely but you wouldn't let me. So, now we play it my way. The bus is open and empty—it'll still be warm and a nice private place to get acquainted."

He lifted her with one arm and carried her and her bags as if she weighed nothing. She kicked and wriggled and screamed behind his hand. She even tried to bite him. But she couldn't break free. God, she wished she had her Ruger, she would've gladly shot his ass.

When he reached the side door exiting to the bus loading area, he had to stop. It wasn't automatic, and he'd have to turn a handle to get out. *Thank you, God.* When he let go of her mouth to open the door, she had enough leverage to bang the back of her head against his face. *Ouch, that hurt.* Since he was not much taller than she, she hit his nose. He let go of her to grab his bloody and, she hoped to God, broken nose. Now free, she ran toward the connecting hallway to the diner, screaming for help.

"Callie!" The roar sounded familiar.

"Risto?" She stopped and looked around, and there he was by the main entrance. She turned to run to him, but her stalker caught her by the waist and swung her around. He had a gun in his hand and waved it wildly.

"She's going with me." He backed away, dragging her with him.

"Let my woman go." Risto's voice and demeanor should've had the guy behind her pissing his pants, but since the idiot was crazy, he didn't release her. Risto swept her with a searching glance from her head to her toes. "You okay, sweetheart?"

"Been better." She attempted a smile but knew it had to be pathetic. "You came. Conn said you would." Tears poured down her cheeks.

"Of course, I'm here—you're mine. You need me—I'm here." He stalked toward them. "And when I take care of the fucker holding you, I'll be putting a ring on your finger so stupid asswipes know you're taken."

"Yes." Tears ran down her cheeks. "If that was a proposal, the answer is yes."

"Baby, that was an order." He turned his gaze to the man behind her. "Let Callie go and I might let you leave here with all body parts attached."

"Fuck you." The crazy man aimed at Risto, the gun held along her right side, just within her peripheral vision. She heard the snick of the release of the safety.

"No!" She abruptly raised her right arm, hard, throwing his aim off. The shot went into the ceiling. The lookee-loos dove to the floor, screaming. And then Risto was there, tearing her out of the bastard's grasp and shoving her to the side, out of harm's way.

She watched as Risto disarmed the man and proceeded to beat the shit out of him. Hearing sirens, she got to her feet with the help of the bus driver. "You okay, miss?"

"Yes. I need to stop Risto—I'm the only one who can." She observed two other men imploring Risto to stop. Her attacker was no longer fighting back and looked unconscious. Risto would kill him. "Marine? I need you. Please … please, Risto … I'm so dizzy." She wove an unsteady path toward him. He held the limp man up by his jacket and looked over his shoulder.

"Callie?" He tossed the man to the floor as if he were garbage and came to enfold her within his arms. "What's wrong?" Holding her tightly against his body, he stroked a bloody, but gentle hand over her face, her hair. "Conn said you were sick. Did that bastard hurt you? Did I hurt you when I shoved you away? God, baby, tell me." His eyes filled with worry, he searched her body frantically for any wounds.

Now that he was here, she wasn't sure how to tell him that the woman he just proposed to was going to make him a father. She shook her head and buried her face on his chest.

"Fuck it, baby, you're scaring me." He picked her up, then carried her to a booth in the small station's diner.

The bus driver picked up her bags and placed them in the booth, patted her arm. He addressed Risto. "She was pretty sick in Milwaukee, according to one of the female passengers. She slept most of the trip, when that bastard wasn't bothering her."

"Callie, do we need an ambulance?" He brushed her sweaty hair off her face and placed a gentle kiss on her lips.

"No." She sighed and kissed him back. "I just need to eat something … something mild." She ran a finger along Risto's five o'clock shadow. "You're really here. I missed you. I…"

"Hush." He kissed her again, then pulled her tightly against his side, blocking her from the view of the interested onlookers. "While we give statements to the cops, we'll feed you. Then, if you look better than death warmed over, we'll hit the road for Osprey's Point and my island."

She nodded and rested her head on his shoulder, her eyes drifting shut, and let him take over. He needed to care for her—and she needed him to do so.

"Callie? Does chicken noodle soup sound good?" She looked up and realized she must've dozed off for a few minutes. A waitress stood by the table, smiling at her. A police officer sat in the booth across from them, his face kind and patient.

"Sorry, I must have … I was tired." She yawned. "Um, yes, I think I could eat the soup. Some saltines. And Seven-Up or Sprite." The waitress nodded and said, "be right back."

"Callie, I've told the officer my end of it." Risto rubbed his cheek over her hair. "The bus driver and everyone on the bus from Milwaukee gave statements about the man stalking you. But we need to hear your side."

"Okay." She took a deep breath and told the police officer everything that had happened since Milwaukee. The man nodded and made sounds, asking few questions.

He flipped his notebook closed and looked at both of them. "That should do it. We'll book him for assault, stalking, attempted kidnapping, possession of an illegal firearm—and for the drugs he had on him. With all the eye witness testimony and the fact he'd purposely changed his ticket from his original destination of Duluth to an open-ended ticket and followed you onto the bus to Escanaba, it's a pretty cut-and-dry case."

"He saw me in Milwaukee and changed his plans so he could follow me?" She glanced at the officer who nodded, then looked at Risto whose face was dark and grim. "I ... God, that's crazy. I ignored him. Told him no—and he..." She shivered and snuggled into Risto's comforting embrace, his warmth and his scent calming her.

"It's okay, Callie. I expect the police will find he has a record of stalking and assaulting women." Risto spoke over her head at the police officer. "My fiancée will be with me. You have my address. Please tell the prosecutor that we'll be at the trial if it goes that far."

"Thank you, Mr. Smith. Ms. Meyers, you put this behind you. You did good—and from the witness accounts, you saved your fiancé from being shot. Good work."

"Thank you." She looked up from the comfort of Risto's sheltering arms. Her right arm trapped tightly against Risto's side, she held out her left hand to shake the officer's when she saw the ring. A cushion cut emerald surrounded in sparkling white diamonds and set in platinum. The officer shook her hand gently then left.

She held her hand up and let the ceiling lights shine off the exquisite ring. "Oh, Risto. It's beautiful." She looked at his smiling face. "When did you get it? When did you know you wanted to marry me?" Suspicion crossed her mind. "What did Conn tell you?"

He frowned, puzzled. "What does Conn have to do with anything?"

Thank God, he doesn't know about the baby. He proposed because he wants me. She shook her head. "Never mind. Answer the other questions, please." She stroked his jaw and watched the ring sparkle. It made her insides melt. He wanted her—forever.

"Baby, I knew within twenty-four hours of leaving you I'd

made a mistake letting you go, but…" He swore under his breath. "I wanted to give you a chance to recover. To think. Then I wanted to court you properly."

"Not a word for two months, Risto." She punched him in his rock-solid abs. He didn't even have the courtesy to wince. "I was dying, missing you. I worried about you. No one would tell me where you were or what you were doing or if you were even alive. I was going to call, but, dammit, I didn't even know if you'd want me to. I figured you were out with other women." She started to cry.

"God, Callie. Don't cry." He pulled her face into his chest and kissed the top of her head, stroking his hand over the length of her hair. "There's been no one else. I thought about you every day. I bought the ring in Cartagena from a jeweler friend of Conn's my last trip there. I would've come to Chicago this week and started courting." He exhaled. "But when I saw that fucktard take a hold of you, I knew I had to stake my claim immediately—you accepted, so no going back for us. I'll just have to court you after we get married."

She laughed, a watery sound. "Well, your timing was impeccable." She hiccupped then sniffed.

"Here, wipe." He plucked a napkin from the holder on the table.

She took the napkin and wiped her face, then blew her nose. "Thanks." She straightened up, but remained within the embrace of his left arm. "How far is it to your island?"

"A little over three hours. You can sleep some more in the Jeep." She nodded and yawned. "Ren already filled me in about Cruz being in the US. By the way, your brothers made it to Sanctuary."

"Then they're safe." She breathed out a sigh of relief, then stiffened as his other words penetrated the fog in her head. "Cruz is actually in the States?" Risto massaged the top of her shoulder. "I'd hoped he just hired some mercs."

"You made it too hot for him to remain in Colombia.

According to the latest intel I got from Ren, Cruz has been ousted as a para-leader and told by Paco he'd be piranha food if he ever returned."

"Oh, God, he'll want to kill me." She held her stomach and choked back the bile threatening to come up. She reached for the lemon-lime soda the waitress had dropped off and sipped some to calm her stomach. "Crackers. I need saltines."

Risto signaled the waitress. "Can we have some saltines right away, please?" The woman nodded, throwing a concerned glance at Callie.

"I won't let Cruz get you. I protect what's mine." He rubbed his cheek over hers. "Now, tell me about your illness? You have the stomach flu?"

She turned into his body and cradled his rugged face. "I've been feeling unwell for weeks. I went to the doctor yesterday and I found out…" his eyes filled with fear at her words, "… no, it's nothing fatal." She took a breath and blew it out. "I'm pregnant. You're going to be a father in about seven months."

His dark eyes warmed and his lips broke into a wide smile. "How? We only … um, you had birth … um, how?"

He kissed her before she could answer. His tongue thrusting into her mouth. He angled her face to take the kiss even deeper. She moaned and placed her arms around his neck to pull him closer, to keep him kissing her forever. God, she'd missed this, missed his taste, his scent, his touch. And now, she wore his ring and carried his baby. Her life was looking good—except for the serpent in the garden, Cruz, her life would've been fabulous.

Risto broke the kiss and then peppered her face, hair and neck with dozens of smaller kisses. "God, baby…" Kiss. Kiss. Kiss. "…I love you." Kiss. Kiss. Kiss. "A baby. Our baby." He touched his forehead to hers and looked lovingly into her eyes. "But how?"

"The birth control failed." She peered at him. "You really don't mind being a husband and a father so quickly?"

"Hell, no. I envied Ren when he found Keely and she got pregnant right away. Never thought I'd be lucky enough to find a woman who'd fit into the world I'd chosen." He kissed the tip of her nose. "Then you leapt into my arms in Colombia and from that moment on proved there was such a woman. And, damn, baby, you wanted me back. How freaking lucky are we?"

"Very lucky." Her stomach gurgled loudly and she laughed. "That is your son or daughter, though I'm leaning toward it being a boy, telling me he is done making me throw up for a while and I need to eat."

Risto cuddled her. He picked up a package of saltines, opened them and handed one to her. "Been bad?"

She munched on the cracker, signaling one minute, then took another sip of the soda. "God, I needed that. Yeah, it's been hell. There doesn't seem to be a schedule. I just get sick. The doctor says I have an extreme case. Hormones, lots and lots of hormones. We're hoping I'll get over it by the end of the third month."

"So, you're two months along." He counted on his fingers as she ate her soup. "That means our baby will come sometime in late June of next year."

"Yep. The shower room in Ungaía will always hold fond memories for me," she said. He grinned. She crumbled some crackers into the soup. "So, we'll be living in the U.P.? I'll need to get pre-natal care set up soon. The doctor in Chicago did an ultrasound to make sure the fetus was attached solidly." She dug into her tote and pulled out a small manila envelope and handed it to Risto.

He opened it and looked at the images. His smile was broad. "Yep, that is a fetus. No way to tell the sex yet."

"No, but I'm pretty sure we'll have a boy. I remember Mrs. Walsh saying she was the sickest with all her boys and then Keely was a dream pregnancy. Probably not scientific, but I'm going with it until proven otherwise. Do you want to know?

The doctor said we could try another ultrasound in a few months and see if the baby would pose so we could tell." She giggled and Risto's eyes lit up at her laughter.

"What's so funny?"

"He was a jumping bean. He moved the whole time they did the ultrasound. I'm surprised you don't see wave motion in the images. I suspect when he gets bigger, he'll be an active baby and keep his momma up nights."

"I'll be up with you, then. Rubbing your tummy, your back and telling him to settle down and let his momma sleep." He kissed her, his hand covering her stomach. "I love you. And as to where we'll live—once we take care of Cruz, we'll go to Idaho. We can get married there in less than twenty-four hours. I have a large apartment in the main house at Sanctuary. We'll make that our base until I can build us a cabin there."

"But what about your Michigan place?" She frowned, her hand covered his on her stomach. "We can live here. I don't mind. I adore the Midwest."

"Too isolated. Sanctuary, while also isolated, has people I trust to guard you while I'm on assignment during your pregnancy. Plus, you can work alongside Keely and Tweeter. She has a good ob-gyn in Coeur d'Alene and Ren is talking about attracting a doctor for the Sanctuary area, for operatives and their families and the other employees who work and live in the area."

"Fine. But I'd like to visit Michigan from time to time—it's closer to my brothers and their college."

"Not a problem, honey. I inherited the island. It'll be a great vacation place for your brothers. Plus, Ren wants to use the island as SSI-East. I would head it up, but for now, someone else can run it. Until the baby is born and we make sure the DOD traitor doesn't come after you, I feel better about you being at Sanctuary with Keely and the others." He frowned.

"Why the frown?" She traced the downward curve of his lips. When he didn't answer, she added, "For your information,

I'm sure I'd be fine in Michigan on your island. I'm betting you already have excellent security in place. Plus, you'll be there, and when you aren't, I can go to Idaho."

"We can discuss where we'll live later. We have more pressing concerns. Conn and Berto are heading here. The plan was to use you as bait to draw Cruz to the island in order to take him down." His brow creased with worry. "You're pregnant. Sick with it. We'll have to figure another way."

"I'm pregnant. Not disabled—and not so sick I can't help. We need to get him out of the way now while he's on the run and off-centered, before he can regroup. Now is better than later, when I'll be as big as a Hummer and unable to move."

Risto's lips thinned. His eyes were dark and stormy. But she knew she'd won when he let out a long, slow sigh. "You're right. Now is better than later."

"Good. I need to eat something else. Then can we leave? I want to see your island fortress." She was already planning her campaign for living in Michigan. Idaho was fine for a visit from time to time, but she wanted to live in Risto's home and closer to her brothers—the DOD traitor be damned.

He grinned. "You having cravings already?"

"Yeah. Banana cream pie. I want some, and I see a piece with my name on it." She pointed to a refrigerated shelf under the cash register.

"You got it." He signaled the waitress and placed the order.

Callie sighed and nestled against him. What had been a horrible and stressful twenty-four hours had turned into one of the best days she'd ever lived. She laid her head against Risto's shoulder and enjoyed the flashes her ring made as she massaged his chest.

Chapter Seventeen

*Early Wednesday morning,
Highway 2 in Upper Peninsula Michigan.*

For what could've been the hundredth time since they'd left the bus station in Escanaba, Risto glanced over to check on Callie. One hand on the wheel, he reached over and swept a lock of hair from her eyes. She murmured briefly then went still. She was in a deep sleep. He cursed silently as he noted once again the dark circles under her eyes and the lack of color in her face. He'd make sure she took better care of herself in the future. He could see the need for him to be with her at all future obstetrician visits so he'd know what she needed to be doing for both herself and their baby. His little soldier had a way of not telling him what she needed or when she felt bad.

Their baby. A smile formed as he placed his hand over where their child was safely ensconced. A boy. A girl. He didn't care as long as both Callie and the baby were healthy.

Both hands back on the wheel, he concentrated on getting them all to Osprey's Point, the small town on Thousand Island Lake. At least he had a safe and secure place from which to launch the final battle to eliminate Cruz from Callie's life. His paternal grandfather had been an architect trained in the schools of Saarinen and the mid-twentieth-century Brutalists.

The house, a modern masterpiece of glass, metal and cement, was built into the side of a hill overlooking the lake. Other houses on the island, used for guests, were as equally sturdy and looked as if they had grown out of the rock formations. The whole island and all of the permanent structures and several limestone caves had all been wired for security. No one stepped onto the island, or even approached it by air or water, without Risto knowing. Last Spring, Keely while still in her second trimester of her pregnancy, along with her brother Tweeter, had helped him install the same three-dimensional security system they had at Sanctuary. His island was literally Sanctuary East, and as much as he looked forward to heading up this branch, he could wait until after all danger to the women of SSI was eliminated. Callie was not only targeted by Cruz, but like Keely was also a target of the DOD traitor.

He smiled grimly, his hands fisting on the steering wheel. No one was going to take Callie from him. Anyone stupid enough to try was a dead man.

His phone rang. He answered it through the steering wheel, chancing a glance to see if the noise had bothered Callie. Her gray eyes blinked at him and she yawned. "Sorry, baby," Risto said.

"When did you start calling me baby, you dumb fuck?" Conn's baritone rumbled over the open line.

"Conn. Callie's here with me. Watch your language, asshole."

Callie giggled. Color came into her cheeks. He grinned and winked at her. "Say hello to Conn and Berto, sweetheart."

"Hi, guys. Ignore Risto, he's still in shock about the baby." She looked around her and frowned. "It's really bad outside. Where are you guys?"

"Hey, sweet cheeks. Berto says *hola*. Glad your man found you." Conn paused. "We're in Marquette, trying to find a small plane to charter to get to Watersmeet."

"Risto?" Callie sent him a scared look. "It's not safe ... is it?

This is a blizzard."

"Yeah, Conn. Callie's right. It might be okay in Marquette right now, but this shit is heading your way. You'd be flying in a whiteout." A particularly fierce wind hit the Jeep and Risto wrestled with the steering wheel to keep the vehicle in the middle of the barely plowed lane. "The conditions are deteriorating fast. We'll be pushing it to get to Osprey's Point and then to the island."

"Hadn't planned on leaving until this blew through. Midday is what they're predicting before we'll be able to fly to Watersmeet."

"No need to kill yourself to get here any sooner. The bad guys will be riding this out, also. Just call when you get in. I'll come get you."

"Okay, Berto and I will bunk down at one of the airport hotels for what's left of the night. We'll fly into Watersmeet later today, count on it. A little snow never stopped me, although Berto is freaking." A loud protest in vulgar Spanish came over the speaker. Risto snorted and noticed a slight smile on Callie's lips. "And, Risto, be careful. I know you want to get Callie to your island fortress, but the lake will be bad."

"Give me some effing credit, Redmond. If I can't get her there safely, we'll hole up at Big Earl's at the landing. But ... trust me on this, I've boated this lake in absolute white-outs and two-foot plus chop and made it every damn time."

"Yeah, but you have more to lose this time than your ass."

"I know it. Just take care of your asses. I'll take care of Callie's."

Conn laughed. "Got it. Talk to you later today."

Risto punched off the line then looked at Callie. No anxious hair-twisting, her hands lay relaxed in her lap. Her gaze took in the black-and-white landscape illuminated by the Jeep's headlights. "You okay?"

"Yeah, I've been in worse. Dad was stationed in Alaska one tour. Man, that was desolate. And I've been on lakes with rough water in a blizzard before." She patted her tummy. "I'm feeling human now—but if I get sick on the boat ride, I can blame the baby and not the weather. I really am a better sailor than a flier. A helicopter in gusty winds would make me sicker than a choppy boat ride."

"See if you can get the Weather Service report on the satellite radio, okay? I need both hands to keep us on the road. The cross winds are a bitch. We're almost to the Osprey's Point turn-off."

"Okay." She punched the car computer and located the controls for the radio. He noted she was very much at ease with current technology, which shouldn't surprise him since she used computers to track dirty money. "There it is."

The National Weather Radio announcer was reporting on conditions in the Great Lakes region and it was pretty much as he'd expected—a whole load of snow and winds hitting upwards of fifty miles per hour through at least midday with continuing chances for heavy snow, wind and low temps through the weekend.

Callie, showing no concern about the weather or his driving, had sat back. Her hands went to her stomach. He smiled. He'd often noted pregnant women covered their stomachs a lot—Keely Walsh-Maddox had—in all stages of pregnancy. He couldn't begin to imagine what it felt like to have a life forming inside. Women were just fucking amazing, his woman most of all.

"You okay?"

She glanced at him curiously. "Yeah, why?"

"You're holding your stomach."

She looked down and shook her head. "I've been doing this ever since the doctor told me I was pregnant. Not sure why. Well, that's not quite true, when I feel like coughing up my guts, it makes sense. But at other times like now, everything is good. Nervous gesture, maybe?" She smiled, a dreamy look in her eyes. "It makes me feel better, not so sure about the baby."

"I think our baby will adore his mother petting him. And when we settle in for a nice sleep, I'll be helping you comfort our child."

"How long have you been up?" A crease between her brows showed her concern. God, he'd missed her during the time they'd been apart, no one had ever cared about how he felt before.

He hurried to reassure her he was well-rested and alert. "I'm fine. I slept on the plane from Bogotá to New York and then had another nap between New York and Marquette. I'm good to go. I'll get us safely to the island."

"I'm not worried about that." She paused, and he shot her a quick glance. Her color was high.

"Then what are you worried about?" He lifted a hand from the wheel and touched her cheek with a finger. "You're flushed. Don't be embarrassed, baby. If you need to stop, if you're sick…"

"No, it isn't that … uh, I want you to make love to me. I've … I've dreamt of you every night. God, Risto, I ache with wanting you. I need you in me, making me yours. Especially now."

His dick turned steel hard at the desire in her voice. "I want you, too, but the baby … are you sure? Sweetheart, you've been sick, stressed … I don't want to hurt you." God, the way he felt right now, he'd be too rough. He'd hurt her. He'd cut off his own dick before he did that.

"Risto Smith, I'm pregnant, not dead." She gripped his thigh and squeezed. "I expect to have lots and lots of balls-to-the-wall sex before I deliver our child. So get used to the idea. I know when I get as big as a hippo, you might not want…"

"Shh, Callie," he pulled the hand petting him to his mouth and kissed the tips of her fingers before placing her hand on the hard-on threatening to burst through his jeans, "you could be as big as an elephant, and I'd want to make love to you. It's just I don't want to hurt the baby."

"I asked the doctor—in case you came after me—and she said I was good to go for sex. Might have to change positions as my stomach gets bigger, but anything else is fine. And I know for a fact Keely had lots of sex right up until she had her baby because she told me so. And she's a dainty fairy-like girl compared to me."

Risto nodded. He recalled many a time at Sanctuary when Ren and Keely excused themselves after dinner to go to their house. The following mornings at breakfast Ren had appeared extremely satisfied. "When we get home, you want sex—you get sex."

"I think this first time after being apart, it will be love-making, a seal on our commitment." Callie hesitated. "Well, at least it will be for me."

Jesus, she thinks it's just sex for me?

"Callie, when I have sex with you, it's always love-making. Always. From the first time, I knew it was different than what I'd experienced with other women. I may have been a stubborn, thick-headed, dumb fuck as Conn named me, but never doubt that I knew you were the only woman for me. I love you, Calista Jean Meyers."

When she didn't respond, he turned his head. She was smiling and crying, a hand massaging her tummy and her other hand fisted on his thigh. "Why are you crying?"

"Because I'm happy." She unfisted her hand and stroked his thigh. The ring he gave her sending off flashes of light. "I love you, Marine." She sniffed and laughed.

"Is there a manual on this pregnancy shit a father-to-be can read so I don't fuck up or say something to hurt you or the baby?" He was one guy who always read the instructions.

"The doctor gave me a book." She patted her bottomless tote bag with her free hand. "I'll give it to you once we get home."

Home. She'd said home. A warm glow of contentment permeated his body. She loved him. She desired him. She accepted his protection and the home he could provide for her and the baby. What more could a man want? Nothing but the elimination of all danger to her. And with any luck, that would happen sooner, rather than later.

He slowed down and took the narrow county road, cleared much better than the state highway had been, to Osprey's Point. Luck on their side and the weather calming down long enough, he'd have Callie home within the next hour or so.

Callie stepped into Big Earl's, the small grocery slash diner slash marina office which comprised the largest commercial building in the tiny municipality of Osprey's Point. There were several other small businesses, all closed this time of the morning, or maybe for the season. Early winter in the U.P. wasn't mild. She imagined the busiest time of the year would be high summer, July and August, when people came to the Cisco Chain of Lakes region for weekend vacations and breaks from the heat of the cities. Through the swirling clouds of snow, she'd caught glimpses of a lot of darkened cottages and mini-mansions along the lake shore and the single road into town.

"May I help you?" A grizzled giant, taller and far broader than Risto, stepped from the diner area into the small grocery. He carried himself like a soldier. "You have car trouble or something?"

"No. Risto Smith dropped me off. He's parking in his spot."

"You a lady friend of Risto?" He looked her up, then down. She saw recognition in his eyes. He smiled. "I know you. You're that model on the swimsuit issues." He stepped forward and offered his hand. "I'm Earl. My friends call me Big Earl."

She took his hand and noted how gingerly he treated her much smaller one. She smiled. "You consider Risto a friend?"

"Yes, ma'am. We went to school together from third grade through high school graduation. Since he lived here year round, we became buddies."

"Then I'm Callie, and I'll call you Big Earl."

"Good enough. You need a cup of coffee or something?" He pulled her into the diner and seated her at the counter.

"Hot chocolate would be great if you have it." She took off her gloves and shoved them into the pocket of her woven wool coat with its sheepskin lining. Again, she mentally thanked whoever watched over her that she'd worn her warmest coat and boots to the appointment yesterday. She shrugged out of the heavy coat and laid it over an empty stool next to her. Her tote she hooked on the purse hanger under the counter.

"Here ya go." He placed a steaming mug with whipped cream and chocolate sprinkles on top in front of her, then glanced at her left hand. He touched the engagement ring lightly with a finger the size of a cigar. "Ahh, you're Risto's for sure with this ring. Just so you know, you are the first and only woman I've ever seen him bring here. Ever. Honest Injun." He held up his hand in a parody of every television Indian she'd ever seen.

"You Native American, Big Earl?" She was pretty sure, like Risto he had some in him. His darker skin looked natural and not a tan. He had dark eyes and hair. The facial hair came from the other part of his heritage, she was sure.

"Yeah, with some good Swedish thrown in to boot." He wiped the sparkling clean counter with a cloth. "Here's your man. Risto," he yelled, "your lady's in here, drinking some of my fine Belgian hot chocolate."

Risto came up behind her and kissed her cheek, then sat next to her, shrugging off his coat and placing it over hers. "Hot chocolate sounds good. You want some breakfast, sweetheart? I've got the boat engine warming up. I want to give it another half hour. It's damn cold out there."

She touched her stomach and thought about how she felt.

"How much chop will we be experiencing?"

"Winds are dying down. Maybe a foot to a foot and a half. My island's only ten minutes from the dock." He turned to Big Earl. "What do you think?"

Big Earl stared at the hand on her abdomen and a knowing smile curved his lips. "You should be fine. You a good sailor, Callie?"

"Normally, yes." Her stomach growled, and the two men laughed. "Oatmeal sounds good if you have it. Nothing greasy or smelly for now."

Big Earl looked from her to Risto and back. "Oatmeal for the lady. What about you, you lucky dog?"

"I'll eat oatmeal also and a nine-grain bagel with cream cheese."

"That sounds good, can I have a bite of your bagel?" She turned to Risto who put an arm around her and pulled her to him then kissed her.

He spoke against her lips. "You can have a bite of anything of mine."

Big Earl threw back his head and laughed, the sound echoing around the small diner. "Behave yourself, old buddy. This is a decent family place."

"Shut the fuck up, Big Earl. You've never been decent a day in your life." He stroked Callie's face. "We'll need to keep an eye on my old friend and make sure he doesn't put poison in my oatmeal. The man would try to steal you from me in an instant."

Big Earl chuckled as he began to make the oatmeal from scratch. Callie had expected instant. Her taste buds salivated, she loved real oatmeal. "Callie, if you ever want a real man, you come to me."

Risto snarled, "Fuck you, Earl."

"You'll need to clean up your language with a lady in your life." Big Earl winked at Callie then said, "Old Annie was at your place two days ago, getting things ready for your arrival.

She stocked up on dry goods and stuff for your freezer. Told me to tell you that you only needed fresh fruit and vegetables and maybe some milk."

"Got it." Risto smoothed a hand down her back. "You drink milk?"

"Not usually, but the doctor said it would be good for me and the baby. Skim milk or two percent would be fine. I don't usually do well with milk." She patted her tummy again and Risto's hand covered hers. His possessive yet gentle touch made her vaginal muscles clench and her clit throb. She noted the bulge behind his jeans and smiled. He wanted her just as much as she wanted him.

"You have any skim milk, Earl?" Risto asked.

"Yeah, blue label. Freshest at the back. Try some cottage cheese, Callie. Just as much calcium and something about the processing lessens the side effects from lactose intolerance." At Risto's raised eyebrow, Earl added, "My sister had the same problems with milk so she figured out alternatives when she was pregnant." He shot Callie a grin. "You got a good multi-vitamin?"

God save her, another over-protective alpha male. Maybe going to Sanctuary until after the baby came was a good idea. At least she'd have Keely on her side. "Yeah, the doctor recommended one. I bought some in Chicago. I guess you figured out I'm pregnant."

"Sort of added it all up. Congratulations to you both. When's the newest little Smith hellion due?"

Risto snarled. Callie giggled and answered, "About seven months—so middle of June."

"June's a fine month around here." He placed a bagel and cream cheese on the counter between their place settings. "Go get the groceries, Risto. I won't steal your lady. Oatmeal will be ready in about four more minutes."

"We won't be here in June, Earl. I'm hiding Callie away at my place in Sanctuary until after the baby is born—for her safety."

"Danger?" Big Earl shot him a questioning glance.

Risto exhaled and ran a hand through his hair. He looked tired and angry all of a sudden. "There's a really bad-ass fucker stalking Callie."

"Why is this fucker still alive?" Big Earl slapped a hand on the counter, his pleasant face turning ugly. Even with his gaze on Risto, Callie could tell Big Earl was searching for potential danger around them. He was like Risto and every other superbly trained soldier she'd ever met. She'd bet her new engagement ring he was ex-Special Forces.

"He's alive because I had to get Callie out of Colombia—and he was hiding when I went back for him." Callie gasped. No one had told her the SSI missions Risto was on were about getting Cruz. She would've been catatonic with worry if she'd known. "He's a Colombian paramilitary leader and muscle for a drug cartel centered in and around Cartagena. Well, he was. Messing with Callie got him ejected by Paco, the head of the cartel."

"Fucking Jaime fucking Cruz is after your woman?" Big Earl braced his hands on the counter. "How in the fucking hell did a sweet woman like Callie get on that fucking bastard's radar?" He looked at her. "Excuse my language."

She waved it off. "Marine brat here. And the asswipe saw me, decided he wanted me, and bribed my agent into getting me to Cartagena for a modeling job. When I arrived, he told me he was keeping me—if I didn't cooperate, he'd kill my younger twin brothers."

Big Earl turned away and muttered something vile sounding under his breath, then turned back. "So, SSI sent Risto in to get you." It was a statement not a question which told her Big Earl knew all about what SSI was and what Risto did for them.

"Yeah. I spent most of my formative years at Camp Lejeune and grew up alongside the Walsh kids, so I turned to Keely's husband when I knew I was in trouble over my head."

"I've met most of the male Walshes. Good men." Big Earl smiled. "Know Ren Maddox also. He just sent me a picture of him and Keely and little Riley." He walked over to a small desk area, picked up a framed picture and brought it over. "Damn fine looking family. I expect a similar photo from you two." He set the picture on the counter and turned back to his oatmeal.

Risto picked up the picture so they could examine it together. "Damn, they look happy. Just think, that'll be us by the end of next summer."

"Yeah. I've held Riley. I fell in love with him. He smiled at me and cooed. God, I want to hold my baby now."

He kissed her. "It'll happen. We'll hold him together. What were you doing in Sanctuary? I must've been out of the country when you were there. I thought Keely told me you were doing your work from Chicago?"

"I was. I was also in Idaho for a week—maybe while you were chasing Cruz?" She poked him in the ribs. "No one told me. Why did you…"

"Shh, Ren sent me. Cruz needed to be taken down. But Paco had already scared him off by the time I got back to Cartagena. We have a good idea of where he went and that would've been my next mission. But he's here and will come to us. We can take him out on our turf."

She nodded. "Home field advantage works for me. Plus, he and his men aren't used to the snow and cold. We'll have Mother Nature on our side."

"You," he tapped her nose, "will be safely locked away on my island. And we men will be taking care of Cruz and his thugs. Now, what were you doing at Sanctuary?"

If he thought he would tuck her safely away when she could help, he had another think coming. "I was training on their software systems before I began my search for the hidden accounts. Keely's program is far superior to what I used in college. Also, Ren wanted me to pass his weapons certification so I could get a license to carry concealed in Idaho for when I'm there. I already had a license in Illinois and Chicago, but that wasn't good enough. Keely just laughed at him when he said he wanted to see how out of practice I was."

Big Earl placed their bowls on the counter. "Eat, Risto. You have time to get your groceries later. There's supposed to be a calm between the weather systems, might as well take advantage of the break so Callie won't get sick on the ride to the island." Then he looked at her with something akin to reverence. "You shoot?"

"Oh hell yeah, she can." Risto laughed as he put brown sugar on his oatmeal and tossed some raisins on it. "Tell him, baby."

"Expert-rated with both sniper rifle and hand gun." She took the raisins from Risto and added them to her oatmeal along with maple syrup. "I used Keely's sniper rifle, she has a really sweet Lapua, and scored one hundred percent kills at every distance. Scored a hundred percent kills with three different pistols, none of which were fitted for a woman. Ren shut up then and asked me if I wanted to train to be a field operative rather than an analyst. Said he needed some female operatives for personal security jobs and some undercover HUMINT work."

"Fuck no. Not gonna happen. Keely might want to do..."

Callie touched his chest and turned into the body which had automatically surrounded her at the perceived threat. "Calm down, tiger. I told Ren no. I can't fight hand-to-hand worth a damn. I'm an analyst—period. And while I did okay in Colombia and Chicago when confronted with a threat, I couldn't live like that. I want to be there when you come home so I can help you decompress and shut out the rest of the world."

"Sweet Jesus, I'll love coming home to you and our babies and the home you'll make for us." He touched his forehead to hers. "I can't handle you being in danger, baby. But just so we're clear, you've handled everything thrown at you better than anyone could've ever expected. You are one of the bravest women I've ever met, and I know you'd defend our home and children until I could get to you. No warrior has ever had a better woman by his side."

Callie leaned her forehead on Risto's shoulder, hiding the tears his praise brought to her eyes. She sniffed. "Damn hormones."

Risto laughed and kissed her ear, then nuzzled her neck. She lifted her head and kissed him, then turned back to her oatmeal.

"You are one lucky son of a bitch, Risto. Got any sisters, Callie?" Big Earl smiled at them, but his eyes held sadness.

"Sorry, Big Earl. Just eighteen-year-old twin brothers." She took a bite of the oatmeal. "Yum. You'd make some woman a great husband—you can cook. Did you train as a chef? I noticed some unusually gourmet items on the menu."

"No trained chef." Risto spoke before Big Earl could. "Earl's a former Army Ranger. He worked some joint covert ops with Ren while they both were in Special Forces. He came home to Osprey's Point when he mustered out and decided to be a regular civilian. We resumed our childhood friendship when I came back home after I left the Marines. He was one of the people who sent me to the Maddoxes when I couldn't adjust to civilian life as well as he did."

Callie smiled at the big man. "Well, I'll keep any eye out for just the right woman for you, Big Earl."

Earl chuckled. "I'd appreciate that. Ex-models who can shoot and like to nest would suit me just fine. But I figure you're one of a kind. I'm happy my friend managed to find you." He turned serious. "So, I need to keep my eyes peeled for Cruz and his mercenaries? I'd heard through the ex-military grapevine Paco threatened old Jaime with the whole Colombian neck tie if he ever showed his face in the country again. I had no idea you were involved in all that. Some bad shit, brother."

"I've got help coming, but we'd appreciate all the extra assistance you're willing to give. I'll be flying to Watersmeet to pick up Conn and one of his men, Berto, later today. Ren told me he's sending us the Walsh twins, both just left the SEALs within the last week. They're coming from Chicago. We're setting a trap for Cruz."

"Conn Redmond?" Risto nodded. Big Earl smiled. "Haven't seen old Conn since, well, it's classified, but it's been a while. Count me in, buddy. You know several of the locals are ex-military and can cover your asses. Just yell."

Callie looked between the two men. "Cruz doesn't have a chance with men like you on the job." She glanced out the window to see a sliver of sun shine through a break in the snow-filled clouds and sparkle off the steel gray waters of the lake. She smiled. "Damn, I love cold, snowy weather. No anacondas. No mosquitoes. No heat stroke." She turned to Risto. "I can live here, Marine. Here or Sanctuary. Either place I can make us a home. As long as you come back to me, I'll be happy. And if you don't, I'll come find you."

"Shit, Risto." Big Earl punched Risto in the arm. "I said it before but it bears repeating, you are one hell of a lucky man."

Risto took Callie's face between his hands. "Yeah, I know."

Then he kissed her, right in front of Big Earl, as a ray of sunshine came through the windows and warmed their bodies. She took it as an omen that whatever happened, it would be a cold day in hell before a cretin like Cruz could take this new life away from her.

Chapter Eighteen

Later Wednesday morning. Risto's island.

Risto entered the unlocking code, then a security disarming code on the front door to his house, then ushered Callie inside. "Make yourself at home. I'll bring in the groceries and your other bags."

Awe-struck, Callie turned around in a circle, taking in the large open room. She'd been impressed with the size of the island and the house's exterior but the interior stunned her. This was *Architectural Digest* gorgeous. She sat on a contemporary version of an Amish settle and took off her snow-covered boots, then stood up and walked into what she would call a great room.

The main living area was open-concept. The great room flowed into the kitchen and eating area. A wall of floor-to-ceiling windows, some with French doors, overlooked the lake and a patio area carved from the escarpment upon which the house had been built. She wiggled her toes on the stained-concrete floors and found them warm to her stocking-covered feet. The house had radiant heat, very eco-conscious. The furnishings were contemporary, mostly Scandinavian in design, with touches of Native American textiles and accessories. The rugs scattered about the room belonged in a museum. While contemporary rooms often seemed cold and sterile, this one was warm, lived in.

She walked to the bar counter separating the kitchen from the great room and placed her tote on top of the black granite and her coat on a bar stool. When she heard the low beep of the security system, she turned and eyed Risto as he brought in the rest of their things through a side hallway off the kitchen leading to another exterior door. She waved a hand around. "This is amazing."

His face blank of all emotion, he eyed her closely. After a few seconds, he nodded, then smiled. "You like it. Good. That's good. If you want to change … um, redecorate…"

This place was important to him and she hurried to reassure him. "You've never seen my house in Lincoln Park. While the exterior is early twentieth century Chicago-style, its interior could be almost a duplicate of this house. I have different accents, mostly items I picked up in places I modeled, many of them are primitive pieces and textiles. When we close up my place, I'd like to bring some of those pieces and mix them in. They'd blend nicely."

"You don't have to close your Chicago house, Callie. We can afford both places. You might want your brothers to have it someday. And, of course, you should bring some of your treasures here. This is your home now."

Risto set the groceries on the counter top and approached her. He pulled her to him. With her head resting against his chest, he smoothed a hand over her tousled hair. "We'll also have a cabin in Idaho once we build it. Right now, my suite of rooms is in the main lodge at Sanctuary. You'll have to take some of your things there also." He kissed the top of her head. "Want to help me put the groceries away?"

"Sure. I need to learn where everything is so I can cook for you." She stroked a hand over his chest. The flare of his nostrils indicated he liked her touching him. Good, she intended to touch him a lot more once the groceries were stored.

"You can cook?" he teased. "I thought models existed on air, water and lettuce."

She punched him on the arm. "Yes, I can cook. I had two brothers otherwise known as bottomless pits. I can also grill and I make a mean barbeque." She had an outdoor kitchen on the patio. She swept a hand over her torso. "Plus, do I look as if I missed many meals?"

His dark eyes held lambent heat as he scanned her body. "You look perfect."

She blushed. As many times as she'd heard those words, they meant so much more coming from the man she loved. "Good genes. Lots of exercise. And keeping junk food binges to a minimum. But I love meat, potatoes, any carb form you can name. My man won't starve." She winked then walked around the counter and began to take things out of the sacks. "I'll unload. You give me the tour of the kitchen and show me where things go."

"Okay." He walked around the kitchen, gesturing as if he were a realtor. A fun side she had never seen in him before. She was enchanted. "Here we have your gourmet gas range with a pop-up hood." It was opposite the bar counter which had a built-in sink and a dishwasher underneath. "We then have a double oven, one is convection and one, microwave. And here is the all-important, big-ass stainless steel refrigerator. There's a stand-up freezer in the mud room, just off the kitchen. The laundry facilities are there as is an exit to the covered boat dock." He gestured to the hall he'd used earlier.

"And here," he opened a door between the gas cook top and the refrigerator, "is the walk-in pantry where all the dry goods go." He took some of the items she'd set out and put them away in the pantry. "The kitchen cupboards contain all the usual dishes and cookware. Feel free to poke around."

"Spices? Are they in the pantry?" She liked to make spicy food and she wanted to make a list of any additional spices and herbs they might need to purchase. Idly, she pulled open a drawer next to the sink and found dish towels.

"All dry seasonings are here, next to the gas cook top." He opened an upper cupboard and showed her a highly organized set of spice shelving. "By the way, the gas supply for the cook top and the steam radiant heat is propane, and the tanks are full. I have them checked monthly." He cornered her against the counter, then gathered her into his arms. It was nice to know she wasn't the only one who needed to touch. "You think you can be happy here?"

She leaned back and looked at him. He sounded worried—looked it too. Her dominant, drop-him-in-the-middle-of-nowhere-and-he-could-survive marine was insecure as far as it concerned her. That was unacceptable.

She rushed to reassure him. "I'm happy wherever you are. Here. In Idaho. On a boat on the Atrato River. In a hovel in the middle of Siberia. Anywhere. You complete me."

He smiled, the coming-from-his-heart-and-soul smile she wanted to see more often. "God, baby. I feel the same way." Then his smile dimmed somewhat. "I don't want you on any more boats in the Darien Gap. And a hovel in Siberia is out, also. I can't stand the thought of you in danger."

She petted his chest then trailed a hand to his face where she swept her thumb over his mouth. He kissed it. "I really liked the people in Ungaía. It's not the place that's bad, Risto, you know that. Those people were living their lives just as we do, but it's people such as Cruz and his kind who spoil such places for everyone else."

"I agree. But from here on out, you are an analyst—and analysts don't need to physically go out and nab the bad guys. Agreed?"

"Agreed—after we get Cruz out of our lives."

"I'll get Cruz out of our lives."

She mentally sighed. Whether he liked it or not, she would be right there with him when he and the others were taking Cruz down. There was always a role to play—she could be back-up, but one thing was for damn sure, she refused to be stuck away on this island while he was out there risking his ass. But that argument was for later—now was the time for loving.

Risto took the hand touching his face and placed a kiss on her palm, then enfolded it in a gentle grip and held their joined hands against his chest. "Let's get the perishables put away, Callie. I want you to lie down and rest before the men get here. I'm betting you haven't had more than short naps in the last twenty-four hours."

"You'd be right on that point." She looked up. "I haven't slept well since the last time I was in your arms at Conn's."

His eyes dilated and the heat she sensed earlier now glittered in his gaze. "I remember. You were like quicksilver in my arms, made to fit only me. I loved holding you as you slept, protecting you with my body. I knew I wanted you forever, but I was afraid…"

"Afraid?" She kissed his chin then scolded him gently. "Yeah, Conn told me what you were afraid of. How could you think you weren't what I needed? I knew instantly you were the man I'd waited for all those years. A man like my father and the men he trained. A brave and honorable man. A man who'd protect me with everything in him. What woman wouldn't want a man like you?"

He laughed and shook his head. "Lots of them. But I'm sure as hell lucky I found the one woman who wanted me as I am. I'm not sure I could change."

"As I said before, you don't need to."

"Well, you might want to domesticate me somewhat before the baby arrives." He chuckled. "If we have a little girl, I can't see her wanting to play survival games during playtime." Callie giggled. He arched a brow. "What?"

"Um, Keely and I used to take our Barbies and dress them in GI Joe outfits and play war with them in the sandbox. I just had an image of you on the floor, playing war-dolls with a little girl with your hair and my eyes."

He grinned. "I like that image. A lot."

"So do I."

Risto crowded her against the counter. His thick erection pulsed against her stomach, branding her with his heat. Her knees grew weak at the memory of how his cock filled her tight channel as he'd born her weight and taken her against the door in Ungaía. His strong hands, calloused from years of shooting and fighting, smoothed up and down her arms, creating an exciting friction which went straight to her clit. She clung to his waist as arousal swept over her. His hips circled, rubbing his hard-on against her. Her womb clenched and her panties got wetter. He slipped a hand under her sweater and deftly unhooked her bra. If she didn't stop him, he'd take her against the counter. And as much as she would like that, she felt icky and wanted a shower and then a bed for their first encounter since Colombia.

Rubbing her cheek over his chest, she eyed the items yet to be put away. She shoved at his waist in an attempt to put some distance between their lower bodies. He didn't budge. "Hold that thought, tiger ... the milk is getting warm. Let's get this stuff put away so I can take a shower before we take this to our bed. I've been in these clothes for almost twenty-four hours. I smell like sweat and stale bus air."

He leaned over and nipped her earlobe. "You smell like my Callie." He sighed. Visibly controlling his ardor, he moved away. "But a shower with me to assist sounds fun." He swept a finger over one beaded nipple poking against her sweater. "I recall our last shower with great fondness." He leaned down and took the perked tip into his mouth and suckled it through the thin wool of her sweater.

"I'd love your assistance." She also recalled the showers she'd previously shared with him with great fondness and a lot of lust. "Don't get my hair wet, mister. It takes forever to dry, and I don't want to go to bed with wet hair."

He saluted. "Ma'am, yes, ma'am. Your wishes are my

wishes." He picked up a bunch of vegetables and walked to the refrigerator.

She handed him the cottage cheese Big Earl had suggested and the milk. "You'll be going to bed with me?"

"Until Conn calls." He grinned. "Plus, I plan on doing more than going to bed. You requested some love-making, if I recall. I think you need me to relax you so you can get a good rest."

Callie snorted. "Is that what you're calling sex now? Relaxation? So, any time you think I need relaxing, you'll make love to me?"

He laughed. "There's that attitude I love." He flicked the tip of her nose with a gentle finger. "Your nose wrinkles up so cute when you sniff at me."

She passed him some fresh fruit. "Answer the question."

He leaned over to kiss her. "Quality sex—my love-making—is better than muscle relaxants."

Callie's nipples budded even more tightly. "I recall it working at Conn's house."

"Yeah, and just think, I can put you to sleep that way for the rest of our lives." He cupped her breasts and stroked his thumbs across her aching nipples. "You know the nicest thing about quality sex with me, Callie?"

"There's an unlimited supply and it's free?" She shoved a bag of shredded lettuce into his chest, forcing him to let go of her breasts in order to catch it. If he didn't stop teasing her, she'd drop to her knees and put her mouth on his cock. Turn-about teasing was fair play.

"Well, those are good things, but I was thinking more along the lines of quality sex is also the best way to wake up in the morning." He shot her a wicked glance as he shut the refrigerator door.

"My goodness," she said with mock reverence. "You mean sex is both an upper and a downer?"

"It's all in the technique." He held out a hand. "That's the last of the groceries, Callie. Let's get you in the shower. I'll reset the security then join you."

She placed her hand in his. "Lead on. I can't wait to see the master bedroom and bath. If they're anything like the main living areas, I'll think I've died and gone to interior decorating heaven."

Risto raised their joined hands to his lips. "I love having you here, Calista Jean Meyers. I love the fact you're carrying my child. I worship and adore you. And if ever a day goes by and I forget to tell you, kick my ass."

Tears streamed down Callie's cheeks. "Those have to be the nicest words anyone has ever said to me."

He let go of her hand and placed his arm around her waist and walked her into a huge bedroom with another beautiful view of the lake. But it was the bed which drew a gasp from her. It was a king-size, four-poster made of black iron. The four posts, headboard and footboard had intricate metal work depicting mountains, trees and animals native to North America. It was a dramatic piece of art. The woven bedspread, just like all the woven area rugs in the house, probably belonged in a museum.

They walked toward the bed. "Like it?" He rubbed her waist.

She traced the metalwork. "This is exquisite. Who made it?"

"My maternal grandfather. His metal pieces are in museums. My maternal grandmother wove the bedspread—and all the area rugs. The bedspread reminds me of your coat."

"I bought the coat in Canada from a museum shop on a reservation." She stroked the woven cover; the weave was so fine it felt like satin. "This bedspread is worth a small fortune. I'm almost afraid to sleep under it, what if I get sick…"

"Callie, my grandmother made the spread for me to sleep under with my wife. It's not a museum piece here. It's our bedspread on our marriage bed. It will wash."

She nodded. "Um, Big Earl said you never brought women here…" She couldn't voice her question. She wasn't sure she really wanted or needed to know the answer.

"Callie." He tipped up her chin. "Open those gorgeous eyes and look at me." She did as he asked and saw love and understanding in his gaze. "I've had a lot of women over the years—and they meant nothing to me beyond immediate sexual satisfaction. No other woman has slept in that bed, under that blanket. This house was my refuge. No other woman has ever stepped inside the house other than Old Annie, my cleaning lady. You are the only woman who will ever sleep in that bed with me."

She swallowed and opened her mouth to say something. He stopped her words with his mouth. Once he'd kissed her into silence, he continued, "Let's clear the air about a few other things. You're fairly inexperienced. Our few times together, I've been pretty dominant and at times rough. I can't change my nature and you've not asked me to, but, baby, if I ever do anything…"

"Shh, Marine." It was her turn to cut him off; she covered his mouth with her fingers. "It's my turn to clear some things up." His eyes crinkled with laughter and his lips curved into a wide, natural smile under her fingertips. He nodded. "Okay, I like you in control sexually." His nostrils flared at her words, his fingers tightened briefly where he held her chin. "You make me feel wonderful. And, I'm sure you can make me feel a lot better as we explore our sexual needs together. I'm not a prude and am open to learning from your experience."

He groaned, his high cheekbones flushed red with his arousal. He moved her fingers from his mouth. "Callie…"

"Enh, I'm not done." He nipped her lower lip in a mock punishment and rubbed his cock against her lower body. "I also like that you're possessive and protective of me in certain situations outside of the bedroom. It might not be a popular feminist viewpoint, but it's mine. As long as you respect my intelligence and capabilities, I have no issues giving control over to you in dangerous situations. If you go all cave man when I don't think I need it, I'll let you know."

Laughing, Risto hugged and rocked her within the circle of his arms. "Does that mean I can tie you to our bed some day and give you so many orgasms you'll beg me to take you?" He waggled his eyebrows.

Callie moaned. "God, yes. I think I just had a mini-orgasm thinking about it." She peered up at him. "But no sadistic shit."

"God, sweetheart, I'm not a sadist. I'd never mar an inch of you. I like to make my women scream with pleasure and then take my own—again and again. I've found bondage heightens the pleasure for some women. I enjoy giving a woman more pleasure than she thinks she can handle."

"All that pleasure giving of yours is mine now."

"I'm definitely a one-woman man from now on. My maternal grandparents had a happy fifty-year marriage. I heard rumors grandfather was pretty kinky and my grandmother loved it." He winked.

"They're dead?"

He nodded. "Grandfather went first, massive stroke. Grandmother lived for a few more months and then died. Of grief. She told me she couldn't live in a world without him, so she literally willed herself to die and joined him in the next life."

"That's the way it would be with me. I know after the last two months, I don't want to live in a world without you."

"I feel the same way, sweetheart." He brushed a kiss over the top of her head. Patting her on the butt, he moved her toward a set of double doors. "Now, let's get you in the shower."

Risto checked all the windows and doors and made sure the security system was set for its highest alert. If anyone approached the island by air or water, if anything tripped the perimeter security to the house, the system would blare a warning. He had more to protect now than just a house and SSI technology. He had the safety of his woman and unborn child to ensure.

Entering the bedroom, he heard the steam shower and imagined Callie naked, enjoying the wet heat. No worries about there being enough hot water for the shower sex he wanted, he had put in a state-of-the-art, hot-water-on-demand system. He walked to the bathroom, stripping his clothing as he went. Naked, he opened the glass doors to the huge shower with its multiple heads and jets and steam vents.

Callie sat on the built-in bench, her towel-wrapped head braced on the tile wall and her long, perfectly curved and deliciously naked body stretched out on the bench. Her eyes were closed and a slight smile curved her lips.

"What are you staring at? You've seen me naked before." She opened her eyes. They glittered like silver gems under the shower's indirect lighting. Her gaze covered him quickly, zeroing in on his erection. She licked her lips.

Yeah, I want those beautiful lush lips on me, baby. He hadn't let her finish him in Ungaía, he'd been too eager to enter her pussy.

"I've never seen you this rosy pink before." He nudged her legs to the floor of the shower and sat next to her. He stroked a finger along her neck, down the middle of her chest to her belly button, then into the neatly trimmed triangle of blonde curly hair above her sex. He stopped there, swirling his fingertip through the silky curls. "You were waxed before, but I like this better." He traced her labia and found them free of hair. She whimpered with each stroke of his finger, her hips arching as if begging for more. "Oh, yeah, I like this a lot." She'd be so easy to eat out, sensitive, but with the feminine curls pointing the way.

"Risto," she encircled his cock with her hand, "do I finally get to suck you?" Gripping him tightly, just the way he liked, she pumped his cock slowly, her thumb sweeping over the tip each time she reached the top.

He covered her hand with his and pulled it away. "Hell, yeah, I want your mouth on me, Callie. But only if you're up to it."

She immediately dropped to her knees and in between his legs. She took his cock back into her hand and swiped a gentle thumb over the small drop of precum oozing from his slit, then licked the moisture from her thumb. "Yummy."

Fighting the urge to thrust into her mouth, he forced himself to lean against the tile wall. He searched her face for any signs of discomfort or illness. "Callie? You sure? You were so tired earlier … we don't…"

She tightened her hand around his steel-hard length. "Oh, yes, we do." She licked at his cockhead daintily like a momma cat licking a kitten. Every third lick or so, she swiped the taste of him from her lips with her tongue and hummed. Her eyes had darkened to slate gray with lust. "I'm fine. This time you come in my mouth. You stopped me in Ungaía."

"Yeah, I remember." He caressed her face as she balanced his balls in one hand and her other held onto his cock. "Yeah, take the edge off, baby. I want to last forever when I'm inside you."

She sighed. "I want that too. I love the feel of you in my pussy. I've dreamt about it. I've been so empty, so cold without you."

"No more dreaming. You're with me now and I'll never let you go again." He angled his head and nodded toward the hand caressing his dick. "You plan on teasing me forever? Or, are you going to put those sexy lips around my dick and make me cum?"

Callie looked at him, worry in her expression. "What's

wrong?" He tipped her chin up. "Tell me."

"I don't have much … well, not really any … just one time … um, I want to do it right." She scrunched her nose. "I'm pretty A-type."

He chuckled. "Well, sweetheart, from a guy's point of view, it's pretty hard to mess up a blow job. Biting is about the only way I know of. Although there are guys, myself included, who get off on a scrape of teeth when highly aroused. Men just like a pretty girl's mouth on them—anywhere."

Callie pursed her bottom lip while absently fondling his cock. He could almost see the wheels turning in her head. Finally, she leaned over and licked around and over the head of his cock several times, then lifted her head to look up at his face. When he grunted and nodded, she repeated the motion, but this time licked the head and up and down his shaft as if cleaning up a messy ice cream cone. "That's very good, baby. Just like that." His hips jerked and he knew in the future he'd get hard watching her eat a cone.

She stopped and licked her lips. "Salty. I like your taste."

"It felt good. Do it again."

Callie grinned then licked his cock from root to head several times, pausing to flick her tongue over the tip. The feel of her tongue had him groaning. "So good. Now, suck me."

She frowned and he realized her insecurities had risen to the forefront of her mind again.

"Like this, sweetheart." He placed a hand over the one holding his cock for her tongue and moved it. "Put your hand here." He wrapped her fingers around the base. He was thick and her fingers did not touch but her grip was firm and felt so good he almost shot his wad right then and there. He throttled back the urge to cum; he wanted to cum in her mouth.

"Hold on tight." She squeezed him and stopped adding pressure at the touch of his finger. "That's good. You control how deeply I can thrust." He moved his hand from hers and cupped the back of her towel-covered head. "Now, take me in your mouth." She placed her lips over his cock head and took him in to the base of the glans and stopped. The hand not fisting him fondled his balls.

"Fuck, your instincts are good. I love my balls fondled." She nodded, forcing his cock to move even farther into her warm mouth. He jerked. God, her mouth was so hot. He was so close. The mere thought of her sucking him off had him primed to blow as soon as he entered her sweet mouth. All that was keeping him from thrusting into her was his need to make sure she was comfortable with what they were doing.

He begged. "Jesus, baby, take more of me, please. I want to be fucking that sweet mouth when I come."

Callie moaned in the back of her throat and took another inch or so into her mouth. "That's the way. Just take me in at your own pace. It feels so good. Your lips and mouth are heaven." She tightened her grip on his cock and moaned low in her throat as she took in another bit of him. He arched his hips forward, gently thrusting into her hot little mouth. "So fucking good. Loosen up with your mouth, let me do the work."

She widened her lips and allowed him to thrust in and out of her mouth. He gritted his teeth and forced himself to keep his thrusts shallow. She wasn't ready for deep throating him yet. He wanted her to enjoy giving him head, not fear the experience.

Then she relaxed her grip around his cock to take in another inch. As she caught on to his rhythm, she hollowed her cheeks and took control of his cock, moving up and down on his length. He stroked her face with one hand, while petting her breasts with his other. The pressure to come was there, but he enjoyed the sensations so much he wanted to push his orgasm off as long as he could. He knew it would be worth the wait. When Callie added a slight scraping of teeth to his shaft on her upward motion and lots of tongue on her downward, he swore under his breath as he fought not to go wild and thrust like crazy. "Fuck that feels good. God, you're a natural."

Her response was a long lick to his shaft. Tightening her lips around his cock, she gently squeezed his balls, adding a stroking finger to his perineum. "Fuck!"

All control was out the door. The teeth had pushed him to the limits, but the finger near his ass took him over. He gripped the back of her head and took back control, thrusting, his hips lifting off the tiled bench. Moving hard, fast, his groans and muttered curse words harmonized with her throaty moans until he shouted his release and poured his seed down her throat. Callie swallowed and licked as he lost all semblance of reality and floated on the sexual haze her mouth had wrought.

Risto released his grip on her head once his cock was spent. He laid his head weakly against the shower wall. All the pent-up need which had built ever since he'd left her in Panama was now gone. Unable to be apart from her for even a second, he pulled her from the floor and placed her across his lap. He cuddled her. She circled his neck with her arms. Between peppering kisses over her face, he murmured. "I love you … you looked so beautiful … loving me with your mouth. God, I love you. Don't ever leave me."

Finally, he took her mouth, red and swollen from pleasuring him, in a deep and hungry kiss. He tasted his seed mixed with her unique flavor. His cock came back to life with a vengeance, wanting a turn in her snug, hot little pussy.

After he sampled every bit of her mouth, he pulled away and looked at her. Her cheeks were rosy with arousal and her eyes shone with happiness and her love for him. She traced his mouth with a shaky finger. "Did I do okay?"

"Baby, if you'd done any better, I'd be lying on the shower floor in a puddle of goo."

"But I really didn't do anything," she blinked, "just sort of let you take over. Aren't I supposed to work a little harder? Like twine my tongue around your cock and do patterns and things?"

Risto chuckled. "You can do those things, later, maybe after I've had you a thousand times. I was too turned on to let you tease me. Right now, any time my dick is anywhere near you, it's gonna want to explode."

"I can understand that." She sighed and rubbed her nose against his throat and sniffed. "I think I had a small orgasm when you came in my mouth."

Risto nuzzled the damp hair around her forehead. "God, that is so sexy." He shifted her to sit next to him, then took one of her hands and placed it on his semi-aroused cock. "I don't think I've ever recovered this fast, at least not since I was a horny sixteen-year-old."

Callie snickered and stroked his dick with a finger. "I remember those years. I washed my brothers' sheets and underwear. Trust me, I know how easily teenage boys climax." She smoothed her thumb over his blood-swollen glans. "I'm all clean now. I want you to take me in that big beautiful bed. Reclaim what's yours."

"Oh, hell, yeah." Risto stood with her in his arms. He carried Callie to the computerized controls to the high-tech shower. "Hit the off-button." After she shut off the shower, he carried her out and set her down. Then, holding her to him with one arm, he reached for a heated towel and carefully dried her from her neck to her toes. He pulled the towel turban from her head and ran his fingers through the tangled tresses. "You have a brush?"

"In my tote. It's in the bedroom."

"I'll brush your hair before you go to sleep then." *After I've messed it up even more making love to you.*

"I'd like that." Callie took another heated towel from the rack and began to dry him. She went to her knees and paid particular attention to his cock and balls.

She was teasing him again. The little minx was playing with C-4 and her touch was the detonator. "Callie." He pulled her up from where she kneeled at eye level with his randy package.

"I want to make this erection last."

Her sultry smile had to be similar to what sailors had seen on the legendary Sirens' faces just before they wrecked their ships on hidden shoals. How a sexy woman such as Callie hadn't had a string of discarded lovers in her past would never cease to amaze him. He was just glad she was his now.

She turned and walked to the bedroom, throwing him the same sexy glance she'd had in Cartagena, the come-hither look she used in the perfume commercial he liked so much. This time he got to follow through and take his little sex goddess to bed. *Hoo-rah.*

Chapter Nineteen

Risto took in every luscious naked inch of Callie as she led the way to his, now their, bed. She pulled back the woven bed spread. Carefully folding it, she placed the spread at the end of the bed and out of the way. She smoothed a hand over the softly worn surface as if it were a priceless treasure.

"This is so beautiful." She turned shining eyes toward him. "Your grandmother was a true artist. You must be so proud." She stroked the sheets. "You are a naughty boy. Black sheets."

Her purred words pulled him from a vision of him holding her as their child suckled her breast, covered by the spread into which his grandmother had woven so much love. "*Your* naughty boy. You'll look gorgeous against them. Your creamy skin and blonde hair against all the dark."

Hell, he almost made himself come just picturing it. He moved quickly. Picking her up, he swung her over the bed and gently laid her in the middle. "Spread your legs and don't move." He positioned her hands by her head. "Leave your hands where I put them. No touching me—or I'll go too fast. I want to feast this time. I didn't get the chance before."

She watched him through narrowed lashes. Her breasts rose and fell with her rapid breaths. Scared or excited? He needed to know.

Risto crawled onto the bed and settled between her thighs, spreading them even wider so he had the perfect view of her glistening pussy lips. He sat back on his heels and placed the palm of his hand over her heart and felt it pounding. "Are you frightened?"

She wrinkled her forehead. "No, should I be?"

"Your heart rate is elevated, and you look as if you'll hyperventilate any second."

"I'm just excited. I ache. I need your cock in me."

"That's good. I never want you to be afraid of what we do in bed." He smoothed his hand over the swell of her right breast, barely touching her puckered nipple. Her breath hitched and she let out a faltering breath.

"Are your nipples more sensitive?" He stroked a finger over the right one and it beaded even more tightly. "They seem larger. Darker."

"Yes, from the baby." She swallowed. Her gaze moved from his hand to fixate on his cock, which was once again fully roused, its head leaking precum. She licked her lips and his greedy dick throbbed, wanting more of her mouth. He took several deep breaths and vowed he'd go slower this time if it killed him. She deserved foreplay—and goddamn, she'd get it.

"Risto?"

He focused on her face. Her eyes crinkled at the corners and he wondered what the imp in her would come up with next. "Yes, baby?"

"What if I move? What happens?" Her gaze glittered with excitement. "Will you tie me to the bed?"

"Nothing will happen … this time." The idea of her bound for his—and her—pleasure had him tightening his groin muscles to halt the climax threatening to overtake him. He coughed past the sudden constriction in his throat. "Tonight,

I want you to remain still so I can take my time. If you move, if you touch me, we'll be done before we get started."

She inhaled sharply then let it out slowly as she glanced toward his cock which moved toward her as if it were made of iron and she was the North Pole. A mischievous quirk to her lips had him grinning.

"What if I want you to tie me up? The doctor said strenuous sex would be okay until about the last month or so." Her hands fisted beside her head, but remained where he'd placed them. She was giving him *carte blanche* to play. He was excited and grateful to have found a woman willing to play in bed. "I'm not sure I can keep my hands to myself, Marine."

"Fuck, baby. Don't tempt the beast. I want to make this good for you."

She flashed him a wide smile. "I think I'd love your beast, but I'll try to behave … this time."

"Good girl." He leaned over and braced himself above her on his forearms, his hands holding hers to the mattress. She moaned as she tested his grip.

"God, that excites you. I smell your arousal." He brushed a kiss over her chin before taking her lower lip between his teeth and nipping it. He soothed away the tiny bite with his tongue, then thrust inside her mouth for a better taste of her. He ravished her mouth until her throaty moans and arching body drove him insane with lust. His cock leaked precum onto her smooth stomach.

Breaking off the kiss, he lifted his lips a whisper's length away. He released her hands. "This time is for you." He said the words, more to remind himself than her. She was being an absolute angel. It was his impatient dick that wanted to come inside her—and wanted it now.

"Risto?" She moved her hands from where he'd placed them and cradled the back of his head, urging him toward her lips. "I'm aching. Go slow some other day." She tugged his hair and met his mouth, her tongue demanding entrance.

He pulled back and gasped out hoarsely. "Jesus, baby, let me at least give you some foreplay this time."

"I'm ready now. You can do foreplay another time." She pulled him back to her mouth and kissed him hungrily.

God, she was just too fucking sweet and sexy. Steadying her head with one hand, he dueled her tongue and took back control of the kiss. His hips in collusion with his cock seemingly had a mind of their own. His body had instinctively aligned with her pussy; his cock sliding over her folds was covered in her copious juices.

"Shit, so wet. So hot. So fucking sweet." He let go of her face then leaned back. He used one hand to anchor both of hers above her head. With his free hand, he brushed the tip of one finger over her labia and clit. She gasped and bucked her hips to meet the light touch. He grinned. God she was so responsive.

"Watch me, Callie." He brought the finger he used to trace over her folds to his mouth and sucked her juices off it. "Yum." He swept the finger around her sex once more, drawing intricate patterns over her labia and clit, spreading her moisture around.

"Risto!" She wrapped a leg around his lower back and used the position to lever her hips even farther upward. "Cock. In. Now!"

"We'll get there." His finger tickling her opening, he lowered his head and took a puckered bud into his mouth, scraped it with his teeth. She mewled, then inhaled sharply when he gently bit the abraded tip. He soothed the nipple with his tongue. "Patience is rewarded."

"Patience is highly overrated—and pay back's a bitch." She yawned and closed her eyes.

Little tease. He laughed. "Am I boring you, baby?"

She opened her eyes and fluttered her lashes. "As I said, patience is overrated—and exhausting. I may just take a nap."

"Well then, let's see what I can do to wake you up."

He licked the nipple he'd teethed then sucked the skin around her areola, careful to avoid the highly sensitive bud. He moved to the other breast and teethed, sucked and licked it, spreading the pleasure around. He still shackled her hands with his while his free hand moved away from her opening and smoothed up and down her torso.

"Hold on to the headboard." He moved her hands and waited until she grasped the wrought iron. "Now, leave them there. Don't let go until I tell you." Her eyes widened and she nodded.

He used both hands now to stroke her torso from shoulder to breast to stomach and then down her legs, avoiding her pussy. He wanted to sensitize her whole body, adding to the sensations building in her sexual organs. Her body trembled with each sweep of his hands. She teethed her lower lip as she moaned low in her throat. Her eyes, dilated with her increasing excitement, followed each and every movement of his hands.

His arousal flared in response to hers. Her reaction to his touch, her absolute trust in his experience, were the greatest aphrodisiacs in the world. The love glowing beneath the trust made him feel as if he could conquer the world.

He sat back on his heels, giving each of them a break. He wanted both of them to simmer at the breaking point. He cuddled her breasts, cupping one in each hand, but made no move to stimulate her nipples. Her creamy breasts looked so fair against his darker skin. The disparity was exciting. "No other man will ever touch you in this way."

"No one." She stared him in the eye. "I was yours from the first moment I leapt into your arms in Cartagena."

"Damn right you were."

He released her breasts and pulled a pillow from the head of the bed. Lifting her hips with one hand, he shoved the pillow under her to support her lower back. She watched him curiously but said nothing, her hands still clutching the headboard. He moved farther down the bed and positioned his body so he could kiss the insides of her thighs. She shuddered. "So beautiful, all wide open for me."

A hand on her lower stomach, holding her in place, he nipped her inner thigh at the juncture with her pubic region. Callie inhaled and her stomach muscles tensed as she attempted to move her hips toward his mouth and close her thighs at the same time. His shoulders held her legs apart so she couldn't move away from anything he wished to do to her. He nuzzled the small cluster of curls at the top of her mons. He inhaled her scent and his mouth watered. "You smell good, as good as you taste, baby."

Braced on one forearm, he used that hand on her stomach to continue to hold her to the bed. With his other hand, he petted and smoothed the area above her folds as his lips and tongue began a journey of discovery to see what places gave her the most pleasure. Beginning on one side of her pussy, he licked a path up the outer labia, across the area at the top of her clitoral hood, then down the other side. He reversed the path, but this time increased the pressure above her clitoris. She gasped and let out a whispered "oh fuck."

"Good?" He repeated the motion, this time twirling his tongue around her clit, adding even more pressure.

"S'good. Nice. Makes me ache."

Her stomach muscles quivered under his trapping hand. He massaged them with gentle fingers. Her hips moved in a circle under his hand. "No moving until I say."

"Risto!" She attempted to throw his hand off so she could move into his tongue as it danced teasingly over her folds. He thwarted every wiggle and shift. "Beast! I'm so close … God, so close."

"You can take more." He nuzzled her thigh, his two-day-old beard reddening the tender skin. She attempted to close her thighs around his head. "You like having your thighs touched." He recalled how she'd reacted in the car in Colombia when he'd touched her thigh.

"Yes. I like you touching me anywhere." She shimmied her ass against the bed. "Stop teasing me. I need you inside me, Marine."

"Not yet." She swore and he chuckled. "Language, baby." He licked one inner thigh then the other before he went back to her cleft. This time he added teeth to the labia, tugging on them before resuming his licking path. She groaned, the sound somewhere between pain and pleasure. "Hurt or good?" he asked.

"Good, so good. More … I need…" She arched her head back against the pillow, struggling for breath.

"What do you need? Tell me." He nibbled her clit, scraping his teeth over the bundle of nerves to heighten the sensation before he moved to tongue her opening. He fucked her with his tongue several times, stopping when she attempted to meet his thrusts.

She lifted her head and glared. "Stop asking me questions—and just do it."

He massaged her tense stomach. "Calm down. I just want to make sure I'm pleasuring, not hurting you. I hurt you in Ungaía."

"Fuck … is that what this sexual torment is all about? You feel you need to make it up to me for that last time?" He nodded. She released the headboard and her hands went to his head. She stroked his hair with urgent, shaky fingers. "You didn't … you've never hurt me. Now or in Ungaía."

He stared. "Don't lie. Dammit, you gasped with pain in Ungaía when I took you against that fucking door. I never want to hear that sound from you again."

She snorted, the little get-a-clue sound making him hornier than he already was, then tugged his hair sharply. "Listen up, Marine. I loved what you did to me in Ungaía. And if you want to take me up against doors, on floors, over the backs of couches or in bed with me tied down seven ways to Sunday—I'm there. Understood?"

He examined her face. She was serious. She'd loved the rough sex they'd had in that hell hole. "Yes, ma'am. I'll add all those sex acts to the list of things to do once Cruz is out of our lives."

He kissed her stomach above her curls and easily slid a finger into her drenched slit. Her muscles tightened around the intrusion. "Now, where was I?" He pulled the finger from her and idly stroked around the opening.

"Um, you were sucking and lightly biting my labia and clit. I liked it. I really like the clit suckling, and the tongue or finger in my pussy are good choices also."

Her tone was not quite sarcastic, not quite helpful, but a blend of the two. He nipped her clit and elicited a moan from her. "Watch the sassiness. This is a learning curve for both of us. Hands on the headboard … now." She obeyed instantly.

He snickered at her mumbled "damn slow learning curve if you ask me." His woman was a piece of work and he loved it.

Continuing the soothing massage on her stomach, he nuzzled her inner thigh as he separated her labia with his fingers. He licked around her before resuming his kissing and suckling of her pussy lips and clit. He loved the kittenish noises his tasting evoked. Slipping a finger inside her, he continued to lick and nibble her folds and inner thighs, mixing up the sensations so her excitement would build upon itself. His hand on her stomach was now extremely necessary to keep her hips from moving away from the increased intensity of his ministrations. The sounds coming from Callie were all mewling whimpers, gasps, moans and the occasional "oh fuck."

When she yelped "goddamn, fuck, shit" several times, he grinned and added another finger to her pussy, scissoring them to stretch her for his cock. A deep throaty groan told him she liked the intrusion and was ready for more—but that was for later. He wanted to give her an oral climax this time. His throbbing cock wanted inside her now, but it could wait. He planned on coming inside her before the evening was over. Timing and preparation were everything.

"Risto!"

Her cry was the result of his adding a third finger into her pussy. He chuckled, his breath on her clit causing her to curse. "Fuck, just fuck. Payback is a bitch, bub."

He couldn't help it. He laughed, leaning his forehead on her lower stomach. His lips skimming over her dewy curls. "I look forward to your efforts. Now, lie back and enjoy."

"Promises, promises." She shrieked and screamed, "Oh my fricking God," as he added his thumb to her clit and stroked her G-spot with his fingers. He resumed licking her sex as his fingers and thumb incited her first orgasm.

Callie screamed, a high, breathy sound. Her body bucked against his hold and it took all his strength to hold her hips to the mattress. A quick glance at her face provoked a satisfied smile. Her head tossed back and forth on the pillow and her hands fisted the headboard as she rode the strong contractions. She took all he had to give her.

But he knew she could take more. She would take more.

Keeping up a steady finger-fucking, he applied extra pressure to her clit and tongued her lightly. He prolonged Callie's orgasm for at least a minute.

Petting her tummy in a circular motion, he brought her down with gentle brushes of his lips around her sex, his fingers stilling within her and his thumb soothing her clitoral hood. Her gaze on him was unfocused. Her breathing rough as if she'd just run a very hard race.

"Was that okay, baby?"

"Oh hell yeah." Her voice was low, husky from her screams and gasping for breath. She lifted a hand from the headboard and crooked a finger. "Come up here and put that cock inside me. I bet he's so purple with engorged blood he's ready to burst."

"Nun-unh." He nipped then kissed the top of her mound.

She hissed and jerked. He soothed her by massaging her quivering, sweat-sheened stomach. With the fingers still inside her, he massaged the spongy spot on her interior vaginal wall and applied more pressure to her clit by a firm circular motion of his thumb.

"Oh… Risto … no…"

"Oh fuck yeah. One more time and this time, I'll come into you when you scream my name."

"No, Risto. I don't think … sorry … I'm all done." Letting go of the headboard, she reached for him. "Just come in me. Take what you need."

"Hands, baby." She put her hands back on the headboard. "And you will come again, because I'll make sure of it." He kissed her belly button then moved his thumb so he could take a loving lick of her clit. He built her up again using his fingers, setting up a rhythm of several fast, deep strokes, then a pause before he curled and massaged the G-spot. His tongue never left her clit, laving the distended bud with a firm caress.

Callie's breathing grew more and more erratic as she strained for her orgasm. "Risto. I can't … it's there … but…"

"Shh, baby. It's my job to see you get it. Just let go. You're thinking too much."

A several second pause in her breathing and her sex clenching his fingers like a vise told him she was ready. He moved the hand from her stomach and took a nipple between his thumb and finger then pulled and twisted the rosy tip as he drew her clit into his mouth and suckled it. The added stimulation on her breasts was all that was needed to tip her over.

"Oh my God. Oh my God. Risto! Please … please…"

He moved quickly up her body. Grabbing her ass, he lifted her lower body and thrust into her in one strong motion of his hips. She screamed as her orgasm took her over. Her muscles fisted his cock, clenching and unclenching as a powerful orgasm raged through her. Her hair billowed around her tossing head as she emitted animalistic grunts with each thrust of his hips.

He held back his climax for as long as he could, wanting her to have all the pleasure she could take. He rode her with a steady, deep motion, his pubic bone grinding her clit with each downward movement. Leaning over, he took her lips, then tongued her mouth, matching the rhythm of his hips. He swallowed her guttural moans and gave her back his hungry growls.

When a particularly strong contraction fisted him extra tightly, he broke from their kiss and bellowed as searing pleasure tore down his spine. The pleasure was so great his toes curled into the mattress as he poured his seed into her depths. Her interior muscles milked him and sent shards of pleasure up and down his body, so much pleasure, more than he'd ever known. Every muscle trembled and his body shook.

Finally, he slowed his hip motion, riding her through several small spasms. Each time her muscles tightened around his cock, he groaned and muttered variations of "fucking good" and "love you, baby."

Callie's hands had left the headboard and stroked his sweaty hips, soothing him, as if to say "there, there."

By the time he could force himself to slip away from her warm haven, she was half asleep and her body was as limp as overcooked pasta. Her lashes lay like dark brown feathers against her flushed cheeks. Her lips were slightly parted as her breaths slowed to sighs whispered into the pillow.

When he moved to lie next to her, she turned on her side, curled into a ball and snuggled her hips against his torso. He smiled. Sweeping her hair out of the way, he kissed the spot where her neck joined her shoulder. She moaned and shivered and moved her sweet ass over his relaxed cock.

"Sleep, love." He got up and pulled the sheet and down-filled blanket over her so she wouldn't get chilled. He padded into the bathroom and cleaned himself up, then took a warm cloth into the bedroom to clean their fluids off her so she could sleep more comfortably. She slept through his ministrations with only a few incoherent mumbles escaping her lips.

Placing a kiss on her stomach where she carried his child, he covered her and added his grandmother's spread. He smoothed some tousled strands of hair from her cheek, tucking them behind her ear. She muttered "Risto" and then snuggled into her pillow, a smile curving her lips. His heart ached with all the love he felt for her in that moment. He should be planning how to take down Cruz, but instead he crawled into bed and spooned her. He could take this time to be with her … just until Conn called for pickup. He buried his face in the hair strewn on his pillow and fell instantly asleep.

Callie woke and stretched like a cat. She'd never known orgasms could be a combination of pleasure and pain before. But then she'd never had multiple orgasms before meeting Risto. If that was a sample of what their sex life would be like, she needed to build some stamina. Her pussy clenched around emptiness, eager for more when she should be exhausted. Yeah, she'd need to eat her Wheaties for sure.

"Risto?" She listened and heard no reply, no sound indicating he was in the house. She frowned and tried to remember what had happened earlier. A phone had rung. Risto kissed her and tried to wake her. Okay, she seemed to recall him telling her he had to pick up Conn and Berto. So, he must not be back yet.

She sat up on the side of the bed. The room spun around her. Nausea ensued. "Damn." She patted her tummy. "Sorry, baby, I know you don't mean to make mommy sick."

Throwing the bedclothes off, she ran into the bathroom and made it to the toilet in time. Coughing and choking, she vomited until she thought her lungs and guts would come up.

Finally, she stopped.

A cold sweat covered her naked body. Breathing heavily, she slumped against the wall next to the commode, afraid to get up in case she began to heave again. She shivered violently. She was naked. She needed to clean up and find something to wear. Groaning, she tried crawling. The world didn't spin so she kept moving.

Making her way to the vanity first, she found a cloth. She rose to her knees and wetted it, then wiped her face, neck, upper body and her pussy. Then she used a new toothbrush and some toothpaste she found in a drawer and brushed her teeth. Sitting back on her heels, she looked around the bathroom, finally eyeing a closed door. It had to be a closet.

Reluctant to stand and upset the status quo, she went back to her hands and knees. She made it to the door and opened it. Yes, a walk-in closet. All neat and organized just like the marine Risto had been. She entered and found a shelf with neatly folded T-shirts and picked out a drab olive green one, well-washed and soft, with the USMC Force Recon logo on it. She pulled it on and found it covered her to her upper thighs. She felt warmer already. A couple of drawers later, she found some boxers and selected a pair to match the shirt. She sat on the carpeted floor and wiggled them up her legs and over her butt. A little loose in the waist but not so much that they would fall down.

Exhausted from her efforts, she leaned against the built-ins. "Just wait it out, Calista Jean. You used up all your energy. Just sit here until you find the strength to crawl back to bed."

Which might never happen, because the bed was at least three feet off the ground and she'd have to stand to get into it. Well, she could pull the covers off and nest on the bedroom floor until Risto got back.

"Note to self, put saltines and water by the bed to hold off morning sickness." Well, it had to be late afternoon, but same difference.

She was starved now, but too damn wiped out to do anything about it. She prayed she'd have the shortest duration of morning sickness on record, but the doctor hadn't held out much hope. She needed to call Keely and see how her friend had coped. Keely had mentioned something about having morning, noon and evening sickness from hell for about four months. "Four months!" She groaned.

As she sat in the closet, she glanced about her, assessing the space. She blinked and yawned. "More than enough room for my stuff." She'd rent out the house in Chicago until the boys decided whether one or both of them wanted it. She'd live with Risto here and in Sanctuary. She didn't need her own place any longer. She yawned again and slid down to curl up on the comfy carpet covering the radiant-heated floor. Just a little nap, then she'd get up and find something to eat.

AFTER SHOWING CONN AND BERTO to one of the island's guest houses and arranging for them to meet him at the main house in a couple of hours for an evening meal and planning session, he disarmed his security and entered the house, rearming it behind him. He hung his coat in the mud room then went to the kitchen and pulled the makings for beef stew out of the refrigerator. Throwing together the dish, he put it in a slow cooker on high. It would be ready for supper.

Then he went to check on Callie. She wasn't on the bed and it looked as if the covers had been thrown to the side in a hurry. "Callie!"

Panic hit him in the gut, then calm reason took over. The system hadn't been disturbed. She was here somewhere. No one could have gotten inside, no one could have gotten to her, taken her away from him.

He entered the bathroom. The slight smell of sickness still

hung in the air. "Callie, where are you?"

Then he noted the closet door was ajar. And there he found her, curled on her side on the floor, wearing some of his old Corps BvDs, sound asleep. She must've woken up and gotten sick. Why hadn't she gone back to bed? He'd ask her later. Now, he'd just tuck her back into bed and crawl in with her for another nap. Just the thought of curling around her, protecting her with his body as she slept, made him happy, made him whole when he'd never known he'd been incomplete before.

He picked her up. She muttered something and flapped a hand at his chest. "Shh, love. It's just me."

She made a little sound and snuggled closer, her fingers grasping his shirt, her nose sniffing his neck.

He kissed her tangled curls. He'd enjoy brushing all that hair later. Her naked body against his. Him naked surrounding her from behind with his arms and legs as they sat on their bed. He'd stroke the brush through her hair, pausing to kiss her neck and shoulders from time to time. Once he had all the tangles out, he would arouse her with more kisses to the sensitive area around her ears as his hands stimulated her breasts. Then he'd turn her around until she straddled him. This time she would ride him. He'd be able to pay even more attention to her beautifully formed breasts. The hair he groomed so carefully would brush against his skin … shit, he imagined himself into a steel-hard boner.

"Chill, Smith. She's sick. She doesn't need a randy bastard poking her now." His cock wasn't listening, but he'd deal.

Carefully laying her on the bed, he pulled the covers back over her. He quickly stripped to his skin and crawled in behind her, pulling her ass into him. His erect cock cradled along the seam of her sweet little butt. Taking deep, controlled breaths, he willed his cock to a semi-erect state, probably the best he could hope for under the circumstances. Just lying with her this way made him happy, replete. Sighing, relaxing around her body, he went to sleep.

CHAPTER TWENTY

Wednesday afternoon, Risto's Island.

Risto kept an eye on the closed double-doors to the main level master bedroom as he, Conn and Berto went over the plan to draw Cruz and his men into a trap. Callie hadn't awakened when he got up from his nap and kissed her sleep-warmed cheek. Her deep sleep reassured him; she'd need to be well-rested over the next few days, when he hoped to get Cruz out of their lives permanently.

"Stop watching the door." Conn chuckled. "She's safe. No one can harm her here. Hell, the fucking White House has less security." Berto snorted back a laugh and just shook his head at his boss's words.

Risto regarded the two men who'd dropped everything and flown all day and night into a winter storm to get here. "Have I thanked you yet?"

"This would be the fifth time," Berto said. "I'd have flown ten times as far. I owe your woman for avenging Javier and saving the traitor for my family to take care of."

Risto had heard how Berto's family had taken care of Ricky and frowned. "Callie doesn't need to hear what was done to Ricky. I don't want that time to touch her any more than it already has."

"Won't hear it from me," Conn said.

"Nor me," said Berto.

Risto turned back to the most current intelligence report he'd received on Cruz from SSI. "You'll be happy to know that our Uncle and the Colombian government have decided to allow SSI to handle Cruz's illegal entry into the USA any way we see fit."

The mission to eliminate Cruz now fit into the murky area of black ops. Homeland Security, the FBI and the Michigan version of Homeland Security had all been informed by the National Clandestine Service that NCS's contractor, SSI, had Cruz covered. The other intelligence agencies hadn't been happy, but since it would have taken them days to mount an op with any chance of success, they ungraciously ceded the mission to SSI, which had boots on the ground and the home field advantage. The other agencies would come in and secure the scene after Risto called to give them an all-clear. Plus, the other agencies would take all the credit—which was fine with SSI. SSI liked working under the radar.

"Generous of them." Conn's tone was sarcastic. "Since the fucking bureaucrats never saw fit to shut the asshat down as he terrorized and killed innocent Colombians, kidnapped foreigners, and protected one of the largest drug cartels in South America."

Risto grunted. "Plausible deniability has always been Uncle's middle name in situations such as these. Cruz had a 'use' until now." He turned back to the report. "On the also bad news for Cruz front," *since I plan on killing the bastard and making everybody happy, but just in case,* "Paco has issued a shoot-on-sight, no-questions-asked contract on Cruz if he ever shows his shit face in Colombia. Just goes to show, never cross a drug dealer."

Conn nodded and smiled grimly. "I heard Paco went ballistic. He killed all of Cruz's top men stupid enough to remain in Colombia. He appointed one of his most trusted aides to take over Cruz's paramilitary organization and had the rank-and-file guerillas swear allegiance—or die. No one in Colombia will assist Cruz—not if they know what's good for them."

"Keely has questions about how Paco might proceed against Callie." Risto frowned down at the papers in his hand. The cartel leader would never touch her, but he still wanted to know what he might be facing. "What have you heard from Tom and Rosa?"

"Rosa talked to Paco after he'd instructed his men to find you and Callie while you were still in the Darien. She told him our version of what had happened." Conn shrugged. "For a murdering drug lord, Paco is a chivalrous son of a bitch. Oh, and I hate to tell you, but you didn't get all the back-ups of the video from Callie's suite."

Risto swore violently.

"Chill, Paco obtained them. Anyway, after hearing what Cruz had done and viewing some of the footage, Paco destroyed the back-ups. He called his men off the search for you two and advised them that Cruz was a pornographer and a disgrace to his Catholic upbringing." At Risto's snort, Conn smiled. "Yeah, go figure—a devout drug lord. At that point, Paco stated Calista and her man had every right to take the videos, the DVD was considered collateral damage. Conclusion is, Paco doesn't blame you two and he began covering his financial ass before Callie was even out of Colombia. Bottom line, it was all Cruz's fault."

"Cruz's prior bad acts trumped ours." Risto nodded. "A logical approach."

"Yeah. Plus, Paco doesn't know as far as I could tell that it was Callie who actually tracked Cruz's information to the few of Paco's accounts which he couldn't protect quickly enough." Conn grinned. "He just figured it was the US government who nailed his assets."

"Which is good for Callie. Paco's chivalrous nature

could easily vanish if he knew she was capable of tracking his money. To him, she is a super-model whose privacy was cruelly violated," said Berto. "But what bothers me is Cruz's continued pursuit of Callie. He risks a lot following her to the US. He has Mexican citizenship and a fortress outside of Mexico City. There, he is safe, but still he came into the US illegally and went to Chicago. Me? I think he has more reasons for his pursuit than depraved lust." The Colombian's cheeks flushed slightly.

"Keely agrees with you." Risto's lips twisted. "Her take is Cruz found out that Callie was instrumental in using the data on the disk to get to his money." The anger churning in his gut threatened to overwhelm him. Unfortunately, the target of his ire was not within reach yet … but soon. "Cruz isn't chasing her to get in her pants."

"So, the fucking traitor in Defense sold her out? Ren suggested as much when I spoke to him yesterday." Conn's expression was dark and ugly. Berto drew his knife and began to polish the already pristine blade, a habit the man had when he was extremely pissed.

"Yeah. What we all suspected has been confirmed. Keely's trapping program intercepted a message sent to Cruz at his estate in Mexico. The message informed him about Callie's role in his downfall. Keely's conclusion is Cruz wants to take Callie back to Colombia and hand her over to Paco, to serve as his get-out-of-getting-tortured-and-killed card. Although it is far too late for that, she isn't sure Cruz is sane enough to understand that little fact."

"Why hasn't the fucking traitor been caught yet? There can't be that many people high enough in the DOD with this kind of clearance." Conn spat the words as if he had a vile taste in his mouth.

"Not my expertise. But Keely and Tweeter along with Callie's help have been following threads and narrowing those that have access. I just want the fucker, whoever he is, gone. He's aimed his greedy, treacherous eyes at me and mine now. SSI has plans in place to nail the fucker and all his little moles. And when they do, I want a few private moments with him." Risto shoved the papers away. "He sold my Callie out, knowing full well Cruz would attempt to capture and kill her."

"But that just gives us another thread to pull." Callie's soft tones drew all three men's eyes to her.

She stood in the doorway to the bedroom, holding on to the door. Her face had more color, but was still too pale for his peace of mind. She had that just-out-of-bed tousled look which roused his simmering libido. Her hair lay tangled about her face and shoulders. Her body, covered in his marine T-shirt and boxers, looked both sexy and cute. God, he still couldn't believe this beautiful, precious woman was here—and all his.

At Conn's sharp inhalation and lowly muttered "Jesus" and Berto's "*bonita*," he shot them both a hands-off glance and muttered, "mine." Conn, asking for his balls to be lopped off, snickered.

"The more info the traitor sells, the more electronic trails SSI has to follow." She shoved away from the doorway and walked slowly toward the dining area where they sat. "And as soon as we take care of this problem with Cruz, I'll get on the computer and help with tracking the asshole. The traitor made a big mistake. If Cruz paid him through any of the accounts we left open and are tracking, I will find the payment and should be able to match it to an account associated with one of the men Keely has her eye on in the DOD. It will take a while, but I'm sure we'll eventually tug on the right string."

When she stopped and swayed, she halted a sure tumble to the floor by placing her hand on the back of a low-slung leather chair. Risto shot up and was at her side in mere seconds. He swept her into his arms and carried her to the couch in front of the fireplace and its warming blaze. He placed her gently on the sofa, her back supported by the couch's arm and her legs stretched along on the cushions. He snagged one of his grandmother's woven throws and covered her bare legs.

Stroking hair away from her face, he peered into her gray eyes. "Were you sick again?"

"Yeah." She smoothed a hand over his bristly jaw. "I think a package of Saltines by the bed is going to be standard operating procedure for a while."

He frowned. "Will they help?" She looked slightly green and all that vomiting couldn't be good for her or the baby. Hell, he didn't know. Being an only child raised by an old man, he'd never been exposed to pregnant women. He needed to read that book the doc had given her. He definitely needed to get her to a doctor and sit in on the examination. He wanted to know what danger signs to look for.

"I called Keely on my cell as I was resting on the floor of the bathroom—and I really appreciate your heated floors. She said bland crackers helped her. You can't get any blander than Saltines." She wrinkled her nose. "I'll try anything. I hate throwing up. My doctor in Chicago told me the queasiness is caused by extra estrogen and progesterone. An empty stomach exacerbates the problem and she recommended eating a lot of small meals."

"What kind of meals? You craving anything other than banana cream pie?" Risto asked, a smile on his lips. "Do I need to stock up on pickles and ice cream?"

Her lips twisted and her eyes glimmered with amusement. "I haven't found the urge to dip pickles in my dessert—yet. The crackers are the only thing I need, preferably before I get out of bed in the morning. Other than that, I'll just approach each meal as an adventure." Her tummy rumbled. All three men laughed. "Guess I need to feed."

Risto covered her hand as she rubbed it over the complaining organ. "I have some beef stew. It's mild—I left out my usual spices so you could eat it. Or, I can open a can of chicken noodle soup, if that sounds better. The guys and I haven't eaten yet. We were waiting on you." He leaned over and kissed her cool forehead.

She thought for a few seconds. "Meat and potatoes sound good. I think we'll try that."

"We?" he asked.

"Me and the baby." Callie looked down at her still flat abdomen. "The doctor said to go with the flow and then laughed at me. She told me she'd always hated beets and then craved them throughout her pregnancy." She turned toward him, a solemn expression on her face. "If this baby decides he likes something gross such as pickled pig's feet or tripe, I'm going on record now—ain't gonna happen."

Risto threw back his head and laughed. Callie's voice held a lot of disgruntlement.

"Don't laugh. I meant it." She tugged on his shirt until his lips were close to hers. "It will be your responsibility to talk to the baby and convince him that I refuse to eat stuff I can't stand the sight of. Got it?" She bit lightly into his lower lip then let it slide from between her teeth.

He cradled her jaw and took control of her pouty mouth with a deep, wet kiss. Later tonight, he'd make love to her again, then hold her close all night. He had that right now. And the next morning, he'd be there to help her when she was sick. He wanted to make it clear that she wasn't alone any longer—she had him to back her up.

The clearing of a throat forced him to halt the kiss, which had begun to turn carnal. Callie moaned as he pulled away and his erection strained against the zipper placket of his jeans.

Callie looked at him with dilated eyes. When she licked her lips, he groaned and brushed another kiss over her bruised mouth. "Sorry, I was rough."

"Don't be. I love when you go all He-Man on me." She nipped his chin. "I love you." He smiled and zeroed in on her mouth once more.

"Ahem," Conn said even more loudly than before. "Give two single men a break, would ya?"

Risto stroked his thumb over Callie's lips and mouthed "sorry," then glanced over and spotted two grinning faces. "Stuff it, Conn. I'm busy here."

"I can see that, but there are the little matters of, one, feeding that sweet thing you're mauling, and, two, finalizing the plans to protect her from Cruz and his thugs. The bastard is probably already on his way to Osprey's Point. The DOD traitor and his minions would have access to all your Department of Defense records and would've sold Cruz your permanent residence's address."

"Sorry, I've been sort of distracted lately." Risto nuzzled the focus of his distraction. She giggled.

"Well, hell yeah, you have." The smirk on Conn's face drew a scowl from Risto. "So, stop kissing and cuddling your woman. Let's eat and plan how we're gonna take out the bastard."

When Risto released Callie, she rested against the couch's arm with a sigh. He stuffed an extra pillow behind her, giving her back more support. "Let's eat here so Callie can stay warmer by the fire. I have trays for the food."

"No need for trays. Berto and I can sit on the floor and use the cocktail table." Conn led the way to the seating area in front of the fireplace, bringing over the reports provided by SSI.

Risto took the thick stack of papers from Conn and handed them to Callie. "Here, sweetheart, this is the most current intel from Sanctuary." He stood. "I'll get us all something to eat while you read them over."

"I'll help get the food," Berto said.

The three men went to the kitchen. As Risto pulled out bowls and spoons, he kept an eye on Callie's expression as she skimmed the analyses Keely had prepared. He knew when she'd reached the part about Paco and the extra back-up of the videos.

He must've made some sort of sound at the fleeting expression of fear which swept over her face, because Callie looked over and smiled. "I'm okay. If Rosa confirmed the video footage was destroyed, then it's gone. And as I told you back at Conn's house, a video can't hurt me." He heard her words but her expression told him she was relieved. "So, at least for now, I don't have a vicious, but chivalrous, drug lord after me, just an angry, nearly broke, former paramilitary leader who can no longer go home because of me."

There was distinct touch of hysteria in her voice; his little soldier wasn't as unfazed as she pretended. He wasn't the only one who'd heard it.

"Go to her." Berto shooed Risto out of the kitchen. "I have this. Your woman needs you."

He left Berto and Conn putting the meal together and swiftly went to Callie's side, sitting on the edge of the couch, his hip nestled against her legs. He massaged her thigh, his fingers grazing the sensitive inner portion, and noted the slight change in her breathing, indicating the beginnings of her arousal. She sent him an "I'll get you for that" look and he grinned. She wasn't totally upset if that slight touch could distract her.

"None of this goat-roping is because of you," he said. "It's because of *me*, baby. I'm the one who took Cruz's accounting DVD. The bastard wants me almost as much as he wants you. He realizes getting to you and hurting you would bring me into the open."

She shot him a look of incredulity. "So, that's the frigging plan? Lure him here with the idea he might get to me but then you parade in front of him and hope you kill him before he kills you?"

He didn't say a word. There was nothing to say. He'd be the one to lure the fucking bastard to his doom.

She punched him on the arm. "That doesn't make sense. Me … he wants alive, so he can use me to get back in Paco's good graces." Fiery anger blazed from her opalescent eyes. "You," she poked him in the chest, "he wants dead." She threw the report onto the cocktail table. "Dammit, Risto, it's not acceptable to dangle your so-fine ass out there in place of mine. He'll just shoot and kill you on sight." Tears filled her eyes as she covered her stomach with one hand and twisted a strand of her hair with the other. "I want our baby to have his father."

"I'm hard to kill. Plus, our plan is a tad bit more refined than me parading my ass to get shot." Her angry snort had his lips twisting into a grim smile. "The bastard is never getting near you again. The fact he'll be within a quarter mile of you is barely acceptable. So, don't even think about offering to be live bait."

She muttered, "Fucking, alpha-macho-bloody male."

Approaching the couch, Conn laughed. "She's got you pegged."

"Shut the fuck up, Conn." Risto snarled the words at his soon-to-be former friend.

Berto brought a tray for Callie and Risto and set it on the cocktail table, then went back for his and Conn's. Risto picked up a bowl and handed it and a spoon to her. "Eat."

Callie took the spoon and balanced the bowl on her lap. After taking a couple of bites and chewing thoroughly, she put the spoon in the bowl. "So … what's the plan?" Her eyes glittered with silver fire. "Have you slink around your island until one of his men kills you? If the man hired a decent sniper, he could make the kill shot from any high point in Osprey's Point. Hell, I could make that shot. All your high-tech surveillance equipment isn't worth the cost of parts if they have a merc sniper who's halfway decent."

Callie was crying. The sound made his heart hurt. "Fuck, baby." He stood, took her bowl from her unresisting hands and put it on the cocktail table, then lifted her into his arms. Sitting down, he cradled her across his lap and rocked her. "Please stop crying. You'll make yourself sick again."

"Shut up." She sniffed loudly, wiping her wet cheeks on his

turtleneck. "I have the right to cry. You wouldn't have a target on your forehead if it weren't for Cruz's hard-on for me."

"Callie," Conn leaned forward in the chair he'd pulled to the cocktail table, his arms braced on his knees. "Look at me, sweet cheeks."

Risto growled. "She's not your sweet anything, Redmond. And don't even talk about her ass."

Callie snickered, then sniffled against his neck. "I like it when he calls me that. He sounds like a forties private eye talking to the ditzy blonde in trouble, but who is really the deadly *femme fatale*." She turned her head so she could see the two men sitting in the chairs across from the couch. "What did you want to tell me, Conn?"

She petted Risto's chest and he released some of the tension which had stiffened his body when she'd begun to cry. He didn't want her afraid for him, but he refused to allow her to place herself in danger. What kind of man would he be if he didn't protect her—and his unborn child—from scum such as Cruz?

"We'll be taking out the bad guys in Osprey's Point. Our plan keeps Cruz and his men from even leaving shore. Berto and I will have Risto's back. Plus Keely's twin brothers will be here. They're on their way. Can you trust the four of us to protect your man, little momma?"

Callie rubbed her fingers over her face, wiping away the wetness. Risto hugged her closer into his body. She sighed and rested her head back against his shoulder. "Yeah, Loren and Paul are good. However, I'll point out, I shoot better than both of them and they'll tell you the same."

Berto shot a wary look at Risto. "Our plan could use the addition of a sniper."

Risto glared at Conn's right-hand man. "No fucking way … the twins are SEALs, one of them can be the sniper."

"Listen up, Marine, and use your head." Callie petted his chest. "Berto thinks I can do it and that's good enough for me."

Conn nodded. "Berto does have a good point. The only weakness I saw in the plan was not having someone high up to feed us intel and cover us with precision shooting. Callie would be far out of harm's way, at least a thousand meters and maybe more depending on the rifle and her skill. She could cover Osprey Point's whole downtown area with the perfect sniping position."

Risto took her hand in his and kissed the tips of her fingers. His gaze fixed on her. She met his eyes, unflinchingly. His brain refused to engage, pure emotion drove his reaction. "I don't want you anywhere near the battle zone. You'll be locked down here, safe on my island, where nothing but a nuke from China might reach you."

"So, you're assuming Cruz won't ever make it to the island before you spring your trap? Shit happens, Marine. What if they have rocket launchers? I'd be a sitting duck in this glass house." Callie waved a hand toward the expanse of glass. She turned toward the others. "I'm safer in Osprey's Point with you all, so you might as well use me. Tell me your plan."

"Callie!" Even he heard the fear in his voice.

She cupped his face with her hands. The look in her eyes was fierce, determined and filled with fear for him. "Risto, I love you. But right now, you're being a recalcitrant ass. I'm not a helpless female who needs to be placed on a shelf for safe-keeping. We've had this discussion." She shook his head for emphasis. "I know my limitations. Getting out of Colombia on my own was not in my skill set. Fighting hand-to-hand in a running street battle in Osprey's Point isn't either. But I *am* an expert sniper. I've proven I can take out a live target. I can make a difference and save lives—your life."

"Callie ... sweetheart..."

She covered his mouth with her fingers. "Shut up, Marine." Then she snorted, one of those elegant, disdainful sniffs which made him harder than titanium steel in a nanosecond. "You insult me—and your friends—if you think any of us would endanger the baby I'm carrying. And, since I'm essential to the live birth of our baby, that means, *ipso facto*, the danger to my person would also be factored into my decision."

Conn choked back a laugh. Berto coughed. Risto swore in Finnish and several other languages before staring the other two men into silence. He pulled away from her hands and took her lips in a rough, rapacious and all too brief kiss. "We'll discuss who's the boss in this family later—in private."

"Sweetie, we already discussed that—last night. In the bedroom, you're the boss. Outside, however, we're a team. I expect to be treated as the intelligent equal partner I am."

"Fuck, Risto. You're the boss in the bedroom? Way to go, man." Conn gave him a thumbs-up. He shot a naughty wink at Callie who giggled. Conn really needed to stop flirting with his woman or Risto would be happy to remove the man's favorite dangly parts.

Conn continued to bury himself by adding, "You have to admit, she's smart and can think on her feet. She doesn't panic. Plus, we really could use her shooting skills. The Walsh twins would be of better help on the ground. Ren told me she out shot him and Price Teague and is Keely's equal. I'm betting she can make a fifteen-hundred-meter shot with that fricking Lapua you have in your armory, even in a high wind with snow."

"Yes, I can. I shot Keely's Lapua every day I was at Sanctuary. It's sweet." Callie petted his chest as if soothing a rabid animal. "Even if I don't make a kill shot at that distance, I can still do a lot of damage to the enemy at that caliber. My shooting might tip the psychological advantage to our favor. Sniper kills, according to my dad, demoralize invading troops."

"Fuck, just fuck." Risto wiped a hand over his face. He was out-numbered and worst of all—they were right. He just didn't like it. If it had been anyone but his Callie, he would have agreed from the get-go. He heaved a sigh. "You're all correct. I just … Callie…" He cuddled her closer and gently kissed the lips he'd bruised earlier. "I just found you. I can't…"

"I know. I know." She nuzzled his neck and petted him. He sighed and let her comfort him with her touch. "I feel the same way about you risking yourself, Marine. I want to make sure we have years and years together. This is my way of making sure that will happen."

He had to trust her. She'd handled everything thrown at her since he met her in Cartagena. She'd proven that she was smart and knew her limitations. If she needed help, she'd let him or the others know. Plus, he'd make sure one of the Walsh twins backed her up as a spotter. Two sets of eyes at high ground were better than one. Plus, the spotter could be armed as a back-up sniper.

"Tell her the plan." Risto held her as close to his body as he could. Her stomach growled loudly. His lips quirked. "Our child needs to be fed and so does his mama." He reached over and retrieved the bowl he'd set aside. "Eat."

She took the bowl from him and began to eat. She paused, a spoonful of stew halfway to her mouth, and spoke before Conn could begin. "It's a good thing I'm not showing yet since I have better accuracy lying on my stomach using the bipod."

Risto groaned. Okay, maybe he had given in too soon. This whole thing had cluster fuck written all over it. "Callie, maybe…"

"Risto, I'll handle it. I can do this. Anyone tries to kill my man is dead meat." She took her next bite and chewed the beef as if it were Cruz.

"Fine. But you'll be at the maximum range for the Lapua. Fifteen hundred meters. And the position will be elevated and protected so they can't get to you easily. Plus, and this is non-negotiable, you'll have one of the Walsh twins as a spotter and back-up sniper. Got it?" He swept all of them with an evil eye.

"Sure, old buddy, sounds like a plan to me." Conn smirked. Yeah, the man wanted to sing soprano.

"*Sí,* Risto."

"Yes." Callie hugged him, endangering her bowl of stew, then kissed the edge of his clenched jaw. "But it can be less than fifteen hundred if I'm elevated. From what I saw last night when we arrived, I'm not sure the whole downtown of Osprey's Point is much more than twelve hundred meters in length."

He shook his head and let out a disgusted breath. "I've got to be nuts to even consider this." Absently, he massaged Callie's shoulders, finding the motion comforting.

"You're not nuts," Callie rubbed her cheek against his jaw line, "just using all the resources at hand. You'd trust me to protect the baby if you were on a mission, wouldn't you?"

"Yes. Absolutely." But he planned to have her safely at Sanctuary when he was on extended missions after the baby arrived. He was sure Ren would conspire with him to give Callie assignments during those times.

"Then trust me to protect the baby's father."

"Fine, but if you even get frost bit, I'll tie you to the bed and never let you out of my sight again."

"Risto, you were going to do that anyway." She poked him in the chest with the hand holding her spoon.

Conn and Berto roared with laughter. Risto shot them a nasty glance. "Just wait until you get women of your own. You'll know exactly how I feel and I'll be happy to remind you of this moment."

"Can't wait, old buddy. But I doubt I'll ever find a woman to match Callie." He winked at her. "You sure you don't have any sisters, sweet cheeks?"

"Sorry, none."

At Conn's continued flirtation with Callie, Risto muttered several pithy swear words in Finnish. He received an elbow in his ribs. "What was that for?"

"I don't know what you said," she massaged the area she'd elbowed, "but I'm sure it wasn't complimentary."

"Hell, I can't even get away with swearing at my former friend's suggestive behavior toward my fiancée in my own house."

"Nope. Plus, it's our house, you said so, and Conn and Berto are guests. So be nice."

"Yes, ma'am." Then he muttered against her ear, "Did you know that sassy mothers-to-be get spanked?"

She grinned. "Promises, promises. Now, dish on the plan." Looking toward the kitchen, she added, "Didn't we buy bananas? All of a sudden, I'm craving a banana." She stared him in the eye and licked her lips. "A nice big one."

When Conn hooted with laughter once more, Risto swore. "You are a dead man, Redmond."

Chapter Twenty-One

Late Wednesday Evening, Big Earl's in Osprey's Point.

Big Earl had agreed to host the final planning meeting. Since the wind and snow had died down, Callie, Risto, Conn and Berto boated to the mainland rather than use the helicopter. While in town, they'd scout the positions Risto wanted to use in the street battle with Cruz and his hired army. Callie had insisted on coming along. After all, she had to find her sniper's nest from which to shoot. No sniper worth his or her salt allowed someone else to scout out their sniping post.

Sitting at the diner counter, Callie watched the group of men argue over various vantage points and nursed the glass of red wine she had to argue with Risto to get. In the end, she was forced to resort to the baby book she carried in her tote and pointed to the passage which stated an occasional glass of wine was allowed. Muttering, her stubborn marine acquiesced. Big Earl winked when he poured her the glass of Shiraz and whispered, "Keep him on his toes, Callie." She hid her grin by taking a sip.

The team to trap and take out Cruz and his men had swelled to include Loren and Paul Walsh who'd driven into Osprey's Point over an hour ago, and several locals who were also ex-military and year-round residents. The four men, who hadn't been introduced to her by name, looked tough. They were like Risto and the other men—the kind of men who could be dropped into a wilderness with just a knife and come out alive. The Yoopers, as the locals were called, had come to the meeting fully armed and ready to go to war against the be-damned guerilla invaders.

Cruz's force was in the U.P., but was still well away from Osprey's Point, stuck at a Comfort Suites on the outskirts of Watersmeet. The U.P. was difficult enough for those in the know to navigate in the winter weather, let alone for strangers. The intel had come from a friend of Big Earl's in Watersmeet who'd been given the heads up to watch for the invading force. Strangers in this part of Michigan stuck out like men in a lingerie store.

Big Earl leaned his large, muscled body against the diner's counter. "So, Risto's ignoring you, huh?"

"Yep, and he isn't too happy with you, either. You became a traitor to the cause when you poured the wine." She grinned as Risto shot another in a series of glaring looks at the diner owner. "Better watch it, Big Earl. He might shoot you for corrupting the pregnant lady with demon alcohol."

Big Earl grunted. "I can put that boy on his ass and he knows it."

She looked at his broad shoulders and muscled forearms covered by a skin-tight ski turtleneck. "Maybe. But he fights dirty. All marines fight dirty."

The big ex-Ranger grinned. "Pansy-assed wusses, the bunch of them. I'll put my old Ranger buddies up against a unit of marines any day."

"I heard that," Risto shouted across the room. "Leave my woman alone or I'll show you who's a pansy ass."

"Chill, Marine, Earl's keeping me company." Callie set her glass on the counter and pulled on her coat. "In fact, I'll just let Big Earl show me the best vantage points for sniping."

"Just let me get my parka, Callie, and I'll give you the grand tour." Big Earl placed a hand under her elbow, leading her to where the jackets were hung. "You'll want some elevation to get the best view of Main Street and the marina area. I have a couple of places in mind."

"The grand tour only takes five minutes tops." Risto put on his parka and moved to her side, shoving Big Earl out of the way. The man laughed and cuffed Risto on the back of the head. Risto slapped Big Earl's arm out of the way. "We'll all go and get the lay of the land. It's dark and starting to snow again. We'll need to leave soon to get back to the island before the next bout of weather comes through. I want Callie to get some more rest so she'll be ready for our pre-dawn arrival back here."

"We won't be leaving until I find my post." She turned to smile at the Walsh twins. "Which one of you hunky SEALs is going to be my spotter?"

"They aren't that hunky," Risto grumbled and anchored her to his side with an arm around her waist.

The Walsh brothers laughed at the signs of Risto's jealousy. Loren, the twin with green eyes—Paul's were blue, eye color being the only difference between the identical twins—answered, "I am. I lost the toss."

Callie punched Loren's arm. "Ass! I'll tell your sister you flipped a coin to see who'd be stuck with me."

"Go ahead," Loren said, laughing. "I can take the imp."

Paul snorted. "Ren has taught Keely new moves since the last time you wrestled her. I'd bet on the imp."

Loren shook his head and cuffed his brother. "The day I can't take our little sister in hand-to-hand is the day I admit you're smarter than me—and that ain't ever gonna happen."

Callie laughed. The twins were always attempting to one-up each other. From her previous experiences, the two were evenly matched in most respects. "Well, Loren, you need to come along with us. As my spotter, you'll need an even more expanded field of vision."

"What're you shooting?" Loren asked.

"I'll be using a Lapua with all the extras. Risto has a sweet arsenal. He even had a hand-held targeting computer, though I like to check the computer targeting calculations against my own through the scope. What are you carrying?"

"My Barrett M107," said Loren. "It's accurate to two thousand meters. How far out you planning on being, Callie?"

"She'll be at the maximum for the Lapua—fifteen hundred meters," Risto stated, a don't-mess-with-me tone in his voice.

"She can hit a moving target that far away?" one of the locals asked, his skepticism clearly etched on his face.

The other three Yoopers displayed the same incredulity. They'd see tomorrow. The killing would take an additional emotional toll on her, but Risto would be there to help her process through it. She wasn't alone anymore. She had a man who cared and would stand between her and anything.

"Yeah, I can," she reassured the men before Loren or Paul spoke for her. They knew her training; they'd shared it growing up on marine bases. "I may not make the kill shot every time, but the .338 cartridge can take down a hippo. So, any mid-torso shot should do the trick."

Loren nodded. "That's for damn sure." He turned to the Yoopers. "I'll be backing her up, not that she needs me. My .50 caliber rounds will obliterate anything she can't. Any further issues?" Each man shook his head.

Callie liked the idea of Loren covering for any misses she might make. "Loren and I won't allow anyone to sneak up on you guys."

Risto shot the cynics a glare. "I can assure you Callie can shoot and hit what she aims for. She took out three tangos in Columbia in a close range battle and held it together. At long range, I've seen her stats. She's expert-rated." The Yoopers perked up and looked at her with new-found respect and awe.

Risto leaned over and whispered in her ear. "Dammit, Callie, if you weren't pregnant, I'd beat that butt of yours until it's bright pink for insisting on being involved."

She brushed her lips over his ear. "Don't let me being pregnant stop you if it'll make you feel better. I've heard some spanking can be very erotic." His sharp inhale made her lips quirk. She rubbed a hand over his chest. "I need to do this. I'd go crazy being locked up all nice and safe on the island while you and all these men took care of my problem."

"This cluster fuck is not your fault." His voice carried to the other men who observed them with expressions running from mild interest to outright concern.

"He's correct, Callie," Conn said. "Cruz is at fault. He needs to be stopped before he becomes another country's problem terrorist."

Callie knew he was thinking of Mexico, where Cruz had moved after running from Colombia. God knew, Mexico had enough terrorist and drug cartel problems of its own and was another country just a drug lord away from anarchy.

"And, Risto, your woman might look like she just walked off the cover of some ladies' fashion magazine, but she's got bottom." Conn looked Loren over. "Plus, I don't think Loren will let her get hurt, will ya?"

"Nope. Keely would kill me. My little brother Tweeter would kill me—and Risto would tear my limbs off, then kill me. I've got to stay alive and intact so the ladies of Michigan won't be disappointed."

"Michigan?" Callie looked at Risto. "Loren and Paul will be living in Michigan?"

Risto nodded. "Yeah, Ren confirmed it after you fell asleep last night. They and one other guy yet to be named will make my island their base. I'll shuttle back and forth from Idaho to run SSI-East as we're calling it. After our baby is born and you've recovered from the birth, we'll pretty much operate from here with odd trips to the place I'll build us in Sanctuary."

Callie was still upset that he felt the need to put her in Idaho during the pregnancy, but wouldn't fight him on it. His worry was valid while she was carrying and right after the birth, and it would give him peace of mind knowing she had Keely and the others around her during this special time.

"That's so neat." Callie moved from Risto's side to hug the twins. "It'll be just like old times back in Camp Lejeune."

"Well almost, except Tweeter won't be here to moon all over you." Paul tweaked her chin. "We older boys always hoped you and Tweeter would get together so you could be our sister for real." He shot a grin at Risto who'd visibly stiffened at Paul's words. She winced. It was too much to hope that Risto hadn't been listening. "Guess it didn't work out that time he and Keely visited you in Chicago. Your dad died the next week, right?"

"Callie?" Risto grabbed her arms and turned her into his body. "Wasn't…"

Shit, she'd hoped Risto would never find out that Tweeter was the one who'd taken her virginity. Damn Paul and his big mouth. "We'll talk about it later, okay?"

"Count on it." He took her chin in his hand and held her for a rough, deep, territorial marking kind of kiss. All he needed to do was beat his chest and snarl "mine" at the other men to make her day. If he did, she might just knee him in the balls.

"Well, that was cave man," Big Earl said as if he were commenting on the weather. "But time is flying. We need to find Callie her shooting blind, and Loren his spotter position, and map out the other positions we discussed."

Risto nodded. He placed his arm around her waist and pulled her into his body. "Let's go, baby."

It was a short tour. Osprey's Point was small and had few year-round residents. She was pretty sure Big Earl and the other four Yoopers represented over fifty percent of those. Many of the businesses were seasonal and aimed at people who had summer residences on the lake. Those homes were dark and shut for the winter. Big Earl, being Mayor and the constable, had keys to many of the shuttered homes for security reasons.

"What do you think, Callie?" Loren stood at her other side, viewing the marina from the vantage point of the front porch of a two-story Victorian home. "You on the roof-level widow's walk, sheltered behind the slatted wood railing, would have the best view of the main street, the marina and most of the streets leading to it."

She eyed the panoramic view which was more than decent from the porch. "Yes, from up there I'd definitely be able to see most of the town's business district."

In urban battles, not that Osprey's Point was in any way, shape or form similar to a major urban area, line of sight was often impeded by buildings. Here, she'd have almost a Google Earth picture of the streets. She could warn her guys where the enemy was and target the bastards if they endangered Risto and the others. Running gun battles moved fast, and snipers could only kill what they could get in their sights. She would rely on Loren to back her up. She didn't want a mistake on her part to harm their men.

"It's good. Excellent line of sight. I'm well within the Lapua's maximum range," she said.

"It looks less than eleven hundred to any point in town." Loren squinted at the dark street.

"Where would you be?" Callie looked toward the east where Cruz's men would approach from Watersmeet. Another advantage for their side was there was only one main street in and out of town, the Victorian was situated at the far west end on the way out of town.

"That concrete and glass house, the second structure in from the eastern entrance to town." Loren pointed down the street to a modern version of a cottage on the same side of the street as her Victorian.

"Looks good. It also backs up on the hillside, so no one will be coming at you from behind," she said. "Well, not without a lot of trouble anyway."

"Yeah, and I'll have pretty much the same elevation as you'll have so I can police the side streets also." Loren shoulder-bumped her. "And an expanded view of the complete marina area."

"What about being sky-lighted? You think you can hunker down enough?" The modern monstrosity had no widow's walk with a railing to hide behind. The roof looked fairly exposed from this vantage point.

"Calista Jean, I'm ashamed of you. I'm a fucking Navy SEAL. We blend into the shadows, baby girl." He tugged a curl escaping her wooly hat.

"Watch your hands, Walsh." Risto approached them from the shadows of the wrap-around porch. He'd gone to the backyard to gauge the accessibility from the cliff behind the house. He pulled her into his arms.

"Down, tiger. Loren is like another brother. All the Walsh boys are." She rubbed her cold cheek against Risto's chest and shivered. "Sorry, Loren, I forgot all you Special Forces types were super-human."

Loren chuckled.

Risto kissed her forehead. "You cold, baby?"

"Uh-huh. I've seen enough." She looked at Big Earl who stood at the bottom of the porch steps. "Big Earl, you got the keys for this house and that modern one down the street, right?"

"Yep. But even if I didn't, all us super-human ex-Special Forces operatives have never met a building we couldn't breach."

A chorus of "damn rights" came from all the men, including the four locals. She'd guessed correctly as to the Yoopers' background. The odds had been in her favor since this part of the country was famous for reclusive, rough-edged types. Her dad had once said many Special Forces men couldn't handle what stood for civilization once they left military service. Quite a few gravitated toward the more isolated areas of the country such as the U.P., and the less populated western states such as Idaho, Montana and Wyoming. But you couldn't ask for better men to have at your back in a fight.

She smiled. "Thank you all for helping us. I'd give you all a hug and a kiss, but my marine might turn rabid. He's very territorial." The men laughed.

One of the locals called out, "If you were mine, I'd be the same damn way, ma'am."

"No kissing and hugging the men, sweetheart," Risto kissed her forehead, "until after the battle."

"Until after the battle." She captured each man's eyes in turn. "Count on it."

Another local nodded and smiled. "Well, damn, ma'am, that's better than bonus pay." He rubbed his large hands covered in what she recognized as military-issue cold-weather gloves and said, "Bring that Colombian a-hole on. I've got me a supermodel to hug."

The men's raucous laughter echoed off the shuttered buildings in the clear, cold night air. Even Risto chuckled, but she didn't fool herself into thinking he wouldn't demand some answers about Tweeter and his presence in Chicago the week before her father died.

Chapter Twenty-Two

Wednesday night, Risto's Island.

The trip to the island was made in silence. She didn't know what Conn, Berto, Paul and Loren were thinking, but assumed they were mentally preparing themselves for the battle to come or just thinking about getting horizontal and sleeping.

The silence from Risto was more ominous. Paul's loose lips about her and Tweeter had roused Risto's possessiveness. She anticipated some hot and heavy lovemaking once they got home. He'd want to reclaim what he considered his—and she had no problem with that. She didn't want him entering into battle tomorrow with any lingering doubts—she loved him and only him.

His dark gaze glistening from the glow on the boat's dash captured hers. "Cold?"

"No." She moved to stand closer and slid her hand under his parka, grasping his waist band to steady her on the bouncing deck. "Just thinking."

"About tomorrow?" He tensed against her. "You can always remain on the island. No one would hold it against you." She heard the "I'd rather you stayed on the island" subtext in his statement. "Loren can be the sniper and Paul can spot him."

"You need all the men you can muster on the streets. Cruz will bring a small army." She rubbed her cold face against his arm. "It's bad enough you have to spare a man to spot me."

"If it's not tomorrow that has you twitching, then you're worried about what's gonna happen when I get you alone." It wasn't a question.

"Maybe a little." She slipped her gloved fingers farther down the back of his jeans and stroked the top of his buttocks. He had on ski underwear and no briefs or boxers. His skin warmed her even through the gloves.

"Good." He nipped her jaw where it met her ear. "I'm pissed I had to hear from a Walsh that one of them had taken your virginity—so you get to soothe the beast in me."

She trembled at the promise in his tone. Tonight would be about fucking and taking the edge off her man. *Hoo-rah.*

"I won't hurt you, baby." He kissed the spot where he'd bit her. "I just … need…"

"I know. I need you that way, too." She snuggled against his side, her fingers massaging the top of his tight ass, teasing him. His glutes tensed under her ministrations and a low growl rumbled through his chest. She hid her smile against his parka sleeve. This primitive claiming would go both ways. She loved Risto's brand of male dominance, but she wasn't a wuss. She knew with just one lick on his penis or the stroke of her fingers over his superior ass, she could control him—and wasn't that a heady amount of power for a woman to possess?

Risto docked the boat. "Go up to the house, Callie. I'll get the guys situated. I'll be in as soon as I can."

"Shouldn't I check over the weapon I'll be using tomorrow?"

Risto didn't answer immediately, but took several deep breaths. She should have kept her mouth shut, mentioning weapons and herself in the same breath was the same as waving a red flag in front of a bull.

She raised a hand to stroke his arm when Loren snagged it and looked her in the eyes. "Do you trust me and Paul to check over the rifles, Callie?" Obviously, her brother-by-choice was keeping an eye on the dynamics between her and Risto.

"Sure." She would have time in the morning to get the rifle set up for her reach. "I'll need a scope which can handle the early morning glare. And a hand gun."

"You'll have everything you need," Risto said as he helped her onto the dock and then patted her on the ass. "Go on, get inside where it's warm and dry." There was her over-protective male, even pissed, he took care of her.

She climbed the steps from the sheltered, floating dock to the side entrance to the house. When she looked back, all the men stood, watching her. She waved and entered the codes for the house locks and security alarm then went inside.

Hanging her coat on the hooks in the mud room, she took off her wet boots and placed them on the boot tray. She entered the kitchen, pulled out a bottle of orange juice then hunted out the bananas. For some reason, she craved the combo.

Sitting at the kitchen bar counter, she ate the fruit and sipped the juice. The queasiness, which had begun on the bouncing boat ride from Osprey's Point, went away. She imagined she could hear the baby "coo" with relief. She smiled and petted her tummy. "You were hungry, weren't you?"

"Everything okay?"

Squeaking, she startled, her hand covering her suddenly pounding heart. She turned to see Risto enter the kitchen from a doorway which looked to lead to a basement she hadn't realized the house had. "You scared me!"

"Sorry. I forgot I hadn't shown you the underground tunnels." He walked to the refrigerator and took out a beer. Twisting off the cap, he took a long draw from the bottle, his dark eyes fixed on her face. "They connect the other houses on the property and also lead to the armory—and to a sub-basement where we house the 3-D security array and computers."

"Just like the Bat Cave in Sanctuary?" She sat motionless,

watching him watch her. Was he testing her for fear? Or, was he plotting her sexual downfall? Probably both, she decided. She returned his concentrated stare with what she hoped was a calm facade.

"Just like." He drained his beer and set the bottle on the counter, gently, making no sound, then walked, no stalked, toward her. "Your first lover was Tweeter? Why didn't you tell me?" His voice was devoid of all emotion, but she knew he was anything but emotionless. He used his body to keep her on the stool, surrounding her with male heat, musk and muscle.

Outlining her face gently with a single finger, he continued, "Especially in light of the fact you'll be working with the man, often closely, while I'm out in the field." The muscles in his face were tense, emphasizing his rugged bone structure. A muscle in his jaw jumped, but his touch never hardened in any way.

She captured the finger and swirled her tongue around the tip, then held his hand against her heart. "I didn't love Tweeter. He was there. He was safe. He was a friend." Some of the tension left his body with her words. His silent seething had been more about this than her being involved in taking out Cruz. *Good.*

"Go on. You did it twice with him. I can see once for curiosity's sake, but why did you do it again?"

"Maybe *he* thought we could be more than friends, I don't know." She shrugged. "I was ... excited that an older man, even an inexperienced one, wanted me. He was twenty-two to my eighteen. He'd spent his early years protecting Keely. I helped my father raise my brothers. Neither of us had lived yet. We both wanted experience." She sighed. "The first time was uncomfortable." Risto winced. "Awkward, you know?" He nodded, his face expressionless except for the clenching muscle in his jaw.

"The second time was ... better, but the awkwardness didn't go away." She took the hand she clasped and brought it to her face, rubbing his warmth against her still-cold cheek.

"He was like a brother to me. We finally realized that feeling would never change, then laughed at our silliness in thinking we could be anything other than siblings by choice."

She brought his hand back to her chest, over the heart that pounded just for him. "Tweeter's never mentioned those two times to me again. I would never have sex with him or any other man. Do you understand? I love you. The feelings I have for Tweeter or any of the Walsh boys are the same feelings I have for my brothers."

"Good." The muscle in his jaw relaxed. He drew his hand from hers, then lifted her off the stool. With a firm hand on her lower back, he ushered her to the bedroom. He closed the double-doors. The snick of the lock sounded like a gunshot in the quiet, dimly lit room. "Get naked, Callie."

His voice was rough, guttural. She turned and shot him a concerned look. "Didn't you believe what I just said? Tweeter means nothing to me."

"I believe you. I trust you." Risto approached, his movements akin to those of a large cat stalking prey. She backed away until the back of her thighs hit the end of the bed. She reached back to brace herself on the mattress. "But I'm worried about your safety tomorrow and that ... stresses me. And when I get stressed, sweetheart, I need a release. Since I can't kill Cruz right this minute, I'll take that release in the form of sex."

He stopped about a foot away and tucked some hair behind her ears, then traced a finger down her neck, along her collar bone and down the center of her chest. "And since you," he tapped her sternum lightly, "are the cause of my tension, you can be the designated release valve." His glittering dark gaze swept over her body. He cupped her ass and pulled her to the evidence of his arousal. He massaged her bottom with both hands. "So, strip, baby."

His voice was a sexy rumble. His anger over being scared on her behalf—because she didn't believe the stressed argument for a second—had morphed into lust. Her body flushed with an answering desire, her intense arousal soaked the crotch of her leggings. Her breath came in short gasps.

"Callie? You want me to take your clothes off for you?" He brought his hands to the front of the flannel shirt she'd scrounged from his closet. "I can't ... can't promise to be gentle. I'll rip them off. I'm that close to losing control. I don't want to scare you, just fuck you."

God, he needed her—and she wanted to give him whatever he wanted.

"Rip them off." She smiled and placed her hands over his and pulled. The shirt tore open, buttons popping off. "Fuck me. Just like in Ungaía. I loved it. Lose yourself in my body. Take me until you find the balance you need."

Risto's nostrils flared and his lips twisted into a sexy smile. "Fuck, I love you."

With one quick pull, he tore the shirt from her body, then did the same with the T-shirt she wore underneath. Her unbound breasts heaved with her excited, erratic breaths. He lifted her to sit on the end of the bed and pulled the leggings from her, then removed her socks. He stepped away. His breathing slow and controlled, he scanned her nudity. The lust blazing in the depths of his eyes had her flushing.

"Crawl up the bed. I want you on your knees. Head down. Butt in the air."

Callie swallowed hard. "Are you going to spank me?" He'd threatened to do so in the past and again earlier today, but she'd thought he'd been teasing.

Risto grinned evilly. "We'll see. Now get in position."

She nodded, biting her lip. She scooted farther back onto the bed, then turned over and crawled to the middle and assumed the position he'd dictated. She swore she could feel his fiery stare on her bare ass. "Like this?" She wiggled her butt, teasing him.

"Almost perfect." His purring voice came from her right

side. His hand smoothed over each buttock. Her pussy got even wetter and goose bumps popped up all over her body at his touch.

Several seconds passed without any further action on Risto's part. She heard the sound of a zipper and the rustling of clothing. She turned her head toward him then inhaled. He was gloriously naked. Every muscle sharply defined by the indirect lighting of the bedroom. Her pussy tightened around the emptiness, demanding to be filled. His cock was fully erect, the plum-colored head glistened with precum. "Um, why almost? You sure look ready to me."

"You'll need some support in this position." He pulled a couple of pillows from the head of the bed and tucked them under her stomach. "This should take some of the strain off your back. Now, stretch forward. Reach for the headboard. Head between your arms."

"Like this?" She laid her head sideways so she could breathe.

"Here," he tucked a pillow under her head and arranged her arms to lie on either side of the pillow. "Comfortable?" He swept a hand over her back from the top of her spine to her ass, again and again—petting her, soothing her, exciting her.

"Yes."

"Good. You'll be there for awhile." On his next stroke down her back, he fondled her bottom, caressing each globe. "I want you comfortable. You hurt or get a cramp, I want to know. I don't want to upset the baby." He smacked one butt cheek lightly then massaged it with firm fingers. She gasped and shot him a questioning look. He smiled. "Just a warm-up tap." He spanked the same area two more times. "You pink up quickly. Barely any jiggling." He squeezed one of her ass cheeks as if testing it for ripeness. "Nice and firm. You have a gorgeous ass, sweetheart." He leaned over and licked the area he just fondled. She squirmed. His tongue tickled and was cool against the heat of her skin. She shivered.

He fingered her pussy. "You liked that. You're getting

wetter." It wasn't a question. "I liked doing it." He climbed onto the bed behind her, his legs on either side of hers, blocking her in. He slapped her other ass cheek several times, then eased the slight sting with his tongue. She blushed at the intimacy of his mouth on her bottom. Her clit throbbed with each touch of his hand and his tongue. He checked her sex with his finger again, taking his time to touch her labia and clit. "Sweet Jesus, you're so responsive. So beautiful like this."

She wiggled her butt—and he laughed. Risto slapped each ass cheek until she felt her skin heat up.

"Perfect color, all rosy just for me." He covered her body with his. His arousal snuggled against the seam of her butt. His pubic hair scratched the sensitized skin of her ass. He supported himself with his left arm placed alongside her outstretched one. He nuzzled her hair away from her neck then kissed and teethed the shoulder he bared.

"Risto!" She thrust her butt to meet him. "In. Now."

He nipped her shoulder sharply. "Not yet. Behave." He cuddled a breast with his free hand, his thumb rhythmically brushed over her aching nipple again and again.

She gasped, jerking away from his touch. She clenched her inner muscles against the ache. She was so ready to come and would as soon as he put his cock in her—if he ever would. "So sensitive." He kissed the top of her spine and nibbled down the vertebrae. Her back had become one giant erogenous zone. She shuddered as he slowly detailed each inch of skin along both sides of her spine. He continued to tease her right breast, altering the pressure on her nipple with each pass of his thumb. "Did Tweeter take you this way?"

His words jerked her out of the almost euphoric state his lips and hands had created. No matter what he'd said, it still bothered him her first sexual experience had been with a man he considered a friend and colleague. A man he'd have to face every time he went to Sanctuary. Only time and her love would take care of his insecurity.

"No ... no ... just you." She moaned as he sharply pinched the nipple he'd stimulated. The pointed pain translated as pleasure to her clit.

"Fuck, I'm glad." He kissed his way back up her spinal column then rubbed his cheek over the same area as if he were a male cat rubbing his scent over his mate. He moved his hand to the other breast, caressing it, arousing it to the point of pain-pleasure. All the while he kissed, licked and nibbled along her neck, shoulders and spine until he had her whimpering. Her juices were dripping down her inner thighs now.

She shoved her bottom against his hot, hard, pulsing erection. His cock slid along the seam of her ass. She could feel his precum dampening her. "Dammit, Risto ... take me. Fuck me. Hard."

"Not yet." His voice was harsh with sexual tension. She was glad she wasn't the only one suffering. He moved his hand from her breast down over her tightened stomach muscles to her sexual folds. A firm finger stroked over and around her opening. He managed to miss her aching clit each and every time.

Damn him for being a tease.

"You are so wet for me. Just for me." He shifted slightly to nip a butt cheek.

"God, yes ... only you." She panted and rubbed against him, tempting him in the only way she could as he surrounded her with his body.

"Good, 'cause I'm going to pound you, baby." *Thank you, Lord.* "Going to release all the fear clawing at my gut over you endangering yourself." He spanked her pussy right over her clit. The small bite of pain had her yelping into her pillow and almost threw her over into orgasm. "Going to claim what's mine and will never be Walsh's again." He rubbed his thumb over her engorged bud.

She whimpered then gasped as he shoved two fingers into her pussy and thumbed her clit, setting a punishing rhythm.

"Only yours. God that's so good, so good … God, please, fuck me now. I need you. Only you."

Risto snarled something dark and gritty against her back as he fucked her with his fingers, his thumb on her clit, pushing her to a climax she wasn't sure she'd survive. She could barely breathe, let alone scream, for the pleasure building within her.

She reached blindly for the arm he'd braced alongside her. She gripped it hard as her orgasm overtook her. She shouted her pleasure again and again into the pillow. He held her in place and continued to ply her pussy and clit, drawing out her enjoyment. And just when she thought the powerful release was winding down, he pulled another intense peak out of her by stroking her G-spot with his thrusting fingers.

"So fucking gorgeous." He kissed and nipped her back from her neck to her bottom. Finally, he pulled his hand from her sex, but even then her body continued to convulse with minor aftershocks. "Look at me, baby." He turned her onto her back, pulling the pillows out from under her until she lay flat on the bed.

She watched him lick her fluids from his hand. His dark eyes filled with heat and enjoyment. "You taste like heaven."

He stroked her sides, gentling her, as he sat back on his heels. She smiled at him and felt herself slipping into sleep.

"No sleeping yet. I'm not done with you."

"Oh, damn, you haven't come yet." She eyed his erection. It jutted from his groin, its tip almost reaching his navel. She reached for him with one hand as she supported herself with the other arm on the bed. "Come into me."

"Hands down." He positioned her hands on each side of the pillow supporting her head. "Leave them there." He tipped her chin so he could kiss her. She tasted herself in his hot mouth.

Once again he surrounded her, anchoring her with his body, this time face-to-face. It was so hard not to touch him, but she sensed he was on a short fuse and wanted to take this at his own pace. She wasn't going anywhere until he allowed it. All she could do was answer his kiss with her tongue and mewl in the back of her throat as he took her mouth.

When he broke off the kiss, she gasped for breath. He straightened and pulled away from her, the chill of the air caused her to whimper at the loss of his heat and weight.

"Easy, baby. I'm here. Not going anywhere." He slid his erection up and down the folds of her sex, hitting her distended clit, still very sensitive from her orgasm. She moaned at the acute sensation and knew it wouldn't take long for her to climax again. Holding her hips steady, he angled her pelvis and slipped his cock into her with one steady thrust of his hips. He stopped as she adjusted to his girth and length. "Am I hurting you?"

"I'm fine ... Risto ... please." She writhed against the bed. "Move, dammit."

"I'm too close, baby. I want you with me." He firmed his grip and stopped her movement. His face was taut with his pleasure.

Leaning over, he nibbled a path of biting and suckling kisses along her shoulder to her neck. Taking her earlobe between his teeth, he tugged her ear. She shivered, letting out a low cry. "Fuck, your ears and neck are so sensitive." He slipped the tip of his tongue into her ear. She sobbed his name. He nuzzled the skin behind her ear. "So sweet. So responsive. All mine."

"Yours. All yours." She cried out when he pulled away from her neck. "I love you, my marine. No one else."

"I'm so glad. But I am in control in the bedroom." His lowly muttered "because it looks as if I'll have fucking little control anywhere else" caused her to laugh.

He leaned over and took her mouth, forcing his cock even farther into her. She moaned low in her throat and ate at his tongue. With his cock fully lodged, he rotated his hips, causing his pubic bone to press on her clit. She broke away from his kiss, her head tossing on the pillow. Callie clenched her teeth. "God, Risto … that is so … fucking … good … ahh!" She fisted the pillow, clawing for the pleasure which was just out of reach. "Risto!"

Risto supported himself on his forearms and began to thrust in and out of her pussy. The motions started slow but increased in speed and force with each push-pull of his hips until he pounded her bottom into the mattress. As he took her, he kissed and licked her heaving breasts.

When he bit the tip of one nipple, he snarled, "Now, baby. Come now."

And there it was, her release had been hovering just at the edges of her consciousness, waiting for him. The strength of her climax forced her ass up and away from the bed, lifting his greater weight and impaling herself on his cock even more fully. "Risto! Ohmygod. Ohmygod." Her inner muscles clamped down on his cock like a vice, not wanting to let go, wanting to make the feelings last forever. His thickness and length stroked her swollen inner tissues, touching every sensitized nerve.

Just like a leaf sucked up into a maelstrom, she was buffeted on currents of never-ending pleasure—hers and his as their pleasure fed upon each other's. And just when she couldn't scream anymore, she fell back to earth.

Risto shot his seed into Callie's body as her inner muscles continued fisting him even as the rest of her body went lax. He brushed kisses over her face and hair as his hips continued to undulate, drawing this closeness and contentment out for as long as possible. The climax was the strongest he could ever recall in his long sexual history. Callie responded to his every move so beautifully, just the right mixture of sass and compliance. He could see long years of equally mind-boggling, dick-wrenching sex—that is, if she didn't get her stubborn little ass shot first. He lips curled into a silent snarl. She whimpered and he brushed a kiss over her pouty lips. She settled at his touch.

"Not gonna happen, baby. Not on my watch." He nuzzled the side of her neck, licking over the pulse throbbing just under her creamy skin. "I'll protect you any way I can."

Callie moaned when he pulled his cock from her sex. He rolled off her body then lay on his side. Murmuring soothing nonsense, he pulled her back into the curve of his body. Surrounding her with his bulk and heat, he stroked her stomach, his hand dark and rough against her pale smooth skin. Brushing a kiss over one pale shoulder, he smiled as he visualized their child nestled safely within her.

She murmured in her sleep and snuggled into him, her rosy pink ass rubbing against his cock. He groaned and promised himself to make sure to add the erotic spanking into their regular sexual repertoire. She'd enjoyed his hand on her ass—and he'd enjoyed doing it to her.

He whispered words of love and appreciation over the sensitive flesh behind her ear, taking the lobe gently between his teeth. She shivered and muttered. "Shh, baby. All done. Sleep."

He frowned as he noticed dark circles under her eyes. He traced a gentle fingertip over the one closest to him. Had he pushed her too hard? No, he wouldn't second-guess himself or belittle her strength. She'd been with him one hundred percent, giving him everything he asked for and more. He—they—had needed this time to bond, become closer. He knew he hadn't hurt her, had only given her pleasure. And his Callie was a strong woman who would've told him if she couldn't handle what he gave her in bed. His lips quirked. Besides, she'd enjoyed every second of the sexual encounter. Her screams of pleasure attested to that fact. Thank God he'd had the foresight to put the men in the guest cottages. He laid her flat on her back and leaned over to kiss her belly where his child grew before getting out of bed.

After cleaning both of them up, he tucked her under the

covers. He made the security rounds one more time, then grabbed a bottle of water for both of them and a sleeve of Saltines for Callie. After drinking his water, he took the other items to the bedroom. He placed the morning sickness precautions on the bedside table so Callie would see them when she awoke.

Once he was satisfied that he'd taken care of ensuring Callie's safety and comfort, he climbed into bed and pulled the love of his life into the curve of his body, spooning her, sheltering her for what was left of the night. Burying his face in her silky hair, he sighed and fell asleep, vowing to protect her precious body and the child it bore with all that was within him.

Chapter Twenty-Three

Before dawn, Thursday morning, Osprey's Point.

Callie sat at Big Earl's counter and ate small bites of his home-cooked oatmeal, allowing each spoonful to settle before chancing another bite. So far the Saltines Risto had hand-fed her before she was even completely awake were doing the trick. The oatmeal wasn't triggering any morning sickness, either. It looked to be a good day on the hormone front. The heat of the soothing breakfast staple did double duty and warmed her up after the cold, wet boat ride from the island. The pre-dawn morning was overcast, just below freezing and windy with snow ranging from flurries to white-out conditions. A typical northern Michigan winter's day. She smiled. Cruz and his crew, used to hot, third-world hellholes, would hate this. She, however, loved it.

"You okay?" Risto's arm curled around her waist. He nuzzled her neck, right over the spot he'd sucked, licked and teethed this morning as he'd cuddled her awake.

"Just fine." She angled her head and kissed him. "Baby is happy with crackers and oatmeal."

He swiveled the bar stool around so she faced him, then looked her over with a critical eye. "The Kevlar vest seems to fit okay."

"Yeah, if you like the Poppin' Fresh Doughboy look." She looked down at the extra-layer of protection Risto and the Walsh twins had insisted upon. "Good thing I'm tall and busty or it would fall off my shoulders." She plucked at the bulky bullet-proof vest and the thermal underwear beneath it. Both items belonged to Tweeter and had been left behind after he and Keely had helped Risto set up the security array on the island. "Tweeter's ski underwear is just the right size, though." She stroked his cheek. "Yours would've swamped me."

Risto's dark eyes glittered with simmering sexuality. "But you like me big, dontcha, baby?"

"Yep, I love the fact you can lift me as if I were as tiny as Keely." She touched her forehead to his chest. His heart beat slowly, his breathing slow and calm. He acted much less stressed this morning. *Guess the mind-blowing sex last night was worth it.* Just the memory of the orgasms he'd given her had her heating up from within, shoving away the cold of the day.

"Hey, Smith, leave my sniper alone." Loren came over to stand next to them. He scanned her face. "No nerves there."

Yay, I've got him fooled. Risto was another matter. He'd sensed her nerves and had come to distract her with his always present sexuality. It had worked.

"Reminds me of my baby sis." Loren patted her shoulder. "Ready to get set up?"

"Yeah." She kissed Risto, letting him hold her close for a few seconds more, since her next chance might be some hours away. Loren snorted in the background and a couple of hoots from the other men didn't dissuade her from taking her time. When she broke away, she licked her lips, tasting his morning coffee, mint and him, then fixed him with a stern look. "Protect that ass of yours, Marine. I still have a use for it."

Risto hugged her tightly and muttered against her hair. "Don't take any chances." He leaned back and shook her, his hands gentle on her arms. "Stay safe—you hear me?"

"I'll be fine." She shot him a cheeky grin. "Trust me, I don't want to get shot. Plus, I'll be in the safest spot next to Loren's. It's the rest of you I'll be worrying about." Running gun battles on streets and around corners of buildings could be tricky at best and lethal at worst.

Conn came over, captured her hand and squeezed it gently. "Don't hesitate to take your shot when you have one, Callie. You'll have the best view of the battleground. Don't warn us, just take it. All of us have been in battle with sniper protection before, we'll know where you are and stay out of your line of sight the best we can."

She nodded then frowned. "I just don't want to take my first shot too early, tip them off and allow them to get cover."

"That's my call, Callie." Loren squeezed her shoulder. "As your spotter, I'll give you the cue to take the first shot and feed you intel as to crucial shots as I see them." He picked up her rifle bag and his. "Come on, kiddo. Let's go. You got your communications headset?"

She held it up and slipped it on, then pulled a thermal-lined balaclava over her head followed by a wool ski cap. Risto tucked away an errant strand of hair, his finger sweeping over her cheek in a loving caress, then helped her into Tweeter's arctic-weight parka, which was the closest they had to fit her. A trip to a ski town in the U.P. was needed to outfit her more properly for winter weather until she could get back to Chicago and pack up her clothing. Whether they lived here or in Sanctuary, she would need heavier outwear.

Risto pulled her into his arms for one last quick kiss, then turned her over to Loren with a pat on her bottom. "See you soon."

Risto's lips might be smiling but his eyes were sober with worry. She sighed. She couldn't take away his fear—he would always be overprotective and a worry-wart about her safety—she could only survive and prove yet again she had what it took to be a warrior's mate.

She waved at the other men who shared a similar look in

their eyes to Risto's. *Sheesh.* She had to survive intact to prove her worth to all of them. No pressure there … much. She followed Loren out the back of Big Earl's. He had Big Earl's set of keys and the security codes to the private residences they'd be using for their designated posts. They made their way along Osprey's Point's main street in the frigid pre-dawn air, flurries blowing all around them on the stiff breeze coming off the lake. She scanned the empty marina area as they walked up the hill to the Victorian they had chosen for her position. The quiet was preternatural; nothing moved in the early morning darkness except for the snow, the wind and the waves on the lake. The new snow under her booted feet crunched slightly, evidence there had been a temperature shift overnight. It was colder than a witch's tit now.

When they reached her shooting site, she stood guard on the front porch of the two-story house, a Glock in her hand, her back to Loren, as he got them inside.

"We're in." His monotone carried no farther than her position. Sound would travel easily on the brisk wind.

She turned and followed him into the house, closing and locking the door behind her. Both of them used small Maglights to light their way up the stairs. Big Earl had told them the door to the widow's walk and the rest of the roof was through the attic. The access to which was a set of stairs at the back of the house from the second floor. Once in the attic, the door to the widow's walk was at the front of the house between two huge dormer windows.

The view from the walkway was fantastic. She had a panoramic view of Osprey's Point's main street and commercial area and all of the marina, but for the part blocked by Big Earl's building. Behind the house was an impassable crag which had gone a long way in reassuring Risto that it would be hard to sneak up on her position from behind. She eyed the steep cliff. Well, maybe not totally impassable, a determined bad guy could rappel into the backyard. She could do it with the proper gear and a climbing buddy, so Cruz's hired help could possibly do it also. Worst case scenario to her way of thinking would be if someone knew to climb up there; they'd have the same shots into the town she would. They wouldn't be able to shoot her, though; the pitch of the roof protected the front of the house and the widow's walk where she would be.

Standing next to her at the west corner of the house, Loren eyed the cliff, also. "The front of the house is well-protected from the bluff. Let's get you situated."

She headed for the place she'd chosen to set up her rifle. "Here look good to you?"

Loren moved to where she'd left her rifle bag and eye-balled the view. "Perfect. I only hope my position is as open and all-encompassing. I want to check walkway access from the back of the house." He moved off and she began to unload her bag. The guys had partially assembled the Lapua so she didn't have much to do but check over their work.

Several minutes later, Loren came at her from the opposite direction from which he'd started. "There's another walkway egress than the one through the attic." He motioned her to follow; they walked around toward the rear of the house. "See?" He pointed to something attached to the side of the house. "The owners installed a series of external drop-down ladders from the attic-level to the ground. Probably an alternate fire escape in case the residents are trapped above the first floor."

She nodded. "The ladders would also give an enterprising person a chance to get up from the ground. All they'd have to do is get into the backyard and then pull down the first ladder and then again for the next one. Maybe with a grappling hook?"

Loren took her arm and urged her back to the front of the house and her setup. "Yeah. I'll keep a close eye out on the top of the crag. My roof is so flat I'll have a three-sixty view." When they reached her position, he turned to her and tapped the end of her nose. "Okay. Headset on?" She nodded. "Listen for my cue on the first shot. After that, take any you feel are necessary. I'll alert you to any others I see that are dire." Meaning one of their guys was in danger of getting his ass capped.

"I'm worried I might miss and…" Shooting live humans was far different than hitting targets. The kill shots she'd taken at Conn's had been different—she'd been in direct danger then. Sniping was planned, not reactive—more a calculated choice to take a life, not an instinctive one. If she froze, if her brain decided to rationalize the shot … someone, Risto, could die because she got wussy.

"I'm not worried. You'll hold it together. What did our dads always tell us about shooting in battle situations?"

"If you're going to shoot, shoot to kill. If you aren't going to shoot to kill, then what the fuck are you doing on the battlefield?"

"This is definitely war. Cruz and his men are coming here to kill your man and take you. We have been sanctioned to take them out as enemies of the state. You have the skills, use them. Don't think, just shoot. If it helps, picture them as targets, not people." He leaned over and brushed a brotherly kiss over her chilled forehead. "Take care—and good hunting."

She kissed his cheek. "You, too. Go. I can handle my set up."

"I know you can." He nodded. "There are five pre-loaded magazines and enough ammo to reload. I'll use the emergency ladders at the back of the house so no one sees me leave."

She nodded and hoped to hell twenty-five shots would be enough. The Lapua mags she was using held five .338 cartridges. Re-loading magazines in the cold and while a battle ensued would be tough; she was used to indoor shooting and had trained in a warmer climate. She waved at Loren as he disappeared around the corner of the house. She listened carefully and couldn't hear the ladders drop. But then SEALs were trained to be swift, silent and deadly.

She laid her rifle aside on the bag, then cleared a spot on

the widow's walk on which to spread a waterproof tarp. She sat on the dry surface and attached the bipod to the rifle since she didn't plan on moving around to take shots. The bipod would give her the maximum stability for her shots and was much more desirable than using a bean bag or some other mobile positioning device some snipers used when changing their sniping positions. She also checked the butt pad for proper spacing as compared to the length of her arm from her hand to her shoulder and for comfort. Loren or Paul had guessed correctly and she would not have to make any adjustments to the butt pad spacing.

Finally, she looked over the three scopes the guys had put into the bag. She attached a scope that could deal with the unique glare provided by cloud cover and snow. The Weather Channel had predicted the snow would not end for the next twenty-four hours; so clouds were assured. If the sun peeked through for a bit, well, the scope could handle it also with a slight adjustment. Then she plotted and tested distances against her hand-held targeting computer and her scope's site.

The gusting winds were tricky and would have to be accounted for. The Lapua was made for cold-weather shooting and had been used in much harsher weather than today's. She patted the stock.

It didn't take long to get the rifle positioned, and only a few minutes more to locate targeting points and find their ranges. To check her scope sightings, she plotted every nook and cranny of Osprey's Point within her direct line of sight into the computer. She sighed with relief when the computer data matched her skills with the scope. Every shot she might need to take was less than the maximum range, upping her chances to make a lethal or crippling shot.

Everything done, she had time on her hands until Loren gave her the word. She lay on her stomach and sighted through her rifle scope toward the roof where Loren should be setting up. She couldn't see him.

She tapped her headset, putting her on the private link to Loren. "You set?"

"Yeah. You?"

"Roger that. I can't see you."

"Good. I can't see you, either."

"Should we go to the group frequency?" she asked. She suddenly needed to hear Risto's calm voice.

"No, not until we see the bad guys. Then we'll need to talk to the guys and let them know who's on their asses. Right now they're scouting and it would be distracting for them and you." She heard the emphasis on *you* and knew if she hadn't been there, Loren would be on the group frequency with the guys, sharing in some sort of pre-battle ritual bullshit. "I don't see any bogies yet," he said.

"Okay. Since I don't have to shoot yet, I'll put my hand warmers on." She had Thinsulate shooting gloves made specifically for cold-weather shooting. She slipped on her ski gloves with built-in battery-powered heating units to keep her joints limber. "It is frigging cold up here."

Loren's chuckle came over the headset clearly. "Yeah, my dangly parts aren't happy, either."

"Way too much information."

He snorted. "You're not shocked. I can remember we boys used to moon you and Imp to get you to shriek and giggle."

She laughed. "That you did. But my marine would cut those puppies off if you did that now."

"That he would. Just checked your six. Didn't see anyone on the cliff behind your position. This flat roof does have a nice view."

"Appreciate that." Her gut clenched at the thought Cruz might have found local help who'd know all the various approaches to the town. "Going to silence."

Callie could hear Loren's slow, calm breaths and the whistle of the wind over her headset. She rechecked her set-up once more and was happy with it. Bored and needing to do something, she picked up a set of mini-binoculars to scan the road leading in and out of Osprey's Point. Yeah, that technically was Loren's job, but two sets of eyes were always better than one.

The town was located on an inlet of Thousand Islands Lake and surrounded by the Ottawa Forest. Thick stands of trees hugged the main roadway in and out of town, only interrupted where a house or a commercial building was located. The woods backed up to most of the residences along the main street, except where the rocky crags were located; there, the trees grew right up to the edge of the cliffs. If Cruz and his force decided to come in through the forest, she and Loren wouldn't see them until they popped out. Vigilance was paramount.

She scanned the marina area and the few side streets to the extent of her field of vision. She saw no movement anywhere—from bad guys or her guys, which proved to her how good their side was. Big Earl's was the only building of any type, commercial or residential, lit up. It stayed open 24/7 for the year-round residents. Closing it would have made anyone who'd scouted the town suspicious.

Making another full sweep of the area, a movement at the edge of town caught her eye. She focused the binocs on the road coming from Watersmeet where it entered the town's limits. There it was again, a shadow cast on the snow-covered berm; no, there were several shadows and they were in motion. "Loren. My three o'clock, south side of the main road, just before the gas station."

A several second pause and all she heard was Loren's slow, calm breaths. "Good eye. I've got more movement on the north side. See it?"

"Switching to my rifle scope." She set the binocs down and sighted through the rifle. *There you are.* The scope was so powerful she could almost count the facial scars on the first man she made out. "Yeah. Got 'em. They're just under fourteen hundred meters from my position."

"Roger that. Get ready. Shit is about to fly." Loren's voice was unruffled.

She had to remind herself to breathe slowly when all she wanted to do was pant as the adrenaline flowed into her bloodstream. Breathe in. Breathe out. Keep the heart rate down so she could hear Loren and the others instead of her heart thudding like a marching band's bass drum. Her eye still on the scope, her breath stuttered. A man in Arctic snow gear scuttled along the ditch, paralleling the shoulder, on the south side of the main road. This was the movement she had seen first. He ran up and over the road and disappeared into the north side ditch. She could barely see his white-hooded head move toward the docks. "Loren! Marina approach."

"I see the fucker. Wait for my signal. Switch to group frequency, Callie." She did so and heard Loren tell the others, "Heads up, guys. We've got company coming from the east. One tango is going for a boat. I see maybe ten others approaching. Could be more behind them. Fuckers have Arctic battle whites."

A series of calm acknowledgments came over the headset.

The plan was premised on two facts: one, the bad guys didn't know they were anticipated and, two, they would need a boat to reach Risto's island. Big Earl's was the only place on this part of the lake with a year-round dock navigable at this time of the year with boats available. They'd taken the chance that Cruz wasn't savvy enough to obtain a boat elsewhere, tow it to the general area, and then attempt to launch in the early winter snowstorm from a public launch site farther up the shoreline. Even if the Colombian had thought of the latter scenario, all the public launches would be under six feet of snow and ice, making it damn tricky and near impossible to launch a boat safely. So, the trap would be set and sprung at Osprey's Point Marina.

Their premise had a ninety-seven percent probability. The

other three percent, an air approach, was covered by Keely and Tweeter who monitored the lake area using the feed from an NSA satellite miles above the Earth. They'd have called if Cruz had found a way to accomplish an air approach.

Loren's voice startled her from her brain fade. "We've twenty bogies total, gang. They have snow gear and are loaded for bear. Fuck, they've got a rocket launcher." Several different voices swore.

Callie's narrowed gaze swept the line of men approaching the marina. She singled out the guy with the rocket launcher. His scarred skin was swarthy against the white of his hooded parka. He didn't look Hispanic, more like Middle Eastern. Maybe a survivor of the war in Bosnia or any number of places in the war-torn deserts of Asia Minor and Africa.

The rocket launcher was on the man's back and extended above his head. He could do a lot of damage with that weapon. And wasn't she glad she wasn't stuck on the island at the mercy of that thing. She'd remember to tell Risto that very fact ... later.

Callie pulled off her mittens, flexed her fingers encased in the thinner shooting gloves, took a deep breath, blew it out, then sighted for the shot, her trigger finger at ready. She acquired his forehead, her target centered between his thick bushy eyebrows and up a quarter-inch. She also checked a shot for the bag the man carried, probably containing the rocket-propelled grenades for the launcher. She had two shots she could take. No matter which, the shot was less than a thousand meters and moving ever closer. If the man headed toward a boat dock behind the profile of Big Earl's she'd lose her shot. She couldn't wait.

Her finger was poised on the trigger, she increased the pressure slightly, waiting for Loren. She could take out the man or the bag. If the bag exploded, it would take care of the explosives, the gun and the man. The chatter in the background washed over her as she debated. The first shot wasn't her call.

It was Loren's. "Loren, if I take out the bag, will my shot blow the munitions?"

Loren's voice, "Fuck, maybe, if you hit a grenade at just the right place with enough percussion."

"Go for it, baby." Risto's calm, confident voice came over her headset. "If nothing else, it will start something. We're all in position and ready to rock. The fact they have a rocket launcher is all we need to justify shooting first."

The theory being, no one would come armed to the teeth if they hadn't wanted to start a war. She took in a deep breath and let it out. Her eye to the scope, her world narrowed to the bag as the man carrying it trotted along the road. On her next breath, she took the shot as she exhaled slowly. The bag decimated, but did not explode. The man went down, the bullet passing through his hip. He might manage to crawl, but he wasn't walking anywhere for a while.

Loren's voice, "Good shot. I'll take the kill shot on him, Callie. I have the better angle."

Callie checked her scope and noted she had no head shot, the man had fallen with his feet toward her, the bag next to his legs. She sighed with relief, letting Loren take the burden from her. The crack of the Barrett came over the headset. The downed man's body jerked from Loren's high-caliber round. She swallowed heavily, glad she had no view of what had happened to the man's head. Her dad's voice came to her just as it had in Colombia, *"Callie, don't think. Just do. Worry about what you did after the battle is over."*

All hell broke loose after Loren took his shot. Her ears waiting for Loren's commands, she phased out the men's chatter as she noted movement coming from the side of the dead man. A bad guy was going to retrieve the rocket launcher and the ammo bag.

Not waiting for Loren, she took the bogie out with a shot to the head, incapacitating or killing him. She saw the blood spurt and swallowed. She took a deep breath, then set her sight back on the bag. It bugged her that the damn bag had not exploded. Her .338 cartridges could stop a rhino and destroy an engine block; it should have pierced any ammo in the bag.

"Good shot there, Callie." Loren's voice. "Bogie on Conn's ass. East side of Big Earl's front door. Don't worry about the RPG, we can cherry pick any tango stupid enough to go for it."

Loren's logic made sense so she switched her scope to the diner and saw a man approaching a position where one of her guys must be hunkered down. She took the shot. The bad guy was down.

Conn's voice, "Thanks, sweet cheeks. He's toast."

She had two shots left in this magazine, sweeping the area, she took out another man going for the rocket launcher. Then another. They must've really wanted to blow things up.

"Reloading," she said, her voice thin from the stress threatening to choke her. She'd taken out four men and a bag. She swallowed several times and closed her eyes as she switched out the magazine by feel just as her dad had taught her. She remembered practicing in the dark for hours until she could assemble and disassemble a sniper rifle, switch out magazines and load ammo into magazines fast and efficiently. He'd given her a Bob Mackie Barbie to reward her proficiency.

She opened her eyes and readied herself. All was silent. When had that happened? *Okay, breathe. Everyone's reassessing the situation.* Cruz's people just realized this wasn't the turkey shoot they expected and the good guys were ready and capable. She scanned the streets through the scope and then looked around her position on the walkway. She was still alone as far as she could tell.

"What's up?" she whispered into her cheek mike.

"They're thinking they're up shit crick." The drawling voice was one of the local men.

"Okay, that's what I thought. How's my six?"

Loren's voice, "No one coming your way that I can see.

Don't worry, I've got you covered."

"And I've got you." She took aim and took out the man approaching the house Loren was perched on. "Move, Loren. They know you're there."

"Thanks." She heard Loren's movements. "Bugging out and heading your way."

"No. I'm fine. If they find me, I'll go down the back and find my way into the woods." She swept the area around Loren's position. "Stay down, Loren. Another one coming your way." She took the shot.

"Good shooting, baby." Risto's calm, low tones steadied her. "I'm going to cover Loren's six while the other guys take it to the badasses. Cover us."

"Got it." She eyed the area around the modern house where Loren was located, saw movement and knew it was Risto by his size and how he moved. A shadow slithered along a side street on an intersecting path. "Bogie coming your way, Marine. Intersect path, west side of the Confectionary Store." Risto's low snarl made her womb clench. "Target acquired. Drop, Risto!" She took the shot and winged the guy. "He's wounded, not wiped. Wounded, got that?"

"No worries." Loren had somehow gotten off his roof unseen and approached the man she crippled from behind then slit his throat.

She gagged at the sight of the arterial blood spray turning the snow around him red. She turned her head from the scope and vomited away from her weapon and ammo. She scooped some clean snow and used it to wipe her mouth, then spit.

"Callie? Baby? You sick?" Risto's breaths were loud over the headset and she knew he was hoofing it alongside Loren.

She cleared her throat. "Fine. Don't risk your ass. The blood got to me." She took a calming breath and placed her eye back on the rifle's sight. The sound of shots echoed off buildings as both sides escalated, the bad guys trying to kill Risto and Loren, and the good guys, protecting. She spotted

Berto moving to cover the other two. "Berto, heads up. Guy on your ass."

"Go for him." Berto dove behind a trash container and Callie took out the man bearing down on her friend. "Kill shot, *chica*." He slithered into the shadows to rejoin the battle.

She had one more shot in this magazine. She swept the area in front of the marina and found another man crawling toward the rocket launcher. She took him out.

"Reloading." She practiced breathing slowly as her gloved fingers, cold and trembling slightly despite the high-tech material, switched out the magazines. "Ready."

Her eye back on the scope, she noted the wind and blowing snow had picked up. A draft down the side of her neck had her shivering. She readjusted the neck gaiter. When would this end? *"Patience Callie,"* her dad's voice rang in her ears, *"the patient soldier wins more often than not."*

How many were down? She'd taken out nine and a bag, ten rounds. The men on the ground had to have taken out some silently which she wouldn't necessarily know about. She had fifteen rounds left, loaded. Should be enough to get the job done. Maybe she should load the empty mags. She reached for an empty magazine and pulled five cartridges from the side pocket of the bag and loaded them as she braced herself on her forearms, her gaze divided between the two duties.

"Baby?" Risto's voice came over the headset. His voice, though calm, held concern.

"I'm fine." She placed the loaded magazine next to her others and then began loading the other empty one. "Just reloading the empty magazines. I need to do something."

"I understand. Waiting for shit to happen is a learned skill. You're doing super." He paused and let out a noisy breath. "However, you won't be doing this again—ever. Over my dead body, will you ever do this again."

"We'll see, Marine." She knew he needed soothing, but it was hard to do over a shared connection. "We'll be using some more of your stress relief method later." His sharp inhale had her seeing images of heat in his eyes. "Where are we at now ... exactly?"

"They've dug in, sweetheart, mostly because of your fine shooting. They couldn't figure exactly where the shots came from which is why they went after Loren's position when they spied him. By the way, Loren's coming to you now through the back of the house. So be warned."

"I won't shoot him. I promise."

Paul's voice, "You have my permission to shoot him. I've always wanted to be an only twin." The sound of several of the men's laughter came over the headset. Callie shook her head. Her dad and Colonel Walsh had often spoken of battlefield humor, but this was her first real experience with it.

"Permission to come on the roof." Loren's voice came from behind and to the side of her. The dormer blocked her view of the attic door.

"Permission granted." She angled her head away from her scope for a second and smiled as Loren crawled onto the widow's walk.

"Hey, kiddo." He looked her over. He spoke into his headset. "She's pale, but holding, Risto. No worries. She's fine."

"Thanks, Loren." Risto's tone was filled with relief. He had to be as worried about her as she was him. "We're going hunting. Just watch for bad guys retreating. No one gets out of town. No one."

Several choruses of "got that right" peppered with several anatomically impossible suggestions for the bad guys came over her headset. Callie shook her head, scanning the marina. The rocket launcher was still attached to the dead man's back, and the bodies of the men who'd tried to liberate it were still lying in the street, their blood creating red Rorschach images in the snow.

"Loren, you set?" She didn't look away from her scope.

"Yeah." His voice came over the headset even though he was only twelve feet or so away. "No one has tried for the rocket launcher since you took those men out. Good shooting, kiddo. Let's keep an eye on it. If the tangos get that weapon, you, I and this very nice house would be toast."

She coughed and sniffed as her nose began to run from the cold and the wind. "They know where we are, don't they?"

"Yeah—it's the only other place for the types of shots you've taken. Their job now is to get to us without placing themselves in our scopes. We might get a chance to take some out from up here, but at this point, our main job is to keep the badasses away from the rocket launcher and off our roof."

"Gotcha." Or keep them off other roofs. She quickly checked the other buildings along the main street, most of which were single story. No danger there so far. She spotted movement on ground level, approaching the house where Loren had been. "Who's near Loren's old site? I've got movement."

A chorus of "no ones."

Loren's voice came across, "I see him. Good eye, Callie. I have the better shot." A shot rang out from Loren's Barrett and the shadow went down. Callie could see the man's head had been partially blown off.

"You..." she choked and swallowed the bile, "got him." She took several deep breaths. "What do you have in that thing? .50 caliber? Right?"

"Yeah." Loren paused then added, "Take a break, Callie, if you need to."

She appreciated the sentiment, but... "My marine is out there. I'll take a break when this is done and we're safe on the island."

"That's my woman." Risto's voice rumbled over the mike and instantly warmed her. He was alive and safe—so far.

"Callie, you sure you won't come to Cartagena and be my woman? I have a much bigger dick than old Risto and would treat you like a queen." Conn went silent and a shot rang out.

"Got the fucker."

Callie snickered when Risto said, "Don't believe him, baby. His pencil dick is half my length. The only thing he can shoot off is his mouth and that Glock he's carrying." The other men chortled.

The crack of Loren's Barrett had her scanning the area. "What did you see, Loren?"

"Eastside of town. Something at the edge of the woods. Along the north side of the road heading into the marina."

"You got him, buddy," one of the local men said. "Fucker had hung back."

"Was it Cruz?" Callie asked. If it were, the others might retreat.

"No such luck," the same local said. "Some Asian merc. Asshole hired a whole bunch of outside talent."

Callie's gaze swept back to the center of the street. No action near the rocket launcher. She wondered aloud. "Why didn't the ammo bag explode when I hit it? Are the rockets like plastique and need a triggering device?"

Big Earl answered. "Possibility, but not likely. Just need the right percussion to set them off. Loren, maybe a hotter bullet will do the job. You got a shot?"

"Hell, yeah. Callie dropped the fucker perfectly for this angle. Bag is just a sitting duck. You want me to try and make a nice hole in the middle of the street? I'd have done it before—all you had to do was give me the word."

"Appreciate the restraint, buddy. What the fuck … go for it." Big Earl chuckled. "I'm the fucking mayor after all—and the law. We got money in the budget to fix the damn street."

The crack of another shot from Loren's rifle echoed off the buildings. She watched the impact and then the explosion. Flames and smoke shot up from where the man and the bag used to be. She made a mental note not to look at the area too closely. Her stomach was upset again. She patted her tummy. "Calm down, little guy. Momma is okay."

"Callie, you sick?" Risto's voice was strained. *Shit, I forgot he could hear me.*

Loren belly-crawled to her then checked her over. He smiled and stroked her cold cheek. "Here." He handed her something. She choked out a laugh and took a couple packets of Saltines from his hand. She mouthed "thank you."

"Will someone … gotcha fucker," a shot rang out and the thud of Risto's running boots sounded, "…talk to me. Callie? Loren?"

"I'm fine. Loren just gave me some crackers." She shoved one in her mouth and put her eye back to the scope. Loren patted the top of her head and slithered along the walkway back to his post. "I need to remember not to look at the dead bodies, that's all."

"Think of this as a single-shooter role-playing game, Callie." Paul's voice made her smile. She remembered weekends where she and her brothers would stay with the Walshes and play video games until her dad came back from wherever the Marines had sent him.

"I think you and Loren still owe me for one of those times I beat your asses at Patriot Games."

Loren chuckled. "She's got you there, bro. Should've kept your mouth shut. What did we owe you?"

"Taco Bell, three full meals."

"We'll pay up when we get these yahoos taken care of," Paul promised.

She thought about it. "Ya know, a Burrito Supreme, extra sour cream and some green sauce sounds yummy right about now." She inhaled and then on her exhale took a shot at the bogie coming around the corner of Big Earl's.

"Good shot, *chica*," Berto said. "He was on my tail. Cover me. This seems to be a popular destination. I'm going up to better defend."

Callie, along with Loren, said, "Roger that." She kept her eye on the area around Berto. "Loren, is that a bogie by the marina's gas pump?" Big Earl only had a single diesel pump for the boats.

"Fuck yeah. There's a wood support in my way. I don't have a clear shot." He cursed. "Don't want to blow the pump."

She eyed the area. She had a head shot and took it. "Did I get him?"

Big Earl let out a rebel yell which reverberated around the marina area. "Damn fine shooting, little girl. Wish I had you covering my ass in the Gulf."

"Thanks." She blew out a breath and did a mental count on her ammo in the current mag. *Three more shots in this one.* Loren had done most of the shooting since her last switch out.

She blinked. "Losing my vision here. Damn cold is making my eyes water."

"Go inside the house, baby," Risto urged. "Take a short break. Use the restroom. Pregnant women snipers are allowed breaks. Right, Loren?"

Loren chuckled. "Go, Callie. Stay low. I've got the guys covered."

"Thanks. I could use a potty break and a face wash."

Not to mention washing out the sick taste in her mouth. Scooching backwards, she turned and belly-crawled around the corner of the dormer and toward the door to the attic. When she was less than a yard away, the door burst open. A man barreled through, a Glock in his hand. He moved first toward Loren's position.

"Loren! Behind you," she whispered urgently into the cheek mike.

The fucker had either ignored her as a threat or hadn't realized there were two snipers on the walkway. He shot at Loren. His sharp gasp of pain made her wince. Loren's return shot sent the tango back her way as he took shelter on the other side of the dormer closest to Loren's position. Loren sent several more shots the bad guy's way, keeping him pinned down. The man didn't know it yet, but he was caught between the two of them and wasn't getting off this roof alive.

Tuning out the background shouts for status on her headset, she rolled and rolled until she could get around the edge of the dormer closer to her gun set up.

"Hold on, Loren," she spoke in a toneless voice into the headset. She pulled out the Glock from the back holster. Peeking around the corner, she took a shot at the ass of the man still trying to kill Loren. Her shot took him down, but she could tell by his angry bellows he wasn't mortally wounded and still a danger.

"Loren! He's down," she shouted now. The only response over her headset was labored breathing and Risto's and the other men's increasingly frantic demands to know what was going on.

She took a look around the corner and found the wounded man crawling toward the attic door. He had no easy shot, his arms fully engaged in pulling himself along the walkway. She came around the corner low and took her shot. The tango was down, his head half blown off.

Carefully, she duck-walked toward the body, keeping below the widow's walk fencing, then shoved his gun away from his hand and removed a knife from a scabbard on his thigh.

Then and only then did she check on Loren. He smiled at her, but she could tell he was in pain. He held his shoulder, applying pressure, but was bleeding profusely.

"Bad guy's dead. Loren's hit. It looks bad. Position is compromised. I need help."

"Coming, sweetheart. Cover the attic door. We'll be coming up through the house, clearing it. Any bogies in the house will be shoved ahead of us toward your position."

"Got it." She turned worried eyes to Loren. "Loren? The shot went through your vest?"

"Cop-killers. Fucker was too close." Callie made a move toward him. He would need help in stopping the bleeding. "Stay there, kiddo. I can cover the door." He released the pressure on his wound long enough to switch his hand gun from his dominant side to the ground on his left side. He grunted. "You get your eyes back on that scope and cover our guys' asses."

She nodded, stayed low, and shut the attic door which flapped in the circling winds. Using her lower body strength, she used a balustrade to brace herself and shoved the dead man's body with her legs, effectively blocking the door. Anyone trying to come onto the roof would make a lot of noise before they could move the obstruction out of the way.

Loren gave her a thumbs-up. He had a field dressing on his shoulder now, he must have had a field med kit in his sniper bag. He seemed to be handling his side arm just fine. "Callie blocked the attic door with the d.b.," Loren spoke into his headset. "So when you need to come out, let us know."

"That's my woman. We're almost there."

"Take your time, Marine. We're fine." Callie took several calming breaths, gobbled down another cracker, then took up her sniper position once more. She blocked out Loren's harsh breathing and the noise of the other men working their way through the town. Gradually, her heart rate slowed back to that of a mild jog rather than that of an all-out sprint. The sick feeling in her stomach subsided to a manageable ache. Blinking away the wetness in her eyes, she scanned the marina. She spotted several of the locals taking out their targets. As she continued her surveillance, movement by the boats had her narrowing her vision. "Action near berths five and six."

Big Earl swore virulently. "Those are my fucking boats." Heavy thudding footsteps and harsh breathing indicated Earl and someone else were on the run. Several seconds later, she spotted him and another local. A flurry of shots and the two men approaching the boat docks were down. "Got those assholes. Good eye, Callie. You take care of old Loren and you, ya hear?"

"Roger that. Loren's taking care of himself." She shot a

glance to her side to make sure that was so. He winked at her. His Glock in his non-dominant hand was aimed at the doorway. His position protected his body from shots from below.

A bullet struck the door to the attic, high and in the middle. The shot came from a similar elevation to theirs. "Loren? Where did that come from?" She'd already begun a search of all the roofs north of their position, keeping in mind Berto had said he was going to the roof on Big Earl's.

"Trajectory indicates the Bait Shop or the one just west of it." Loren said. "Berto, what do you see from the diner?"

"Nada, the roof line here blocks the buildings to the west." Berto's answer was immediate.

Callie zeroed in on the Bait Shop which was two doors away from Big Earl's, west along the main drag. Her vision tunneled and she watched for movement. There. The fucker was readying another shot. "I see him."

She took the shot and the guy jerked, his hand clasping the shoulder of his gun hand. She shot him again at the same time as Loren. Both shots hit. She peered around the corner at her childhood friend. He'd taken the shot, one-handed, his non-dominant side. "How can you shoot a Barrett one-handed?"

"Practice, honey. Way too much fucking practice." He slumped down against the side of his dormer, his sniper rifle lying at his side and his Glock back in his hand. "How many shots left in your mag?"

She thought. "Um, one, I think."

"Reload, Callie. I've got the door."

"Reloading." She swiftly took out the partially empty magazine and shoved in a full one.

"How are your back-ups?" Loren asked, his voice shaky.

"I reloaded them. The one I just took out is the only one not full." She crawled to him. He was really pale. Pain pinched the corners of his mouth and his skin seemed stretched extra-tight over his cheek bones. "Risto, Loren doesn't look so hot."

"Paul and I are in the house clearing the floors. Conn's on the front door. They bring the fight here, they're dead meat. Hold on."

"Okay." Loren's lips attempted to form a smile but failed abysmally. "Um, Loren said okay too."

She went back to her sniper rifle, then swept every roof. She couldn't see Berto but knew he was there because shots were coming from the area. Satisfied no other tango was on a roof that she could see, she began to quarter the area around the marina. As she methodically checked every square yard of the town, something nagged at the back of her mind. Her neck itched and she shivered and knew goose bumps had broken out all over her body. It wasn't the cold—she'd been beyond cold for quite a while. Something wasn't right.

"Risto?"

"What is it, baby?"

"Something's wrong. Not sure what. I need to check the perimeter of the roof. Now."

She peered around her dormer and found Loren's narrowed gaze on her. He frowned then nodded. He felt it too. He mouthed "go" and indicated he was fine. She nodded and crawled toward the west corner of the house, away from Loren. When she got there, she peered around the corner to the back of the house. Some sixth sense told her to look up. Two men were coming down the side of the crag. She hissed into her mike. "Two men rappelling into the backyard from the cliff."

"I see them out the kitchen window." Paul's voice was calm. Two shots rang out and the men fell to the ground. "Two men down."

"There could be more. Get back to Loren, baby."

Two sharp gasps came over the headset. *Loren.* Something was wrong.

She crawled back to the front corner. "Loren, you hurting?" she called out, not bothering with the mike. "I'm coming."

"Please do, *puta*. I have my knife at your friend's throat."

Cruz's voice came over the headset loud and clear. Either he hadn't seen Loren's cheek mike or didn't care. The others would have heard Cruz's words. Risto and Paul would be coming, but they might not make it in time.

She couldn't assume Cruz didn't have Loren's headset, so she switched to the private channel which would take her to Risto and only Risto. Always have a Plan B, her dad had said. Risto was trained the same way and made this arrangement in case the plan went tits up. "Cruz has Loren," she murmured into the mike. "He wants me to come to him."

"Don't do it. Paul and I will get onto the widow's walk from the rear of the house."

"Calista," Cruz shouted. "I will kill this man if you do not appear in the next twenty seconds." The damn Colombian sounded way too smug.

"I don't think Loren has that long." She flipped off her headset. She needed to calm down and plan her move. The men's voices, Risto's voice, wouldn't aid that goal.

"I'm coming. Don't hurt him." She stood up and hoped the other bad guys would be too busy running from her guys to worry about what was happening on the widow's walk.

Shots from Berto's position on Earl's diner's roof made her smile. Her guys on the ground began to yell and shoot, making a lot of noise and confusion. All of them were harrying the bogies, giving her the room to figure out how to take out Cruz.

"I'm waiting, Calista." His sneering voice made her skin crawl.

"Don't come, Calista Jean!" Loren's shout was cut off.

She clicked her headset back on and hit the variable frequency the men would have switched to when it was obvious Loren's position and communications might have been compromised. "Berto?" she whispered. "Do you have a shot?"

"No—the *pendejo* is too close to Loren. He has his arm around Loren's neck and a knife in his other hand, near the carotid. Only a head shot will save Loren, maybe—and I do not have that." The "without taking off Loren's head" also went unspoken.

"Callie, wait on us." Risto's voice was calm, but authoritative. That tone, she would have to tell him, only worked in the bedroom. This was her decision to make and she would make it.

"Sorry, can't do that." She shut her headset off on Risto's anguished roar.

She would only have one chance. She hid her Glock along her side and walked around the corner. "I'm coming. Loren, you okay?"

"Yeah." His voice was raspy, but he was alive.

"God, this reminds me so much of when we were kids." She rambled, hoping Cruz would take her mutterings as a sign of fear. "Remember that time I played the hostage? Keely saved me?"

They'd used laser-guns and worn suits and headgear which would register the lethality of the hits. Keely had taken out Paul who had held Callie in a similar hold by shooting him in the forehead, the suit signaling a kill shot with a high whine.

"Yeah, you were always the hostage." Loren choked as his voice was cut off.

"Enough talking. Come now. This man can't afford to lose any more blood."

"I'm almost there. I have to step over this body." She lied, she was already at the second dormer, using it to hide her presence. She visualized Loren's last position and imagined how Cruz might be holding him. They would be down and to her right when she came around the dormer. She would only have a split second to adjust her aim.

"I'm…" she swept around the corner, her gun in a two-handed grip, "…here." She had guessed the two men's positions almost perfectly. She adjusted her aim to her left and up and took the shot faster than she could even think about it. The

Glock had a stronger recoil than the Ruger she was used to, but she managed to take the shot and made the adjustment to take another shot, following Cruz to the floor of the walkway.

Loren had moved to the right as soon as she had spoken and had gotten cut for his efforts to give her the best head shot. He was covered in so much blood and brain matter she wasn't sure how badly he was hurt.

She moved to him, her gaze passing over Cruz. Since there wasn't much left of his head after two shots, she could turn all her attention to Loren.

"Loren?" She touched his good shoulder.

"I'm fine, kiddo. Fucking good shot."

Chapter Twenty-Four

"Shit, shit, shit!" Risto shot a look at Paul. "She's going to help your twin."

Paul nodded, a grim look on his face. "Berto, you sure you don't have a shot?"

"None. Cruz is plastered to Loren. They are also below the railing."

"Conn," Risto spoke into the mike, "no one gets in this house but our men."

"Got it."

Big Earl's voice came over the headset. "One of my guys is going onto the roof with Berto. He was a sniper in the Gulf. He's picking up my sniper rifle along the way and will see if he can get a shot at Cruz."

"I don't think we have that much time." Risto made his way to the back of the house, shoved open a window and looked up. The emergency ladder was within reach and he pulled it down, blessing the owners for buying quality and keeping it oiled. "We're going up the back."

Just as he began to climb the ladder, he heard a single shot.

Hand gun, sounds like a Glock. Then another shot.

Icy fear swept down his spine and all color bled from the world. *Callie! God. No, please.* He climbed faster. He practically leapt onto the widow's walk and ran toward the front of the house. He prayed every step of the way. His Glock clenched in his fist and his knife in the other hand. He sensed Paul on his heels. As he peered around the edge of the house, he swore. He couldn't see past the damn dormers. He duck-walked toward Callie's sniper position, staying below the railing so he wouldn't be skylined. Paul was so close behind, he swore he could feel the man's body heat through his parka.

"Callie? Loren?" Risto whispered into his cheek mike.

"It's okay, Risto. Cruz is dead." Callie's voice, shaky, but alive, came over the com system. "I needed to take care of Loren first. He's bleeding pretty badly."

Risto stood and ran, uncaring who saw him. In the background, the men cheered.

"Get your damn ass below the railing, Risto, and take care of them," Big Earl said. "We've got the ground covered. Berto and my sniper are covering us." The crack of a sniper rifle echoed in the clear morning air. Automatic weapons fire punctuated the sniper's shots.

"Thanks, Earl. I'll be down as soon as I get Loren and Callie secured inside the house."

Risto dropped and then maneuvered around the dead man blocking the door to the attic. Paul's muttered "Jesus Christ" blew by on the wind.

As he rounded the second dormer, Risto found Callie with Loren in her arms as she held a field dressing on his neck. The SEAL had another bloody dressing on his shoulder. Both of them had blood, bone and other organic matter all over them. Cruz lay on the ground, not moving, for a very good reason.

"She blew Cruz's fucking head off," Paul said for the others on the ground's benefit. He moved past Risto to get to his brother's side. "I'll take him, Callie." He dragged his twin into his arms and sheltered them from ground fire against one of the dormers. He quickly and efficiently began to check out his brother's condition. "Jesus, bro, you look like something out of *Friday the 13th*."

Loren cursed a blue streak. "Fuck, you ham-handed ape. I want Callie. She has a much lighter touch."

A crack of gunfire and splinters flying from the top railing on the balustrade had Risto pulling Callie under him.

She touched his face with a bloodied, gloved hand. "Couldn't wait for you. Sorry."

She shook within the shelter of his arms like an aspen in the wind. He rubbed her body, warming it. She was shaking from both aftermath and cold. His little soldier had pushed herself to the limit and beyond. "Damn, I'm proud of you, but enough is enough." He kissed the top of her head. "You're done. The men can handle the rest. Cruz's mercs will be on the run once they know the man paying them is dead."

"O-o-kay." Her voice was as tremulous as the rest of her. She held on to him and buried her face in his parka.

"It's okay. You're fine." Risto wasn't sure who he was reassuring—her or him? It had been close—too close. He groaned and clutched her more closely against him. "Sweet fucking hell, when I heard those two shots, I died inside."

She petted his chest. "Sorry. I couldn't take the chance the bastard wouldn't kill Loren right in front of me."

"Poor Loren is fucking grateful you didn't hesitate. The bastard would've killed me as soon as he had you within reach," Loren said as his brother worked on his neck. "Watch it, dipshit. I want Callie back."

Paul laughed, tears in his eyes. "You'll live." He slapped another field dressing over the cuts and taped them down. "Just nicked you. Most of this shit on you is Cruz's."

"Head and neck wounds bleed like stink, dad always said." Callie stretched a hand to pat Loren's good arm. "Check his shoulder wound, Paul. I think the sniper's slug went through, but it needs to be cleaned out to make sure nothing got in the wound."

Paul nodded as he peered under the dressing. "We'll need to irrigate it to be sure. We can do that inside. We need to get off this fucking walkway." Proving Paul's point, another bullet hit the dormer right above the twin's heads. Paul swore. "Loren's stable to move. Let's get the fuck out of here."

"With you on that one." Risto looked down at Callie. "You ready to move?"

"Yes, please. I was heading inside when everything turned to shit." She looked from Paul to Risto. "I'll stay with Loren. You need to help the others. We'll be fine."

"God, sweetheart, you've done enough." Risto couldn't imagine any woman doing what she'd just done—well, no woman other than Keely Walsh-Maddox. He looked to the cloudy skies and mouthed "thank you" to her father and God for watching over her. He kissed her cold forehead. "Okay, turn over under me. Belly crawl to the attic door. I'll be right behind you so I can move the other dead body out of the way."

She sighed and turned over with his help and began to slither her way along the walkway. "I have to say I'm getting kind of tired. This will be over soon, won't it?"

Risto followed on her heels. "Soon, baby. Big Earl and the guys are doing cleanup. We'll tuck you and Loren in bed here. Paul and I will remain in the house to watch over you. No one else will be shooting at you today."

"No, go help Big Earl and the guys. I can watch Loren." She stopped crawling a couple of feet from the dead body blocking the door.

"Let me move the body." He scooted past her and shoved the man along the walkway until he cleared the doorway. "How did you move this bastard?"

Callie sighed. "Women's lower bodies are very strong."

He grinned. "I love your lower body." She smiled weakly and buried her face in her arms as if she'd fall asleep right then and there.

No way would he leave Callie alone to guard Loren. She was exhausted and Loren needed pain meds and would be useless to take care of himself, let alone Callie. God knew, he might never let her out of his sight again. None of them ever expected a scenario where she'd put her life on the line for the ex-SEAL. But he wasn't surprised she'd stepped up and handled it. After all, she'd dashed into a raging battle zone in Ungaía to save the Mayor's wife, a perfect stranger. Why would she do any less for a man who was like a brother?

He'd always known true courage was doing what had to be done, when it needed to be done. His woman was the perfect example of the adage. She proved it again and again. Damn, he was a lucky man.

"Let's get inside, love." He opened the door. She raised her head and resumed bellycrawling into the attic. Paul supported his brother's bad side and they tandem-crawled behind Callie. "Find them a bed, Paul," Risto said. "One room so I can defend them easily. I'll want you and Conn back out to help the others. I'm going to get a sit rep and do some cleanup of the widow's walk."

Paul's eyes widened, then his lips quirked. "Yeah, clean up sounds good." He shoved his brother inside. Loren protested the rough handling. "Stop whining, bro." He winked at Risto and shut the door.

Now that the others were inside and out of sight, Risto breathed easier. "Big Earl? Berto? Conn?" He spoke into his mike. "Someone report. What's going on?"

"The house is still secure, but the gunfire is heading this way. You off the roof?" Conn sounded his usual bored self which meant he had shut down all emotion and was ready to fight all Hell's minions to protect the house and those within.

"Callie and Loren are being put to bed by Paul. Stay on the front door until I relieve you."

"Got it."

"Conn is correct," Big Earl said. "The rats are working their way to your position. Guess they want to see what happened with their employer. Callie okay?" Several shots rang out. "Chalk up another dead tango."

"Callie's fine." His little soldier spoke for herself. "Are all our guys okay?"

Everyone reported in as a-okay. Loren spoke over his mike, pain evident in his voice. "Well, hell, guess I'm the only lucky one."

"Big Earl?" Risto eyed the dead, practically headless bodies of Cruz and the other man who'd attempted to take the roof and failed. "What do you think would happen if Cruz and his equally dead buddy fell over the widow's walk and landed on the ground in front of the house?"

"Might bring the rest out into the open or make them run. Dead men don't transfer money into mercenaries' off-shore accounts."

"That's what I thought." Risto smiled grimly. "Watch for the garbage dump. Be ready to take care of the resulting chaos."

"Gotcha." Big Earl sounded way too happy. But he wouldn't be after Homeland Security and a bunch of DOD types came to crawl all over Osprey's Point. That would be a real goat roping in just paperwork alone. Callie as the intended victim couldn't be kept out of the resulting investigation. His protective nature told him to swear every man present to secrecy about her sniper's role, but the practical side of him said to detail her deadly skill in the official report. The knowledge would then get back to the DOD traitor and he might think twice about aiding and abetting anyone wanting to go after Callie. He'd have to think about that, ask her what she wanted to do. He knew she'd have a definite opinion.

Risto rolled the body by the attic door to the widow's walk railing, then muscled the man up and over. Then he crawled to Cruz and did the same to his body.

"Fucking A! Little Callie did a number on old Cruz's head.

The fall finished the job." Big Earl's voice was low and rough. "Damn good shooting, Callie. Oops, no time to talk, the rats are leaving town—and in an all-fired hurry." Automatic gunfire sounded, echoing off the buildings.

With a few adjustments, Risto manned Callie's rifle and provided additional coverage to his team. He wanted this done and over so he could take Callie home and take care of her.

Shower. Food. Cuddling. And sleep, in that order. He'd deal with the official aftermath of this morning's work tomorrow.

"Big Earl. No one makes it out of town. No one." He found his first target and took the shot and went into the zone.

ONCE BIG EARL ASSURED HIM the invading force was either dead, dying or captured, Risto searched the second floor until he found the bedroom Callie and the twins had taken over. He sent Paul to relieve Conn so that man could help with clean up. Paul would stop anyone who might have escaped Big Earl's net from entering the house.

A noticeably cleaner Loren smiled weakly, pain etched on his forehead. Naked from the waist up, the white dressings looked stark against his deeply tanned skin. Callie, minus the heavy outerwear and blood, lay on the huge bed next to the wounded man, sound asleep. Risto frowned. "How's Callie?"

"She's fine—not a scratch on her. Paul and I convinced her she could keep a better watch over me by lying down on the bed rather than sitting in a chair." Loren smiled down at Callie. "She fell asleep in seconds. Ren told me once that Keely did that a lot early in her pregnancy."

"Good thing this is a big-ass bed, 'cause I'm joining you." Risto approached the bed and edged onto it next to Callie. He kicked off his boots, then stretched his legs out. Needing to touch her, he smoothed some errant curls from her wind-burned cheek. "You do consider yourself a big brother to Callie, right?"

"Yeah, why?"

"Well, I'd hate to have to kill you." His lips twisted at the look on Loren's face.

"You're teasing, right?" Loren narrowed his gaze. "You're not. Fuck, Risto. She's just as much a sister to me and my brothers as Keely is."

"That's good to hear. Though, Tweeter didn't think that way at one time." Risto idly detangled some of Callie's curls, the backs of his fingers gently stroking her neck with each pass.

Loren cursed under his breath. "Paul and his big mouth. Trust me, Tweeter only told us about that time after four shots of tequila. He said his body liked the experience," Risto hissed and Loren held up a hand, "but his head told him it was wrong. Hell, I recall Devin kicked his ass a couple of times about it and threatened all of us with emasculation if we touched Callie in that way."

Risto nodded. Devin was a marine and a mean son of a bitch, which weren't mutually exclusive. He knew Ren and Trey wanted to recruit Devin and Andy Walsh to come aboard at SSI when they got out of the Marines. "Tell Paul if he ever mentions that incident in Callie's past again and I find out about it, I'll take care of removing his balls and shove them down his throat."

"Got it." Loren winced, then laid his head against the pillow propped on the headboard. He looked down. "We'll need to replace the homeowner's bedding and towels. It took both Callie and Paul to clean the shoulder wound. One to hold me up and the other to irrigate. The bathroom looks as if an ax murder occurred there."

Risto snorted. "Big Earl will handle it. He has access to a crime scene cleanup service."

Footsteps coming up the stairs had Risto pulling his handgun. He covered Callie with his body and aimed at the doorway.

"It's me," Paul's voice called out.

"Come in, slowly," Risto responded, not letting down his guard until he saw Paul and the local who he knew was a fireman/paramedic on the Osprey's Point Volunteer Fire Department. The man had a huge metal box with a red cross on the side. "Everything quiet?"

"Yeah." Paul moved to his brother's side. "Shit, you're bleeding again, twin." He looked at the paramedic. "If he needs blood, I'm your man." The medic nodded and opened his kit and began to pull out what he needed.

Risto swung his legs over the side of the bed and found his boots and put them back on. "With all of you here, I'll go get a report before I move Callie to the boat and take her back to the island. Paul, have Big Earl loan you one of his boats to get to the island. Conn knows the security procedure for my dock."

"Got it," Paul said. "Big Earl's leaving the dead where they lay until the State Police and Homeland Security and anyone else coming to the party do their thing. The live ones are locked up in Big Earl's jail." Paul chuckled.

Risto laughed. Loren looked at his brother then Risto. "What's so funny?"

"Big Earl's jail is an old root cellar under his diner," Risto answered, his fingers stroking over Callie's blanket-covered legs. "It's colder than the dark side of the moon in that shit hole. He uses it to keep produce and meat fresh for his convenience store and the diner."

"The bad guys will be thrilled to go to a real jail after that." Loren gasped then cursed as the medic peeled off the dressings sticking to his neck.

Both Paul and the medic applied pressure to stop the renewed bleeding. The activity and the ever louder and creative curses Loren issued didn't even rouse Callie. With one last stroke of her leg, Risto left the room. The sooner he spoke to Conn and Big Earl, the sooner he could get Callie home.

Eight hours later, Risto's Island.

Risto licked and stroked Callie's pussy lips and clit. Her moans and tensed abdominal muscles told him she was close to her climax. "Don't come, baby. I want to be in you this time."

She laughed, then her breath stuttered as he thumbed her clit harder. "You said that the last time."

"And you came so I had to start all over again." He rubbed his beard-roughened cheek against her inner thigh and she trembled.

He'd woken her an hour ago with her first orgasm and had taken her to the edge and over one more time since then.

"This time I mean it." Giving her clit one last lingering lick, he pulled her over him. Bracing himself on his elbows, he watched as she guided his erection into her moist opening. She wiggled her ass as she took his cock fully into her.

"God, you feel so good in me." She moaned and arched her back, settling his cock even more firmly within.

"You okay?" He loved this view. Her lean muscled body topped by full breasts hovering above him. He stroked a hand over one luscious breast. He cuddled it, massaging the rosy red nipple with his thumb. He lay back against the pillows and pulled her to him so he could nuzzle along her hyper-sensitive jaw line to her chin, which he nipped, then proceeded to nuzzle the other side of her face. Her hips moved up and down on his cock, her inner muscles fisting him tightly. With each downward movement, she circled her hips, grinding her clit against his pubic bone. Her breaths came in gasps and moans as she used his body for her pleasure—and his. He gritted his back teeth, holding back his orgasm as long as possible.

When she reached her pleasure, he wouldn't be far behind. Her pleasure always came first—always.

"Love you, Calista Jean Meyers." He sucked on her earlobe. She sighed and closed her eyes. She shivered both within and without and began to ride him faster. His hips rose to meet her. "You're my heart. My soul. Mine." He licked the outline of her ear.

Her silver gray eyes opened. She smiled and reached for his face with one hand, her other remained on the bed by his shoulder. "I love you, Risto Smith." She kissed his chin then nipped his lower lip with her teeth. "Mine." She squeezed his cock and he groaned. She took the sound into her mouth, kissing him deeply. He held her head to him. She lifted her mouth and whispered over his lips. "Come with me. Now."

"God, yes." He took her lips in a ravenous kiss and met her hips, faster, deeper, harder. He held her to him so she couldn't move away from his hips as he took over the depth and speed of their mating.

As Callie went wild above him, he released her lips to shout his own climax. "Callie!"

She rode him until her spasms faded away and his cock softened within her. She collapsed on top of him, her body a sweet, female-smelling blanket. He circled her with his arms, rubbing her back with long, slow sweeps of his hands. Tugging the covers up over their cooling bodies, he kept her on top of him, her head nestled in the crook of his neck.

"Risto?" she said on a yawn. She kissed his sweaty chest.

He kissed her forehead. "Yeah, sweetheart?"

"What now?"

"We'll go to Chicago. Pack up what you'll need for a long stay at Sanctuary. Make sure your brothers get back to their lives okay. Then we'll move to my suite of rooms in Sanctuary until after the baby is born." And maybe beyond that, depending on the lingering danger from the DOD traitor. Nothing would be allowed to happen to Callie or their child.

They were his future.

She moved her head until she could see his face. "Why go to Idaho at all? Your island is safe. We have Big Earl and his buddies and the Walsh twins. Why can't we live here?"

"It's not secure enough. Cruz found us too easily—and that has to be chalked up to the DOD traitor. Next time, we might not be forewarned." He shuddered at the thought of a rocket attack on his island. The DOD traitor had access to all sorts of technology and weaponry and mercenaries who would do anything for money. He kissed her lips, swollen from his lovemaking and her teething on them through the orgasms he'd given her. "I *need* for you to be safe."

"I don't want to be separated from you."

"You won't. I'll only be here when Paul and Loren need me."

She scrunched her nose. "I hate that you have to change your…"

He cut off her words with a kiss. "I *need* to have you safe. I also want to be with you—watch as you grow big with our child. Ren understands. We're all good. So, stop worrying, okay?"

She nodded. He smiled and kissed the tip of her nose. "Once I feel sure you aren't a target of Paco and the DOD traitor, we'll move back here." He rubbed his cheek over her hair. "The Sanctuary move is temporary. We have our whole lives ahead of us to live in Osprey's Point."

"I look forward to each and every year I can be with you." She snuggled into his body and sighed. "Hold me while I sleep. I love waking in your arms, all safe and warm."

"And I love holding you." Risto closed his eyes and enjoyed the feel of her body lying safely over his. No one would take his woman, his child, from him. Anyone who tried would die.

Epilogue

The following Monday, Washington, D.C.

His hands stuffed into the pockets of his wool overcoat, he walked along the Reflecting Pool, just another person enjoying the mild, sunny November day. The intelligence briefing he'd just left had him steaming.

Once again an SSI operative and the woman he'd chosen had managed to escape his carefully crafted plans. Using client Jaime Cruz's misfortunes in running up against SSI in Colombia hadn't worked to his benefit as he'd hoped. Instead, the private security organization had managed to destroy one of his better-paying clients and damaged any chance he had of getting Paco's drug cartel on his client list.

He'd begun his campaign to destroy SSI, a thorn in his financial backside. But the mercs he'd hired failed to take out Maddox and his team in Argentina. He'd then tried a two-prong approach: sending mercenaries to attack Sanctuary and aiding Reyo Trujo to gain access to Sanctuary in order to kidnap Maddox's woman, Keely-fucking-Walsh, the woman who'd foiled the attack in South America. Both those attempts had failed abysmally.

After another couple of attacks by his operatives from within and without Sanctuary failed to take out Keely

Maddox-Walsh, he'd decided to lay off her and SSI for a while. He became determined to work around SSI and the genius bitch Maddox married.

He'd had only minor success; Maddox's bitch-wife's NSA trapping programs made it too hot for him to do any major selling of US intelligence to his former client list.

Cursing silently, he sat on a bench and stared sightlessly at the sparkling water, the Washington Monument unheeded in the background. Now, he had Calista Meyers, soon-to-be Smith, assisting the Maddox bitch in putting the pressure not only on his network of moles but also on his financial assets.

They hadn't singled him out … yet. But he was aware they were looking and getting closer than he'd like.

Even his lower level moles in NSA had told him they were being watched. It was only a matter of time before the two bitches' systematic approach and some really bad luck on his part would see him uncovered. His many clients wanted to buy US military intelligence, but until he shut down the eyes and ears SSI had on the intelligence community through their NSA contract, his hands were tied.

It was time for direct action again. SSI needed to be taken down permanently. Sanctuary had to have a weakness.

He pulled a throw-away cell from his pocket and pressed speed dial for the only number entered.

"Talk to me." A low, gritty voice snarled the words.

"I have a job."

Silence met his words. He muttered under his breath then ground out the words once more. "I said I have a job."

"I heard you. We need to meet. Face-to-face. I'm not taking your jobs without a meet."

"Why the fuck not?"

"'Cause the last guy who took one of your so-called jobs got dead. Him and a bunch of other guys, some of whom I knew and worked with. Good guys. The best. So, we meet and you can tell me why I should take this job. I'm not working for you unless I know who you are."

Shit. He'd been afraid of this. Mercs talked to one another. The word had gotten around in the insular world of soldiers-for-hire. This would cost him. The merc was buying himself some insurance—of the potential blackmail kind. If the guy survived the job, he might just have to kill the man to get free. He'd killed before, he could do it again.

"When and where?" he asked.

"This Friday night. Late."

"I've got tickets to the Georgetown-Purdue game."

"Fuck basketball. It's this Friday or nothing. If I spread the word I turned down this job, you won't be able to find anyone willing to take your calls."

He mentally snarled. He had no other choice. If he didn't destroy SSI's intelligence-gathering team and capabilities, he'd be on the run, living in third-world hellholes for the rest of his life—or dead, because the good ole US of A still sentenced traitors to death.

"Okay. Friday night. Georgetown's Main Library, Fourth Floor Lounge, ten fifteen p.m."

"Won't there be students?"

"The game." He left "asshole" unsaid. "Plus, it's Friday." Obviously the merc had never attended college. Fridays were party-nights. "The library will be deserted, trust me. The game's televised so it will start later. Ten fifteen will be around half-time. I can slip away from the game and be back before anyone misses me."

"Fine. See you then."

The static of the open line buzzed in his ear. He punched off the phone, then smashed it under his foot. He picked up the pieces, walked to the Reflecting Pool and tossed them as far as he could. The resulting plops were slight. He stood and watched the ripples until they faded away. Then he headed back to pick up the Metro to return to work.

THE END

About The Author

Monette is a lawyer/arbitrator living with her retired pathologist husband in Carmel, Indiana. She also writes under the pen name Rae Morgan. You can visit her web site at http://www.monettemichaels.com.

Printed in Great Britain
by Amazon